Broken Spirit

A Novel

John Shivers

CRM BOOKS

Publishing Hope for Today's Society
Inspirational Books~CDs~Children's Books

To

Marc Ethridge
April 17, 1955 - September 9, 2004

Spirit and determination...
devotion...
but most of all, faith.

Though Marc was mortal and Sallie fiction,
both were children of a loving God,
kindred spirits with merry hearts
and a deep and abiding faith,
especially in the face of adversity...

ACKNOWLEDGMENTS

"Where do you get your ideas and how do you turn them into a book?" This question, in one form or another, is one I've heard frequently since my first book, *Hear My Cry*, was released.

This book, and a behind the scenes look at how it came to be, is probably the best way I can satisfy my readers' curiosity.

Broken Spirit was born on a cold, January afternoon in 2004 when my wife Elizabeth and I passed the Boswell Regional Center campus north of Magee, Mississippi, previously the state tuberculosis hospital. As I glanced over at those aged buildings dating to that earlier era, the little voice behind my left ear that is far wiser than I began to ruminate. What was it like to be a patient there – especially before the advent of antibiotics? How did those patients face each new day while death struck all around them?

From that genesis, this story was born. But it was neither a quick nor a dovetailed delivery. The basic premise developed in a matter of hours, where the main character seeks to discover the definition of faith and to understand how God answers prayers through those He places in our lives.

Writing the book itself was a much longer process, propelled to completion by the contribution of a number of individuals, all of whom I truly believed were placed in my life specifically for this purpose.

For starters, there is the Boswell Regional Center, formerly "the Sanatorium" and Dr. Raymond Johnson, director. He quickly put me in touch with staff members who went far beyond the call to assist me. David Tedford and Kara Kimbrough were my two main contacts that lent their expertise, memories and unfailing encouragement. In addition to two days on site, there were many e-mails and phone calls among the three of us, then a few more quick visits before the manuscript was complete.

Mr. and Mrs. Billie Duckworth's contribution cannot be appraised highly enough. This couple, whose entire life centered around the Sanatorium, spent several hours sharing their memories. Hers' recalled what it was like to come there first as a patient and later marry an employee. They didn't know they were telling me Sallie's story, the one I had committed to paper three months earlier. But they were the validation that this story should be told.

Many thanks to Jackson, Mississippi pulmonary surgeon Richard Yelverton, Sr., M.D., who made time after a long, hard day in O.R. and caused his wife wait, so he could to talk with me about his residency at the Sanatorium and explain tuberculosis in layman's terms.

Three more capable armchair guides to the intricacies of Boston than Suzanne and Peter Read and Dr. Linda Cibrowski will never be found. Their assistance in directing me via long distance to the city where Saralynn Reilly grew up can never be adequately repaid. Via e-mail and over the phone, these three directed me to an area in South Boston where the Reilly home might have been and located the various businesses and landmarks that Peter, Saralynn and Marc would have frequented.

Broken Spirit is a work of fiction. Neither Sallie McIntire Watson nor Saralynn Reilly exists except within the pages of this book, volume one in the "Renew a Right Spirit" trilogy. Readers can, however, if they travel to Simpson County, enjoy a real Zip Burger at Windham's and get home-cooked catfish at South Fork. Most of the landmarks mentioned, such as the Simpson County Courthouse and the Mendenhall Grocery & Grain are very real, as visitors will discover firsthand.

As I began to set the story in Simpson County, my main character required an anchor and an advocate to help her to overcome the tragedies in her life. Enter the family of God that is the Rials Creek United Methodist Church, a small rural congregation located between Magee and Mendenhall. They may be small in numbers, but their spirit of family and love is gigantic, as Elizabeth and I discovered when we visited them the same weekend the idea for this book was conceived.

Many thanks to Bro. Tommy Stephenson and his members who allowed me to incorporate their congregation into the book and who have literally adopted us in the process.

Thanks also to my pastor, Dr. Brian Clark, of First United Methodist Church, Calhoun, Georgia, who gave in to illness on a Sunday morning for the first time in his pastoral career. His absence from the pulpit placed staff associate, the Rev. John Ponders there instead, where he explained to the congregation in a simple but dynamic one sentence, the basic definition of faith that I needed for my readers.

Much appreciation is due Lori Lewis Ethridge and her children Lindsay, Graves and David, who allowed me to dedicate this book to their beloved Marc. Through his conquest of death, even as he flew away, he taught all of us a little more about the importance of living and he was my inspiration for Sallie.

Writing a book is a solitary task; the job definitely doesn't lend itself to the committee approach. However, there are many ancillary chores that can pull the wordsmith away from his craft. Thanks to Dale Lowman, my "brother by choice," I've been assisted in a variety of ways at every turn in the road. "I believe in what you're doing," he told me early on. Then he put feet under those words and made a difference.

Many have offered encouragement during this process and for that I am eternally grateful. Among them, my daughter and son (he's more than a son-in-law) Sarah and Lindsay Lewis. My grandchildren, Grant and Lillie Lewis, have kept me grounded because to them, I'm just Papa and I write books. Thanks also to Catherine Ritch Guess and Elmer and Corene Ritch, for their prayers and support in a multitude of ways.

Last, but certainly not least, Elizabeth, my writing partner in this marriage. Without her constant and unwavering support, I could not do the work that I love most, or carry out the mission that I feel called to perform. Fasten your seatbelt, Elizabeth… it's time to start on the next book!

John Shivers
December 31, 2005

Renew A Right Spirit Trilogy
Book One

"A merry heart doeth good like a medicine: but a broken spirit drieth the bones."
Proverbs 17:22

Chapter 1

The cold shudder of death and the weight of unspeakable loss enveloped Saralynn Reilly.

"Peter!" she sobbed, her hysteria piercing the darkness as she fumbled for the light. "Peter! Someone's in trouble." Heart pounding, she clawed frantically through a drowsy fog, desperate to find the mournful wail that still hung on the night's blackness. It was the tortured scream of a woman that wrenched her from a sound sleep.

The sudden illumination from the bedside lamp revealed an empty spot on the other side of the bed... Peter would never be there...would never share her bed...again... Her husband and her son, Marc, were lost to her forever. Then she understood, once again, that the panic-stricken scream was her own.

There, in an unfamiliar small bedroom with its white painted plank walls and low, sloped ceiling, she realized the dreaded nightmare had returned. Even more than a thousand miles from home, grief still stalked her. Obviously her tormentor was not to disappear quietly and, indeed, seemed determined to follow her to the ends of the earth.

Running footsteps on the other side of Saralynn's bedroom door were quickly followed by the entrance of an older woman whose face was swollen with sleep and still showed lingering traces of night cream.

"Tell me you didn't have another dream." The woman settled on the edge of the old iron bed, her added weight causing the well-worn springs to creak. She sandwiched Saralynn's hands inside her own. "I hoped those terrors were gone for good."

"I thought they were."

I know why the dream came back, but I can't tell you, Mama. You'd probably burn those old notebooks.

"Can you go back to sleep? I'll stay with you, if you'd like."

"Thanks, Mama, but I'll be alright. You can go back to your bed."

"You're sure?"

Saralynn flashed what she hoped was a convincing smile.

"Just remember, I'm not that far away." Her mother disappeared, closing the door behind her and leaving the troubled young widow again alone with her tormentor.

She made no move to extinguish the light. *I can't trust the darkness. That's when I think most about going to be with Peter and Marc.* Instead, she lay still, staring at the ceiling, counting the knots in the antique heart-pine lumber that had been there well over a hundred years. In her mind, she replayed the events that had led her to this small, southern rural town at a time in her life when she truly believed she had no reason left to live. *I'd be with my guys if I weren't such a coward...*

Saralynn spotted one interestingly shaped knot that she hadn't before noticed. The grain in the wood made it look like an explosion, reminding her of the unexpected explosive events that had transpired only a few weeks before.

It was those diaries that brought back my old nightmare. Their contents caused Peter and Marc to die all over again in my memories and it hurt so badly. But that won't stop me from searching to know more about my grandmother. Not after all these years of wondering. Those diaries are the door to her past. I'm certain of it.

When she finally put out the lamp in the little corner bedroom, Saralynn recalled a similar night only a couple of weeks earlier. A few nights before her arrival in this town her grandmother had called "home."

Similar heart-wrenching screams had awakened the young widow on that night as well, and the horror had been overwhelming then, too. Helpless, she had curled into the fetal position, where she stayed as the tears spent and rejuvenated themselves with a rhythm not unlike that of the tides. Another night's rest had escaped her.

Then it was dawn.

A new day, another twenty-four hours that she had to try and make it alone, without any obvious reason for existing. The remodeled Victorian-vintage townhouse in the south Boston neighborhood, where the three of them had been so happy, was now a mausoleum, imprisoning the memories of what had been a thriving, laughing family. It threatened to entomb her as well, but she didn't care. *If I can't will myself to go to them, maybe I can be taken like they were.*

The phone rang, but Saralynn didn't answer. She heard the outgoing message on the machine, the lines Peter had recorded and that she refused to erase. "Greetings." His distinctive, clipped accent had been what first endeared him to her. "You've reached Peter, Saralynn and Marc Reilly. Leave us a message and we'll call you back." But there was no message. Instead, she heard the click of a hang-up, followed by the droning sound of the dial tone.

The phone rang again and the machine picked it up, only to be rewarded with another abrupt hang-up. Saralynn lost count of the number of times the scenario repeated itself before, finally, she fell into exhausted sleep.

But it wasn't a restful slumber. Her internal video system continued to replay the scene where her husband and son were taken from her, like bad TV reruns that wouldn't go away. They'd dashed out on a whim to Picco, Marc's favorite place for ice cream. *And never come home.*

Marc so loved to go there and poor Peter, he could never stand to disappoint his only son. Oh, Peter, if only you'd said "No."

She had sworn off the frozen treat forever. It was "a dangerous substance and should be outlawed," she had screamed after one-too-many well-meaning callers patted her hand and reminded her that life was difficult to understand.

Looking again into her mind's eye, she saw herself standing at the front door of the home they had so lovingly restored. The tortured expression on the face of the police officer told her the worst: Would she please come with him?

She tried to comply, just as she had done on that earlier afternoon, but the marble-tiled floor in the foyer trembled beneath her feet. She couldn't keep her balance. *It must be an earthquake. Only we don't have earthquakes in Boston. Do we?*

The shaking continued. The officer was calling her name. "Saralynn? Saralynn! You've got to wake up!"

How does he know my name?

"Saralynn! Talk to me!" This voice belonged to a female. *The officer that came to the door was a man.*

"Talk to me! Why didn't you answer your phone?"

The sergeant disappeared and there was only darkness. Just like it was the day her guys were taken from her.

The shaking became more jarring and she clawed at the blackness, desperate to find something to latch on, to steady herself. She had to go to the hospital. But which way was it?

"Please wake up, Saralynn! Darling, if you don't wake up, I'm going to call 911."

"Help me," Saralynn pleaded with the unseen voice in the shadows. "I've got to… to get to… the hospital to… to see… see about Marc." She choked back a sob that caught in her throat. "Won't somebody please help me? He killed my husband."

"Darling, it's Mama… Saralynn, it's me. Wake up so I can help you. Whatever you need, I'll do it, but first you have to wake up."

The younger woman, wrapped cocoon-like in the covers of the spacious king size bed, opened her eyes and stared directly into the anxious face of the older woman who hovered above her.

"Can you bring back Peter and Marc? Can you, Mama?"

"Darling, if I could, I would have already. You just don't know…"

Saralynn fought the comforter that bound her and, with the help of her mother, managed to sit up. "I wish you could, too," she sobbed, unconcerned that her rescuer's red suit jacket was getting the brunt of her salty tears.

Alicia Bankston sat down beside her daughter and took both of the younger woman's hands in hers.

She's always taken hold of my hands like this whenever things were bad.

"I can't bring back your husband... or my grandson, but I'm not going to stand idly by and allow that drunk driver to steal you, too."

"He hit them head on, Mama." Saralynn offered the facts as if they were new information. "Did you see their car? The motor was pushed almost into the back seat. But his big dump truck barely got dented. He walked away with only a bump on his head."

"I know, darling. I know." Alicia hugged her daughter to her. "It isn't fair, but this is one thing Mama can't fix."

Almost as if she hadn't heard, Saralynn continued, "I'll never get to see my son grow up. Peter and I won't get old together and have grandchildren. We'll never make love again or hold hands or wash the dishes together. There won't be any more late night eats at Metropolis Café after a Boston College hockey game."

"But you can still have a life," Alicia consoled the distraught young woman. "You can't give up, Saralynn. I won't allow it." She rose from the bed and began to pace the spacious bedroom. "You're all I've got left and I will not sit by and watch you self-destruct. As God is my witness, I won't! Do you hear me?"

"Mama... you don't believe in God!"

The older woman hesitated before finally admitting, "And just such as this is why I don't. Did you have to lose your husband and son so senselessly? But you're not the only one who's hurting, you know? I lost a grandson that I adored, and a son-in-law who was more like a son. I'm very angry with God because He already owes me."

Saralynn's puzzled expression was slowly replaced by one of grudging comprehension. "I never thought about it like that, Mama."

"You wouldn't have. Your own pain hasn't allowed you to see that others are also hurting. But I promise, they are."

"Oh, Mama, what am I going to do?"

"Come with me to the kitchen. I could use a cup of hot tea and I suspect you could, too. When's the last time you've eaten?"

Saralynn stared at the ornate crown molding she and Peter had rescued from the salvage yard, especially for their dream house, before she answered. "I don't even remember. In fact, I'm not sure what day it is."

But I do remember the day Peter and I found this beautiful woodwork. It was at Bostonian Restorations and we both knew the minute we saw it that we'd found what we wanted. If only life were so perfect and so simple now.

When the two women were finally seated across from each other at the wrought iron bistro set that held center stage in the spacious pecan and granite kitchen, Saralynn asked again, "So what am I going to do?"

"For starters, you're going to get out of this house. It's like a poison in your system."

"Please," Saralynn begged, "this is all I have left of Peter and Marc. I can't lose it, too."

"I'm not suggesting a move, but you have no hope of finding a way out of all this grief as long as you're cooped up inside these four walls day after day." Alicia added more tea to her cup and offered her daughter a refill. "Do you have any cookies or something to snack on? You need something in your stomach."

"You'll have to check the pantry." Saralynn examined her hands, turning them over and over. "I don't want to go out. Friends notice me and it's written all over their faces, 'There goes poor Saralynn Reilly. She lost her husband and son to a drunk truck driver.' When they look at me, I feel like I'm something to be pitied. Or like they're afraid it's catching; like their family might be taken, too."

Alicia Bankston hugged her daughter and the two clung to each other in awkward silence.

"I can't stand that, Mama. Please don't make me leave here because I have nowhere else to go." She felt tears flooding the backs of her eyes again. Tears she couldn't stop.

"Listen, and hear me well. Marc was only four years old, but you had him long enough to understand that when he hurt, you hurt, too. That's the way it is with mothers and children. I'm hurting because you hurt. You simply don't realize it."

Saralynn absently stroked her mother's shoulder-length auburn hair with the back of her hand. "I don't know what I would have done without you these past few weeks," she confessed. "But I don't know where I'd go either, even if I wanted to. I don't feel like a vacation."

"You're not going to feel like doing anything as long as you hold yourself prisoner here. How long has it been since you put on any make-up or even brushed your hair? You might as well go somewhere because you certainly aren't giving any attention to your clients."

"How am I supposed to think about work, or how I look, when I'm hurting so bad?" A fresh crop of tears was born.

"Because, my darling, the cruel reality is that you have

lost a major source of your income." Alicia handed her daughter a tissue. "You got a good insurance settlement, but you can't live on that forever. Sooner or later, you've got to go back to work. Your loyal clients won't always be so sympathetic." She took hold of Saralynn's hands again. "Trust me, they don't want a designer who looks worse than a bag lady."

She ran her fingers through her daughter's matted curls. "You've got to take that first step. Get out of here long enough to get a new grip on life and put some of the sparkle back into those green eyes of yours."

Saralynn couldn't shake the feeling that if she turned loose of even a little of what remained of her husband and son, she risked losing both of them forever.

I don't want to end up like Mama. Daddy left her before I was born and her own mother didn't love her. She won't admit it, but she's always been so bitter, so hard and difficult. If that's what loss does to you, then I don't want to lose anything else.

"So where would I go? If I have to go by myself, I'd rather stay home."

"You can go with me to Magee, to settle Sallie's estate."

"You want me to go to Mississippi? Why? What's there for me?"

"Nothing. But as my mother's executor, I have to do this. Otherwise, I'd never cross the state line again. Won't you please go and help me?"

"You're not just saying that to get me out of Boston?"

"Honest... I do need you. You have no clue how uncomfortable I am going back to that house after all these years. I need you to be with me. So it's really a win-win situation."

"Can't you just hire movers?" Saralynn stared at her hands

again, trying to remember how long it had been since she'd had a manicure. *These are really looking rough.* But even seeing where she had gnawed her nails into the quick wasn't motivation enough. *If Mama's right, the rest of me looks pretty bad, too. So what?*

"It's more than just moving a few pieces back. I've got to dispose of all her possessions and sell the property. So will you go?" She put her daughter on the spot.

"I'll have to think about it. You remember, I didn't even go to Sallie's funeral."

As long as Saralynn could remember, there had been some kind of problem between her mother and her grandmother, although she had never been able to discover what it was.

I never knew what it was like to have a grandmother. Sallie Watson was no more than a name to me; Mama called her by her first name.

Her grandmother sent gifts every Christmas and around her birthday with cards signed "I love you, Granny." Alicia would sniff with disapproval each time she looked at one of her mother's notes. "Granny! Can't she ever get past being an old country woman?"

I wonder what Sallie called me? I'm not even sure how old she was… 74, I think. Or would she have been 75?

Having just experienced a double loss, Saralynn found herself second-guessing her earlier decision to forego her grandmother's funeral. Now that she was faced with the prospect of visiting the home where her grandparents had established housekeeping in the late 1940s, she was ashamed to go. After all, she had never given Sallie a second thought while the woman was alive.

It feels almost sacrilegious. I never even sent her birthday cards or anything. I don't even know when her birthday was.

"If you think about it too long, you'll never do it. Give me an answer."

Saralynn hesitated while she wrestled with her guilt. "In the morning. Will that be soon enough?"

"I guess I can wait one more day. Just remember, though. I have to go and you're going with me. This is not going to be a piece of cake for me, either."

The idea had been planted and as the day went on, the prospect of going back to Mississippi blossomed as she worked to recall what little she knew about this woman who had been a grandmother in name only.

Now, just in the short time Saralynn had been in Magee, she'd discovered that her long-distance notions were far off the mark.

As she lay with her heart pounding, wide awake in the house where her grandmother had lived, she could feel the bloom of real understanding stirring within her. *This is the house where Mama grew up and I'm sleeping in Uncle Tony's old bedroom. At least I got to see Sallie twice. I don't even know what Uncle Tony looked like.* The preconceived image she had of her grandmother was nothing like the woman who had already assumed a three-dimensional quality. *I've only read a few of her journal entries. Oh, Mama, I want so badly to share what I've discovered, but you're not going to want to hear it. And I don't want to be robbed of my only chance to know Sallie.*

Obviously Saralynn's grandmother was not the person Alicia Bankston had painted her to be. Not if the diaries Sallie had kept since she was a teenager diagnosed with tuberculosis were to be believed.

I just want to know her. That's all, Mama. Please don't think me disloyal.

The discovery of the precious diaries had come after she convinced her mother that someone should climb into the attic portion of the old farmhouse. *Just to be certain that nothing of value is up there.*

She had tried to make a joke of the whole thing. "That's where they always hide the good stuff. Don't you watch old movies? If Sallie hid a fortune, you don't want to leave it for the new owners to find."

Alicia laughed, although an undercurrent of irony was clearly evident. "There's no chance of that. Mama never had enough money to be able to save any. Stuff like that only happens in books and movies."

But in the end, after changing into some of her grandmother's old yard clothes that were still hanging on a hook inside her bedroom door, Saralynn managed to squeeze through the small, square hole cut in the plank ceiling of the center hallway.

She and I were practically the same size.

The middle of the attic was tall enough for Saralynn to stand erect. She balanced on a wide plank while she took a look around.

I'm not sure what I'm searching for. I just hope I don't find something I don't want… like mice or hornets… or worse yet, a snake. Just thinking about what she might encounter almost sent her scurrying back to safety.

"Find anything?"

"Uh-uh," the hot and sweaty detective yelled back. *Of course, the attic opening isn't large enough to get much up here.*

Saralynn was about to concede defeat when she saw, only

a few feet away, what looked like an old suitcase. *What's that? Luggage is always where they hide the money.* She picked her way cautiously across the hand-hewn joists, through the shadowy blackness, until she reached the unknown treasure. It was a small overnight bag. Even through the pancake layer of dust and grime covering it, she could tell that the case was ancient.

Wonder if it's locked?

She fumbled with the latches that, while they obviously weren't secured, were rusty and stubborn with age. Finally one popped and then the other. When the lid was raised, though, instead of packs of currency, all she found was a number of assorted old notebooks.

What th...?

"Saralynn? You've gotten awfully quiet. Do you hear me?" her mother's voice demanded from below. "Don't make yourself sick up there. You won't find anything. Honestly, I don't know why I let you do this."

"I'm fine, Mama, I'll be down in a minute."

I'm not leaving this attic until I figure out what I've got here.

She balanced between two of the old, rough beams and pillaged through the notebooks.

"Are you coming down? It's not safe up there, you know."

Mama doesn't ever try to hide her true emotions.

"Just be a minute."

As her eyes adjusted to the attic's semi-darkness, Saralynn was finally able to focus on the flowery script that covered the first page of the notebook she held in her hand. As she thumbed through the pages, her eyes read snatches of entries all written in the same cursive penmanship.

She struggled to see the faded pencil impressions until she

finally made out a date: September 1957. Saralynn brushed the page with the back of her hand, as if that simple motion could wipe away the years of fading and deterioration. Whether it actually helped or not, she was able to make out a few words about a place called "Sanatorium" and the information that the writer's husband had been admitted. She quickly scanned other pages, those where she could make out the dates... August 9, 1957... November 1, 1957... December...

Sallie must have kept a daily journal or a diary! These are her books!

"I'm coming up there if you don't come down right this minute. It's time you got out of that hot place before you get sick."

I want to go through these books. But I can't do it now.

"Coming, Mama," she called back through the attic opening as she carefully closed the lid on the little case. "Don't get so wadded. "

When she gets this way, it's easier to just give in. But it took me a long time to learn this lesson. These should be safe here for a while longer.

She backed cautiously down the rickety old ladder and caught sight of herself in the wavy antique mirror that hung in the hall. "I need a bath bad. That place hasn't been touched in years."

"And you didn't find anything." It was stated more as a foregone conclusion.

I can't lie. "Well, I sure didn't find any money." *Hope Mama doesn't read between the lines.*

Alicia left to drive to town to pick up their lunch and Saralynn was in the tub, scrubbing off the attic grime, when she remembered her tangled emotions during those days prior to their departure from Boston.

On that morning the trip had first been proposed, Saralynn was surprised to discover that she had something new to think about. It had been a welcome diversion, especially since her nights were still held captive by bad dreams and many tears.

She had, however, continued to question their destination. *If only it weren't to Mississippi. Why can't we go to some other third-world country?*

But like a robot going through its paces, Saralynn dragged out the luggage she and Peter had bought for their honeymoon. The pieces were heavy, but not as weighty as the reminder that they would never travel together again as husband and wife. *It's no fun traveling alone, so it might as well be Mississippi.*

Those memories still hurt, even now as she reached for the towel to dry her body so she could get dressed for lunch. The thought of their honeymoon luggage reminded her again of the old suitcase in the attic.

Saralynn didn't even take time to debate the merits of what she was about to do. Instead, she jumped back into the filthy clothes she had just discarded and headed for the center hallway. The rough, wooden ladder they'd found in the barn was still in place below the attic opening.

Can I manage to raise the trap door without help? If I wait for Mama, she'll want to know why.

Using all the strength she could summon, Saralynn managed to push the door back out of the way. *If I get stuck in here, I'll have to confess.* She wiggled through the opening and turned in the direction of the old case. By scooting just a couple of feet across ancient, rough lumber on her belly, the sought-after valise was within her grasp. *That hurt. I wonder if I've got any skin left?* She slowly pulled it toward her and inched her way backward to the top step of the ladder.

The sound of car tires on the gravel outside alerted her that Alicia was back. Without a second thought of how far it was to the floor below, Saralynn yanked on the case, pulled it through the hole and shimmied down the ladder. There wasn't time to replace the door. *Will Mama notice?*

But there was another, more pressing dilemma.

Where can I hide this? Mama's here and I've still got to get back in the tub. Where? Where? I know… the bed. Under my bed.

Her feet obeyed even before her mind had completed the command. She dashed to the small room on the back corner of the house, where she gave the suitcase a shove under the high iron bed. By the time it hit the wall on the other side Saralynn was already in the bathroom.

Her mother's voice sang out, "Are you still playing like a rich woman in that tub? You'll be wrinkled as a prune. Come on out and let's eat. I'm starved."

"Be there in a sec." She had shed her clothes in one motion and was back in the tub for a second, cleansing dip. "I'm just finishing up."

As the two enjoyed the home-style burgers Alicia had bought at Windham's Restaurant, the older woman reminisced. "I used to think these burgers were the best things. Before Daddy got sick, we'd go into Magee once a week to shop. He always insisted that we stop by Windham's for a burger. Mr. Windham, his name was Zip, was alive then. In fact," she said, as she wiped catsup off her chin, "these are still called Zip Burgers."

"They are delicious," Saralynn agreed. "Sounds like you do have *some* good memories of growing up here."

"Yes, I guess I do," her mother admitted. "To tell you the truth, I had completely forgotten about Windham's. I was getting gas when I heard a woman in the next line mention it. So I thought, why not? It's not where it was when I was growing up, but the food smells just as good as I remember."

They made quick business of lunch, and it wasn't long before Saralynn was wiping off the Formica-topped table in the corner of Sallie's kitchen. "What's on the agenda for this afternoon? Where else can we look for treasure?"

Alicia laughed. "You might as well forget the idea of hidden treasure." Her arm made an arc as she said, "What you see is all the treasure there is. Speaking of which, I do need to contact a real estate agent and possibly an appraiser to see what I have to do to put this on the market."

"Will it be hard to sell?"

"Who knows? The sooner I get that ball rolling, the sooner we'll have the answer. Do you want to go back to town with me?"

Saralynn looked across the kitchen to a mirror that hung beside the sink. The scrubbed face and unruly hair that stared back caused her to recoil in alarm. "I think not." She ran her fingers through the disheveled mop of hair. "By the time I get myself tamed and looking presentable, the afternoon will be half gone."

That was how Alicia went to town alone, and her daughter got down on her hands and knees and crawled under the big double bed of an old Mississippi house to retrieve an abandoned suitcase.

It was to be an afternoon of discovery.

Saralynn wasn't sure what she expected to find, but she was elated to know she had uncovered such an intimate link with her grandmother. She dived eagerly into the first entry, only to be rewarded with concern instead of insight. She did some quick math on her fingers. *From the date on the front of this journal, Mama would have been about 10.*

⬤▭

Ralph is bad sick. He's been trying to hide it from me, but he seems to forget that I've been there. He's been losing weight for several months now, and his clothes are just hanging on him. I've seen what he coughs up when he forgets to hide it from me. He don't want to hear it and I can't bear to think about it, but he's going to have to go to the hospital. He's got the tuberculosis unless I miss my guess, and I can't take the chance that he might infect Alicia or Tony. For sure, I can't get sick again. Then there'd be nobody to care for the children or this farm. He's going to be mad at me for going behind his back, but I've made an appointment for him to see Dr. Yelverton at the Sanatorium tomorrow. They've got to help us. As long as he worked for them, they owe us that much. I'm so scared, but it ain't the first time I've had to face the likes of this. I just say a prayer and trust that He'll hold my hand and take care of everything, just like He did the day I left Fishtrap Hollow. That was a long time ago. I don't want Ralph to die, but I don't want to see him suffer, either. So God, it's Your will be done. And I know it'll all work out for the best. It always does, whether we understand it or not.

⬤▭

These were Sallie's most private thoughts. No wonder she hid them.

18

Saralynn was not sure how long she combed through the notebooks before being struck with the realization that if she read them in chronological order, the entries would paint a picture of Sallie McIntire Watson's life. As much as she wanted the whole picture, she was too excited to get organized. Instead she bounced from one book to another, from one diary entry to another, in no particular fashion.

I'll come back later and read everything from beginning to end.

Just reading about Sallie's worries created an all-too-familiar ache in her heart and she was crying quietly by the time she finished. *What Sallie had to face is so heartbreaking. But I can't handle her grief and mine.*

The prospect of further reading postponed, she curled up on the old candlewick bedspread and, just as she had back home in Boston, felt the first wave of emotion and tears carry her out to the deep waters of grief. And she wondered again if there would ever be a day that she didn't cry for her guys. *But now I'm confused. Am I crying for me or for Sallie?*

Chapter 2

I can't stop moving…reality hurts too much.

On the morning that Saralynn first learned she'd be traveling to Mississippi, she began to wander aimlessly about the house. It was a habit she had developed shortly after the memorial service because if she sat still, the enormity of the situation overwhelmed her.

She started her journey that day in the master bedroom on the second floor, and circled through Marc's room with its nautical theme and into the guest room before descending the elaborate staircase into the front foyer. Even now, more than six weeks since that fateful Saturday afternoon, she couldn't resist stealing a look out the leaded glass sidelight, hoping she'd see her husband and child approaching the front door.

Peter would never use the front door. He'd have to walk all the way around from the back.

Whether it made sense or not, she still allowed herself to feel the anticipation, only to then brace herself under the disappointment when the front walk was empty. From the foyer, she wandered through the formal living room, the dining room, into the kitchen and breakfast room, the family room, and then finally into Peter's study where the manuscript he'd been working on, before he and Marc headed out for ice cream, was still open on the antique desk.

Saralynn had bought that desk for Peter at Christmas, the same year Marc was born, because it was a link with his Irish heritage that he so cherished. Now she ran her hand lovingly across the patina of the old pine piece hoping desperately to connect with the love of her life. It was a desk from the old sod for a grandson of the sod.

She'd always envied Peter. He'd not only known both his parents, but his grandparents and their parents before them, and about his lineage stretching back many generations to the Gaelic soil.

Mama's the only family I've ever known, so how can I understand who I am and what I'm going to do if I don't know who I was? I might as well go to Mississippi.

Staying now in Sallie's house, added to the discovery of the diaries, Saralynn believed for the first time that she'd made the right decision in accompanying her mother to Magee. As she reread the passage where Sallie revealed that her husband was seriously ill, she was reminded how wrong her perceptions of this grandmother were. A glimpse through those few brief sentences hinted at a certain quality within the older woman, the trait that her mother had called "faith."

But Mama made this faith sound like anything but good.

She found herself delightfully intrigued, and more than a little envious. *Exactly what is this faith thing?* It was something she couldn't identify, but that she recognized as something special. *I don't think Mama has it either. I'll never know, though, for I'm afraid to ask her. Mama's not big on answering anything that deals with her past.*

Nonetheless, the young widow began peppering the conversation with questions even before they stopped for lunch on the first day of their trip south. Already she denoted the issue had been pushed farther than Alicia wanted.

"Why drag up the past?" Alicia countered when Saralynn inquired about her grandfather, who had died when Alicia was still a young woman.

"I realized the other day that I know more about Peter's family than I do my own. It's not some deep dark secret or something, is it? I mean, your dad wasn't a bank robber was he?"

"Now you're letting your imagination run away with you. He wasn't a bank robber. Or a horse thief, either. Basically, he wasn't anything."

Mama sounds like she's ashamed of him.

Saralynn let that answer tumble as she tried to process a suitable response, while watching the brilliant flashes of gold and russet and salmon that displayed themselves on the rural Massachusetts foliage lining Interstate Highway 90.

Maybe I should try a different tactic.

"How many times have I been to Sallie's? I only remember two trips... once when I was about five or six, and the other when I was fourteen." She scratched her head. "But surely there were more?"

Alicia didn't answer for the longest time, causing Saralynn to wonder if she had even heard the question.

"No, it was just those two times, and if I'd had a choice, you wouldn't have gone then."

It's like Mama has to force herself to answer.

Saralynn had abandoned her quest at that point and let the conversation fall silent. Instead, she searched her memory for a face to match with her grandmother. *If I'm correct, she was only about 53 the last time I saw her. That's how old mama is now. It's funny. Sallie looked a lot older to me then than Mama does now.*

One thing she could remember from her childhood was the interesting design of the house where Sallie lived. In later years in design class, she'd discovered that the house, built in 1853, was called a dogtrot. There were two big rooms on either side of a center hall. Four smaller rooms attached, one on each corner, creating a covered porch on the front with a similar porch on the back of the house. The back porch of Sallie's house had been enclosed to make a bathroom and a sewing room.

That was the first time she'd ever seen such a plan and when she asked Alicia about it, the only answer she received was a forbidding look of stony silence. She hadn't asked again.

Mama's nervously uncomfortable talking about anything that has to do with her mother or growing up in Mississippi. But why?

Instead of family for the remainder of the ride, the two talked about the Boston Ballet - one of Alicia's pet projects - and other upcoming events at the Boston Center for the Arts, located only a few blocks from Saralynn's home.

"I'm sorry, but I'm really out of the loop on what's happening. They could have entirely closed down Boston and sold it to Pittsburgh and I wouldn't know the difference."

"Then it's time you started to make your way back to the world of the living. You are still living, you know."

Saralynn felt the tears beginning to travel their now all-too-familiar course. "I'd hoped maybe I wouldn't cry any today," she blubbered. "I'm desperately tired of crying."

"I wouldn't worry too much. A certain amount of tears in a situation like you've come through is healthy. It's when you go too far to the extreme that problems arise." Alicia looked directly at her daughter. "Like when you can't get out of bed because you can't stop crying."

"You got me there. But I haven't cried nearly as much in the past week."

"That's because you've had something besides grief and loss to occupy your mind."

"I suppose you're right. Now if only the bad dreams would go away. Say, are we still in Massachusetts? You didn't say how far we're going today."

Alicia didn't answer immediately, but concentrated instead on negotiating a crowded highway access ramp to merge with the late afternoon traffic.

Is there anyone who isn't going south? Saralynn wondered between a brief spell of daydreaming and napping.

"We'll be on the road for the better part of three days," her mother said finally. "I'd like to drive another couple of hours before we stop for the night. Somewhere in Pennsylvania."

"I guess I hadn't really considered how long it would take." Saralynn gave a girlish giggle. "Surely I wasn't dense enough to think that we'd ride down the street and be there."

"We could do it in two days – two long, hard days – but it's over fourteen hundred miles. We're not that tight on time."

"Where did you make motel reservations?"

Mama never goes anywhere unless she knows beforehand where she'll be laying her head at night.

"I didn't. Can you believe it?"

Saralynn gave her mother a discerning glare. "You're serious, aren't you?" She was rewarded with a sheepish grin.

"I know it's totally out of character, but I decided to live dangerously for once in my life."

"Oh, whoo hoo hoo! I never thought I'd see this day. Are you feeling okay?"

"Feeling has nothing to do with it," her mother said in a voice that vibrated with a slight trace of irritation. "It's just I didn't want to be chained to a schedule. If we get tired and want to stop, we'll stop."

Saralynn giggled again.

"Case closed."

There's more going on here than Mama wants to admit. She's really uptight.

As the sun began to glare directly into the eyes of the southwestern bound duo, Alicia spotted a sign for one of the popular chain motels. "How about that one?" she asked, pointing at a colorful billboard adjacent to the interstate highway.

"Sure. Why not? Says it's a new property. After all, we're not buying the place. For one night it can't be too bad."

They were pleased to discover that their room with two double beds was both comfortable and clean. After they'd eaten dinner and gotten dressed for bed, Saralynn decided to repeat her try for a window of answers.

"Mama, I would really like to know something about your parents. Anything. Surely you have some stories you can tell."

Why should I have to justify wanting to know about my own grandparents?

Alicia, who had been propped up on pillows surfing the evening's TV offerings, didn't answer immediately although, as Saralynn recalled later, her expression spoke legions. "You're not going to let go of this, are you? Why is it so important? And why now?"

"I wish I could explain, Mama. Really, I do." She punched at her own pillows, trying to get more comfortable, before she continued. "Up until a few weeks ago, I guess having family and knowing who they were wasn't that big a deal. But in coming to grips with Peter's death, I'm... I'm... well, you know..." *No, I don't guess you do.* The young woman struggled to find the right words.

"I know that losing both your husband and your son has been very difficult. But this trip is supposed to help you get past all of that. It'll never happen if you keep dwelling on it."

Saralynn twisted in the bed so that she could look directly at her mother. "I'm not thinking about Peter. Or Marc, either. At least not in the way I would have at home. But their deaths have caused me to realize that I actually know very little about my background."

She traced around the paisley pattern on the bedspread with her index finger as she fought to maintain her composure. *Don't lose it. Don't break down!*

"Both my parents – your grandparents – are dead. It's been over 40 years since my father died. "Just what is it that you think will make a difference?"

"I don't know where I came from. I don't mean Mississippi. I mean, who were my ancestors? It's one thing not to have known them. It's another when you don't even know who they were or where they lived and worked. I don't even know anything about my daddy."

"Well we're not going to talk about him."

"And I'm not asking you to tell me about Daddy. I want to know about Sallie. And... and Ralph, was that his name?"

"I still don't see how any of this will make a difference for you in getting on with life."

The impatience in Alicia's voice threatened revolt.

"Maybe it won't. But at least it would satisfy my curiosity. There's nothing wrong with that, is there?"

"Don't be silly." The words were delivered with deliberate cadence. "Of course there's nothing wrong with wanting to know, but why haven't you asked before?"

I have asked. Mama just doesn't want to remember, and when she gets angry, she doesn't forgive easily. I don't want to make her mad, nor do I want to walk home.

"I guess it never really mattered before. Besides, more than once I've gotten the idea that you didn't want to discuss them."

As she spoke, Saralynn watched her mother's face harden and turn dark. She could actually see the turmoil boiling in Alicia's system as it struggled to expend itself.

"I never talked about your grandparents because it would have forced me to think about them again."

"And you didn't want to do that? Why?" Saralynn tried to visualize how she could deliberately forget her own mother. *Or what about Peter... or Marc?* She railed at the prospect.

"You didn't want to think about your own parents?"

"It would have brought back memories... memories I didn't want to revisit," came the answer at long last. "Because I promised myself I didn't ever have to." Alicia wrung her hands as she spoke.

"But now, Sallie's got the last laugh." The bitterness in her voice was undisguised. "She fixed it where I have to go back. Even in death, she's still getting her way."

Alicia's words, "She's still getting her way," echoed repeatedly over the ensuing days. Now, as she sat cross-legged on the old country bed with the precious journals spread around her, Saralynn had to acknowledge the contradictions she was discovering. Try as she might, she couldn't reconcile her mother's vague description of Sallie with the woman she was now meeting through the pages of the journals.

They simply aren't the same person. Mama will soon be back from town, but I've got to read as long as I can. I have a hunch if I can read enough, I'll discover the problem between Mama and Sallie. From the looks of these diary entries, Sallie poured out her heart on every page.

Proof that there was indeed conflict had revealed itself in that same motel room earlier in the trip when Alicia had gotten so emotional. Saralynn remembered the resulting tension when she asked, "Were there problems between you and Sallie?"

"Not the way you think. There were merely some things we didn't agree on. Things that brought about hard feelings... painful feelings."

"Painful enough that you never talked about them?" Saralynn asked. "I think that's part of what's bothering me. There are strangers on the street that I know more about than I do my own grandparents."

"You're not going to give me any peace on this, are you? Is this cross-examination what I have to look forward to until we get back to Boston?"

"Not if you really don't want to talk about it. As much as I'd like to know more about my ancestors, if it's too painful for you, then I can respect that."

"Thank you," Alicia said without fanfare. "I appreciate your understanding."

Saralynn reached for the TV remote and began to flip through the available channels until she came upon an old movie already in progress. Judging by the automobile styles, it was a story set in the Deep South in the late 1930s.

"Mind if we watch this?" she asked. "I love old movies."

"It doesn't matter. I'll fall asleep in no time. We've had a long day and there's another one just like it ahead of us tomorrow."

Saralynn got comfortable and soon found herself transported into the sultry, sticky climate of the southern summer that was unfolding on the screen across from the foot of her bed. Two women, with partially filled buckets of peas at their sides, were bent low over bushy green plants in a large garden. Saralynn could feel her back breaking every time the two straightened to lift their pickings and move on to the next plant.

"Saralynn?" The voice came from the next bed.

It took the young woman a few seconds to free herself from the clutches of the southern humidity and travel back to the reality of the motel room. Before she could get there, her mother's voice called again, "Saralynn?"

"I'm sorry, Mama." She finally understood she was being paged. "I need to turn off the TV so you can get some rest, don't I?"

"It's not that, but if you could turn it off, we need to talk."

Saralynn hit the power button on the remote. The room was plunged into near blackness, where everything was dark and quiet, before her mother began to speak.

Alicia's voice was quiet, almost a whisper, as she attempted to ask with more conviction, "So you want to know about my mother and daddy... your grandparents?"

"It's okay, Mama. It bothers you to talk about them and I shouldn't have insisted."

I'd really give anything to know, but not at the price of making you uncomfortable.

"Sometimes you do what you think you have to and, in the process, other people get hurt."

"I'm afraid I don't understand."

"Neither did I," her mother replied. "I could never under-stand why she had to be so stiff-necked. Still don't, but it's too late to do anything about that."

Alicia was quiet for a time and Saralynn could literally hear her ragged breathing.

Is she crying? "Mama, is something wrong?"

Out of the darkness surged a sharp intake of breath. Then the unmistakable sound of a sob. Saralynn threw back the covers.

"You're crying, Mama." She scooted to the edge of the other bed. "What's the matter?" When she reached out for her mother, she found Alicia hunched over in tears, her body trem-bling. Saralynn put her arms around the older woman who didn't resist, and instead, cried harder.

"Whatever it is, Mama, it's okay," she crooned as she ran her hand down her mother's back. "It's okay. Obviously this both-ers you much more than I realized. We don't have to talk about it anymore. I promise."

"Tissue...," Alicia stuttered between sobs. "Please... get... get me something... to blow my... nose."

Saralynn ran to the vanity area, grabbed a wad of tissues

and sprinted back to the bed. Alicia took them and began to wipe her eyes. The tears were subsiding.

"It's my fault. I shouldn't have upset you," apologized the daughter.

Alicia sniffled. "These tears have been here forever. Tonight is the first time I've given in to them in years. Who knows? Maybe that was the wrong thing to do."

"I don't know about that," Saralynn offered thoughtfully, "but I think it's time we moved off this subject and got some sleep. As you said, we've got another long day tomorrow." She got up and moved back to her own bed. "And tomorrow I'm going to help you with the driving."

Alicia didn't answer and Saralynn didn't press for a response.

A few minutes later, when there had been no further sound from the other bed, she was startled to hear Alicia's voice.

"Saralynn?"

"What is it, Mama? What's wrong?"

"I didn't know if you were still awake."

"I'm about to drop off."

"Can you stay awake for a few more minutes? I think I'd like to tell you the story you've been asking to hear. I can't turn off my mind, so maybe it'll do us both some good."

Saralynn immediately forgot the fatigue that had been leading her toward sleep. She lay quiet and still for what seemed an eternity before Alicia took her back to the 1940's Mississippi, where she met strange names and unseen faces, now long dead and gone.

※

There were times the next day, as the two women pushed south through Kentucky and into Tennessee, that Saralynn regretted the short amount of rest she'd gotten the night before. She didn't, however, regret learning what Alicia had revealed. Instead of answers, though, she arrived in Mississippi with even more questions.

They were questions that dogged her every waking moment. At the forefront among them stood one question: Why would Alicia have presented such a contradictory picture of her mother?

Will these diaries have the answers? she pondered now after a couple of days in Sallie's house.

That was the dilemma that prompted Saralynn to finally organize the notebooks, from oldest to most current. She was seated on the bedroom floor, in mid-task, when she heard the sound of more than one automobile in the drive.

A quick peer between the unbleached muslin café curtains with red rickrack accents, that she presumed had been sewn on by Sallie, revealed that the lead vehicle was Alicia's van. It was followed by a black SUV.

That answers that question. But like everything else, it asks two more!

She tossed the notebooks into the small suitcase and pushed it back under the bed. Grabbing her brush, she attempted to tame what looked deceptively like a massive case of bed-head. Once she'd done all she could, Saralynn opened the bedroom door just in time to hear her name being called.

"Coming, Mama."

The visitor turned out to be a man who not only had known her mother when they were both in school, but was now a real estate agent and an appraiser who'd come to look over Sallie's property. What started out as a simple preliminary visit to talk about land values turned into a full evening when Walter Kennedy insisted that both Alicia and Saralynn be his guests for "supper," as he called it.

"Do you like catfish?" he asked. "We've got several places here in the county that can fix it any way you'd like, but I'd personally recommend South Fork Fish House."

So South Fork it was, although - as Saralynn commented later - the local fish house wasn't anything like The Dish, with its wood-fired pizza, where Alicia loved to eat back in Boston. Still, the restaurant had a comfortable fit that Saralynn couldn't quite identify. Besides, she found the southern fried catfish to be both different and tasty.

The two ladies insisted on driving their own vehicle, so their host wouldn't have to bring them home afterwards. While on their way back to the dogtrot, stuffed with "all-you-can-eat" fish and hushpuppies, slaw, turnip green and trimmings, Saralynn confronted her mother.

"Mr. Kennedy seems kind of sweet on you. Were you two an item when you were growing up?"

"Don't be ridiculous! Whatever makes you ask that?"

"I saw how he looked at you. More than once I saw it."

"What you saw was that 'southern hospitality' that I couldn't wait to escape. Where men treat women like they're too fragile to think or handle problems. Thank goodness people in Boston don't smother you like they do here."

"You act like he was patronizing us."

"He was."

"I didn't see it that way. In fact, I kind of liked being treated special. I thought Mr. Kennedy was very gracious."

"You call it 'gracious.' I call it nosey and goodie-goodie. Now let's drop the subject. Walter Kennedy is only interested in making a commission. He could care less about either of us."

That always seemed to be the way it was with Mama. As much as I love her, I can remember time and time again when she would "drop the subject" and build a wall, and that was that. No one got around it. Even Peter saw it a few times.

It had been that way the morning after the midnight motel confessional. In the harsh light of a new day, it had appeared that Alicia had second thoughts about all she had revealed. There had been a definite nip in the air when the two women loaded their luggage – a temperature reading that wouldn't have shown up on a thermometer.

She replayed that morning, hoping to ascertain more of the reason for the wedge between her mother and grandparents.

"The leaves haven't totally changed, but autumn is definitely just around the corner," Alicia had commented once inside the car. "The seasons change later the farther south you get, so the fall colors aren't as vivid here. By the time we get to Magee, it'll look more like late summer."

We never talk about the weather! Is she merely making conversation?

"I wouldn't have thought there to be that much difference." Saralynn decided to play along. "Simpson County is that far south?"

"Only about two hours north of the Gulf coast. It's definitely a different world from what we have in Massachusetts right now."

In more ways than one, if everything Mama told me last night is true.

The travelers had set out before eight o'clock on that "morning after" with Saralynn behind the wheel.

Alicia couldn't seem to stop yawning.

"It's a good thing you aren't driving. You're not even good and awake yet."

"I didn't sleep all that well last night," Alicia confessed. "I never do the first night away from home, when I'm out of my familiar bed."

Or when you've been as emotional as you were last night.

"If you don't mind, I'm going to close my eyes and see if I can sleep for another hour or so." Alicia shifted in her seat and released the back to a reclining position. "Do you know where you're going?"

I do, but not in the way that you mean it. Are you really that sleepy or is this your way of ensuring that I don't ask any more questions?

"All I have to do is follow this wide highway. How hard can that be?"

"Great. Wake me if you have a question."

I'm going to find my roots in those two people Mama told me about last night. That was a real love story. I just wish she could accept them for who and what they were.

"What they were," according to Alicia, "was a country farming couple that preferred to work twice as hard as necessary and never spend any money. Or enjoy even a minute of life, if it cost them anything."

"I think they were happiest when they were depriving themselves," she had explained. "Then Daddy died without ever really living, so what little money he'd squirreled away didn't do him any good. And Mama wouldn't spend it because Daddy wasn't there to enjoy it with her. It nearly drove me crazy."

"Is that why you and Sallie didn't get along?"

"That's a part of it," Alicia admitted. "But it goes much deeper than that."

Seeing that her mother was finally asleep in the passenger seat, Saralynn allowed herself to concentrate on the story of the teenager who almost died, and the man she loved, who did die tragically young.

It reads almost like a made-for-TV movie. Only it wasn't a film, or even a book. It's the real story of my grandparents. For the first time, I feel like I have a past.

Saralynn's mind had been anything but quiet following Alicia's tell-all. She hadn't rested that well, either, after her mother's confessions. The weary traveler consoled herself with the fact that it wasn't the first night of lost rest she'd suffered in the past two months. Only this time, instead of combating her grief, the young widow from Boston discovered that it was because she was so captivated by the enticing story her mother had just shared.

With the van's cruise control set, she leaned back in the driver's seat, oblivious to the mountain peaks and rural landscape flashing by her window. Her body might have been behind the steering wheel, heading south to Mississippi, but her heart and a good part of her mind were way ahead of her. Already there… looking. Waiting.

She was anxious to learn more about the desperately ill, yet beautiful, young woman who caught both the eye and the heart of a groundskeeper at the Mississippi State Sanatorium for Tuberculosis. In her mind, she called the roll of current Hollywood stars, wondering who might be cast to play Sallie. *But do I know Sallie well enough to make that decision? There's still so much I never knew... never even dreamed was in my background.*

"Your grandmother," Alicia explained the evening before, "Sallie McIntire was her name, was from north Mississippi, from a little place called Fishtrap Hollow. It's not too far from the town of Iuka, in the northeast corner of the state. When Sallie was sixteen years old she became very ill and almost died before the old country doctor realized that she had tuberculosis."

"I've read about that," Saralynn acknowledged. "They used to call it 'consumption.' That's what that character in *Little Women*... you know... Beth... that's what she had."

"They called it that because the patients wasted away to nothing. The disease totally consumed its victims."

"But obviously, Sallie didn't die."

"At one time TB was an almost automatic death sentence. It wasn't until effective antibiotics were discovered in the 1950s that the disease began to disappear. When she was diagnosed, Sallie's only hope was the state TB hospital in Simpson County," Alicia explained. "Before she was even grown, she was carried in the back seat of the doctor's car – a long, hard day's travel over rough and mostly unpaved country roads – to the Sanatorium."

"She must have been terribly frightened." *I know I would have been!*

"My heart used to break when I'd hear her talk about it. Only you know what? I never once heard her say she was angry. But Sallie was frightened. She admitted that. No one went with her, and up until then, she'd never been more than twenty miles from home."

"That's hard to believe."

"It's true, though. Rural Mississippi in the 1940s was more

like the rest of the country in, say, 1920."

Saralynn had lain quietly in her bed, biting her tongue to keep from asking the ten thousand questions that were exploding inside her head. *I don't know why Mama has suddenly decided to talk, but I don't want to do anything to make her clam up.*

"Sallie was very frightened. She truly believed she was going to die, especially after she heard her father's final words.

"Why? What did he say?"

"He just told her that if she got well, they'd come and get her, and if she didn't make it, they'd see that she got a decent burial."

"How could he be so cruel?" Saralynn yelped, her earlier vow of silence forgotten. "Didn't he love her?"

There was utter quiet, broken only by the whap, whap, woo of a nearby police siren. Finally… "You have to understand… in that day and time, parents and children had a much more distant relationship. But, yes, he probably loved her. He was also a very practical man – that's the only way people got by in those days – he simply said what was on his heart."

How could anyone be so callous? "It sure doesn't sound like love to me. Any loving parent would have put on a smiling face to encourage his daughter, even if the situation were hopeless."

"I thought so, too," Alicia answered. "At one time. But after I was grown and understood the era and the Mississippi that existed when Sallie grew up, I saw things differently."

"I don't get it. What does one have to do with the other?"

"I asked Mama… uh, Sallie about it once, when I was around fifteen. I've never forgotten her answer.

"'Times were so hard,' she said, 'that facing reality was the only way people could survive. Death and dying were just an accepted part of living, and people didn't believe in sugar-coating anything.'"

I could never be that cold and calculated. Peter and Marc were stolen from me and there is nothing that will ever make that acceptable.

"How did Sallie do it?"

"I asked her that, too," Alicia explained. "I'll never forget that answer, either. It's the same thing she said when Daddy died. And when my brother, Tony, didn't come home from Vietnam alive."

"I don't understand."

Alicia sat quiet for a bit in the other bed before her response cut like a razor edge through the night darkness. "She said, 'as long as she had God on her side, He would keep her strong and everything would be okay.'"

"Was Sallie religious?"

"I wouldn't say that," Alicia replied. "As a matter of fact, she would have told you that she wasn't. Her word for it was 'faith.'"

"Faith? That's it?" Saralynn asked incredulously.

"That's how she saw it."

"I take it you didn't agree?"

"Sallie was always so quick to tell everyone how good God had been to her. But I never saw any of that goodness."

The daughter heard a strangled sob and longed to comfort her mother, but feared she would sidetrack the story she had waited so long to hear.

The voice in the darkness continued. "Never mind that she was dirt poor, then took tuberculosis before she even had a chance to grow up. And when she was fortunate enough to be cured, she yoked herself right back to another hardscrabble farm that got her nothing but a husband who died long before his time.

'Show me the good,' I always said."

Her mother's words had echoed in Saralynn's head during the remainder of the trip, although the two women didn't discuss specifics again. It was almost as if the soul and the secrets that had been bared during the night-time tell-all had now retreated behind their closed doors, never to be seen or heard from again.

Just because they were out of sight didn't mean that Saralynn had put them out of her mind. She'd replayed her mother's story daily since then and by the time they returned from the catfish house, Saralynn was frantic to delve back into her grandmother's memoirs. *If only I could pick back up where I was interrupted this afternoon.*

Alicia, on the other hand, was restless – up and down between her bedroom and the kitchen – while Saralynn was finding that her loss of sleep from the previous weeks was finally catching up with her. *I've waited this long. One more day won't matter.*

"Goodnight, Mama. I don't think I can keep my eyes open much longer," she admitted shortly after the two had locked the door of Sallie's house behind them. "Tomorrow is another day, and I'm going to have to let everything wait until then."

Including reading more of Sallie's journals.

"Sleep well. I hope you won't have nightmares again tonight, but I'll be right here if you need me."

"Thanks, Mama. I love you. And I also hope, for your sake and mine, that I won't wake up tonight. I'd gotten rather used to sleeping without those dreams."

It was the bright sun of a south Mississippi autumn morning that roused her a few hours later, not the brutal visions that had stalked her since Peter and Marc were taken away. Although the first few nights in Mississippi had been held hostage by the haunting nightmares, things had gotten a little better with each passing sunrise. *Until I discovered those journals.*

Saralynn wondered, as she squinted against the blinding, buttery rays, what the day would bring. Certainly she couldn't expect another treasure like yesterday's diaries. Instead, she hoped she'd get the chance to visit again in Sallie's world, where supposedly God was good.

The concept of God was, for the most part, foreign to her. Religion had never been a part of Saralynn's life growing up, and she assumed the good life they enjoyed had been accomplished without need of or help from a higher being. *Now I can't help but wonder…*

Sallie's belief that God had been good to her, especially in light of all the hardships she'd suffered, was both intriguing and questionable to this granddaughter.

I'd have to agree with Mama on this. All I can say is, "Sallie, you're going to have to show me."

Chapter 3

*W*hen Saralynn stumbled into the kitchen, a note was propped against the old chrome napkin holder on the table. Sallie's entire kitchen was a study from the 1950s, down to and including the small, chrome rack meant to hold folded paper napkins.

This is so old it's back in style – retro. Once a decorator, always a decorator. I guess it's like breathing.

The note advised that Alicia had gone into town to the supermarket to stock up on groceries. The two women had spent the better part of their first few days cleaning out cobwebs, vacuuming worn rugs and getting the house livable. Eating every meal out was quickly getting old for both of them. They had agreed the previous evening that it was time to start cooking for themselves.

Alicia's last line indicated she would stop by a fast-food place to get take-out breakfast, so Saralynn contented herself with waiting a little longer to satisfy the hunger pangs that punctuated her stomach.

I should go back to my room and read more in those journals. Yet I don't want to get started and have to stop. So... I think I'll wait.

As if to validate her decision, she heard Alicia's van in the drive. Saralynn hurried out to meet her mother and help bring in the groceries.

"Hey," she noted when she saw the number of bags in the cargo area, "you planning to fix food for the public or something? There's enough here to feed an army."

"I'll admit that maybe I got carried away."

Saralynn caught the fleeting grin that flashed across her mother's face. *Mama doesn't do that often.*

"You have to understand what a novelty it is for me to be able to shop for groceries here. When I was growing up, we had the Jitney Jungle on Main Street. Mr. Henry Stephens owned it. But he didn't stock anything like what the stores did in Jackson, you know, the capital city. You bought just the basics here, with maybe a few frills, and that was it. Otherwise you grew your own food. Or we could go to O.L. Stephens, which was a combination dry goods and grocery."

"It must be strange for you to be back here after all these years, what with all the memories."

Alicia paused at the bottom of the back steps, holding several plastic bags of groceries as she looked at her daughter. "In some ways, I feel like I'm on the outside looking in. In other ways, I feel like I'm still a prisoner and I fear they'll close the borders before we can get out again."

Poor Mama. She sounds so haunted. I wish I knew why.

After they had stowed the groceries and enjoyed take-out bacon, egg and cheese biscuits and hot coffee, Saralynn ventured,

"So what're we up to today?"

"We need to inventory this house and make a discard pile for anything not worth keeping or selling. I think I've identified the pieces I want and I'm ready to start winnowing out the rest."

"How long do you think that'll take?"

"Why? You don't have anything pressing on your social calendar, do you?"

"No. I was simply thinking it would be nice to get out for an afternoon. You know, to explore."

Alicia turned toward her daughter and put her hands on her hips. "Okay, what did you do with my daughter? She's not perfect, but I'm kind of used to her so please bring her back."

Saralynn was laughing so hard she could barely respond. "Have you... have you lost it?"

"You're *not* my daughter! My daughter is an absolute hermit. I practically had to dynamite her house in Boston to get her out, so if you're anxious to spread your wings, you can't be Saralynn."

The younger woman collapsed in a heap on the kitchen floor, cackling until tears ran down her cheeks. "Oh, Mama. You're ex... exaggerating," she managed to gasp between big gulps of air. "I wasn't that bad."

"Not to hear you tell it, but there were those of us who were afraid you'd retreat into a shell and never come out."

Mama usually tells it like it is. I must really have been a mess.

"Well, I'm curious," Saralynn replied, obviously on the defensive. "When we get back to Boston, if anyone should ask me what I did in Mississippi, I'd hate to have to tell them that I didn't see at least some of the sights."

"The sights!" This time it was Alicia's turn to laugh. "Just

44

what sights do you think there are? Magee isn't exactly a tourist Mecca, you know."

Now's the time to play my hand.

"If I want tourist I can wait 'til I get back home and go to Old North Church. This is probably the last time I will ever be here, and I'd like to see whatever there is. To at least have some memories to take back with me."

"I wish I could leave all my memories behind when we go," Alicia sighed. "But I guess we can find something."

She sounds so sad. Or is she frightened? "Let's put in a good morning's work and then after lunch, I want to see whatever there is to see," Saralynn proposed.

The two women started in the big room to right of the center hall. It had originally been Sallie's bedroom, but in later years, had served as both her bedroom and everyday sitting area. Saralynn had already decided that the other big room was the company living room. The non-descript sofa and matching chair were obviously ancient, if style was any indication, but they looked as if they'd barely been used.

Her grandmother's bedroom was another matter. Saralynn couldn't denote a label for the style of the cedar bed with its four massive posts and the matching dresser. A chest of similar design stood against a side wall; on one side of the bed was a squat little nightstand. "This is obviously a matched suite," she told her mother. "But matched to what?"

"Design wise, I don't know that it has a name, other than homemade. But it's right in keeping with both of my parents. There used to be a big cedar tree there in the side yard. When I was about four, it went down during a terrible storm. Daddy limbed the trunk and had it sawed into lumber."

Alicia ran her hand over the top of the headboard and came away with a wad of dust, which she wiped on the cleaning rag she had tucked in the belt loop of her jeans. "A man in the carpentry department at the Sanatorium took the lumber and built this set and it's been here, in this room, ever since."

Saralynn did the math. Almost fifty years. *If my clients kept the same furniture for fifty years, I'd go broke in a hurry.* Until now, she'd never fully appreciated one of her steady customers who insisted on completely redecorating every two years.

There was a carpentry department at the Sanatorium? At a hospital? It somehow seemed hardly the place.

Her mother, who'd been pulling clothes out of the small closet – a later addition in one corner of the large, boxy room – held up half a dozen dresses that now hung limply on rusty wire hangers. The fashions appeared to have all been cut by the same pattern from a variety of gingham prints. Obviously they were homemade, although on closer inspection, Saralynn discovered that their workmanship was excellent.

"Look," Alicia groused, "These are all the everyday clothes she had. One dress for each day of the week. And there are that many more hanging in here that she would have worn to church or to a funeral. That was our Sallie… frugal to a fault. Why make it easy on yourself when you can work all day and then sit up nights sewing things that could have been bought ready-made?"

Her bitterness wasn't lost on Saralynn, who recalled another of the diary entries she'd read the day before. *Something about making a dress for Alicia to wear to a dance at school.* She hadn't attached any importance to the passage then. *But is there more here than meets the eye? Did Mama resent having to wear homemade clothes? Surely the problem's deeper than that.*

"It was her who dreamed up the idea for this furniture. I remember Daddy working for two days to get that tree cut up into a size he could manage. Then he got the neighbors to help him load the logs to go to the sawmill."

"It isn't an especially pretty style," Saralynn noted, "at least not by today's standards. But it's obviously well constructed. I wish I could find craftsmen in Boston who would do as well. I'll bet it cost a dollar or two to get this built, even back then. What are there, four pieces?"

"Five," Alicia answered, settling into the well-worn recliner that had obviously been Sallie's personal chair. "Somewhere there's a matching cedar chest."

"That must have been one huge tree."

"It was. And do you know what Sallie said after it fell? She said, 'God not only spared us and our home, He provided a way to get the new bedroom furniture we wanted but didn't have the money to buy.'"

"Didn't they have to pay the carpenter to build it?"

"Sure, but not with cash. Daddy had a bull calf that was ready to be weaned, and he swapped the calf for the furniture. Sallie got her furniture, and the man had a calf he could fatten to feed his family." An expression of total disgust crossed her face.

It's time to change the subject. Again. This is obviously a sore point with Mama.

"So what are we keeping out of this room? I think we should first move out what you want and stack it all in one place. Then it'll be easier to decide what to trash and what to sell or donate."

Her mother agreed, and began to remove family photos that hung on the wall opposite the bed. "I don't really remember who a lot of these people are, but I know that these really old ones are of the McIntire's in Fishtrap Hollow. This is Sallie just before she got sick," Alicia announced, as she took one very old photo off the wall. She held it, almost tenderly Saralynn noticed, for just a moment, before handing it on to her daughter.

"You know, as much as it pains me to say it, if we compared one of your high school pictures with this one, you and Sallie looked a lot alike at 16."

Well, that's one piece of the puzzle. I never knew which family member I resembled. It surely wasn't Mama. Peter always raved about my strawberry-blonde curls and my green eyes. He said they were what attracted him to me. I guess I should say, 'Thanks, Sallie.'"

"I don't want to walk into a restaurant one day and find my forgotten ancestors staring back at me," Alicia declared. "I'll definitely take all of these pictures."

"We need to find something to wrap them with, some bubble wrap and we need boxes and sealing tape, too. Some of those frames are worth something, even if you don't want the pictures. We can get supplies while we're out this afternoon."

Saralynn picked up a brown, fat but well-worn, leather-covered book from the small table beside the recliner. *Sallie's Bible.* She flipped through it to discover that most pages had scrawled notations in the margins in handwriting she now recognized. Many passages were underlined and numerous newspaper clippings were sandwiched between tissue-thin leaves.

"What about this?"

"If I've had the don't's and shall not's in that book thrown in my face once, I've heard them a thousand times."

"May I have it?" Saralynn knew she was going out on a limb, but she couldn't bear seeing this most personal connection with her grandmother in the hands of strangers or worse yet, in the bottom of a dumpster. "I'd like to have something that was hers."

"I can't imagine why you'd want that. Why don't you choose something else?"

"This is fine. I'll just go put it in my room so it doesn't get lost in the shuffle." *Before Mama changes her mind.* She hurried from the room, her treasure clutched tightly to her chest. *This is something else to tell me more about Sallie. But when am I ever going to find time to read all this stuff?*

The rest of the morning was spent evaluating knick-knacks and miscellaneous pieces of furniture.

Sallie has been dead for almost two years, and this room is just like it was the morning she called her neighbor to take her to the hospital.

Saralynn remembered the story. Her grandmother had been feeding the livestock she kept in the fenced enclosure behind the house when she sensed that something was wrong. A neighbor was summoned, who drove her to the hospital in town. Then an ambulance took her from there to University Medical Center in Jackson, but before the day was over, she died. "Complete circulatory collapse" the doctor told Alicia when he finally reached her by phone.

I can actually feel her in this room! This is the most real she's ever been to me.

"What about the big furniture?" Saralynn asked.

Alicia gave the room another critical glance. "There's nothing here I want. This recliner is ready for the dump, but someone could still use the bedroom suite. We'll have to give it to charity, though. I can't imagine that anyone would be willing to pay good money for it."

"I think it's kind of 'interesting' looking. There's a part of me that would like to have it."

"You've been away from your decorating studio far too long," was all her mother said, obviously not giving her daughter's comment serious consideration.

I guess that one didn't fly. And why do I want it? It surely won't work with anything in my house, although it's really not bad. Refinish it and change out the linens and it could really be an attractive bed. Especially in this room.

Saralynn said no more about the furniture but, with an eye on the clock that was rapidly approaching eleven, threw herself into finishing the task at hand. As her mother indicated an item and its ultimate disposition, Saralynn carried it to the appropriate area. Shortly before noon, the two workers declared their task complete.

Sallie put over fifty years of living into this room. Both Mama and Uncle Tony were conceived here, and in less than three hours, we've destroyed an entire lifetime. It's almost like she never existed.

Saralynn couldn't staunch the tears that sprang to her eyes. Neither could she hide them from her mother who looked at her and shook her head, but said nothing, other than, "Tsk... tsk."

"I'm sorry, Mama. When we walked in here this morning, it was like someone lived here. Now, with everything stripped bare, it made me think about Peter and Marc." She wiped her eyes with the sleeve of her tee shirt.

"You know, maybe you do need to get out this afternoon." Alicia's face brightened. "Tell you what. Let's start our afternoon right now. We're not on any schedule. We'll get our baths and go to Mendenhall to The Revolving Tables for lunch. Cooking at home will start tonight."

"The Revolving Tables. What's that?"

"It'll be a surprise. I'm not going to tell you anything else. You'll have to discover it for yourself. Now hit the showers!"

Both ladies were almost ready to leave when there was a knock at the back door.

"Who could that be?" Saralynn asked as she jerked a brush through her unruly curls. *I'm glad Peter thought my hair was so great. He didn't have to tame it every day.* "And why are they coming to the back door?"

"I don't have a clue who it is," Alicia replied. "But they came to the back door because that's how it's done in the country. I don't know why these people even have front doors!"

It sure isn't like this in Boston.

Alicia opened the door to disclose two elderly women standing on the back porch, each holding a cardboard box.

"I'm sorry," Alicia said somewhat sharply, "but whatever you're peddling, we're not interested. I'm trying to empty out this house to sell."

"Honey, we're not selling anything," the taller of the two said quickly. "I'm Minnie Mashburn and this is Flora Martin," she said, indicating the woman whose snow-white hair was pulled back into a bun and held in place with two tortoise shell combs. "We were friends of your sweet mother."

Alicia said nothing, her silent response causing the two visitors to shuffle awkwardly. It was as if no one knew what to do. Or say.

Saralynn found her manners first. "Won't you come in? We were just on our way out to lunch, but we have a few minutes. Don't we, Mama?" *What is wrong with Mama?*

Both visitors still appeared uncomfortable, but "Miss

Minnie" and "Miss Flora" – as they asked to be called – stepped hesitantly inside the kitchen, each holding tightly to her carton. One box evidently held White Lily Flour, Saralynn realized, and the other contained Number Two size cans of Van Camp Pork and Beans.

Why are they bringing us beans and flour?

"Yes," said Alicia. "Do come in for a minute. We're on our way to The Revolving Tables for lunch, but if I remember correctly, they won't run out of food before we get there."

I wish Mama could have sounded a little more genuine with her invitation.

"Oh, dear," Miss Minnie offered. "I'm afraid you won't eat there. None of us ever will again. The Morgan's closed down the restaurant a year or so back."

"But you won't go hungry," her companion added as the two visitors put down their boxes on the kitchen table.

"Yes," said Miss Minnie. "We didn't know how much cooking you were trying to do, so we've brought lunch."

"You've brought our lunch?" Alicia asked, the amazement she felt clearly evident on her face.

"Honey," Miss Flora said, "I can't count the number of times your mama brought food when it was needed. It's the least we can do."

"That's right," Miss Minnie said. "If we'd known you were down, we'd have been here sooner. Walter Kennedy told us."

"But enough talk," the other woman said. "If you were on your way to Mendenhall for dinner, you're hungry."

With that, each woman opened her box and began to re-move containers. The table soon held a platter of fried chicken, and dishes of candied sweet potatoes, fried okra, corn, Cole slaw, sliced tomatoes, cantaloupe and a jar of home-canned pickled beets, as well as still piping-hot cornbread. The ladies had even brought iced tea, lemon wedges and butter for the cornbread, and banana pudding for dessert.

"We didn't know if you take your tea sweet or un-sweet, so we made it un-sweet," Miss Minnie said. "But I've got sugar here, too, if you need it," she offered.

"Ladies, I don't know what to say," Alicia protested. "We can't take your food."

"Why, sure you can," Miss Minnie assured her. "That's why we cooked it."

"Then I'll have to pay you," Alicia said. "Groceries cost money."

The taller of the two women pulled herself erect with her companion only seconds behind her. "Pay us! I should say not," Miss Minnie vowed. "Whoever heard of such?"

"You've been in the north too long, Alicia. You've forgot what it means to be neighborly."

With that, the two visitors bid their leave, almost as awkwardly as they had entered the kitchen moments earlier.

"All those containers are throw-away," Miss Flora advised as they stepped onto the back porch.

"Same old Alicia," Saralynn heard one of them say to the other. "Lord, how her mama's heart broke over her."

Alicia appeared not to have heard the exchange, and her daughter wasn't about to enlighten her. *Mama, this is the first time in my life that you have truly embarrassed me. Those women were just trying to be friendly.* And she thought about Boston, where she barely knew her neighbors who lived only a few feet away. *You know, I don't think either of them even sent a card when Peter and Marc died.*

"Mama! You were just plain rude to those women. This food looks absolutely delicious. For the first time in weeks, I'm actually starving."

Alicia said nothing.

"We *are* going to eat all this, aren't we? It would be a sin to let it go to waste."

The words were barely out of Saralynn's mouth, when she spotted the angry red that was rapidly staining her mother's cheeks.

"Don't you ever say that to me again," Alicia barked. "I had to hear those words from Sallie every day that I lived in this house. I don't care to hear them from you, too!"

Saralynn was too stunned to reply. Her mother's periodic episodes of aloofness were no stranger, but in this case, she couldn't grasp what she had done that was so terrible.

"I'm sorry, Mama," she offered finally. "I didn't mean to upset you. I'm just hungry and don't see why we can't enjoy this feast those two nice ladies brought us.

"All you see is food. What I see is more of what I've tried so hard to forget. And what right did Walter Kennedy have to put out the word that I'm in town? Busybodies... All of them!"

Between growls from her already empty stomach and her mother's sharp rebuke, Saralynn couldn't decide which to address first. She finally chose her stomach.

"Well, you can do whatever you want. I'm going to chow down and I'm going to eat until I'm full." Taking two of Sallie's plates from the shelf, she washed both at the kitchen sink, dried them, and set two places at the table.

Without further conversation, she took a seat and began to dip into the various containers of scrumptiously smelling food until she had a generous helping of home cooking on her plate.

Disposable cups had been included for the tea, which still had ice cubes floating in it. Saralynn poured for each of them, and then began to attack the food on her plate.

"Ummm, the okra is scrumptious. It's fried, right? I've read about it... sure beats boiled."

Her mother said nothing, although she too had begun to serve her plate.

"I don't think I've ever had corn that tastes like this either. I'd love to know how they cooked it."

"It's called skillet corn, or fried corn. Some people call it creamed corn," Alicia muttered finally. "As for how to prepare it, well, that depends on whom you ask. I guess I've eaten it fixed every way there is. Every cook thinks hers is the best."

"I don't understand," Saralynn questioned.

"If you'd been to as many suppers at Rials Creek Methodist Church as I went to when I was growing up, you'd know that there are as many different recipes for every dish as there are cooks. And every old crow says hers is the blackest."

"Is that where Sallie went to church?"

"Every Sunday and every Wednesday, and any other time the church doors opened, she was there. I've seen her get up out of a sick bed to go to church. She claimed it always made her feel better."

So Sallie was Methodist. I don't guess I ever thought about her religion.

"Every time there was a church supper, which believe me, was too often to suit me, she cooked all afternoon. Many's the time we ate cornbread and milk the next day, because Sallie had taken all the food we had to church."

Mama is really bitter. But it's got to be something more than church suppers.

"Well, if all the food at the church supper was as good as what we're eating now, it looks like you could have stuffed yourself enough that you wouldn't want to eat the next day."

"Saralynn Reilly!" Alicia's cheeks were getting red again. "This is the second time you've thrown Sallie's words in my face! Where are you getting them?"

"I'm sorry, Mama. I'm not trying to be difficult. I'm just saying what comes to my mind."

"Well stop it. If I didn't know better, I'd think you and Sallie were in cahoots somehow."

I'm not sure how to take that. Or how to respond.

The two ate until each professed she'd gained ten pounds. Saralynn stowed the leftovers, which were plentiful, in the recently scrubbed refrigerator, "We've easily got enough here for another meal."

"Let's clean up the kitchen and get out of here," Alicia urged. "Before somebody else comes to visit."

In a matter of minutes they were climbing into the blue van, ready to start the great tour.

"So where do you want to go? This was your idea."

Saralynn had known exactly what she wanted to see when she first proposed the afternoon drive. And since the appearance of Miss Minnie and Miss Flora, another stop had been added to her mental itinerary. *But how am I supposed to explain it to Mama? Oh well, she asked, so I might as well go for it!*

"How far are we from the Sanatorium? I'm kind of curious to see what one looks like."

"You really want to do that? You know the Sanatorium itself is out of business. I'm not sure what's there now."

"If it's not too far, I'd at least like to see where it was."

"Very well." Alicia turned the key in the ignition. "We're actually only six or seven miles away, as best I remember. It's been years, so I hope they haven't changed the roads."

"We could always stop and ask directions if we get lost. After all, we aren't men!"

They both laughed and for the first time since lunch, the emotional wall Alicia had erected began to crumble.

The route from Sallie's house took them between fields where farmers were baling hay and harvesting soybeans. Saralynn spotted grazing herds of red and white cows. Others she saw were black. There was one large herd of black and white cows gathered around a large red barn trimmed in white.

"Those are dairy cows," Alicia explained. "They're waiting for the afternoon feeding and milking. "If I'm right, this was once part of the Sanatorium Farm and the Sanatorium itself is just through those trees. That's old Highway 49 up ahead."

"I don't have a clue what to expect. I know we're talking about a hospital, but from the way you've described it, there's more than just one big building."

Before Alicia could answer, they both caught sight of what could have been a college campus. Many of the stately buildings were shaded by majestic oaks, boldly wearing their early autumn colors.

"Oh, no," Alicia moaned, "the depot is gone. But this is the place."

"The depot? I don't understand."

Alicia executed a left turn, bumped the van over a set of railroad tracks that ran parallel to the main highway and stopped face to face with a large stone sign. "Boswell Regional Center."

"Dr. Boswell... why, I haven't thought about him in years," Alicia reminisced. He was quite a character. Whatever they do here now, I think it's nice that they named it for him. He literally built this place, you know."

Mama is swinging from one extreme to another. Those nice women brought lunch and she became angry and withdrawn. Then we get here, where the memories should be painful, and it's like she's come home again. I wish I understood all of this.

"Who is Dr. Boswell, and what's so special about a depot? Every little town used to have one."

Alicia found a place to park near the entrance.

As she spoke, Saralynn realized that her mother's eyes had taken on a dreamy look, and her face was relaxed in a way that made her seem both younger and more carefree.

"I'd never seen another depot like this one," Alicia explained. "It was built alongside the railroad tracks, but it had a pass-through in the middle of the building, and that's how you entered the grounds. As a child, I always thought it was a tunnel or something magic."

Saralynn tried to envision the structure that her mother could see so clearly in her mind's eye, but knew she was falling short. *I guess you had to be there.*

"The depot was more than just the entrance." Her voice was heavy with sadness. "It was also an exit, for before antibiotics were discovered, a good many people left the Sanatorium from the depot."

"I don't understand."

"The cruel truth is that while patients were sent here with the hope they could be cured, it was mostly to quarantine them from the rest of society. So they wouldn't infect others in their family or in their town. For a long time, more of them died than survived, and many of those who died were sent back to their families in their caskets, loaded onto the north and southbound trains right from the depot here."

The painful reality of her mother's story hit Saralynn very close to home, having recently lost two of the most important people in her life. Finally she managed, "But it looks so peaceful here. It's really beautiful today, whatever this Boswell place is. It reminds me of a little planned community all in itself."

"And that's exactly what it was, a small self-contained village. These roads were paved when most other roads in the county were still dirt, or mud whenever it rained. That was done to keep down the dust. The Sanatorium had its own electricity plant, its own water system, and much of the food served to the patients was grown on the property."

"That's almost unbelievable."

"They even had their own theater. I used to come here to see the latest movies for a fraction of what it cost in town. If I remember correctly," she pointed to a yellow brick building with massive columns that Saralynn could see through the trees, "that was the theater. 'Of course, I don't imagine it's being used for that today."

"I wonder what it is they do here?" Saralynn said.

About that time a young woman came into view pushing a baby stroller along the winding roadway that led back into the heart of the campus.

Alicia hit the button to lower the driver's window. "Excuse me, might I ask you something?"

The woman with the stroller responded with a broad smile and stepped beside the van. "I hope I have the answer."

"I'm Alicia Bankston and this is my daughter, Saralynn Reilly."

"I'm glad to meet you both." The walker extended her hand through the van window. "I'm Katie Brooks, and this little fellow who has finally dropped off to sleep, is Paul."

"He's precious," Alicia said solicitously. "Let's don't wake him."

A baby. I don't want to look.

Saralynn gazed instead at the neat and tidy grounds, anything to keep from seeing another woman's child. *It hurts so badly.* This was her first contact with a little one and she ached again for her own child.

Through her grief, which had returned with a vengeance, Saralynn could hear her mother explaining that she had been gone from the county for thirty-five years.

"BRC is a group-home complex for mentally-challenged adults who don't have anyone at home to help them," the young stranger explained. "It's really a wonderful place."

"But you're not a patient here, are you?" Alicia asked.

Their informant laughed. "No, I'm not a client. But I do live here. My husband, Charlie, is one of the staff therapists, and we have a home right here on the grounds."

The baby in the stroller gave a little cry, and Alicia said, "Thank you for the information. You better get him rolling again before he wakes up."

"We've got special plans tonight so he needs to get a full nap today. I'll go now, but welcome home."

They thanked the woman and Alicia cranked the van and prepared to pull back into the main road. She was about to roll up the window, when they heard, "Mrs. Bankston, please wait."

The young mother returned to extend a small white card through the driver's window. "Here's my phone number. If you'd like to see the campus and what we do here, give me a call. As long as I know the day before, I can get a sitter for Paul and I'll be glad to give you the twenty-five cent tour."

"That's really nice of you," Alicia said. "We might do that when we all have time to plan."

As they crossed the tracks and headed south on the main highway again, Saralynn asked, "You weren't serious about coming back for a tour were you?" *I just wanted to see what the place looked like. I could care less what they do for their clients today. And why do they call them "clients?"*

"I just said that to be polite."

"People here in the south are so open, so different." *Home is never going to be the same again.* Suddenly she felt like a traitor to everything she knew, especially to the two Reilly males whose ashes were back home on the shelf in the guest bedroom. *I never knew what to do with them.*

"Mama? Where are your parents buried?"

Why did I ask that?

"In the church cemetery. Right beside Tony. Why?"

"Would you take me there?"

Alicia stole a sideways glance at her daughter, before she asked, "Do you really think that's wise? You're trying to forget death. Remember?"

"You're talking about Rials Creek?" She avoided her mother's question.

"Of course. That's the only church where my parents ever attended."

"Will you take me there?"

"Saralynn, think about what you're asking. I understand there are some really cute shops downtown in Magee. We're only about three miles from there right now. Wouldn't…" she braked suddenly to avoid a car that turned without bothering to give a signal. "Wouldn't you rather go and explore the shops? Spend a little money?" She looked at her daughter again. "My treat."

"I'm greedy," Saralynn confessed. "I'd like to do both. But today I want to go to the cemetery. Really. I think I can handle it"

"Rials Creek it is, then. I just hope this doesn't bring back those nightmares."

The van reversed direction. On the way, Alicia told her daughter more about the church that had been a mainstay in her growing up years. "If we weren't at home, we were probably at church. I vowed if I ever got away from that provincialism I'd never go to church again."

What was so bad about church? The few times I've been to one, it didn't seem so terrible. But then I didn't feel any different when I left, either, so why go? Mama's probably right.

The van made a sharp right turn, pulled the hill and there, ahead of them to the left of the road, stood a modest, yet comfortably, inviting red-brick church trimmed in white. Its graceful steeple reached into the pristine south Mississippi blue sky. A number of towering trees stood nearby, a few early leaves already dropping from their branches.

"It's so beautiful… so simple," Saralynn whispered. She was totally awed by the picturesque tableau.

"There's the cemetery." Alicia pointed across the parking lot. "All of my daddy's family is buried here."

I've been thinking all about Sallie. But my grandfather had family, too. This is weird. I came down here feeling like I had no family, and suddenly I've got more than I ever dreamed about. Only I don't know who they are.

Alicia brought the van to the edge of the cemetery near some vintage looking stones. "The Watson plot is right over there. To the right. See, just past that tall marker?"

Saralynn easily spotted the distinctive stone her mother had indicated and saw beyond it several stones in a sizable area surrounded by a low stone coping.

"Can we get out? Some of those markers look pretty old. I'd be curious to see just how old."

"If that's what you want." Alicia pulled the key out of the van's ignition. "I just hope you know what you're doing."

The rolling expanse of ground was dotted with clusters of stones in every size and description. When Saralynn and her mother reached the Watson plot, the young woman wandered from monument to monument, reading the names of the unknown dead, all of whom were a part of her.

"Sallie was the last one buried here, but there are markers that are newer than hers," Saralynn observed.

"That's because Sallie bought a double stone when my daddy died, but other family members have been buried since he was. I tried to talk her out of getting a stone for both of them. She was still young. I told her she might get remarried." Alicia ran her hand across the granite that showed some of the ravages of weather and time. "But she got that stiff neck of hers and informed me that Ralph Watson was the only man she would ever love, and that when her time came, she'd be buried right beside him.

"That's Uncle Tony's stone, there beside Sallie. He was only nineteen. I've never seen one so flat and squat. You'd have to be looking for it to find it. The government provided his marker because he was killed in Vietnam."

Alicia's face assumed that peeved expression known only too well to her daughter. "I begged Sallie to buy him a decent one. She could have afforded it. But she wouldn't." In a voice tinged with bitterness, Alicia related the gist of that long-ago conversation. "She staunchly informed me, 'Tony doesn't care what kind of marker sits on his grave, because he isn't there.' When I asked her where he was, if he wasn't buried there, she said he was safe with God."

I didn't know I was going to open another can of worms when I asked that question! Without warning, her thoughts drifted back to the two urns, one large and one small, on the closet shelf in Boston. *Are Peter and Marc safe with God? I've never thought about that. I guess I couldn't get past the reality that they aren't here with me.* Suddenly the enormity of the question and the finality of the cemetery became too much.

"Why don't we go now?" Saralynn struggled to keep down the panic that was rising in her throat. "We came right through town and didn't think to stop and buy bubble wrap and sealing tape. Don't forget, we need boxes, too."

"Guess we had our minds on other things. But we can go, if you've seen what you came for. Personally, I've never liked coming to this cemetery. It bothers me."

Saralynn saw a look of grave distaste cross her mother's face. *Mama looks like she swallowed something rancid.*

"We don't have to have those supplies today. Tomorrow will be soon enough. Let's take the back way, the way we always used to come when I was growing up, and that way you can have something else to add to your memories collection."

"I can't get over how rural this area is." Saralynn moved

to admiring the farmhouses and barns. "Some of these homes are comfortably inviting and the countryside is naturally beautiful, what with the barns and the pastures. Do you realize how far out of Boston you have to drive to see real country? Even then, it isn't nearly as pretty as this."

"Watch out. If the local chamber of commerce hears you, they might put you on an ad or something."

Is Mama being sarcastic?

Saralynn judged that she was straying close to treacherous waters, again, so decided to keep her true thoughts to herself. "It's just that the houses look so lived in, like a family is at home."

"Give me the neatness of the city and convenience of a condo. I got enough of this homey living when I was growing up. Barns that smell and gardens to pick and no central heat in the winter. Thank you, but no."

She paused at a stop sign and looked both ways before making a turn onto Highway 28. "Been there, done that. I wouldn't swap Boston for anything. Say, we're only a couple of miles from Sallie's house."

Saralynn heard a noise that, at first startled her. "Your cell phone's ringing. Who could be calling you here?" She grabbed her mother's purse from between the seats and scrambled for the small phone.

"Hello... no, this is her daughter. She's driving right now. May I help you?... I see." She spotted Sallie's house just ahead. "Yes, I understand... if you can hold for just a moment, she'll be where she can pull off and talk with you."

Alicia flashed a questioning glance as Saralynn held the receiver away from her mouth. "It's someone from your condo association. There's some kind of problem."

Alicia whipped the van into the drive and took the phone from her daughter. As she spoke, Saralynn noticed her expression becoming more and more troubled before ending with, "I'll be on my way back tomorrow."

Alicia replaced the phone and shook her head. "The icemaker line in Mrs. Campbell's condo ruptured. In the wall between us and both units took several inches of water." She put her face in her hands, one of the few times Saralynn had ever seen her mother look defeated. "We've got to leave early tomorrow."

It was a somber duo that pulled out the lunch leftovers later in the evening since, as Alicia said, they needed to eat the food rather than throw it out.

She may not have said it's a sin to waste food, but evidently she still remembers Sallie's philosophy, whether she'll admit it or not.

The supper table conversation was rather one-sided with Alicia bemoaning the fact that she would have to come back to finish the job in Mississippi, and her fears of what she might find back in Boston. Saralynn finally found her courage.

"Mama. I've got an idea, but don't shoot me down until you've heard me out."

"What kind of an idea?"

"Why don't you fly back and leave me here? Then I could continue packing while you're dealing with things there."

"No!" The one word was sharp and cutting. "I am not leaving here without you. It's just not safe... for many reasons."

"Look, Mama. It makes perfect sense. You're talking about nearly a week of driving time round-trip, not to mention what you'll be facing when you get home. The sooner you get there to see what can be salvaged, the more of your furnishings you're likely to save."

"I hadn't thought about that. But I don't feel comfortable about you being here alone. You've been more like your old self the last few days. We don't want to have a setback."

"And I don't want to go back to Boston right now, either. Later... yes, but not right now. I feel perfectly safe here and for some reason, I don't think about my boys as much. Really, I'll be fine."

"But you're a stranger and you don't know your way around. What if you have some kind of a problem?"

"I was a stranger in Paris when I was there after high school graduation. When I needed to know something, I asked questions. I can do the same here."

"But you barely know how to get to town."

"I know Mr. Walter Kennedy. And Miss Minnie and Miss Flora." She laughed, "Besides, if I got into a real bind, I could always call and introduce myself to the chamber of commerce!"

"You're really serious?"

"It simply makes better sense for you to get back there tomorrow. And the only way is to fly. In the meantime, I'll be fine."

"I am anxious to see the damage. You're sure you can manage?"

"You just wait and see how well I can manage." Saralynn began to tidy the kitchen. She could hear Alicia on the phone giving her credit card number and assumed her mother had been able to get a seat.

Alicia paused at the doorway of the little corner bedroom a few minutes later. "We'll have to get up and out of here early in the morning. My plane leaves at nine o'clock and, of course, I have to go through Atlanta."

"So what time do you get home?"

"We land at Logan about three-ten, which isn't too bad. I called Elsie and she's going to meet me. This way, I can get a good look at things before tomorrow's gone and hopefully get a head start on making whatever repairs are needed."

"See, I told you it was a good idea. You can stay at my house while you're there. Everything's working out perfectly." Saralynn fairly crowed with delight.

"Then we'd better get ourselves organized and in bed since we'll need to leave for the airport no later than six-thirty, with all these new security measures."

"I can get up if you can."

"I'm going to get my bath tonight and call it a day. I'd better set my travel alarm right now, before I forget."

"'Night, Mama."

"Sleep well, darling. I just wish I felt better about leaving you here alone. What if you start having the nightmares again?"

"I'll make it, Mama. I'll be fine."

Besides, I won't be alone. I've got Sallie to keep me company.

Chapter 4

*U*nlike Boston's Logan International Airport, Jackson's small terminal was much easier to navigate than either of them had anticipated. As Saralynn stood in short-term parking the next morning, watching the red, white and blue speck that was Alicia's plane being consumed by a cloudless cornflower sky, she was both surprised and somewhat apprehensive. *I feel so free.* After weeks of anguish that seemed to stretch forever, it was suddenly unsettling to feel at peace.

"Call me tonight, after you see how bad things are," she had reminded her mother. "If you need quotes from any of my workmen, I can handle that from here."

Saralynn cranked the van and pulled up to the tollbooth, where she parted with two dollars. The barrier raised and she pulled out into the world. Alone. *If only the transitions in life could be this easy.*

She was soon southbound on the four-lane highway. "New 49," Alicia had called it. Saralynn remembered that Magee was only about two hours from the Gulf Coast. *Maybe we'll go before I leave. I've never seen that ocean.*

Her mother had shown her a shortcut for Jackson by cutting through the country by way of Mendenhall, the county seat with its Victorian yellow brick courthouse crowning the hill above Main Street. *That courthouse reminds me of our house,* my *house, back in Boston.* She noticed the now-closed Revolving Tables across the railroad tracks at the bottom of Main Street.

Another business alongside the tracks that caught her eye and piqued her interest was Mendenhall Grocery and Grain. *That place looks like it's been there forever. I'd be interested to come back and spend an afternoon prowling around inside.* She vowed to do just that when she had the time to indulge her curiosity.

Even though she was alone in totally unfamiliar territory, Saralynn was aware of the intense aura of security that surrounded her. *I don't ever remember feeling this way, even when things were at their best, with Peter… or after Marc came along.*

When Alicia asked how she planned to occupy her time, Saralynn had been careful to answer innocently. "I'll start packing those pieces we're taking back, and then I'll probably kick back and read some."

"I'm afraid you're going to be lonesome without a TV to keep you company."

"Not to worry. I've got something to read, and if I run out, there are paperback racks in the grocery stores and at Wal-Mart. I'll be fine."

I'm sorry Mama's condo was flooded, but this will give me a perfect opportunity to read Sallie's diaries. At first, she had feared that invading her grandmother's most intimate thoughts would be an invasion of privacy. But from what little she'd had the chance to read, it was almost as if Sallie herself were standing in the doorway to the past, welcoming her, even inviting her in.

She remembered the need for packing supplies. *I think I can get to Wal-Mart. I'm going there first. I'll need to stock up on some groceries, too. At least sandwich makings and maybe some snacks. I'm not cooking just for me.*

Saralynn was lucky enough to find a car backing out of a parking space very near the front of the crowded discount store, and congratulated herself. Once inside the massive building, she stopped to read the overhead signs and get her bearings. She was on her way to stationery, when she heard, "Excuse me." It was a woman's voice and very friendly. "Weren't you and your mother the visitors I talked with at Boswell yesterday?"

Saralynn turned to find Katie Brooks and baby Paul in his stroller.

"She choked on the memories that flooded her mind, but finally stammered, "Yes, I'm Saralynn Reilly. And you're... Katie... Katie Brooks, right?"

"It's good to see you again," the young mother jiggled the stroller to keep the golden-haired boy pacified. "I'm sorry I wasn't in a better position to talk."

"Oh, please don't apologize. Say, do you shop here often? Suddenly I'm all turned around. I thought I was heading in the right direction for stationery."

Her new friend laughed with an infectious tinkling chuckle. "They really do make these places too big, you know. Actually you're much closer than you think. It's on the other side of that partition, only you have to go down there and double back." She pointed toward the back of the store and Saralynn could see the opening she indicated.

"Listen," the other woman said, "I was serious when I offered to show you what we do at Boswell. Just give me a call any time."

"Thanks, that's very kind of you to offer. Unfortunately, all our plans have changed. *I've got to make some kind of excuse to get out of this.* "We're here to settle my grandmother's estate and sell the house. Only Mama had to fly back to Boston this morning because of an emergency."

"So you're here all alone? We can't have that."

"We can't?"

"Listen, I've got a great idea. We've got the cutest little restaurant on the grounds at Boswell. It's decorated like an outdoor French café, complete with hand-painted murals and the food is just as good as the décor."

Where is she going with this?

"Be my guest for lunch tomorrow, and then we can tour the campus," the other woman insisted. "I won't take 'no' for an answer."

"But I'm going to be busy cleaning and throwing out and packing," Saralynn protested.

"And you have to eat, too. So it's settled. Can you find your way back to Boswell by yourself? If you're unsure, I'll be glad to come and get you."

Sensing that she was not going to deter her enthusiastic new friend, Saralynn assured her that she could drive herself. "I'm just not sure where to go once I get onto the grounds."

"Tell you what… I'll meet you where you were parked yesterday and lead the way." She looked at her watch. "Let's say eleven forty-five tomorrow."

"I'll be there," Saralynn promised, hoping the dread that she felt didn't show in her voice.

"Great. You'll love it. I promise."

As the two parted, Saralynn heard Katie call back to her, "I can't wait."

What have I gotten myself into? Mama's not even home yet and I'm out here taking all kinds of chances. It wasn't that she feared harm, as much as she didn't want to see any mentally retarded people. *Don't they call them mentally challenged now? Either way, they'll make me uncomfortable.*

After getting her packing supplies and splurging on junk foods in the grocery section, she checked out and headed back to the country. *Mama says she can remember when this four-lane highway didn't exist and all of this area was wooded. I guess progress happens everywhere, only it doesn't seem as intrusive here like it is in the north.*

As she neared Sallie's drive, she met a vehicle driven by Walter Kennedy, their supper host from South Fork. While she was unloading her purchases, Saralynn looked up to see that same SUV pulling in behind the van.

"I'm glad I caught you," the tall, white-haired man said through a toothy-grin as he climbed down from the driver's seat. "I needed to talk to your mother, but no one was home."

Saralynn set her shopping bags on the back steps and walked to meet him. *His hair may be white, but according to Mama, he's about her age. His face doesn't look old.*

"Mama's not here." She shared the circumstances behind Alicia's hasty departure.

"Gee, I'm sure sorry to hear that. Water damage can be

expensive. I hope she has insurance."

"If I know my mother, she's fine in that department," Saralynn laughed. "She probably has insurance on her insurance!"

They both chuckled. "I expect to be talking to her tonight. Is there some message I can give her? Or by chance, can I help you?"

Her visitor reached into his shirt pocket and pulled out a sealed and folded envelope. "These are the figures your mother asked me to get. This isn't a formal appraisal, make sure she understands that. But I've been in the business long enough that it's just a matter of putting the information into the legal format."

He scratched his head. "I really would have liked to talk to her. There are a couple of decisions she needs to make that could affect the bottom line numbers." He paused, as if wrestling with the best way to handle matters. "Just tell her I brought this by, and when she gets a chance, to call me from Boston. She's got my number."

"I'll do that," Saralynn promised.

Mr. Kennedy had already gotten back into his vehicle when he called out, "Are you staying here alone?"

"Now, Mr. Kennedy. Don't you go acting like Mama. I'm perfectly safe. Honest."

"Oh, I don't doubt that," he laughed. "I was thinking more about you having to eat out. Tell you what, why don't you join my wife and me for supper tomorrow. We'll either go out or I may grill some steaks. But you leave that to us."

"That's too kind of you. But I should be asking you out. You hosted last."

"Nonsense. We're not keeping score. I'll pick you up about six-thirty. My wife can't wait to meet you. She was out of town when we went to South Fork, or she would have joined us. She and your mother graduated from high school together, you know."

No. I didn't know. However, she didn't admit her ignorance. "Okay, I'll accept your invitation. Six-thirty it is. But next time, it's definitely my treat."

"You've got a deal. See you tomorrow."

Saralynn carried her purchases into the house and stowed them away. Since it was after eleven o'clock and the ham biscuit she had eaten on the way to the airport seemed so very long ago, she decided to make herself a sandwich before getting down to the real work of the afternoon: reading Sallie's diaries.

She'd bought sliced roast beef and ham at the deli counter, and together with items from the produce department, the hungry sleuth built herself a sandwich of Dagwood proportions.

I hope my eyes aren't bigger than my stomach!

As she devoured the sandwich and some barbecue-flavored chips she'd grabbed on impulse, the task that lay before her was foremost in her mind. She was, she realized, actually talking to herself as she planned how to begin her search to find the real Sallie Watson.

When am I going to stop calling her Sallie like we're on a first-name basis?

Saralynn didn't have the answer. *Maybe when I know her better?*

She had thought a lot about how to make the best use of her time, and come to the conclusion that she should start with the earliest dated entries and work forward. *I'll save her Bible for last.*

Saralynn was surprised to see that her hands actually trembled as she worked to pop the stubborn latches on the old suitcase. *You'd think I was expecting to find gold or something. Then, again, maybe I will discover something even more precious.*

The earliest entry was dated February 11, 1945. Fixing herself a tall, cool glass of iced tea, left from the day before, she went to the front porch where an old swing still hung, enticing. *What a great place to sit and relax.*

Two of the pillows from her bed provided a cushioned backrest, and with all the comfort matters attended to, Saralynn Reilly settled down to meet Sallie McIntire, a sixteen year-old TB patient.

✎➤

I've been here ten weeks yesterday. This is the first time they've even let me sit up. I was getting so tired of the bed. Today is Sunday. I know because some of the ministers came to hold chapel services for those patients who can leave their rooms. I could hear them singing and it made me homesick. I would so love to see Mama and Papa and go to my church again. They tell me that I can sit up for thirty minutes, twice a day, not counting when I eat my meals. The food here is good, but it would taste a lot better if I could eat it at home.

At night is when it's the worst, when I really get afraid. In the time I've been here, somebody on this floor has died every week. So I don't know which way I'll go home. I'm not afraid to die, I don't think. It's just that I don't want to die. Not yet. I can't help it... I've cried myself to sleep almost every night.

I've decided to spend a few minutes each day writing in a journal, so if I don't get well, Mama and Papa will know it's not their fault. Even though I've got a lot of time to make up, I'm going to start back from the beginning, from when I got sick.

But I can't write any more just now. I feel so weak, and Nurse Myra said they would be taking me to have my weekly x-ray this morning. So I'll put this away until tomorrow.

✎

Saralynn dropped the old lined tablet with its blue, glued-top binding and let her eyes wander across the road, where the trees formed a seemingly impenetrable shield. But as she studied the forest scene, she could make out that some of the trees were long-leaf pines while others were short-needle. Some were magnolias, the last of their fragrant blossoms having turned brown and shriveled.

The scenery was far different from what she was accustomed to in Boston, nice though their neighborhood was. Even the small park at the corner of Walker and Tremont Street, where Marc had loved to play, couldn't compare to the view from this vantage point on Sallie's front porch. It was barely possible to make out the nearest neighbor's house in the distance. The two-lane dirt road that ran in front of the house curved into a welcoming embrace for the few cars that passed during a day's time.

Saralynn recalled a few lines from a poem she'd been forced to learn in her high school American literature class. She had not a clue as to whom the poet was. But those lines had stuck with her when all the rest had long been forgotten.

"Let me live in a house by the side of the road – where the race of men go by; The men who are good and the men who are bad – as good and as bad as I. I would not sit in the scorner's seat – nor hurl the cynic's ban; Let me live in a house by the side of the road – and be a friend to man."

She could clearly see Sallie seated on this porch, waving to everyone who passed through the curve. *If there was ever a situation that matched those words, this is it.* So how did she get from Fishtrap Hollow to this house? More importantly, why did she stay? The answer had to be buried in Sallie's own words. *I have to admit, I'm obsessed with knowing.*

What did the next day's entry say? She flipped the page.

February 12, 1945

My x-ray yesterday didn't show any improvement over the one they did last week. Which means I'm still going to be a restricted patient here on the second floor. I used to like the light shade of green paint on the walls, but I'm getting really tired of seeing it. Mama, I wish you were here to hold me and make me better like you used to do when I was a little girl. I can still taste the hot lemonade you'd make whenever I had a cold.

There was a letter from home yesterday. They didn't say a whole lot, just that they missed me. It's like they don't hardly know what to say. Like they're afraid if they say too much they'll get the TB like I've got.

That's why I had to come here. So they wouldn't get it. So I couldn't give it to anybody at school or at church. I didn't even know I had it, but old Dr. McLaurin told Mama and Papa that I had all the symptoms. All I knew was I felt so bad and I had a fever and just couldn't seem to get better. I coughed up a lot of stuff. And I was losing weight. Mama said my clothes were just hanging on me.

Well, here comes my dinner. Wonder what we'll have today? I'll be so glad when I can sit up to eat instead of having to raise up in the bed and have somebody feed me.

February 13, 1945

Dr. Boswell was in the building today. I haven't met him yet, but a lot of the patients who've been here longer than I have say he's real nice, and real plain spoken. It seems he's the one who started this Sanatorium and he knows everything about treating TB. I'd like to ask him what he'd do to treat me.

Old Dr. McLaurin talked to him personally by long distance telephone before he brought me down here. They were in school together somewhere, so they know each other. Dr. McLaurin told him about me, and about my symptoms. Dr. Boswell said to get me here quick.

We left early the next morning. The sun wasn't even up good. I remember Papa with a mask over his face, carrying me to the back seat of Dr. McLaurin's big car. Mama had fixed blankets and a pillow and Papa laid me in there and covered me up good. That was on Saturday, the first Saturday in December. The date was the second and I knew there was no way I would be back home for Christmas.

I was right.

Saralynn's heart ached at that moment for the frightened teenager, afraid she would never see her parents again, who also had to spend Christmas critically ill and so far from home and family. *How agonizing that must have been.*

Then reality hit her. *Where will I spend Christmas this year? The holidays are only a few weeks away but what do I have to celebrate, and who do I have to celebrate with? Peter and Marc, all my reasons for Christmas, are gone.* The prospect of spending the holiday season back in Boston made her sick to her stomach.

Saralynn marked her place behind the last entry she'd read with a scrap of paper and took the notebook back inside. *I can't take much of this at one time.* She looked at her *watch. Mama should be landing in Boston any minute.*

That envelope! What did I do with the envelope Mr. Kennedy left for Mama? Unable to remember, she mounted a full-scale search before she finally uncovered the missing document among the packs of sealing tape in Sallie's bedroom.

I'd have been in a fine fix if I lost this.

Since she was out of the mood to read further at that moment, she decided to get started on the packing. Once the bubble wrap and the tape were close at hand and she had a few large boxes ready, Saralynn began to wrap the family photos Alicia had taken off the wall the day before.

With an assembly-line routine established, she would take a picture, swath it in bubble wrap and secure it with a wide band of the clear sealing tape. Once protected, she placed each piece into one of the boxes. And when the container was full, she closed the top flaps and sealed it with a couple of good applications of tape.

It was only after she had sealed the first carton that she realized she hadn't bought a marker to label the boxes.

Oh, well, I'll be back in town tomorrow. I'll buy one then.

To be sure she didn't forget, Saralynn found some scrap paper and wrote "family photos" on several pieces. She taped her homemade labels to each box as it was filled and ready to close.

It was the photo of the woman she now recognized as Sallie, who was probably in her 60's when the picture was made, that caused her to take a second look. The photo, obviously a recent one, was in one of the more valuable antique frames. All the other old frames held brown-toned pictures, some with age spots clearly evident.

I wonder, could there be something else under this newer photo?

The amateur detective searched until she found a screwdriver, then proceeded to remove the back from the fragile old frame. Her hunch was correct. Sallie's newer picture had been placed on top of an older photo of a young couple with two children, standing in front of the same house where Saralynn was now staying. *This has to be a photo of the Watson Family.*

Remembering her mother's comment on how she and Sallie resembled each other as teenagers, she took the time to study Sallie's likeness carefully.

Sallie would have been almost the same age in this picture that I am now.

She took the photo and crossed to the old cedar dresser with its big, round mirror. There she compared the woman in the old, brown picture to her own slightly grimy features.

Even though this is black and white, I'd judge that Sallie's hair had to be close to the color of mine. And those curls she has look to be natural as well. So she's the one I have to thank for the battle I fight with my blow dryer and styling brush every morning.

She judged that they both were about the same height. *After all, I was able to fit into her gardening clothes.* But what she studied most was her grandmother's wide set eyes. *Were they green, too? There's no way to tell. We definitely have the same turned up little nose that's gotten me so much teasing. And her mouth looks like she's in on a private joke. I'll bet she laughed a lot, too.*

Laughter had been another trait that attracted Peter, he'd admitted one special night not too long after their marriage. *I sure don't feel like laughing now. I wonder if Sallie ever had that problem?*

There was an unexplained feeling of kinship, probably due to the belief that she'd gotten inside her grandmother's skin. She carefully replaced the old photo in the frame and set it aside. *I won't pack it yet. I want it where I can study it again.*

Another hour of work saw the completion of everything from Sallie's bedroom that could be packed. Saralynn double-checked the inventory list on the furniture and knick-knacks that would be given to charity.

Seeing that it was only four o'clock, she decided to put in another hour or so, before calling it quits. Her early-morning trip to the airport was beginning to catch up with her, and she knew that if she sat down this early, she might not wake until morning.

Before going to bed the night before, Alicia had walked through the big living room. It hadn't taken her long to select just three small items to keep. "Everything else in here can go – either to charity or to the dump. You decide."

All of this stuff is out of style, but it's all in good condition. It would be a shame to toss it. She patted the still firm, but slightly faded upholstery on the occasional chair. *Nope. We'll give it to a thrift shop. For someone with nothing, this could look like a million bucks.*

It didn't take long to weed out the throwaway items and list on the inventory those pieces destined for charity. By the time she finished, Saralynn felt like she'd moved a couple of mountains. Since it was after five o'clock, she felt justified in calling it a day.

There's always tomorrow.

Then it hit her. *Tomorrow! I've got to have lunch with Katie Brooks and then eat with the Kennedys tomorrow night. When will I have time to work? Or to read?*

She had one foot already in the tub, preparing to wash off the afternoon's grime, when she remembered her mother's promise to call. *I'd better get my cell phone.*

Sure enough, she'd no sooner gotten the shampoo worked into her curls before the small phone began to chime and gyrate where she had laid it on the toilet seat next to the tub.

She reached out a soapy hand and grabbed it. "Hello."

"I'm exhausted, but I'm here." Alicia's voice sounded weary. *Or is it discouraged?* "And now that I am, I'm almost sorry."

"Surely it's not that bad." *The damage to the condo has to be more severe than she anticipated.*

"Believe me. It is bad. In some places the water was as much as six inches deep, judging by the marks on the walls and the furniture. The floors are ruined. Anything that was in contact with the floor, which was all my furniture, is headed for the dumpster, I'm afraid."

Her mother had worked an entire lifetime acquiring nice furniture, usually expensive and a great deal of it antique. Saralynn was sick over the damage that she could only imagine.

"Surely some of it can be salvaged and refinished."

"I don't know which is going to be the bigger headache, trying to get things restored or the ordeal of shopping for new."

"What about your condo itself?" She got out of the tub, shampoo still in her hair, and pulled on her robe. "How involved is that going to be?"

"All the hardwood floors will be to rip up, along with the carpet. Only the marble in the foyer and in the bathrooms can stay." Saralynn heard her sigh. "And all the walls will have to come down and be replaced."

"Sounds like you're going to have to rebuild your condo

from scratch."

"Pretty much," Alicia agreed. "Could you contact your carpenter... what's his name... Merle? I've got to meet with the insurance adjuster tomorrow afternoon, and I need someone I can trust to give me an estimate."

"Sure, Mama. I'll call him as soon as we hang up, and get back to you. Merle will give you solid numbers."

"Okay, I'll wait to hear from you. Are you too lonesome there by yourself?"

"I'm fine, Mama. Quit worrying."

"I'm a mother. I'm supposed to worry. It's part of my job description," She'd said it in a bantering tone, although Saralynn also detected the hint of an ultimatum. "I want you to eat right, even if you have to go to town to a restaurant."

"Don't worry, Mama. I'm not going to starve; not with the appetite I've had since I've been here. As a matter of fact," she informed her mother, "I'm having lunch tomorrow with Katie Brooks at some little French bistro at Boswell, and Mr. Walter Kennedy and his wife are having me over for dinner tomorrow night."

Mr. Walter left those papers for Mama!

"Mama, I almost forgot. Mr. Kennedy dropped off some papers today. He said it wasn't a formal appraisal, but that all he has to do is plug the information into the legal format and it will be a done deal."

"That was quick," Alicia said. "What kind of value did he put on the place?"

"I don't know. The envelope was sealed."

"Are you where you can give me that information now?"

"Sure. It's across the hall. Won't take a minute to get it."

She dashed from the bathroom and settled on the edge of the bed. Picking up the envelope, she slit it open to find three folded sheets of paper inside.

"Okay, I've got it in front of me. Now let's see if I can figure out what he's saying. Give me a minute to study it."

Saralynn scanned the typed pages, digesting the contents. It seemed that Mr. Kennedy was saying there were two different ways to market the property that would make a difference in the fair market value.

Finally, she said, "Here goes... There's the house and the fifty acres. If you advertise this as a small farmstead, he thinks you can get about eighteen hundred an acre, plus about thirty-five thousand for the house."

"That doesn't sound like very much."

"Not according to Boston land prices, it doesn't."

"So what's the other way?" Alicia asked.

"To list it as development property for a subdivision, you should be able to ask about four thousand an acre," Saralynn read from the documents the appraiser had brought.

"About seventy-five thousand more," her mother reflected. "That would definitely be the way to go."

"Does that mean they'd bulldoze this house?"

"I'm sure it does. I mean, who in their right mind would want it?"

"I kind of hate to see it go, given how old it is."

"Modern families want modern houses," her mother reminded her. "There's no telling how long it would stay on the market waiting for someone to buy it for a home."

"You're probably right, but it still makes me sad."

"Not me. I never liked that old barn, and that's all it is.

Why I'll bet Mr. Kennedy's got a buyer in the wings that wants to develop it. That's why he's giving me both options." Saralynn could hear the anticipation in her voice.

"Listen, Mama, Mr. Walter doesn't need an answer to-night. But I do need to catch Merle. Let me go and I'll call you back before bed."

After a couple of attempts, she made contact with her contractor on his cell phone. "I'm stalled in traffic on Massachu-setts Avenue," he reported. Saralynn could sense his frustration. "It means I'll be eating warmed over dinner again tonight," he groused. "Marjorie goes ahead and feeds the kids and keeps mine in the oven."

I'd totally forgotten Boston traffic in the short time I've been down here. It's always rough at this time of day, especially if you're trying to get over to Cambridge where Merle lives.

"So what can I do for you? I didn't know you'd gone back to work."

"I haven't. I'm on R & R in Mississippi right now."

"Mississippi!" Merle's Boston brogue pronounced it Massassippi. "That's one place I don't ever expect to visit, and I sure wouldn't want to live there," he vowed. "Can't believe you went there of your own free will."

His accent sounds so strange. Does that mean my ear has gotten accustomed to the speech here?

"Look, Merle. I need your help in a hurry." She recounted the problems in her mother's condo and got his agreement to meet Alicia there at seven-thirty the next morning.

"I'll call her back and tell her to expect you. And thanks, Merle. I owe you."

"You've given me a lot of business. It's the least I can do.

Listen," he said, "don't let them hold you prisoner down there. You belong back here in Boston."

"Before I got here, I wouldn't have argued with you. But I'm finding a lot to make me like it here."

"You can have my part of it, then" he said. "Tell your mother I'll see her tomorrow."

"Will do. Goodnight, Merle."

I told him I'm starting to like this place. That's interesting, since I haven't even told myself! So where did that come from?

Unconsciously she put her fingers to her head and her hand came away soapy.

Oh, my gosh! I've still got shampoo in my hair. I've got to get this stuff washed out quickly or there won't be enough conditioner in Simpson County to repair the damage!

She dashed to the bathroom, climbed back into the tub and held her head under the running water for several minutes, before finally wringing out the excess and applying a liberal amount of conditioner.

Curly hair is curse enough without deliberately giving myself the frizzies!

Once she felt she'd done all the damage control possible, Saralynn finished bathing, dried off and went ahead and put on her pajamas.

I'm not going back out tonight.

Dinner, she decided, would be a sandwich with all the trimmings she could find, with one of the pastries she'd fallen prey to while standing at the deli counter. In short order, she had her evening feast ready and on the table. That's when the isolation caught her. She realized that, once again, she was all alone.

Please, God. Don't let me cry. It's not that I'm afraid to be here by myself. Then it hit her. *I asked God to help me. I don't think I've ever done that before. Is Sallie rubbing off on me?*

While she wasn't exactly embarrassed, Saralynn did find it an interesting, strangely warming sensation to have called for God's help. *I'm still the only one here, but suddenly I don't feel alone.*

Deciding that she didn't want to eat by herself in the kitchen, she found a tray and carried her dinner – *I've got to remember… they call it supper down here* – into the little corner bedroom that had become so comfortable. The small, wooden rocker by the bedside table was calling her name and she settled into it, balancing the plate in her lap.

This had been Uncle Tony's room. *Seems like he was about four years younger than Mama.* Her uncle left a week after graduating from high school, when he enlisted in the Marines. When he came home from Vietnam less than a year later, it had been to a plot at Rials Creek Cemetery. There were still traces of a 1960's era teenager here and there about the room.

One item that caught her eye was a photo of an athletic team in uniform. *Uncle Tony must have played football. I wonder what he was like?* After the last bite of her apple turnover, she got up to study the photo more closely. Unfortunately, wearing their helmets, the players all tended to look alike. *I can't make out which one he is.*

Questions about the uncle who had died so young made her think of Sallie's journals again, and she decided there was no time like the present.

I may not have TV, but this story is as captivating as any of the shows on tonight. It'll just be Sallie and me.

She found the notebook she'd been reading from earlier that the afternoon, and piled down on the bed, prepared to learn more about her grandmother's early life. Once she'd punched her pillows into a comfortable backrest, she flipped the old book open and in a matter of minutes, was back in Sallie's room at the Sanatorium. Saralynn found herself mesmerized as the young girl so far from home continued to tell her story.

February 14, 1945

I had company today. Two women from town came through the hospital bringing a valentine to every patient who wasn't in quarantine. I hadn't even remembered that it was Valentine's Day until they brought my dinner tray and the card was on it. I lose track of time when I lay here day after day.

The last holiday we had, it hurt so bad. It was Christmas and I spent it right here in this room. I had prayed all that week before Christmas that if I couldn't go home, Mama and Papa would come here. I prayed, but I think I knew they wouldn't come. And they didn't. There wasn't even a Christmas present from anybody at home. Somebody from one of the local churches brought gifts for every patient. It hurts to think that even your own family is afraid they'll get sick if they write you a letter.

February 15, 1945

When I first got here, I thought this was the most beautiful room. It's a shade of apple green and the walls are tall and the ceiling is white. None of the rooms in our house in Fishtrap Hollow are painted. But I've looked at these green walls so long I've really gotten tired of them. My room is on the second floor, on the corner, and I've got windows on two walls. The first morning I woke up here, there were still enough leaves on the trees that I couldn't see very well laying flat in my bed, the way they make me do. But now, all I see are bare tree limbs. I wonder if spring and green leaves will ever come. I wonder if I'll ever get to go home again.

February 16, 1945

It's very quiet on this end of the hall. Allyson, the patient in the room next to mine, died early this morning. It's not the first time I've known when someone died, but this is the closest it's ever come to me. None of her family was here. Just the nurses. Since I don't get to leave my room except when I go to x-ray, I'd never talked to her. If her door was open, I'd wave to her as they wheeled me down the hall, and sometimes she'd wave back. I thought she looked like she was about 35 or so, but Nurse Myra, my favorite on the day shift, said she was only 22. Oh, Mama, I want you to hold me so bad. I'm scared. Why don't you answer my letters?

Saralynn couldn't stop the tears that coursed down her cheeks and landed on the oversize tee shirt that once had been Peter's. She wore it now as a sleep shirt. A quick shove sent the precious journal out of range of her tears. *Oh, Sallie, I can just imagine how alone and scared you must have been. Only you got through your fears. I don't know how I'm ever going to live by myself again when I go back to Boston. How did you do it?*

She pulled up the hem of the shirt and wiped her eyes. *What was your secret, because I sure need some of it!*

In search of how her grandmother had managed to find what Alicia had referred to as "faith" in the midst of all the fear and loneliness, the young woman picked up the fragile old tablet continuing to read. After scanning the next few entries, finding more of the same, she jumped ahead to the first day of March.

✏️

Tomorrow will start my fourth month here. I'm excited and I'm scared, too. Tomorrow is my weekly x-ray to see how the TB in my left lung is, compared to what it was when I got here on December 2. Myra, my favorite nurse, says that if things look better, I'll be able to move around a little more.

I finally had a letter from Mama last week, but I've waited to answer it, to see if I can give them some good news. Poor Mama. She blames herself for me getting sick, but it wasn't her fault that we're poor and she couldn't cook the food I needed. Nurse Myra says that's one of the main treatments, is to eat good, wholesome food, to build up your body to fight the TB germs.

Also, everything is kept very, very clean. I tried to explain to Mama in one of my letters a while back about the sputum cups, but I don't think she understood. When you have TB, you cough a lot, and the stuff you cough up is called sputum. To keep from spreading the germs, we all have to cough into these little cardboard containers that have cotton in the bottom. Then we throw away the container and all. Nobody spits on the grounds or even into trashcans. That's Dr. Boswell's rule.

✏️

Oh, Sallie, you just have to get a good report. Saralynn found herself half afraid to flip the page to the young woman's thoughts on March 2. *If they tell her she's no better, I don't think I can stand it.* It was almost as if she were there with Sallie, instead of 60 years ahead.

I was so frightened I wanted to hold my breath this morning. I was trembling, I was so nervous. But the doctor in x-ray said he really needed me to breathe normally, so I tried. While I was waiting for Dr. McCallum to come around to see me later in the morning, after he'd looked at my "pictures" as they call them, I noticed that the trees outside my windows have tiny, green buds on them. Maybe spring really is coming. Here comes the nurse. She says that Dr. McCallum's been held up. That probably means somebody's dying. And she says I need to get back into bed to rest. The doctor will see me after dinner. So I don't know if this means I'm better or not. Maybe I'll write more, later tonight.

The sound of her cell phone's ring interrupted Saralynn's visit to the Sanatorium. She grabbed for it just as it stopped playing its catchy tune. "Hello...?"

The "Missed Call" feature showed that the call had come from her home number in Boston. *Mama! I totally forgot I promised to call her.* She punched the buttons to redial the last call received, and in a moment, Alicia was on the other end, saying, "Did you forget about me? I hope you were able to contact Merle."

"Yes, I got Merle. So relax. He'll meet you at your condo at 7:30 in the morning," she reassured the older woman. "I didn't forget as much as I got involved in what I'm reading and the time just got away from me."

"That must be some good book. I might want to borrow it when you finish."

"Well you know you can," she joked with a gaiety she didn't feel. *Something tells me if you had a clue what I'm reading, you'd ban it in Boston and in Mississippi!*

The two women chatted for a few more minutes before Alicia reported that everything at the townhouse was secure, and Saralynn promised her mother that she would be careful, "all alone in Mississippi."

Mama makes it sound like I'm in the wilds of an Amazon jungle somewhere. Granted, this isn't Boston, but it's not a third world country, either. Then she remembered that only a few weeks earlier, back in Boston, she'd referred to the state as exactly that… *a third world country.*

"Well, get back to your reading," her mother instructed, breaking Saralynn's thought train of guilt. "I'm about to call it a night. Seems like it's been forever since I flew out of Jackson this morning."

Doesn't it, though? Was that really only this morning?

"Goodnight, Mama. Call me tomorrow, after Merle leaves. I'm anxious to know what he thinks."

After promising once again to be on her guard, Saralynn punched the button to end the conversation and picked up Sallie's notebook. There had been a wavy line drawn horizontally below the last entry Saralynn had been reading when her mother called. The next section below the line didn't carry a new date, and since the entry that started at the bottom of the page was dated March 3, she concluded that Sallie had indeed added to her day's thoughts on that early spring morning so very long ago.

But do I want to know what those thoughts are?

Unable to resist the temptation, and despite the butterflies in her stomach, Saralynn dived into the passage that was much longer than most of the earlier ones. The writing, while it definitely was Sallie's, had a hurried, almost careless appearance about it. *Was she excited, or was it heartbreak that made her usually neat cursive scrawls more reckless than usual?*

⬤➡

Dr. McCallum finally got here, when I had almost given up on seeing him today. And he looked so tired I knew he'd had a rough day. But I wouldn't ask him about it. Maybe that's selfish, but I could tell by the grin on his sweet face that he wasn't bringing bad news. I only wanted to know about me.

X-rays looked good, he says. We've still got a long ways to go, but he says we're making progress. Says I'm lucky because we caught it fairly early. That's funny, because I've not felt lucky through any of this. I finally got the courage to ask him if this meant I wasn't going to die.

His answer really surprised me. I was sitting in the big chair in the corner of my room, and he pulled up a straight chair right in front of me. He took both my hands in his, and then he said, "I'm the doctor, and I'm doing everything I know to do for you. But I'm just one part of the solution."

When I asked him what the other part of the solution was, because I really wanted to get well, he asked if I was a praying person. I said, "Well, I guess I am. I do pray sometimes."

Then he said, "Well if I do what I know how to do medically, and you and I both pray, and ask God to do what He does best, then I think we have a pretty good chance of pulling you through this."

He released my hands and got up out of the chair. Then he said, "I always pray for God's healing, but I also have to accept that sometimes God's idea of healing and mine aren't exactly the same. And whether I like it or not, I have to accept that my prayer was answered, just not in the way I had hoped."

But when I asked him again which kind of healing he thought I'd have, he said he felt real good that it would be the kind we both wanted. "But remember, prayer is just as much a medicine for what ails you as anything else we can do for you here. In fact, prayer will do what we can't."

He told me that I can leave my room for a few minutes every day to go and sit in the solarium, where I can actually have conversations with other people. But we have to go slow.

Just as he was about to leave, we both caught sight of a young man climbing into the upper branches of one of the big trees right outside my window. The doctor's face broke out in a big grin, and he crossed the room to one of the windows facing the tree. "Ralph Watson," he called out to the man, "What are you doing up that tree? Mighty sneaky way to get in to court the ladies. If you fall, they'll call me to come put you back together, and I'm tired. I've had a long, hard day."

Ralph Watson! He was my grandfather. Saralynn's finger ran over the passage, faded almost to the point of illegibility, as though those second-hand memories could somehow connect her with this ancestor she'd never known. *So that's how they met!*

The young man, who was a stranger to me, yelled back, "Don't worry, Doc. I know what I'm doing. There's a cat stuck up in this big ole tree and it's afeered to come down. I just come up after it."

I saw him snake out a long arm and grab the frightened cat, which he quickly stuck into a tow sack he'd had tucked in the crook of his arm. Then he started back down the tree. I heard him holler, "See ya at th' bottom, Doc!"

Dr. McCallum just roared with laughter. His thick mane of wavy red hair acted like it was alive, he was laughing so hard. "That Ralph Watson," he said, "he's the kindest-hearted soul I've ever known."

I've got to write Mama and Papa tonight to tell them what the doctor said. And I might tell them about the cat rescue I saw, too.

Entries for the next few days held little, if any, new information. Sallie wrote about the news of the war overseas, what she'd heard about a battle at a place called Corrigador and how the tree branches outside her room were getting greener by the day. There was no further mention of the young man who liked to climb among the heights rescuing frightened felines.

How am I ever going to have time to read through almost 60 years of memories? Yet I'm afraid if I skip even one day's entry, I might miss the very thing I'm looking for.

Saralynn glanced at the clock and saw that it was nearly ten o'clock. *That's eleven Boston time, and as much at home as I feel here, my body is still operating an hour ahead.* She determined to read for another twenty minutes or so before putting out the light and calling it a night.

Scanning each day's entries, she read about the Easter services Sallie was able to attend, the coming of warmer weather and open windows through which cooling breezes played mischief with the items on her grandmother's bedside table. Summer came quickly on the heels of spring, and Sallie spoke of the fresh vegetables that patients were enjoying from the Sanatorium gardens.

Other notations, most with dates that harkened to earlier days, contained more clinical information about the regular x-rays, talks with the doctors, still more deaths on the floor, and of new patients being admitted. Saralynn learned that new admissions were evaluated and assigned a color code to designate the severity of their disease. The more ill a patient was, the more restrictions that were imposed. Their regimen of treatment was more extreme.

Sallie continued to write of her homesickness that was, Saralynn believed from the benefit of an outsider looking in, caused as much by her illness as it was by the separation from her family.

They probably didn't have the money to come to Magee to see her, but if what Sallie has recorded in these first six months is any indication, they rarely wrote to her either. They didn't even send her a piece of peppermint candy at Christmas.

Her belief that Sallie's parents hadn't truly loved their daughter persisted, despite Alicia's earlier explanation that the era and traditional parent-child relationships were different.

There is no way you could have kept me from Marc's side, even if I had been on the other side of the world. And the thought once again of the double loss she had sustained brought quick tears to her eyes, at the same time her resolve to discover Sallie's secret strengthened.

She continued to scan the pages, getting very close to the

back of the first book, when a sentence in an entry dated October 11, 1945 caught her eye. She stopped and went back to re-read it slowly and completely. Something was obviously wrong.

◑⟩

I just haven't felt like myself for several days now and Dr. McCallum has ordered another x-ray. It hasn't even been a week since I had my last x-ray. Something's wrong. Even Nurse Myra who's usually so chatty has been quiet today. She said the doctor would be around later this afternoon to talk to me. He's in surgery right now.

So far, I've been spared the surgery, but I know plenty here who have had it. They go in and cut out the diseased part of your lung to get rid of the TB. I've heard some of the other patients talk about how the operating rooms run twenty-four hours a day sometimes. I don't want an operation. Please, God, I don't want to be cut on. Papa always said you don't never come back the same after you're cut on.

Here comes the nurse to help me get back to bed. They're not letting me sit up as much as I have been, and I've not been outside my room, except to go to x-ray, in more than a week now.

◑⟩

The next entry was dated October 13, 1945. It was short, cryptic, and to the point.

◑⟩

Didn't write yesterday. Just didn't feel like it. The x-rays showed that TB has set up in my other lung, and the original location that had been healing has gotten worse. I've been put back to bed full-time, no more even sitting up in my chair. Dr. McCallum is calling Mama and Papa today to talk to them. I don't know what's going to happen. Dr. McCallum promised me that he'd do all he knew to do, if I'd pray for him and healing. And I thought I was. Now I'm afraid we're going to get the healing we don't want.

Then there were no further entries, even though several blank pages remained at the back of the book.

Saralynn's heart broke, and she lay on her bed and sobbed as hard as she ever had for Peter and Marc. *Even though I know that she survived, I hurt so bad for her. And I still don't understand where she got that faith that was supposed to make everything better.*

Finally, when her tears were spent, she got up and replaced the notebook in the small suitcase. *Tomorrow I'll look for the second volume. But not tonight. I'm not sure I want to know what came next.*

After double-checking the locks on the old outside doors, and putting out the lights in the rest of the house, Saralynn pulled back the covers and crawled into the bed that had, by now, become very comfortable and just the right size for her. Almost before the room was dark, she dropped off into a deep, if not entirely restful sleep, where she lived through a dream so ridiculous she vowed never to tell anyone about it. Most especially, not Alicia.

Chapter 5

The nice thing, Saralynn discovered early on, about living in the country without a job to dictate schedules was not being a slave to the clock. The down side was the chance of oversleeping.

The sound of her cell phone, combined with the precise angle of the Mississippi morning sun streaming through a gap in the café curtains, yanked her from a sound slumber.

Oh, my gosh! Am I late? She tried to focus her drowsy eyes on the clock at the same time that she grabbed for the phone.

"I was getting worried. This is the fourth time I've called you this morning."

"Sorry, Mama." She yawned. "I guess I was sleeping really hard." She yawned again. "What time is it, anyway? I can't see the clock."

"It's almost ten o'clock here, so it's nearly nine there. You lay awake half the night scared to death, didn't you?"

"Sorry. I read until after eleven, and then I turned off the light and slept like a baby. I didn't know anything that happened until about three minutes ago."

"Well, I'd much rather you overslept."

"It's been a long time since I've felt so rested. Except I did have a dream you…" Then the full impact of her middle of the night imagery hit her. She knew she could never share it with her mother. *I'm not even going to admit to myself that I entertained such an idea. Not even in a dream!*

"One of your bad dreams?"

"No, no, Mama. Nothing of the sort. It was one of those crazy dreams where you do things that could never happen in real life."

"So tell me about it."

*What do I say? **What** do I say?*

"Now, Mama. You know that if you tell a dream before breakfast, supposedly it'll come true. I haven't eaten yet, so I'm not taking any chances. I'll tell you later."

Her mother's laugh told her she'd gotten away with it.

"What's happening? Tell me about Merle's inspection."

"I don't know where to start. Bottom line, it's going to be a very extensive project. Expensive, too."

Alicia went on to explain that Merle's reputation with the insurance adjuster was a solid one, which would greatly expedite her meeting with the man who would ultimately write the check.

"Basically, I have to completely empty out everything and salvage what few things I can to be refinished and re-upholstered. We'll throw away what can't be saved, and make a decision about what I want to replace. The rest will have to be packed and moved into storage until the renovation is completed."

"Sounds like you're going to have a big job on your hands. When can Merle start?"

"He says he'll put a crew in here as soon as I get it empty."

"Then you won't be back here in the next couple of days like you'd thought."

"That's what's worrying me most. The thought of leaving you down there all alone really bothers me. It may be two weeks or more before I can pull away."

"Not to worry, Mama." *How many times do I have to say this?* "I'm perfectly fine. Okay? Coping well, so don't worry about me."

"You say that now, but what about in another week when the isolation gets to you?"

"I hear what you're saying, but I also think you're making much ado about nothing."

Mama is not going to let go of this. Why can't she tell just by my actions and the sound of my voice that I'm better? It was the first time she had admitted to herself that her grief was starting to lift. Even more surprising was the lack of guilt she felt.

"Just promise me you'll be… oh, oh… there's the bell… Merle's sending over two men to haul off the stuff I'm throwing out, so I imagine that's them. Let me go."

Saved by the bell. Only my mind was wandering again. I don't have a clue what Mama said. Sure hope it wasn't something important.

"I'll call you tonight before bed."

"Okay, Mama. Talk to you then."

If she's gonna call, she's gonna call. I might as well accept it.

Saralynn was ready to snuggle under the covers for a few more minutes, when she remembered her social commitments for the day. Instead of indulging in the life of a lazy lay-about, a term she'd adopted from the British sitcoms she and Peter had enjoyed watching together, she hauled herself out of bed and into the bathroom.

Soon she was behind the wheel of the minivan, driving the country roads to Boswell, once the village of Sanatorium in its own right and now just a part of nearby Magee. She was struck once again by the uncomplicated lifestyle that she saw. True, there were no grand mansions, and some of the homes were acutely in need of TLC. Yet there was an unmistakable aura of flawed perfection that was totally lacking in Boston.

It's almost as if they've got some secret here. Like they've all managed to find the best and forget about the rest.

True to her promise, her hostess was waiting in a small, blue Toyota in the turn-around near the entrance. When the two made eye contact, her new friend waved, indicating that Saralynn should follow.

This is some more maze of roads in here. I'm glad I'm behind her and not trying to follow someone's directions.

Katie swung her car into a vacant parking space surrounded by a number of tall, older buildings obviously from an earlier era. They exhibited a certain comfort and charm. *I still say it reminds me of an old college campus. It looks like a setting for a Judy Garland and Mickey Rooney movie from the 1930s.* Saralynn found a space nearby and parked the van, got out and hit the door lock.

"You really don't have to do that," Katie said, as she walked to meet Saralynn. "Nobody locks their doors here."

Saralynn laughed, suddenly a little uncomfortable that she'd been caught.

"Did it automatically. You wouldn't think of leaving a car unlocked where I'm from."

"That's just one reason I'm glad I don't live there. Hey," she said, grabbing hold of her guest's arm, "Let's hit that lunch line. I think you're going to like this."

When Saralynn found time later, alone back at Sallie's house, she had to admit lunch had been most enjoyable. The large, high-ceilinged dining room had been totally renovated by Boswell personnel volunteering their time and expertise. Complete with hand-painted murals that captured the essence of the French countryside, the LeGrand's food was as impressive as its décor. High-spirited conversations floated along with the delicious-smelling aromas in the room, giving it a comfortable atmosphere.

The people were more than professional colleagues. They were friends, practically family in many ways Saralynn realized, as Katie began making introductions. There was no hierarchy or rank. Department heads were sharing tables with regular employees and no one had an agenda other than the enjoyment of a good meal and a break from their respective duties.

The two women selected their items from the cafeteria line staffed by several cheerful women in regulation hairnets who were determined that no one would leave hungry.

Saralynn was unprepared, but tried not to show it when, once they were seated, Katie said, "I usually say a short blessing before I eat. Do you mind?"

Unable to speak, Saralynn simply bowed her head as a silent response.

"Lord, thank you for this another day, for this new friend, and for this food. Bless our time together and bless this meal to the nourishment of our bodies and they to Your service. In Jesus' name. Amen."

Saralynn didn't know how to respond. *I've been in public gatherings where a prayer was offered, but it always seemed more like part of the welcome, the "thing" to do. But this was different, almost like she was talking to a friend. I hope Katie doesn't think I was offended, I just wasn't expecting it.*

The two attacked their food, which was, just as Katie had promised, delicious.

"I'm so stuffed I can hardly move," Saralynn complained when she finally pushed her dessert plate to the other side of her tray. "That muffin was heavenly. In fact, everything was delicious."

"You can see why this place is so popular. Even people from outside the community often come here for lunch."

"You mean they can just drive onto the grounds to eat?"

"Sure. This is an open campus. Always has been, even when it was the tuberculosis hospital. Unfortunately, in those days, many people were afraid of the place. It's a lot different, now."

"Did you live here then?" Saralynn asked, wondering how her hostess could be so knowledgeable.

"Not on the grounds, but I did grow up about two miles down the road. Both my parents were on staff. They're retired now, so this place has always felt like home. During the Sanatorium days especially, it was like one huge family."

"Are there a lot of people here who have those kinds of connections?"

"The number gets smaller every year, as you might well imagine. Did you happen to notice the remains of what was once an old motel just before you got to the main gate?"

Saralynn admitted she had. "I wondered about that."

"That's where one of the department heads, David Tedford, grew up. He's sitting at that table by the door." She pointed to a man who looked to be in his fifties, wearing glasses. "His parents built that motel so that patients' families who came to visit would have a place to stay that would be convenient to the Sanatorium. It was also a place where TB patient families were welcomed with open arms."

"I'm not sure I understand."

"At one time TB was a very feared disease. People weren't sure how you got it, so they feared what they didn't know. Patients' families would come from out of town to visit their loved one, and maybe they could get a room at the hotels in Magee and Mendenhall, and maybe they couldn't.

"You mean the management was afraid they'd bring the TB germ into the hotel?"

"Precisely." Katie slammed her hand down on the table-top to emphasize her opinion of such discrimination. "David's parents' motel – it was called 'The Sans' – stayed full as long as the Sanatorium was in business.

"And I thought the only discrimination in Mississippi was racial."

"Hate to burst your northern bubble, but race was just one of the injustices that used to live and flourish here."

"You say 'used to'. Is discrimination a thing of the past now?"

"For tuberculosis, sure. When it comes to the mentally challenged, well, we're still working on that. And there are still some race problems, although most will tell you that the past ten years have done a lot to eradicate that as well. Just don't expect to hear it announced on the national news."

"It might destroy the myth, huh?"

"Sure thing. It gives the media a basis for stories if they can perpetuate the persistent rumor that we still enslave African-Americans down here. And to be fair, there are still pockets of bigotry scattered here and there. When one of them erupts, the entire state gets smeared with the same tarred brush."

"You know," Saralynn offered up, "I hadn't thought about it, but the same is true in Boston. If you're descended from Irish immigrants who arrived after 1900, you're not the same caliber as others. That's what my husband, Peter, used to tell me. He was an associate professor at Boston College, but despite his credentials, his roots weren't always pure enough for some of the old line Irish."

"You speak of your husband in the past tense. Seeing as how this would be the middle of fall term, I could assume you left him behind at work. Or am I being nosey?"

Why did I have to mention Peter's name? It's like I can't even remember that he's dead?

"Yes... he's in... in Boston." Then, without warning, the tears began to course their well-worn tracks in her cheeks. "He's... he's dead," she finally managed to stammer, before her luncheon host with the shocked face could inquire further. "He and my son were killed... about two months ago... in an automobile accident."

"Oh, Saralynn? I'm sorry. I shouldn't have asked."

"Why not? It's a perfectly innocent question. Besides, you had no way of knowing." She stopped, and choked up on her own words again, before she was finally able to continue. "You see," she admitted somewhat awkwardly, "you're the very first outsider I've told about Peter and Marc. It came as sort of a shock to me, that I was able to do that."

"If you need a shoulder to cry on, just say the word. And if you want to forget that you dropped your guard and pretend this didn't happen, that's fine too." She began stacking their soiled dinnerware onto her tray. "Either way, let me dispose of this, and we'll go out and walk off our lunch, if you'd like."

"I'd like that very much." Saralynn conveniently side-stepped her host's offer of a sympathetic shoulder.

I'm really not sure if I want to talk about it or not. Katie's the first person who didn't already know. But it did feel good to admit the truth.

Once outside, Katie suggested, "Let's just walk – trust me, we won't get lost – and I'll tell you what each building was when this was the Sanatorium. You'll notice there are a few new structures, too."

"My impression that day Mama and I first met you was that this might be a college campus."

"It does have that feel, doesn't it?" Katie agreed. "Dr. Boswell who founded this place gets the credit, I guess. He was one more politician, in addition to being an expert on the diagnosis and treatment of tuberculosis."

"And he's the man for whom the place is named?"

"That's right. Dr. Henry Boswell. Did you notice as we drove through the campus what used to be a golf course?"

"I wondered about that."

The two had reached one of the older buildings that now stood abandoned. "This was one of the patient buildings," Katie told her as they settled themselves on a nearby bench. "As you can see, it's falling in and will probably be torn down soon. I grieve when I see each one taken away."

"So what about the golf course?"

"Dr. Boswell loved to play golf. Today we'd call him an addict." She laughed. "He played golf every day, even in rare Mississippi snow!"

"You've got to be kidding."

"Nope. He used colored golf balls. And when he wanted something from the state, he'd have the governor come down here. He didn't go to Jackson. That's how powerful he was."

"It evidently paid off, if this complex is any indication."

"But it was a double-edged sword. Dr. Boswell was so good he literally put the hospital out of business. At least out of the TB business. But in its prime, this was Dr. Boswell's kingdom."

Katie leaned over to pick one last zinnia that was growing volunteer in a bed next to the bench. "My mother was on the switchboard one day when the governor called Dr. Boswell. Only Dr. Boswell was on the golf course, so mother asked the governor to hold and sent someone down to get him."

"And let me guess," Saralynn begged. "Let me guess that Dr. Boswell sent word back to take a message, that he'd return the call when he got off the golf course."

"How'd you know?"

"Simple deduction," Saralynn grinned. Then, before she could stop herself, she added, "My Peter would have been exactly the same way." She choked back a sob. "If he'd been on the golf course when I went into labor with Marc, I have no doubt that I'd have driven myself to the hospital." *Not that Mama would have let me.*

She smiled a lopsided, teary grin, and said, "I love him so much. Both of them."

Katie put her arm around this new friend. "I don't want to pressure you, but the offer of a shoulder still stands. Take your pick," she said with a grin. "I've got two. You can have them both if you need them."

For the longest time, Saralynn couldn't answer. *I don't trust myself not to go to pieces.* "May I ask you something?"

"Sure."

"Back at lunch, when I told you that Peter and Marc were dead. And again, just now... you didn't get overly emotional or tell me it would all be okay. So I'm curious."

"Did you want me to tell you that? Have I offended you?"

"No," Saralynn answered quickly, afraid she couldn't get the words out if she thought about them. "I didn't want to hear that. One of the reasons I had become such a hermit in Boston was because. I didn't think I could take one more person patting me on the shoulder and telling me that everything would be okay. Especially when I knew it wouldn't."

"And that's why I didn't respond that way." Katie's voice was soft and patient. "It's never going to be okay – not in the sense that your husband or son will ever come back. Or that you will ever be able to forget them."

"That's how I felt, too. I just didn't know how to put it into words. And I sure don't know how to build a new life without them."

"Well, for starters," Katie counseled, "you don't try to do it without them. You have to do it with them, with all the precious memories that you have. Over time, those precious keepsakes will push the bad memories into the background."

"I never thought about it like that."

"And you build that foundation of memories by talking about them. As strange as it sounds, you'd think you had to keep your memories bottled up to prevent them from disappearing. But it's just the opposite. The more you talk about Peter, was that his name? And your son...?"

"Marc."

"Marc," Katie continued, "the more alive they will be to

you, and to those around you. And the sweeter and the more permanent your memories will become."

"You sound like you're talking from experience," Saralynn observed.

"Yeah, well, life gives you lots of opportunities to practice this philosophy. Some day, because I have a feeling we'll still be friends even after you go back to Boston, I'll tell you about it. But not now."

As they continued to sit beneath the ancient magnolia tree that was losing the last of its creamy blossoms, Saralynn told her new friend everything. Starting with Marc's pleas for ice cream, and ending with the diaries she'd found in the attic and what she was learning about her grandmother."

During the hour-long session, during which Saralynn cried and laughed, and cried some more, Katie never once interrupted. Never told her to calm down, or not to get so upset. At last, Saralynn admitted, "And I don't know how I go on from here."

"You just get up and walk on through life. In exactly the same way that we're about to get up and walk down this path."

"But it's so hard."

"Sure. A lot of things in life are. But just like we're going to walk over to that other building together, you don't have to walk through life alone either."

Saralynn didn't know how to respond. For the moment, she said nothing. But as they strolled side by side beneath the towering trees, approaching one of the original buildings, she found the courage to ask, "Are you religious? You're not a minister or something like that, are you?"

"I'm not a minister, not in the way I think you mean. But I am a Christian and I do go to church. I'm not quite sure that religious tag applies. I don't think I'd want to be labeled."

Saralynn wasn't sure how to respond to that answer, so instead, she changed the subject.

"I wish I could get a better feel for how this place was when Sallie – that's my grandmother – was a patient here in the mid-to-late 1940s."

"But you can. The Sanatorium employees, those who were here when the emphasis changed, worked hard to preserve that era. People are very proud of this heritage. We've got a small museum that has a lot of interesting memorabilia that would tell you a lot."

Saralynn felt as if her head were spinning. "Why do I feel like I'm in a time warp? I don't mean that in a bad way." *I don't want to insult Katie.* "Mississippi is an entirely different world... the people," she stammered, "they... they seem more... more connected, somehow."

Katie smiled, but said nothing.

"I'm not saying that very well, am I? If only I could put into words what I've discovered. But how can I do that when I don't even understand it myself?"

After another awkward silence, Katie came to her rescue, "If you had just offered that explanation to a neighbor in Boston, I assume they wouldn't have a clue what you meant? But to those of us who live here everyday, it's a given."

"So if you understand, would you please explain it to me?" Saralynn asked.

"I didn't say I understood it. I said it was a given. There's a big difference. Sometimes we have to accept on faith those things that we know are right, whether we understand completely or not."

Faith! There's that word again. Mama said Sallie had faith.

But she was talking about church and God. That's not the same kind of faith Katie means. Is it?

Finding herself boxed into another uncomfortable corner, Saralynn again elected to change the subject. "So where is this museum? I'd love to see it."

Katie looked at her watch. "May I give you a rain check? My baby sitter can only stay until three o'clock, and it's nearly that now. You see, the museum isn't open on a daily basis, because right now its as much a warehouse archive as it is a museum. I'll have to get someone from Security to open it for us."

"It's almost three o'clock! I didn't realize we'd talked that long. I'm sorry."

"Oh, don't apologize. I've enjoyed every minute and we're going to do this again."

I'm not uncomfortable with Katie, even though I don't truly understand her. But I want to know her better. "I want us to do this again, too. Only next time, lunch is my treat."

"You're on. And the museum will be mine."

As the two new friends began the trek back to their vehicles, Saralynn told Katie about the damage to her mother's condo, and her dinner invitation from Walter Kennedy. "Mama won't admit it, but she's going to be in Boston for at least another two or three weeks. I just wish she'd stop worrying about me."

"You'll enjoy your evening with the Kennedys," assured Katie. "They're both fine people. I should know; we have a family connection. Their house is interesting, too. It's one of the oldest houses in the county, you know."

"I didn't," Saralynn admitted. "Now you've gotten my curiosity aroused."

"Good. Then you won't get bored. Be sure you tell your

mother that she doesn't need to worry about you. We're going to see to that!"

After goodbye hugs and repeated promises to talk in the next day or so, the two parted company and Saralynn pointed the nose of the van in the direction of the front gate. After only one wrong turn, which she immediately realized and corrected, she pulled onto the public highway.

I'm not sure why I feel so at peace, but I do. Lunch with Katie wasn't at all what I expected.

There wasn't time, once she got home, to delve into Sallie's diaries, even though her appetite to learn more had only been intensified by her visit to the old Sanatorium grounds.

Instead, she busied herself getting ready for the evening engagement, and was ready a good fifteen minutes before her host arrived to claim her. While she waited, she went back over the day's events, starting with her mother's wake-up phone call.

Mama sure didn't need to worry about me today. I've not been alone long enough to do anything more than bathe and change clothes.

The short six-mile trip to the Kennedy home was accomplished in quick fashion, so fast in fact, that Saralynn felt she had barely begun to have a get-acquainted conversation before they turned into a drive that led to a spacious, solid looking home, obviously of older vintage."

This kind of reminds me of Sallie's house. Only it's larger.

"Katie Brooks told me I'd find your home interesting," she admitted as her host escorted her up the back steps and into a huge keeping room-kitchen that was obviously of more recent construction."

"How do you know Katie?" He was unable to hide his surprise.

"Believe it or not, I had lunch with her today."

She laughed at the amazement she saw in his face. "Mama and I drove onto the grounds at Boswell the other afternoon, and she was out walking. We stopped her to ask for some information. Then I ran into her in Wal-Mart again yesterday, and when she found out Mama had gone back to Boston, she insisted that I come and have lunch and see the campus."

"So what did you think?" As he spoke, an attractive blonde woman came from the kitchen area and caught him in the crook of his arm.

"Of Boswell? Or Katie?"

"Well, both, I guess." He laughed. "But first, I'd like you to meet your other host for the evening." He turned to face the woman on his arm, "Saralynn Reilly, meet Virginia Kennedy. She and your mother went to school together."

"That's what I understand," Saralynn replied. "It's so nice of you to have me tonight, Mrs. Kennedy. I told your husband, the next time we eat, it will be my treat."

"We're just glad you could come." Her hostess patted her hand. "But the name's Virginia. Down here, once children are grown, we don't stand on a lot of ceremony." Then she added by way of explanation, "But don't feel uncomfortable later if you hear some of our other guests call me 'Miss Virginia'. They've known me since they were children and old habits die hard." She flashed a wide welcoming smile that Saralynn found contagious.

Did she say other guests?

Saralynn's face must have mirrored her question, because Virginia continued, "I thought it would be nice to introduce you to some of our friends closer to your age, so I've invited four other couples to join us tonight." She hesitated. "I hope you don't mind?"

"I'm truly honored. But that means you're cooking for eleven people. That must be a lot of work."

"Actually, it's twelve people, because Kent and Keri Kirk are bringing Keri's brother who's visiting them. But not to worry." There was that smile that Saralynn found so engaging. "It's just as easy to cook for twelve as it is for three."

"Then you must let me help. What can I do?"

Walter Kennedy took Saralynn by the arm before his wife could answer. "Virginia's got it all under control. Believe me, she's the happiest when she's in the kitchen cooking for a crowd."

"If you're sure."

Virginia Kennedy laughed. "Walter's right." There was a wicked gleam in her eyes. "The only thing I like better than cooking is eating, which you can tell by looking at me!"

"We've got about half an hour before the other guests arrive," Walter explained. "We thought we'd like to have a few minutes with you alone, before the crowd descends. I hope that's alright."

"I don't know what to say, other than thank you. Everyone has just been so nice. I'm really looking forward to meeting your friends."

"By the time you leave this evening, they'll be your friends, too."

What kind of place have I come to? I've got that time warp feeling again. But it feels so good.

"Now, while Virginia finishes up her end of the deal, would you like to see the house?"

"Oh, I would! But may I ask you a question? Why does this house, at least the front part, make me think of my grandmother's house?" When she saw what she interpreted as an amused look on her host's face, she added, "I'm not imagining it, am I?"

Walter threw his head back as he roared with laughter. "Virginia, I told you she'd pick up on it!"

Pick up on what?

"Our house is older than yours. And it's larger. There are several others in the county that are of similar style, but in this case, both our house and yours were built by the same man."

Saralynn was stunned. "Why would he build two houses, especially when Sallie's house is smaller?"

"This house, he built for himself. Your house was built twenty years later as a wedding gift for his oldest daughter."

It had never occurred to me that Sallie's house had a history before her. Although, obviously, if it was built in the 1850s, it would have.

"I had no idea. What else can you tell me about Sallie's house?"

"There's a lot I could tell you. But not tonight. Our other guests will be arriving soon, and I'd like you to see what we've done with this house, while we have a few minutes."

"Yes, please, I definitely want to see."

"Let's go to the front of the house and we'll work our way back."

He led her through a short, glassed-in passageway that connected to a dining room in the main part of the house. "When we bought this place, it needed a new kitchen and a family living area. We raised three children here."

They had made their way to the front door, which Walter opened as he invited Saralynn to step outside.

He really did mean for us to start at the front of the house.

"Have you noticed in your house that this room on the side of the porch is only accessible from the porch?"

"You're right, but I never realized it until just now."

"Do you know why?"

"Don't have a clue, but I'm betting you do."

"It was called the 'parson's room,' and it was kept ready for traveling clergy who always knew they had somewhere to lay their heads. If they got in late at night, they just went in and went to bed."

He laughed at Saralynn's shocked expression. "Things were a lot different then."

"But that's one of the reasons we added on. We needed living space and we didn't want to sacrifice this old front porch. Since the kitchens of that era were detached from the house, we built our addition in that same fashion, connected to the house by what passes for a covered breezeway. Just as it might have been then."

The rest of the tour showed equal concern for detail and architectural integrity, and Saralynn was in a state of amazement by the time they arrived back in the keeping room.

During their walk-through, Mr. Kennedy reminded her, "You were going to tell me about Boswell and Katie Brooks."

"Well, I found Boswell to be very interesting, and Katie is going to take me through their museum as soon as we can arrange it."

"And Katie, what did you think of her?"

Saralynn thought for a minute. "I don't think I've ever bonded with a total stranger as quickly as I did with her today." *I'm not going to tell him I spilled my gut, because then I'd have to explain why.* "She's a very warm and special individual."

"That she is," her host agreed. "She's really a remarkable person. You'd never guess how rough things have been for her. She'll make you a true friend."

I never got the impression that she had any problems.

Before she had a chance to question him further, the back door opened and a man and woman about her age entered the room to exclamations of delight and welcome from both hosts. Right on their heels came the rest of the evening's invited guests. What followed was a blur of delectable food, fast-paced conversation, much laughter, and the feeling of completeness.

Saralynn was amazed to discover that she was thoroughly enjoying herself. *There are ten people in this room that I never knew until two hours ago, who I now feel closer to than people I grew up and went to school with and have known for thirty years in Boston.*

The group seemed equally taken with her. They had, she discovered, as many questions about life in the north as she had about Mississippi. She tried to answer them as honestly as she could.

One of their first questions had been about her accent. "Do you say 'Cuber' like Senator Ted Kennedy does? You don't sound like some of the people from Boston we've heard on TV."

Saralynn had to laugh. "If you think I have an accent, you need to hear a true Bostonian. And I say 'Cuba,' just like you do."

"Not like me, you don't," quipped Dave Hasty. "The way you say it don't sound anything like we say it down here."

She went on to explain that Boston natives drop the letter "R" from any word where the "R" follows an "A," giving it an "H" sound. "You know, like many of you live on a 'fahm.' And you drove here tonight in your 'cahs.'" Saralynn deliberately over-emphasized the unique Boston pronunciation.

The group laughed and Saralynn was surprised to discover that she didn't feel the least self-conscious.

"So how come you don't have that kind of an accent?" The question stemmed from one of the ladies.

Julia? Or is she Keri?

"I don't know if it's genes or living with Mama who has never been able to lose her Mississippi accent. And she has tried."

"But you'll agree that you do sound different than we do?"

"Hey, that's a two-way street. The first few days we were here, I found myself having to listen really hard to understand."

"But we don't talk funny. You do," another of the men joked.

I think his name is Doug. "Go to Boston with that accent you've got, where you make a three syllable word out of a three-letter word, and see how the people look at you," she shot back.

"Touché!"

Then, before she knew it, the evening began to wind down, and she found herself almost emotional, not wanting it to end.

"Hey, everybody, we're going to have chili and fixings on Sunday night right after church," the man named Dave Hasty announced. "Everyone's invited." He turned to Saralynn, "You, too, and we'd love to have you visit us at church."

What do I say? I don't ever remember being invited to a church. He makes it sound so casual, not all formal and stiff. I don't know what to do!"

"I really appreciate the invitation – to both," she added quickly. "May I get back to you, after I find out when my mother is flying in? I'll have to meet her plane." *There's no way Mama will be back here by Sunday.*

"Sure thing," answered Dave's wife, Donna, a dark-haired

petite woman whom Saralynn had learned was also on staff at Boswell. "Just give us a call. We're the only Dave Hasty in the book. Wilson Floyd Road."

"If your mother gets back before Sunday, we'd love to have the both of you," Dave added, as the guests began to bid each other goodbye.

While the original plan had been that Walter Kennedy would drive her home, Doug and Bess Martin, insisted they would pass right by Saralynn's house and that they would see her home.

"It's no trouble," Doug insisted over Saralynn's protest. "We won't take 'no' for an answer."

"Goodnight, and thank you so much," she said to Virginia Kennedy, as her host hugged her neck. "I can't remember when I've had so much fun."

"You can't be with this group and not have fun. Only there are lots more of us out there. I didn't invite them all because I didn't want you to feel invaded."

"People really are different, here. I can't get over it."

"Naw, honey," Walter Kennedy spoke up. "People are the same everywhere. They're all God's creatures. Some of them just don't choose to act like it." He put his arm around her shoulders. "But we're just so glad you've come to be one of us tonight, and you're welcome back any time. I mean that, now." He gave her an extra-tight squeeze. "You need anything, you call."

"And even if you don't need anything, you call anyway. Or better yet, just come," Virginia chimed in.

"Say," her host asked as she was about to start out the door, "Did you tell your mother about those appraisal papers I left?"

I'd forgotten all about them!

"Yes, yes I did. I read them to her last night. She said she'd get back to you as soon as she got things squared away with her condo."

"What was her reaction, do you mind if I ask?"

"She felt like the commercial development approach would be the better one, based on the rough numbers."

"And how do you feel about it?"

"Me? Gosh, I don't know. I hadn't really thought about it. After all, it's Mama's house."

"Well, then, I'll just wait to hear from Alicia before I do anything."

On the ride home, she found the Martin couple to be even warmer than had been her impression in the hectic group setting. He was a rural mail carrier out of the Mendenhall Post Office, he told her.

Bess, it seemed, was a stay-at-home mom to two boys and a nine-month-old daughter. It was a task she laughingly defined as over-time employment with an out-of-work level of pay and loads of job security. "Doug wouldn't last a week if he had to do what I do." Bess poked him lightly in the ribs.

"No argument there. None whatsoever."

Their give and take makes me think so much of Peter and me. And suddenly, for the first time that night, she felt extremely guilty for having enjoyed herself. *Oh, God, please don't let me go to pieces in front of these nice people. They won't know what to think!*

When they arrived at the house, Doug insisted in going inside to make sure there were no problems before they left her alone for the night. "We don't have a lot of crime here, certainly nothing compared to what goes on in the big cities. Just don't want to take any chances."

Once he was satisfied that she was safe, Doug started back through the kitchen, where he stopped and placed one hand on the back of a dinette chair. "This was my chair... where I sat, you know?"

His chair? "I beg your pardon?"

"When your granny used to baby-sit me, this is where I sat to eat my snacks."

"Sallie... er, my grandmother was your baby-sitter?"

"Mine and half the other kids in the community. You met my real granny the other day. Flora Martin. She said she and Miss Minnie brought lunch."

"Miss Flora is your grandmother?"

"My daddy's mama. Course when I was growin' up, I just assumed Miss Sallie was one o' mine, too. I didn't know th' diff'rence."

Saralynn was secretly amused to learn that when Doug talked about his childhood, his speech patterns took on a different, more relaxed timbre. *And he made fun of* my *accent. Don't southerners realize they stretch out words and leave off entire syllables?*

"You'll have to tell me about it some time," she suggested. "I'm afraid I never really knew my grandmother."

"It's a deal. Good to meet you. We'll see you at church Sunday; that is, if we don't see you before."

Saralynn was trying to assimilate the findings of the evening. *I've never before been with a group of people like these.*

She waited until she saw the Martin's car exit the driveway before she turned off the porch light, double-checked the lock on the back door, and made her way to the bedroom. The young woman was suddenly extremely weary, only it wasn't a bad kind of tired.

The minute she flipped on the bedroom's overhead light, she realized she'd left her cell phone on the bedside table. *If I'd gone looking for it, I'd have sworn it was in my bag! I guess I just forgot to pick it up.*

Seven missed calls, the display showed. *And I'll bet I can guess who all of them are.*

Sure enough, when she checked the log, it showed that Alicia had been calling about every fifteen minutes. *Guess I'd better dial her back.* She slipped off her shoes and pulled her feet under her as she settled down on the bed. Before she could activate the redial function, the little phone began to sing it's familiar tune. Call number eight had beat her to it.

"I'm okay, Mama. Really, I am."

"Have you been down there so long you've forgotten the correct way to answer the phone? Where have you been? I've been worried sick."

"Now, Mama, we need to get something straight." Saralynn was shocked by her own brashness. Never in all of her thirty-five years had she been so bold and direct with her mother. "I am fine. So fine, as a matter of fact, that I now have nearly as many friends here as I do there. And I've just come in from a very enjoyable evening with eleven of them."

"Eleven!" Alicia shrilled. "What kind of people are these you've suddenly started running with?" "I thought you were going to dinner at Walter and Virginia Kennedy's."

"That's what I'm trying to tell you, Mama. That's exactly where I was. The Kennedys invited several other couples and I don't know when I've had a more enjoyable evening."

Alicia's only response was silence.

"That was the idea of this trip, wasn't it? You wanted to

get me out again, didn't you?"

"Well, yes, but…"

"Good, because it's working. Now tell me about your condo. That was the real reason you were calling, wasn't it? Surely you weren't calling just to check up on me!"

The conversation did turn to the renovation project where Saralynn offered her mother several suggestions for changes she might want to make while the work was being done. "Now's the cheapest time to do it, and you know you've never been happy with the way the kitchen is so closed off from the back parlor. I'd at least put in a pass-through opening, if nothing else."

"So what are you doing tomorrow?" Alicia asked her daughter, just before the two said good-night.

Gosh, I've been so excited about today I haven't even given any thought to tomorrow.

"Nothing definite. I'll be working on the inventory and packing here for at least part of the day."

"I'm sorry I've saddled you with all that. But it's going to be at least two weeks before I can leave here. Maybe longer."

"I'd already decided that. And it's okay."

"Well, get a good night's rest, if you can, and I'll talk to you tomorrow."

While her body felt very tired, her mind was in overdrive. *No, it's more than just my mind. It's my heart, too. I just feel so full, and yet so empty at the same time.*

The argument waging between her weary body and her overflowing emotions centered around picking up the next chapter in Sallie's journals. Her aching body begged for rest, while her inquiring nature strained to know why the first journal had ended so abruptly.

In the end, her emotions prevailed, but promised her body that she would only read the first entry in the next diary. Then it would be lights out. Saralynn dug through the little suitcase, that now sat in plain sight, until she found one with the first passage dated November 7, 1945.

◐▷

This is the first day I've felt strong enough to write in my journal. Nurse Myra offered to write for me, but I don't want to share my thoughts with anyone else just now. Dr. McCallum says the surgery was a success. But I don't think I'll ever get my strength back. I feel worse now than I did when I first came here almost a year ago.

Mama bought a Greyhound Bus ticket at Jourdan Drug in Iuka and came down to Jackson and someone from here drove his car up there to get her. People are so good. She brought a crocheted afghan she made for me and a copy of The Vidette, our weekly newspaper in Iuka. Mr. R.R. Hamilton, the editor, had put in the paper that I was going to have surgery and asked people to pray for me. When I saw the advertisements for the Jourdan Store, I remembered all the Saturdays I spent in there looking at all the things I couldn't buy while Mama and Daddy took care of their business in town. It really made me homesick and I cried when Mama left to go home. I wanted to go back with her so bad. Only I don't feel so alone anymore, because I've learned something about myself.

◐▷

While her promise had been to read but one entry, Saralynn craved to know more. In the end, she honored her original vow, tucking the notebook away safely before crawling back into bed and turning out the lamp.

There's always tomorrow.

As she lay there, in the few minutes before sleep completely overtook her, Saralynn was sure that her grandmother's belief that she would never be alone again was because in the weeks between journal entries, Ralph Watson had come into her life. That had to be it; everything made sense.

Sallie and Ralph Watson... Ralph and Sallie... my grandparents, Ralph and Sallie Watson. Just saying the words sounded wonderful yet felt so strange. *I'm not certain I even understand what all grandparents do, never having had any.*

Then she remembered something else. Something that made her uncomfortable. *Everybody tonight kept referring to this as "my" house. It's not. It was Sallie's house, and now it's Mama's. Every time I called my grandmother by her name... Sallie... I saw people exchanging funny looks.*

She realized that unless others knew the entire history, they could never understand why she referred to her grandparent in such a detached, seemingly disrespectful manner. But maybe they were right.

I'll think about that tomorrow, too. That way I'll have something else to do.

She was on the very edge of sleep, about to tumble off into rest, when the solution hit her. Doug Martin had given her the answer.

Miss Sallie... I'll call her 'Miss Sallie'... like all her other "grandchildren."

Chapter 6

*I*n a dream that was still painfully real the next day, Saralynn stood in the center hallway of Miss Sallie's remodeled home. As guests crossed the wide porch and entered the double front doors, she was there to welcome them. There were Walter and Virginia Kennedy. The Kirks, Kent and Keri, and Bess and Doug Martin were there. As were Katie and Charlie Brooks. Dave and Donna Hasty and Julia and Don Robinson, the other two guest couples at the Kennedy dinner party, were also there, along with many other friends from her church... Rials Creek United Methodist.

The house glowed in its newly restored state as the native greenery and red-and-gold bows announced the holiday season just around the corner. Everyone was complimentary of her skills as a decorator and her eye for architectural detail and integrity. Each guest commented on the two oil portraits of Peter and Marc that hung between the front door and the door into the living room.

I have never been so happy.

A clap of thunder, followed almost immediately by the zap of a lightening bolt striking a nearby target, jolted Saralynn out of a sound sleep. She could hear rain pounding on the tin roof overhead.

Oh, dear, why did it have to rain on my open house? Now everyone will get wet.

Then it hit her.

What open house? Who would get wet?

Realizing that it had all been a dream, Saralynn lay there in no hurry to get up to face the dreary day. *But it felt so real. So good and natural. Oh, this is ridiculous. All I did was have a dream.* However, she was aware that this dream was much different from those she had experienced over the past two months. *I was a completely whole person again, going on with my life without Peter and Marc!* Just the thought was unsettling. Almost disloyal.

When her cell phone rang with what she'd come to accept was going to be a daily morning ritual, she answered. "Yes, I'm awake. I slept well, in fact I slept very well. And I'm perfectly safe."

"I'm getting the impression my concern isn't appreciated."

"Mama. I love you. I'll always want you to worry about me. But please don't smother me. I'm doing just fine."

"Very well," That tone of voice, Saralynn knew, meant anything but agreement.

"So what else is happening? Surely you've not made any progress on your renovation since we talked last night."

"Don't be silly," her mother ordered. "Of course I haven't. I've been asleep. I do sleep, you know."

Mama's building her famous wall again. I'd better cool it.

"So what can I help you with? Besides advice, that is?"

"I'm going shopping today for several pieces that'll have to be replaced. Then I've got to find fabrics for the furniture that has to be reupholstered."

"Sounds like you're going to be busy."

"Oh, and I have to arrange with the refinisher for those wood pieces that can be salvaged."

"Yep, you'll be busy. Look, you know where everything is in my office. Take my billing information and charge everything to my accounts. That way you can get my cost and we'll settle up when you're through."

She recalled one of her suppliers who was unusually picky about decorators who gave their entire families carte blanche whole-sale privileges. "Look, I'd better put in a call to Carl at Kesslerco and tell him specifically that you're buying for me. Otherwise, you won't get to first base with him."

"That will really help me stretch these insurance dollars. There's nothing worse than trying to live on a fixed income like I have to now. I sure hope it won't take too long to move Sallie's property. I can use the cash."

Saralynn placed the promised call to Carl who had to vent his feelings about people who tried to rip him off. She let him rant while she timed him, and when one minute had elapsed, said, "This is my mother, Carl. I'm out of state, so please show her every courtesy you would me. You and I have always been able to work together."

Since it was raining steadily outside, she decided it would be an indoor day. *I should be able to get a lot done.* It was the first time she'd ever heard the sound of rain on a tin roof. *I'll have to be careful it doesn't lull me back to sleep!*

Breakfast was an absolute necessity before tackling the job that confronted her. She was twisting loose the plastic tie on a loaf of bread when she remembered her mother's words: "There's nothing worse than trying to live on a fixed income." Her mother wasn't destitute. Fixed income certainly didn't mean welfare or food stamps, but for the first time, she found herself bothered by Alicia's lifestyle. It was the same lifestyle she had once eagerly embraced and taken for granted.

It never occurred to me to question how we lived.

Over toast, cereal and hot tea, she thought back to a childhood with a non-working mother and an abundance of material possessions. She had been a teenager before she realized that most of her friends' parents were both employed, and still they didn't live nearly as comfortably as the Bankston's. Alicia had never held a job, but it hadn't seemed to make a difference in their lifestyle.

On those rare occasions when she raised the question, Alicia's explanation had been that they had a trust fund that her husband's parents had established. Obviously, there was more to the story.

And because Mama said it, I just accepted it and never thought about it again. To say she lives on a "fixed" income is somewhat misleading. How could I have been so naïve?

Saralynn had enough friends who were divorced to know that the chances of their ex-in-laws setting up a fund to support them for the rest of their lives lay somewhere between remotely slim and impossible. Human nature being what it was, she understood reality. *If I'm right, it all ties in to why she and Sall... Miss Sallie didn't get along.*

The only thing was, Saralynn didn't know what she was

going to do with her newfound revelation, so she tucked it aside while she cleaned up her breakfast mess. *I think I'll work a few hours and then take my bath. No sense having to bathe twice everyday.*

She decided to concentrate her efforts on the kitchen, where cabinets that towered all the way to the high ceiling bulged with every manner of plate, glassware and knick-knack. If she finished this, she'd move into the sewing room on the enclosed back porch.

As she worked in the small kitchen, crowded by the presence of the breakfast table, she realized that Miss Sallie and "Mr. Ralph" hadn't had a separate dining room. *That means every meal was eaten right here in the kitchen.* Then she realized... *I guess it's okay to call him Mr. Ralph.*

She thought again of the Kennedy home she'd visited the night before. Even though their rooms were larger, the basic floor plan of two large rooms on either side of the center hall and the four corner rooms was the same. And they had three children.

I guess they did have to expand to hold that family. But what a beautiful job they have done of preserving the old and tying in the new in such an unobtrusive manner.

That statement, she reflected, could have been a direct quote from one of the trade magazines that arrived regularly in her studio. But she also realized that the renovation the Kennedy's had done was much more than cosmetic. *They made their house a home first, and a finished piece of decorator art second. That could be done here, as well.* In all her years of decorating, she'd never made that distinction between livability and appearance. Acknowledging this pinched her conscience, almost as if she had short-changed her clients.

Try as she might, as she climbed up and down the ladder, removing the contents from shelf after shelf, she couldn't get her mind off Virginia and Walter Kennedy's house. Subconsciously, she began to plan what could be done with Miss Sallie's house.

She was about to give herself a good scolding when she heard her cell phone ringing. *Mama must be having trouble with one of my suppliers.* Some decorators, she was aware, did abuse their wholesale buying abilities, but Saralynn also knew that she hadn't. Only when she looked at the display did she see it was a local phone exchange.

"Hello?"

"Saralynn?"

"Yes?"

"Hi, this is Donna Hasty. From last night at Mr. Walter and Miss Virginia's."

"Oh, hello, Donna. We did have a good time last night, didn't we?"

"Honey, you don't do anything with Virginia Kennedy that you don't have a good time. You'll learn that if you stay 'round here long enough."

"She knows how to throw a mean party, that's for sure."

"Listen, I hope you don't mind, but Mr. Walter gave me your cell number."

I've gotten so comfortable with these people it didn't even occur to me to question how she knew my number!

"No... no, that's fine."

"Good. He said you wouldn't care. Now here's what I'm calling about. We really would like to have you join us Sunday night. And your mother, too. Have you found out yet when she's coming back?"

I can't lie to this nice woman. "It won't be for a couple of weeks yet, maybe a little longer."

"That's too bad," Donna said. "Well, we'll just have to meet her later. But the good news is, that means you're free for Sunday."

Yes, I guess it does. I walked right into that one.

"Now, we don't want to put you on the spot or anything, but Dave and I'd like to have you spend the entire day with us. We'll pick you up and take you to Sunday School. We'll stay for church, of course. Then we'll go somewhere nice for lunch and show you some of the country that afternoon. Then back to church before coming here to our house for chili and trimmings. And we'll even take you home, if you won't spend the night," she laughed.

Saralynn was speechless. *These people barely know me, and they're inviting me into their lives to spend an entire day. What do I say?*

While she was wrestling with an answer, her caller asked, "I haven't over-stepped, have I? Dave always says I move too fast. I'm sorry."

"No, no. It's not that," Saralynn assured her. "I'm just blown away by your graciousness. In fact, I'm speechless."

"Then I'll answer for you. And the answer is 'yes'."

I don't even know what church they go to! What's more, I'm not sure I'll know how to act.

"That's great, Donna. But may I ask you one question?"

"Sure. Name it."

"What church do you go to?"

"I'm sorry, I thought you knew. All of us who were there last night are members at Rials Creek United Methodist. Where your grandmother was a member."

"No, I didn't realize that."

"That's not a problem, is it? We all just assumed you were

Methodist, too."

"Actually, I don't guess I'm anything," Saralynn admitted, suddenly uncomfortable for the first time in her life that she didn't practice religion.

"Surely you're something," Donna insisted, although not unkindly. "You do believe in God, don't you?"

"Well, sure. I mean, I guess. Well, yes. Of course I do." *I'm just not sure God believes in me.* "You see, I didn't grow up in any church. But I don't have a problem with going, if I'm good enough to start at this late date."

"Don't you worry," Donna assured her, "with God it's never too late. We'll pick you up about nine o'clock on Sunday morning. See ya' then."

"I'll be ready," Saralynn promised.

"Oh, and by the way, don't feel like you have to get all dressed up. We're not that fancy. Bye."

Dressed up! Oh, what have I gotten myself into? All I brought were casual clothes and work jeans. Certainly nothing that could even come close to being dressy enough for church. What was she going to do? *I'll just have to get sick. That's it. I'll get a touch of the stomach bug. That'll get me out of church and the chili as well.*

Satisfied that she'd solved the problem, she got back to work in the kitchen cabinets. Only Donna's question, asked in the most forthright and non-judgmental manner, wouldn't let her alone. "You do believe in God, don't you?"

I do. Don't I?

She continued to agonize over the question as she worked. It was slow going, as the shelves seemed to fill with replacement clutter as fast as she emptied them.

If I don't believe there isn't a God, then that means I really do believe in Him. Right?

Or did it? Saralynn's intensely emotional wrestling match continued, intruding on her decisions about which glassware to pack and which was junk.

Alright, God, if I say I believe in You, will that put an end to this wrangling?

She wasn't sure if she expected a direct answer, and was even more unnerved at the prospect of hearing a deep voice from above respond to her question. *Like in the movies.*

Evidently her declaration quieted the furor, because the voices in her head dropped their haggling and allowed her to concentrate on the task at hand. Before long, three large cabinets were totally empty. It was also lunchtime.

The prospect of another sandwich didn't do much for her taste buds. *Not even if I put on every trimming I have... I want some real food!*

The constant drumming on the roof had stopped, so what was the point of remaining a prisoner indoors? Without even debating her options, she headed for the bathroom, pulling off her dirty clothes as she went. A quick bath, a change of clothes, and she was in the van, on her way to... *Where?*

Mentally calling roll of the places she knew, she finally decided if she got to Wal-Mart, she could find something nearby to satisfy the hunger pangs that were by this time screaming loudly. *Windham's! Mama got those good burgers there. I'd rather have real food, but she said they had that, too! That's where I'll go.*

Saralynn found the restaurant tucked away on a frontage road alongside the four-lane. She surveyed the area in front of the building, looking for a space large enough to park the van. *If a crowded parking lot is any indication, this is a great place to eat.*

Once inside, she discovered that seating space was even more precious than the parking. Her eyes quickly surveyed the room, wondering if she'd made a mistake.

"Saralynn! Is that you?...Over here... Saralynn!"

She was certain someone was calling her name. *But who would know me here?*

There it was again. Someone was calling her name. She scanned the room a second time and realized there was another dining room behind the register station. After she moved closer, she caught sight of an extended hand on the far side of the back room waving to her. "You're welcome to join us!"

Saralynn fought her way through the crowded maze of tables and people, where she discovered the waving hand belonged to one of the guests at the Kennedy's the previous evening. *What's her name? I'm drawing a total blank.*

"Are you eating in?" the caller asked when Saralynn reached the table. "I'm Keri Kirk. We met last night."

"Yes, Keri, I remember you and the great time we had. I had planned to eat here. I just never dreamed it would be this crowded."

"There are only three of us, so why don't you round us out," one of the other two ladies at the table offered. She put out her hand. "I'm Sue Ainsworth, and this is Katherine Amos," she said, indicating the third diner.

"If you're sure... oh, and I'm Saralynn Reilly, she said for the benefit of the other two. I don't know where my manners are."

"Sit down," Keri insisted, "before somebody else grabs that chair away from us! Kay," she called to one of the servers nearby. "Kay! We've got another one joining us."

After Saralynn had asked for unsweetened iced tea, and inquired of her mates on which was better, the country steak and gravy or the fried chicken, before finally deciding on the steak, she turned to Keri.

"I can't believe this. We were all together just last night, and already this morning Donna Hasty has called me, and now I run into you. I expected to be eating alone."

"The three of us work at the bank just down the street, so this is convenient, and the food is good. You'll find us all here lots of days, when our schedules mesh."

Saralynn turned to Keri. "Granted, everything was pretty confusing last night, but why did I think you were a nurse?"

"Easy. You've got me confused with my sister, Julia Robinson. She's a nurse at the Medical & Surgical Clinic here in Magee. But we look so much alike, people are always getting us mixed up."

"But you aren't twins?"

"No, but our brother who was there last night. The single guy. He and I are twins."

"I didn't realize the connection, Saralynn confessed.

"Honey, I'm so comfortable here, I'd hate to know I had to go somewhere new and start from scratch to learn everybody. I'd probably just stay home and become a hermit," offered Katherine, the more quiet of the three. "I'm so shy it's pitiful."

"How do you think you're going to like living here?" Sue asked as she speared a fork full of mashed potatoes.

"Who? Me?"

"We understood you were moving here to take Miss Sallie's house. Where is it you're from?"

"Boston." Saralynn answered automatically. *How could*

people have gotten such an idea?

"I'm not sure where you got your information, but I'm only going to be here long enough to pack up the house and get it ready to sell."

Keri reached for a bottle from the center of the table and attempted to shake some of its contents onto her food. "Kay!" she called to their server as she held the empty bottle aloft, "This one's empty. Could you bring another bottle, please?"

Without missing a beat, she added, "That's a shame. We understood you were moving here. Oh, well, it's our loss. But we'll be happy to have you join us for whatever time you're here. Thank you, Kay," she said as the server set a full bottle of pepper sauce down beside her plate. "Green just aren't greens without it."

"Greens?" Saralynn was confused.

"Turnip greens," Keri explained as she dashed contents of the bottle liberally over what looked like a pile of wilted leaves on her plate. "They're good."

"I don't think I've ever had any," Saralynn admitted. "Not that I remember."

"Food doesn't get any more southern than turnip greens," Keri said between bites of the food in question. "Unless maybe it's grits."

"I've never had them either," the northern visitor confessed. "I guess I've got a lot to learn about southern food." Then remembering the home-cooked lunch from earlier in the week, she said, "But I have had creamed corn and fried okra since I got here."

"Then there's definitely hope for you," Keri reassured her as she caught their server by the hand as she passed. "Hold up a second, I want you to meet Saralynn Reilly. This is Kay Austin," she said to the newcomer at the table. "We always try to get one of her tables."

Saralynn acknowledged the petite, black-haired woman with the infectious smile.

"What'll you have?" the server in turquoise asked.

Saralynn gave her order, after asking how the potatoes were prepared.

"We'll get you fed," Kay promised with a broad smile. As she left their table, two other customers called her name.

"She's a dynamo," Sue said. "Everyone here is like family. The customers and the staff. But we especially like to get Kay whenever we can."

I don't think I've ever eaten anywhere that customers were so informal with the wait staff

"So what kind of work do you do back in Boston? Katherine asked. "You must have a real understanding boss to get off like you have."

"I work for myself. I'm a decorator. And there are days that I question how understanding I am. I'm often tempted to fire me!"

Her lunch companions chuckled and one asked, "So what stops you?"

"I need the money," Saralynn admitted. "Do you have any idea how expensive it is to live in a city like Boston?

"Well if it's any worse than here, I'll settle for what I've got," Sue said, as she speared a bite of steamed broccoli. "Thank you very much, but no thanks!"

"So your husband. He doesn't mind you being gone all this time?" Again, Katherine, the "shy" one was asking most of the questions. "Or is that a sore subject that I shouldn't ask about?

Everybody tells me I'm too nosey."

"I'm a widow," Saralynn answered, offering no further information. *Please, God, don't let them ask me anything else.*

"That's too bad," Sue offered up. "It doesn't matter if you're young or old. When it happens, it hurts. Jack's been gone ten years come January, and there are days I still think, 'I've got to tell Jack about...'" She hesitated for a minute. "And then I re-member... he's gone."

"You're a widow, too?" Saralynn asked.

"That's society's label for it. I'm Jack Ainsworth's wife, only everybody can't see him as clearly as I do."

"Sue leads a 'Surviving Spouse Recovery Group' at the community center, Keri explained. "You've done that what, for about six years now?"

"You wouldn't believe how many people, especially women, surrender their very identities to marriage and then they become non-persons when their spouses die," Sue explained. "Yeah, six years last month. I tell 'em, 'Look, Jack's not eating my food and sleeping in the bed with me, but as long as I have the precious memories we made together, he'll always be a part of me.'"

"That's hard for me to do," Saralynn confessed, "even though I have a separate identity because I was working for my-self before Peter and I married."

"It's like this," Sue explained. "Two years before Jack died suddenly, he and I took a trip to Scotland. We had a ball. He'd been gone about three years, when I got a chance to go back. If I had never been before, with him, I don't think I'd have been inter-ested. As it was, I went, I felt like he was right there with me, and I had the time of my life."

She reached for her tea glass and took a sip. "In fact, I

recalled memories from our first trip that I'd forgotten, memories that are more precious to me than money. So you see, I came home richer for having gone, even though I didn't have Jack there with me. Physically, that is."

"How long has it been?" Keri quizzed. "If you don't mind my asking."

"Eleven weeks."

"You're still a baby in the recovery process," Sue counseled. "Don't beat up on yourself, and don't let anyone dictate how long you should or shouldn't grieve. That's between you and God; only the two of you know what's in your heart."

Her three companions consulted their watches and announced that they had just enough time to make it back to the bank before their hour was up. "We always walk, since parking is usually scarce."

They bid her a warm goodbye and left her to finish the strawberry shortcake she'd ordered to top off the real mashed potatoes with lumps and the pinto beans and pear salad. *They have a lot of different foods here, but I think I could learn to like most of them.* As she savored the simple goodness of what she had on her plate, Saralynn allowed her eyes to wander over the restaurant. It wasn't like any other place she'd ever eaten, certainly nothing like The Butcher Shop or even Hammersley's, both of which were close to their house and had been Peter's favorites.

If I were in Boston, I'd probably avoid Windham's Restaurant, which tells me I've been more of a snob that I'm comfortable admitting.

From a professional decorator's perspective, the facility had little to recommend it. The floor of worn, red square tile was littered with small clumps of dirt that had fallen from the boots of the farmers and workmen who ate there, many of whom were regulars, she'd learned from overheard conversations.

Paintings by local artists lined the walls. Saralynn noticed that the one next to her table was an outdoor scene of a small, red and white calf drinking milk from a bottle. The artist was identified as a Jean White. *She's not bad at all. That's an interesting piece. Makes me think I'd like to see a baby cow sometime.*

The wait staff didn't wear matching uniforms, but they hustled among the tables, responding to multiple demands simultaneously, all the while carrying on a running conversation with the customers. No, this place would never have passed muster in Boston. But where it lacked ambience it more than compensated with great food and warm and friendly service.

It's… it's… genuine. That's it. Genuine. I will be back.

When she went to the register to pay her bill, she was informed that her friends had already settled the tab.

Why would they do that for me? If I didn't know better, I'd think it was because they felt sorry for me. But that's not it. I'm certain. So what is it?

An answer still eluded Saralynn as she slid behind the steering wheel of the van. While she arrived at no satisfactory answer, the advice that Sue had offered, "…that's between you and God; only the two of you know what's in your heart," kept playing in her head.

She said that like she and God were personal friends, just like she's friends with Keri and Katherine. I thought God was someone in a high tower. Are we talking about the same God?

That question continued to bother her as she maneuvered her way out of the parking lot and headed back to the country. When she spotted the façade of a shopping center in the distance, she detoured into the parking lot near a ladies' dress shop.

Before entering the store, she stopped on the sidewalk to check out the fashions displayed in the front window. *Donna said 'casual,' but I'd still feel better about wearing something with a skirt. I don't know how pants would go over.*

After a few minutes of searching the racks, she found a long, simple denim skirt and a patchwork pullover top. *Now all I need is a slip, a pair of flat shoes and some pantyhose and I'll be set for Sunday.* At the last minute, she threw a lightweight cardigan sweater on the counter with the other merchandise and flashed her plastic.

I don't know why I feel so much at peace, but I do.

On her way home, back to Miss Sallie's, her cell phone rang. She pulled off the road and fished in her pocket. "Hello?"

"Saralynn? It's Katie Brooks. I hope I haven't caught you at a bad time."

"No, not at all."

"Listen, I've been able to arrange for a babysitter tomorrow. How would you like to spend the day here and really see the old Sanatorium and the new Boswell?"

"You're sure you can spare an entire day?"

"There's nothing I'd rather do."

"You've got a deal, but on two conditions."

"And those would be?"

"Lunch is my treat, and you let me pay your babysitter."

"I won't argue about lunch, but I'm afraid my aunt would be terribly offended if we offered her money for keeping Paul. She complains now that she doesn't get to spoil him enough."

"In that case, the last thing I'd want to do is hurt her feelings," Saralynn laughed. "But lunch is definitely on me."

The two arranged to meet at nine-thirty the next morning, and Saralynn pulled back onto the road. She was home in record time, she realized, because over the past few days, she'd become so much more comfortable and familiar with her surroundings.

Once inside, she put away her purchases, still uncertain why she had suddenly decided to accept the Hasty's invitation for Sunday. But she was sure that her heart knew. There would be no further anguish over her decision.

The same couldn't be said for the rest of her day's agenda. She'd already invested a half-day's work in the kitchen and there wasn't a definite deadline to finish. But it was something more than simply being tired of the task.

Why do I feel like I'm doing something wrong? This was, no, it still is, Miss Sallie's house. With each piece I take off the wall or out of the cabinets and toss, I'm throwing away a little bit of the woman I never knew. In the few days I've been here, I've come to feel closer to her than almost anyone I've ever known.

She knew what she wanted to do. She just wasn't sure how to make it happen. *God, You'll have to show me.* And this time, she fully understood that she was calling out to a God who had, until recently, been a stranger. A distant, unreachable and untouchable being. *I still can't see Him.*

Saralynn retrieved the journal she'd started the night before and settled down to read, determined to know more of the grandmother that had been denied her. She resumed her habit of scanning the diary entries, stopping to read only when something significant caught her eye.

Miss Sallie had chronicled her slow recovery from the extensive surgery that had been performed, the only hope she had of defeating the tuberculosis that seemed determined to ravage her body. She wrote of the day she was first able to sit up in her chair unassisted. Of the Thanksgiving feast that had tantalized and nourished, and the bare tree branches that sported a rare, south Mississippi December dusting of snow.

A real surprise had been the unexpected birthday present from Mama and Papa. The little figurine of a black and tan puppy that looked amazingly like her dog, Simon, back home in Fishtrap Hollow, had come from the Gritz Department Store in Iuka. Mama never shopped there unless she had cash money, Miss Sallie had noted in explanation.

Oh, God, thank you that her parents finally started acting like they loved her.

On the first anniversary of her admission to the Sanatorium, Miss Sallie's writings reflected on the year gone by, the highs and the lows. She began to speak of staff and fellow patients as family and she still referred often to her parents far away in the northeastern corner of the state. Missing, however, were all the expressions of desperate longing that had dominated in the first hundred entries. Saralynn no longer glimpsed flashes of anger or the fear that had been clearly evident in her grandmother's earlier writings.

Instead, frequent reference was made of a lady named "Miss Dora," and the fact that her grandmother never felt alone any longer. But there was no indication of whom this woman was, or how she figured into the picture.

Even though she read until the hour was late, she could find no further clue to the person or the event that had made such a difference in Miss Sallie's life. When she finally called it quits, at nearly ten o'clock and went to the kitchen to fix a snack – it was too late for dinner... uh — supper – she was more confused than ever.

Once she finally found slumber, she slept soundly. It wasn't until the next morning when she realized that Alicia hadn't placed her nightly call. Concerned, that she had slept through her cell phone's trumpet solo, she was momentarily reassured that the log showed no missed calls.

But then the panic resurfaced. There had been no wake-up call, either. She noted the time, advanced it by an hour and decided that her mother was probably at the condo already at work. She dialed Alicia's cell number. It rang five times, before being answer by a gruff, male voice.

Did I misdial the number?

"Yeah, who's there?" the man's voice demanded.

"This is Saralynn Reilly. I'm trying to reach my mother. Alicia Bankston. Is this her cell phone?"

"Yeah, it's her phone. But she ain't here."

Saralynn heard in his voice the unmistakable accent that was so quintessentially Boston, and for the first time, she found little charm in it. Certainly there was no warmth or concern.

"Well, where is she?" *Why is her phone there and she isn't?*

"She went with Merle to look at some flooring samples. I guess she forgot her phone. I heard it ringing so I answered it."

It's not like Mama to leave without her phone, but then I'm doing things out of character for me, too.

"You want to leave a message? I gotta get back to work."

"Just ask her to call her daughter. And tell her nothing's wrong."

Knowing that she was to meet Katie at nine-thirty, Saralynn made quick work of breakfast, got her bath, and was on her way out the door, when the cell phone in her purse began to sound off. She stopped to answer it."

"Are you okay?"

"I'm fine. It just worried me when you didn't call last night or this morning."

"I got the impression that I was bothering you, so I decided to leave you alone."

I wish Mama could get beyond playing the martyr. I don't have time to indulge her if I make it to Boswell on time.

"Bothering me. No, Mama, you weren't bothering me." But you were obsessing, even after I told you that there was no cause for you to worry."

"Well, I'm a mother and…"

"I know, Mama, it's in your job description. And I love you for it."

"You're all I have…"

"And you're all the blood family I have, but honestly, Mama, you have been suffocating me."

"That's pretty strong talk for someone who couldn't even stop crying long enough to get out of bed as recently as three weeks ago."

"And now I'm better. Much better. Isn't that what we wanted? There will never be a day that I don't think about Peter and Marc. But I'm able to get on with my life without being crippled by their memories. I thought that was the whole idea of this trip."

"Naturally, I'm thrilled, but I don't understand how it could happen so quickly."

Saralynn remembered Sue's words from lunch the day before. "I realize that you may not fully understand, and neither do I. All I know is that for the first time since that horrible Saturday, I don't feel like I want to give up on life. So please be happy for me, and give me some freedom by not worrying about me every waking hour.

"There is a difference in your voice. You sound like you're alive again. Now if you can just keep that spark and get back home where you belong, I'll really believe you're on the road to recovery."

"I'm on the road, there's no doubt about it. But I'm not entirely sure that I'm coming back to Boston."

Saralynn knew she would never forget the responding gasp that echoed across the miles.

"If you don't come back to Boston, just where would you go?" Saralynn sensed the hostility behind the question.

"I'd stay right where I am."

"Over my dead body. I didn't work like I did to escape that prison to allow you to walk in and pull the cell door shut behind you."

"Mama. You're over-reacting again."

"I'll call you as soon as I can get a flight back to Jackson. We'll get you to a doctor as soon as I get there."

"I don't need to see a doctor, Mama. But I am meeting a friend to spend the day, and if I don't go now, I'll be late. I'll call you tonight and bring you up to date."

"I'll be there before bed time."

"Come back if you're ready to come, Mama. But don't use me as your excuse. And don't expect me to see a doctor. I am an adult and they'll not treat me without my consent."

She heard Alicia's hard intake of breath.

"I love you, Mama. Talk to you tonight. Got to run." Then she punched the off button and hurriedly closed the door behind her. *Mama's in one more stew.*

Chapter 7

There's the Boswell entrance ahead. I hate to be late.

The car in front of her slowed without warning, and Saralynn had to stand on her brakes to keep from having an accident. *Guess I better pay more attention to the road and worry less about what time it is.*

Katie had given her directions to the Brooks' home that Saralynn discovered was located on a tree-lined street of similar cottages, very near where they had lunched earlier in the week.

"Come on in," her friend said and the trademark smile she flashed echoed her greeting. "My aunt will be here in about five minutes and then we can go."

Saralynn was ushered into a comfortable, cozy living room that fairly screamed "home, hearth and family." As she settled herself on an overstuffed sofa draped with handmade afghans, she thought about the special throw Miss Sallie's mother had made for her so long ago. *I wonder what happened to that afghan?*

"Do you crochet?"

"Me?" Katie asked in mock alarm. "Hardly. I need an instruction manual to know how to thread a sewing needle."

"Well, someone in your circle can do it without instructions, if these beautiful pieces are any indication."

"Actually, Charlie's mom and my mom are both avid needle workers."

"These are absolutely magnificent. The workmanship is exquisite."

"They are pretty and I love them, so I'm glad someone has the talent. I didn't get any of that."

Maybe not in needle work, but you're a master craftsman when it comes to relationships.

Saralynn noticed another intricate piece of needlework and fabric art hanging over the fireplace. It was of a phoenix done in brilliant primary colors framed in a deep shadowbox.

"Oh, Katie, that is one of the most gorgeous pieces I've ever seen." She walked closer and stepped up on the raised hearth to make a closer inspection. "I've got clients who would pay big bucks for work like this."

"Tempt me with chocolate any time, but money will never buy that."

"Oh, I didn't mean that you should sell me this piece. But if you'll put me in touch with the artist, because that's what he or she is, I'd commission several pieces."

For the first time since the two ladies met, Saralynn saw a shadow cross her friend's face. Then Katie answered softly, almost sadly, "Unfortunately, that artist passed away shortly after this piece was finished. So, you see, there can be no more." She reached up and brushed her hand across the glass in the lower corner of the frame.

"What a loss," Saralynn said.

"Yes, it was," Katie agreed. "In many more ways than one."

"Hello…" a voice called through the screen from outside the still open front door. "I'm here."

"That's my aunt," Katie said. "Come on in."

When the introductions had been made, Aunt Toots, as Saralynn was instructed to call the woman, said, "I've always got room for one more niece. So welcome to the family." She hugged Saralynn warmly. "Now, where's my young man? He and I have great plans for the day."

"He's back in his room. I told him Aunt Toots was coming."

"Well, then… shoo… off with the both of you. And don't look for us back until about six o'clock. Young "Mr. Paul" and I have a lot of ground to cover."

"You heard the lady," Katie said. "Let's be on our way."

"What's first?" Saralynn asked her.

"I'm glad to see you wore comfortable walking shoes." She indicated that they should go to the left. "We're going to explore this place on foot. Otherwise, we'd spend half our day getting in and out of the car. Besides, it's a beautiful day for walking and my figure can use the exercise."

"Works for me." Saralynn checked her pocket to be sure her cell phone was there and operating. "Mama's buying things for her condo today, and she may need me. I promised her I'd be as close as my phone." *I'm not going to tell her that Mama threatened to come back. Dear God, please keep Mama in Boston.*

"Being a decorator must be very interesting. I can easily visualize you in that element, working with colors and styles."

"I can't say this back in Boston, because it would cost me business, but it's more stressful now than it is satisfying, and it's been that way for a while. When Peter was alive, I had the luxury of picking and choosing my clients, because we had his income. Part of me dreads to go back to the rat-race."

The two were walking alongside the yellow brick building that Alicia had pointed out to Saralynn that first afternoon on campus.

"This is the theater," Katie explained. "It's now used for a variety of activities. This is where the local little theater, The Lamplighter Players, stages its performances. But you seem such a natural as a decorator. I wouldn't think you'd ever get burned out."

"My first love is painting; in fact, my major is in fine art and I've got a minor in Interior Design."

"So why aren't you painting?"

"Because artists starve and designers eat, and before Peter and I got married, I had to support myself." *I'm not going to tell you that Mama believed I could have social status and the chance to mix with the better class of people if I was a designer.*

"So do you ever paint now?"

"I haven't had a brush in my hand since before Marc was born. You have Paul, you know the drill."

"Tell me about it. If I didn't have Aunt Toots, I don't know what I'd do some days. Especially since a baby wasn't in our game plan right at this time. Not that I'd give him back for anything," she hastened to add.

Sometimes you don't have a choice.

"So where to first?" *If we keep talking about babies, I'll get all depressed.*

"I thought we'd spend the morning in the past and this afternoon, we can visit the present."

"So we're going to the museum?"

"Security is there now, waiting for us." She went on to explain that plans were to develop the holdings into a first-class museum. "Right now, they're being housed in one of the former staff homes, which isn't ideal. But it's the best we can do."

As Katie had promised, a uniformed man was standing in the yard of a neat little brick bungalow. He greeted the ladies and asked Katie, "Where's my little man Paul this morning?"

"He spending the day with his favorite aunt."

"You better watch out. Toots will spoil that boy so bad you won't ever be able to do anything with him."

"Don't I know it," Katie replied. "She's the best and the worst of babysitters."

"And you'll let her have him any time she wants him."

"You know too much," Katie teased back. "Say, I'm sorry, I didn't introduce the two of you. James, this is Saralynn Reilly from Boston. Miss Sallie Watson was her grandmother, and Saralynn wants to see what the Sanatorium was like when Miss Sallie was a patient here."

To Saralynn she said, "And this is James Dean, just like the late actor, not the sausage baron. He works with security."

"I'm glad to meet you," James told Saralynn. "Your grandmother was one of my favorite people, even if she didn't spoil me as much as Toots does Paul."

"You knew my grandmother?"

"Sure. Spent half my life at her house. Would have spent

the other half if my mama and daddy had let me."

It wouldn't take much for me to get jealous. Everyone knew Miss Sallie better than I did.

"Thanks, James, I'll call you when we're ready to leave so you can lock up."

Once inside, what Saralynn saw wasn't what she expected. Having worked an internship in an established museum as part of her graduate degree work, she was expecting professional displays and staging. *When Katie said things were more archived than displayed, she wasn't kidding.*

Katie explained, "Things used to be in better form, but we had to evacuate all of this stuff from one of the older buildings that was being torn down. No one has had the time, or the expertise, to get it all back into shape."

After a cursory tour of the small home, which had one bedroom set up like a typical patient room of that earlier era, Saralynn found that her grandmother's writings, many of which had been crafted in a very similar setting, took on a whole other dimension.

"Everything looks so severe, so plain. Almost primitive."

"Sure, when you compare it to the standard hospital room of today. Back then, this was about as good as it got."

"Yeah, I hadn't thought about it like that." She walked to the bedside table and picked up an interesting brown, folded pasteboard box-like object. "Now what is this?"

"That is a sputum cup. Do you have any idea what it was used for?"

"It's the cup where patients deposited whatever they coughed up?"

"One and the same." Katie took it from Saralynn. "I'll

admit, it doesn't look much like a cup, not like you think it would look. You see," she demonstrated, "there was cotton in the bottom. And the top closes. The patient would spit, the cotton would absorb it, and it stayed closed when it wasn't being used. Then the entire cup would be discarded."

"Sallie... I mean Miss Sallie, mentions this in one of her diary entries, but I would never have connected that term with something that looks like this."

"Most people don't. Say, would you mind if I ask you something?"

"I don't guess I'll know for sure until you do."

"Why do you call your grandmother by her first name? I get the idea you've just started adding the 'Miss'."

"Well, it's like this. In the first place, I only saw her twice in my life for a total of eight days. Mama and she had some sort of problem years ago that they never did settle and Mama always called her 'Sallie', so that's what I called her too."

"Makes sense. I'll bet she didn't even feel like a grandmother to you. What was their problem, because Miss Sallie was one of the sweetest people I ever knew?"

"I've never understood because Mama won't talk about it. She builds some of the best glass walls you've ever seen.

"That's a shame, because you missed out on one great grandmother."

"Don't tell me. She babysat for you, too."

"You bet. Me and half the kids in Simpson County for a long time."

"And that's why I want to know more about her. All of you got what I should have had." *I know I don't have any reason to be jealous, but I guess I am!*

"Those diaries should be a good start for you."

"Speaking of which, in the last few entries, there's been something else I don't understand." She picked up the sputum cup again. "You clarified this, so maybe you can solve another mystery."

"I'll try. You'll want to be sure to look through these photo albums before you go." She led Saralynn back into the living room, where folding tables held an assortment of memorabilia.

"Miss Sallie has started talking about someone named Miss Dora who evidently made a difference for her, but she doesn't give her last name. There isn't a clue who or what this Miss Dora was?"

"As it happens, I can answer that. Dora Baldwin was a woman in the community who volunteered here for more than forty years. She was one of..." Katie snapped her fingers. "I think there's a picture of her in one of these albums." She began to flip pages, scanning the pictures, some more than seventy years old.

It took nearly five minutes to find the picture in question. "Pay dirt! Here she is. Right there," Her finger pointed to a fading photograph of a middle-aged woman with her hair pulled back into a bun, who was assisting two patients with a crafts project.

"If you asked "Miss Dora" what she did here, she'd say she helped patients pass the time making a variety of craft and art projects. But in truth, she gave them a reason to want to get well. You're never too old to need a mother when you're sick, and to a lot of them, she was the closest thing to a mother they had."

Miss Sallie was evidently one of those patients.

"Miss Dora was a fixture here. She was one of the few people in the state who would contradict Dr. Boswell. When she saw a need, she answered it. Or she got someone to do it. Nobody refused Dora Baldwin."

Saralynn thumbed through the rest of the photos, stopping every so often to ask questions, most of which Katie could answer. There was also the Sanatorium newspaper, *The Pulse*, and from scanning a number of issues, she was able to understand more about her grandmother's daily way of life as a patient.

"Say, it's getting close to lunch time," she said, as she glanced at her watch. "What else do we need to see here?"

"You've hit the high spots," Katie assured her. "And you can always come back any time. Just give me a call and I can arrange it."

"Then let's close down here and go feed our faces."

Katie alerted James that they were ready to leave, and he drove up as they were pulling the door closed behind them.

"Today's the potato bar. You two eating here?"

"That's where we're headed now," Katie answered.

"Well get in. I was on my way over when I got your call. Save your feet."

That's how Saralynn took her first ride ever in a pick-up truck, while Katie explained about the popularity of the baked potato bar with Boswell staffers. When lunch was over, the visitor from Boston was wondering how she could arrange to eat there every Friday.

"We'll walk, thank you very much," Katie informed James afterward when he asked if they needed a lift. "Carbs are our enemies and I know for a fact that those potatoes were loaded with them."

"Yes, but they were some of the nicest carbs I've ever tasted," Saralynn offered as a defense for their entrees and their appetites.

"Thanks, James." Katie said. "See you around. Come on, Saralynn, now I want you to see why we're so proud we've been able to continue the Sanatorium's heritage, only in a different way."

Their first stop was in a building Katie explained had been the Preventorium.

"Dr. Boswell believed that people, especially growing children, were at risk for tuberculosis because their diets and lifestyles were lacking. This is where children came to live for extended periods of time, to eat, sleep, and play under strict supervision."

"Parents just turned over their children?"

"Many of them did, solely because the threat of TB was so horrifying that they would have done almost anything. Others, who were patients here themselves, had no one who could... or would, take their children. They often brought the kids with them."

"I've had problems over how Miss Sallie's parents could have allowed her to come so far from home. And once she got here, it was almost like they forgot that she existed."

Katie was leading the way down a wide hallway. "I want you to meet my husband, Charlie, before we do anything else."

"I'd like that."

"As for Miss Sallie's parents," Katie continued as if there had been no break in the conversation, "you need to understand a couple of things." They came to an office door with glass in the top half and Katie peeped inside. "He's on the phone. We'll wait out here... People were terrified they would get tuberculosis. Some of them were right here in Simpson County. Whenever people drove by the Sanatorium, they'd pick up speed because they thought they could outrun the germs."

"You're kidding?"

"I'm afraid I'm not. Remember, Saralynn, when people

fear something, their behavior isn't always rational. That's how it was with TB before antibiotics were developed in the 1950s. If rest and nutrition, and surgery as a last-ditch option didn't work, tuberculosis was a death sentence. There was good reason to fear the disease, but the ways people demonstrated that fear wasn't always reasonable."

She checked on her husband's availability and noted that he was still engaged in conversation. "He's being long-winded with somebody. There's something else you should realize. Things were drastically different back then. Life was harder and death was as common as birth. People operated in a survival mode, although to us today, it sounds cold and heartless."

That's the same thing Mama said. I still don't see it.

"Charlie's finally off that call," Katie said when she peeped in the window again. She rapped on the glass with her knuckles. "Let's get in there before that phone rings again."

As Saralynn followed Katie into the small office, a tall, dark-headed man with a mustache and goatee rose from his chair and put out a hand. "You must be Saralynn," he said calmly. "Katie has talked about nothing else since you two had lunch the other day."

"This is my Charlie." Katie slipped around behind the scarred old wooden desk, and put her arm around his waist. "Saralynn Reilly, meet Charlie Brooks."

"I'm so glad to finally meet you," Saralynn shook Charlie's hand. "If I'm all Katie could talk about, then you're already bored stiff with me."

Charlie roared with laughter.

"Believe me, she made you sound interesting enough that I managed to stay awake. I didn't want to miss this opportunity to meet you."

What could Katie have told him about me? I'm not royalty and I'm surely not famous.

"No offense meant," Saralynn cautioned, "but either Katie really stretched the truth or you desperately need to get a life."

"Nope," he said, "I think that my first impression was correct." He grinned and squeezed his wife's shoulders. "Katie here usually calls them right on target. Listen, Hon, don't want to be rude, but that call I was on when you got here was about a called meeting across campus. I've got to duck out." He turned back to Saralynn, "I hope you will forgive me. And I hope you'll come back and visit when I don't have to meet and run."

Saralynn laughed. *This guy has a real wry sense of humor. But then I can't imagine Katie married to any other type. Only what did she tell him?*

"Don't give it a second thought, Katie's promised to show me around the campus this afternoon. I'm sure we need to get on our way."

"Thanks for understanding. Both of you." He again hugged his wife, saluted to Saralynn and left the office.

They heard his heels tapping out a rapid rhythm that quickly faded into the distance.

"Poor, Charlie. They just don't make enough hours in the day for him. Come on, let's be on our way." She followed Saralynn out of the office and pulled the door shut. "There's no telling what time he'll get back."

"What does he do here, exactly?" Saralynn asked. "You said he was some kind of counselor, I think."

They exited the building and continued their walk across the campus. Katie pointed out the former electric department, the lake and other former Sanatorium buildings now being recycled for new uses.

"Charlie is an occupational therapist," Katie explains. "Many of our clients work for a paycheck. We have several small industries where we contract with vendors to manufacture or assemble products."

"I guess I thought of this as a warehouse type facility for people. I know that sounds crass, but that would have been my guess."

"You're not alone in that mindset. We have many clients here who work very hard. They are dedicated to their assignments and have a real work ethic."

They had reached a long, ranch-style building, one of the newer additions to the campus, Saralynn judged. Katie indicated they should slip in quietly. "I want to you see in here, but without being seen. You'll understand in a minute."

What greeted Saralynn was an assorted group of adults clustered around tables at the far end of the room.

"We have art and crafts for the clients. Strictly recreational, you understand." She pointed to various creative projects hung around the room. "These are some of the examples of what they make."

Her eyes traveled from one item to another. "I'm amazed at the simplistic beauty of some of these. There are definitely some of your clients – that is what you called them, right? – who have some talent."

"Most people don't know that, because this is a past-time activity, not one of our industries. But I think some of our clients turn out remarkable work. I'd be interested in knowing what you think."

"Tell me something, Katie. I don't mean this the way it's going to sound, but I would never have suspected that anyone with mental impairment could be an artist."

"You and a lot of other people."

Katie finally suggested they should move along. The rest of the afternoon was spent leisurely walking the grounds, where Saralynn was coming to feel more and more comfortable. Clients would pass them and speak, and Katie would respond, calling many of them by name. In each case, she'd introduce them to her friend, Saralynn, and a conversation would result.

By the time they were back at Katie's house, Saralynn's mind was about to explode from all she had seen and done. Her heart was equally full.

"So," Katie asked, "has your day been worth the time invested?"

"You don't even begin to know the half of it. I feel like I'm on overload. I hope you won't mind if I don't stay and visit. I feel like I need to be on my way home. I'm really tired."

"Whatever works for you works for me," Katie says. "You know you're welcome to come back any time."

Saralynn hugged her friend's neck. "Thanks for all I've learned today, but even more, thanks for your friendship. I can't begin to tell you what it's meant to me."

They hugged again. Katie stood on her porch until Saralynn had cranked the van and was backing out of the drive. The two waved and the weary young woman behind the wheel wondered if she could get home before all the starch drained from her system. *I don't know when I've felt so many conflicting emotions and ideas swirling all at the same time. This is how it used to be when I first started decorating. But that was a long time ago.*

She was about half way home when she remembered there was nothing for dinner – er… supper, and decided to run through one of the pizza places on the four-lane for take-out. The detour delayed her by about thirty minutes, but she knew if she got home, she wouldn't venture out again.

She slid the pizza box into the oven at home, and put the salad and bottled soft drink in the refrigerator. *I'm not hungry yet, but it won't be long.*

Saralynn had planned out her evening while she waited for her pizza order. She would lock the doors and soak in a hot tub. Then, after putting on her pajamas, and eating her fill of the food she'd purchased, she could get down to the main business of the evening. *And I'll call Mama while I'm eating. I'm a little concerned that I haven't heard from her.*

She carried her cell phone into the bathroom as insurance. *About the time I get comfortably settled, Mama will call.* But there was no interruption and she relaxed in a tub of hot water and bath salts for more than thirty minutes.

After she'd dried off and gotten dressed for bed, Saralynn piled a plate high with several slices of the deluxe pizza and drizzled oil and vinegar over the take-out salad. She took both plates to her bedroom and came back for her drink, double-checked the back door, and returned to enjoy her feast.

Two large pizza wedges and several bites of salad later, she felt fortified enough to tackle her mother. *She'll be at my house by now.* But after five rings, she was confronted with Peter's voice on the answering machine, and the old pain, the grief that had moved into the background, was suddenly back and even more crippling than she remembered.

I'd forgotten all about that recording. It's just one more piece of confusion to add to the equation. How can I even think about starting over with a new life if I can't hold myself together when I'm confronted with what used to be?

"Don't let anyone dictate how long you should or shouldn't grieve..." Sue had counseled with such conviction only the day before.

Oh, Peter. I can never forget either you or Marc. But I really feel like I want to take the first step to get on with my life. Can you understand that? Will you give me your blessing?

For the first time in many days – *How long has it been?* - tears captured her and wouldn't let go. She had no choice but to ride to the crest of the emotional climax, and then try to swim to safety once the dam burst. When she surveyed her surroundings again, she was curled tightly into a knot near the foot of her bed. *I don't even remember moving from the chair. What else did I do?*

The musical tones of her phone caught her attention and she grabbed it. *Mama got to me before I got to her.*

"Hello, Mama. I was going to call you in just a minute."

"I'm not your mama," a male voice replied, "but I hope you'll still talk to me."

Who is this?

"It's Walter Kennedy. If you need to talk to Alicia right now, you can call me back."

I didn't recognize his voice, but that's no reason to get so spooked.

"There's no hurry." She hoped he couldn't tell by the sound of her voice that she'd been crying. "It's nice of you to call. I really enjoyed myself the other night, but the words 'thank you' just don't seem sufficient."

"Believe me, they're more than adequate. It was a great evening for us, too. But I know you need to talk to your mother, so let me tell you why I called. First, Virginia and I are delighted that you're going to join us at church on Sunday. Donna just beat us to the punch with the invitation, but we'll gladly concede the game point."

"I'm telling you, I don't think I've ever been so sought-after. It's a rather heady experience." *I really do feel overwhelmed.*

"We tend to be a pretty gung-ho group, but please don't feel intimidated. Don't think we've ganged up on you. Everything that's been said or done has been sincere."

"I know that. It's just that you don't find it this way in the north, and I have to remember that I'm in a different place. Why I barely know my neighbors on either side of my house, and Peter and I moved there seven years ago."

"And Peter would be...?"

I've done it again. Why can't I remember that not everyone knows what happened?

Because she felt she had no other choice, she said, "Peter is my husband, but he and our son were killed in an accident earlier this year."

"We're here for you if you need us, but I'll let you be the one to tell the others. When and if you're ready. Either way, we're still looking forward to Sunday."

He didn't pity me, or patronize me.

"The other thing I called about was the listing for the property. I've not heard anything from Alicia, but I know she's got her hands full. When you talk to her, tell her the deadline for the next real estate sales magazine is a week from today, and we really need to get your place listed if she's still planning to sell."

Saralynn promised she would relay the message, and they chatted for a few more minutes before ending the conversation.

Might as well get it over with.

She hit the redial button for her house, and after five rings, got Peter's voice again. This time the pain wasn't quite as bad; the sting of realization that this was the only way she would ever hear his voice again was less piercing. *When I get back to Boston, I need to remove that tape and put it safely away and make a new one.*

Her second call was to Alicia's cell phone, which her mother answered with the advice, "I'm coming back as soon as I can. I just couldn't leave today."

"And hello to you, too, Mama."

"I hope you've had time today to come to your senses. Do you have any idea how upset I was this morning, thinking about you burying yourself in that god-forsaken backwater?"

"We'll talk about this when you get back, Mama. Whenever that is. But for right now, we're going to drop the subject, because obviously we can't discuss it without disagreeing."

"You can bet we're going to talk about it. We'll talk while we're loading the van and I dare anyone to mention the name Mississippi in my presence ever again."

"Change the subject, Mama. Or I'm hanging up."

"You used to be such a good daughter. Something's changed you."

"Mama, after what I've been through this summer, I'd have to be dead myself not to be changed. It's like someone took an eraser and just obliterated a part of my life. I'm sorry that you don't approve, but I'm more at peace today that I have been since it happened. Now, like I said, let's talk about something else, or I'll hang up."

There was total silence on the other end.

She's still there. I can hear her breathing. Looks like I'm going to have to do it all.

"What did you accomplish today? Any problems with my suppliers?"

More silence.

"Mama. I know you're there. Don't do this to me."

"I picked out a beautiful floral for the new draperies in my bedroom. I'm going with a totally different look in there. I want something that's bright and colorful."

How like you, Mama. You could give denial lessons.

"Sounds pretty. You've got a good eye for design. You should have been the decorator, not me."

"You're too hard on yourself. You've done some beautiful projects. Just ask your clients."

Clients who are as two-dimensional as I've come to realize I was. But I'm not going to argue with her. Instead, she relayed Walter Kennedy's message.

"Tell him I'll talk to him when I get there. We'll still make the deadline."

Mother and daughter made small talk for another couple of minutes and then said their goodnights.

Mama's built that wall again.

If anything, Alicia's attitude had strengthened Saralynn's resolve to create a new life for herself, free from all the ghosts of the past.

Chapter 8

*W*here could Marc and Peter be? In her dream, Saralynn worked on the casserole she was preparing for dinner, keeping one eye on the kitchen clock. She'd insisted that they not go for ice cream so late in the day. It would spoil her son's appetite. But Peter had given in to the youngster's pleas.

"We'll be back in a jiffy," he called over his shoulder, as the two Reilly men departed the back door.

How long does it take to drive six blocks for an ice cream cone?

The sound of the front door bell forced her to hurriedly wash and dry her hands. *Who could that be?*

When she released the deadbolt and opened the door, Saralynn discovered a blue-uniformed police officer on the front stoop.

"Yes?"

"Mrs. Reilly? I'm Sergeant Morgan." The man extended

his identification. "May I come in?"

"Certainly. Is something wrong?"

I haven't even had a parking ticket in quite some time. What could he want?

"Mrs. Reilly, I'm sorry to have to be the bearer of bad news, but there's been an accident..."

Saralynn sat bolt upright in the bed with tears raining on her sleep shirt – Peter's shirt. Peter! Where was Peter? There'd been an accident. Was Marc hurt?

She fought to get free of the officer's arms that imprisoned her. He said she needed to accompany him, but he wouldn't let go of her arms. Saralynn thrashed about, seeking to escape the man's grasp.

The impact of the floor rising up to meet her was both sudden and painful enough to separate nightmare from the reality of the moment. *I'm not in Boston. And Marc and Peter have been dead for weeks now. I've had another nightmare. But why, when I've been so happy?*

Then the guilt overwhelmed her. *That's the problem. I don't have any right to be happy so soon after losing Peter and Marc. I'm being punished.*

While her diagnosis didn't at all jive with what she'd been hearing from others over the past week, what else could it be?

I've been disloyal to those I love most, and now I'm paying for it. This nightmare was a signal that I'm not supposed to move on. Not yet, maybe not even here. But why did it feel so right?

She managed, finally, to unwind herself from the pile of covers and throw them back on the bed. Then she moved to the little rocker in the corner to finish out the night. When the sun sneaked between the curtains a few hours later, Saralynn was still seated in the little brown rocker. *This rocking chair is just like my life. I keep moving back and forth but I don't feel like I get anywhere.*

She probably would have stayed there indefinitely. Lacking the will to get up... to get on with the day... with her life. The trill of her cell phone's summons, however, provided the little nudge she needed.

Mama.... I might as well answer. If I don't, she'll be landing at the Jackson airport before sunset.

Sure enough, when she checked the display screen it was Alicia's cell number.

"Hello, Mama."

"You don't sound so good this morning. What's wrong?"

Good old perceptive Mama. I can always count on her to jump to conclusions. Only this time, Alicia was on target and Saralynn knew she didn't dare allow Alicia to discover the truth.

"Sorry, Mama. I'm not good and awake yet. This business of not having to get up at any particular time can get you spoiled in a hurry."

"You're sure nothing's wrong. You're not keeping anything from me, are you?"

Why do I always have to walk a tightrope with Mama?

"Have I ever?"

"That's just it. I'm never sure anymore."

"So how's it going? They've got to be making some good progress by now." Saralynn deliberately changed the subject.

For the next ten minutes she listened to Alicia's laundry list of concerns and questions, and tried her best to reassure, to calm the sense of panic she heard on the other end of the conversation.

If only I could make myself believe that I'd made some headway on my own project.

Saralynn had promised herself that she would spend the day reading in Sallie's journals. Instead, once she had finished her conversation with Alicia, she hauled the covers back up onto the bed and burrowed under them. It was there that she spent the day, crying and dozing, and crying again.

I'm no better now that I was the week after the memorial service.

If the low level of natural light in the little back bedroom was any indication, it was early evening when a persistent knocking at the back door roused her from a frustrated sleep. Once she'd gotten her bearings, she decided to ignore the noise and the unknown visitor making it. However, the banging continued and she could hear voices calling her name.

If I don't answer, they may think something's happened to me and break down the door. Then I'd have to explain to Mama.

She threw aside the already tangled covers and crawled over the foot of the old iron bed, grabbed her robe and tied it over her nightclothes.

Sounds like a man and a woman.

She turned the big skeleton key in the ancient lock and pulled open the door to find Doug and Bess Martin on the other side.

"Is anything wrong?" the couple demanded in unison. "Your cell phone isn't working, and when we saw your van in the drive and couldn't get you to the door, we were about to summon help," Doug informed her.

"You really frightened us," Bess added. "We couldn't imagine what had happened."

"I'm so sorry," Saralynn said contritely. "I didn't mean to

cause problems for anyone." She could tell that her guests were questioning her sleep-worn appearance but were too polite to comment. The looks that were passing between them, however, spoke loudly.

"As long as you're okay," Doug said finally. "We were calling to ask if you wanted to go to Jackson with us to a movie. We'll probably grab a burger somewhere."

All I want to do is go back to bed and pretend that I never came to Magee. I knew I shouldn't have let Mama talk me into this. Instead, she said, "Thanks, but not this time. I think I may have gotten a touch of a bug or something, and I wouldn't want to pass it along."

"Do you need a doctor?" Bess asked. "All I've got to do is make a phone call. We can drive you."

Gee, don't these southerners ever get off that "can't do enough for you" kick? She immediately felt guilty for her harsh judgment. *I sound just like Mama. They were only trying to be helpful.*

"I'm sure I'll be fine by tomorrow. It's just one of those twenty-four hour bugs." She clutched her robe closer around her, suddenly aware of just how disheveled she looked. "But thanks for caring," she added, hoping to disarm her would-be rescuers.

"We'd still love to have you go along," Bess insisted. "It might do you good to get out."

Fighting aggravation, Saralynn said, "Thanks, but not this time. You go on and enjoy your evening. I'll be fine. I just need to rest and let whatever this is get out of my body." *If only it were something so simple that time could heal what is causing me to hurt.*

"Wish you'd go," Doug said, "but if you're sure you can't, we'll leave you to get back to bed."

"Thanks. I really think that's best."

"But you need to check your cell phone," Bess reminded

her. "We tried for almost two hours and kept getting your voice mail."

The couple turned to leave, but Bess added, "I'll check on you tomorrow morning." She then flashed Saralynn a look that reminded the young Bostonian of one of her mother's business expressions. "And if you're not better tomorrow, we'll be calling a doctor."

Saralynn watched the couple walk hand in hand across the yard to where their car was parked. The image reminded her, once again, that her walking mate was gone forever. Then she remembered why she'd spent the entire day mired in grief and despair.

Lord, just get me back to bed. Then, in shocked reaction, she realized that once again she'd called on the God she earlier denied even knew she existed. *Why did I do that? I'm starting to do this automatically, without even thinking. Mama always said God wanted you to do things for Him, not the other way around.*

She spied her cell phone and recalled her guests' parting words. *I need to get that problem fixed. If Mama can't get me, she'll be frantic.*

The small silver phone lay on the bedside table where she'd dropped it after the last conversation. One look at the display told her that the phone had been left on talk mode.

Dead as a doornail. I've got to be more careful about this.

Saralynn dug in her purse where she finally found the charger unit and soon had the phone connected. It showed fourteen missed calls, thirteen of which were from Doug and Bess. The last call was from Alicia's cell number.

I'd better call her right now.

She hit the recall button and in a matter of seconds was rewarded with the distant sound of ringing. And more ringing, until finally, just when Saralynn was about to panic, she heard Alicia's breathless voice on the other end.

"He... hello... don't hang up. I'm here."

"You sound out of breath, Mama."

"Uh... uh... hold on... whew... give me a minute."

"Take your time. I'm not going anywhere."

Her mother's labored speech was troubling and Saralynn waited for what seemed an eternity before Alicia said, in a more normal tone, "I couldn't find where I laid my phone. This place is in so much turmoil. Why didn't you answer when I called?"

"I forgot to disconnect and the power ran down. I just discovered it." *I didn't lie, I just didn't tell her everything.*

"When I didn't get you earlier, I started to get worried. There's no telling what could happen to you there all alone."

"Mama, you make it sound like this is a lawless land or some such."

"As far as I'm concerned, you're in grave danger every minute."

"Whatever, Mama. I'm safe and I'm happy." *Or at least I was happy until I had that nightmare last night. Now I don't know any more.*

"You may think that, but I know better. I'll be back as soon as I can. Hopefully no later than this time next week. It's just every time I think I can get away here, something else crops up."

There's no use arguing with her. She always has a comeback for everything.

"Just let me know when you're arriving."

Almost as if they 'd reached a mutual but unspoken truce, the remainder of their conversation dealt with Alicia's renovation project and the need to sell Sallie's house to help pay the bills.

What do I care if she sells this place? My idea was really dumb. So dumb, I can't believe I seriously considered it. After that nightmare last night, I know where I belong, and as soon as Mama can get back, I'll be headed north to Boston.

"Mama, don't forget Mr. Kennedy needs to talk to you. I think you'd better call him."

"Yes, I guess I had. Give me his number and I'll call him tomorrow. First thing."

"Even before you call me, right?"

"After I call you. We just won't talk as long."

For the first time since she'd been sleeping in Sallie's — *Miss Sallie's* — house, Saralynn acutely sensed the absence of a television.

I never realized how addicted I'd gotten to the TV.

She picked up one of the paperback books she'd grabbed off the rack at Wal-Mart, and piled up on the bed to read. But it wasn't long before she dropped the book beside the bed, unable to get past page four.

I really don't feel like sleeping any more, but I just couldn't get into that book. She's always been one of my favorite authors. Back in Boston, anyway. Maybe I should have gone to Jackson with Doug and Bess.

Saralynn wrestled for the longest time with the voices in the back of her head; voices she had learned, through painful experience, to heed. In the end, she brought the small, soiled valise to the bed and began to dig for another notebook.

I want to read them, but for the first time since I found these old diaries, I'm afraid because I don't know what I'm going to find.

Finally she opened the faded, once-brown cover of the book she had started earlier and began flipping pages.

Broken Spirit

It's been almost three weeks since I wrote in my journal. Dr. McCallum says I've been one sick young lady. I won't argue. One day this week is Thanksgiving, but I've looked at these same cracks in the ceiling so long, I'm not sure when it is. I'll have to ask Nurse Myra.

Funny, a few days ago when I was so sick, I wouldn't have cared if Thanksgiving came or not. I sure didn't have anything to be thankful for. Not then. But now, I don't care if I can't go to the dining room and must lay here in bed and have someone feed me my turkey and dressing.

The doctors say Miss Dora is the best medicine I could have gotten. I think so, too.

There's that woman's name again. Only this time Miss Sallie – Hey! I remembered to call her "Miss" – says she's a medicine.

Saralynn went on to read further, determined to discover what sort of magic power this Baldwin woman had that could make Miss Sallie consider her a healing tonic. Finally, however, fatigue and heavy eyelids claimed first rights over her body, and she was powerless to resist.

It was a sharp, knife-like pain in her neck that first awakened Saralynn the next morning. She had lain at an awkward angle among the mound of bedclothes that crowned her uncle's old bed, her head hanging over the edge.

No wonder my neck hurts. Did I sleep like this all night? What time is it?

177

She grabbed her cell phone, willing her eyes to focus on the small display screen. *If I'm seeing things right, it's six-seventeen.* She rubbed her eyes, trying to get awake.

Once she persuaded her feet to hit the old, worn linoleum floor, she was surprised to discover that she felt awake and rested. *I might as well get a jump on the day, even if it is early.*

When she looked out to check the weather, she was shocked to see a small red and white calf standing in the back yard, looking lost and forlorn. *Whose little cow is that? And what do I do with it? It looks like that little cow in the painting at Windham's. When I said I'd like to see one, I didn't expect my wish to be granted so quickly.* She wrung her hands and paced nervously in front of the window, almost hoping when she looked again, it would be gone. *I don't know anything about animals. We couldn't even have a dog for Marc. Peter said there wasn't room for one to run and play.*

She stopped in the bathroom, where her conscience jabbed her about forgetting to brush her teeth the night before. To salve her conscience, she brushed for an extra minute and almost choked on the toothpaste lather, before spitting the contents of her mouth into the old, yellowed basin that hung on the bathroom wall.

"Maaaaaaaaaahaaa."

Saralynn jumped. *What was that?*

"Maaaaa. Maaaaaaah."

Then she realized it was coming from the back yard. *That baby cow. What do I do?*

Grabbing her robe, she wrapped it around herself, shoved her feet into old shoes beside the bed and, almost as an afterthought, snatched up her cell phone and dropped it into a pocket in her robe. Then she headed for the back yard armed with all of the animal husbandry skills at her disposal. *That little animal is a member of the cow family. Like those dairy cows we saw the day Mama and I first went to Boswell. Only they were black and white and he's red and white. I wonder what the difference is?*

Saralynn had never even been near any animal before, unless you counted the various dogs that belonged to their friends. For certain, she knew she wasn't equipped to do whatever should be done in this situation. She needed reinforcements. Better yet, she needed someone to handle matters for her, while she went back to bathe and dress.

Instead, she eased out the door, sensing that any sudden noise might spook the little animal. *Wouldn't want it to bolt and run. Might get hit by a car or something. I just wish I knew who its owner is.*

When the small calf spotted her, its eyes widened in fear, and it ran in the opposite direction. Then the little animal turned and faced its foe again – Saralynn guessed when it felt safe. She froze, not wanting to frighten it further. They both stood like statues, staring at each other, for what seemed an eternity.

"So there you are," she heard a man's voice behind her say. "Yo' mama is bellerin' her head off looking for you."

Saralynn turned and saw a man she judged to be near her age coming around the corner of the house. He held a rope harness looped around his left arm, and in his right hand, he held the bale of a galvanized bucket.

"I no more get one hole in the fence fixed before you find another," he scolded the calf. "What am I gonna..." Then he glimpsed Saralynn standing near the steps.

"Sorry, miss." The tall man was dressed in jeans, a denim shirt and cowboy boots.

I guess that's what farmers wear?

"Didn't see you there."

"Is this your little cow?"

"Yes'um." A smile played at the corners of his mouth. "She's mine, and her mama is mighty worried. Little booger keeps finding places in the fence where she can squeeze through. Can't seem to figure how to squeeze back in, though."

"I don't think I've ever seen a cow so small." *In fact, I've never seen* any *live cows before I came here.*

The stranger smiled again, unable to hide his amusement. "This little calf is only about a week old. She's got a lot of growing to do."

Saralynn thought about that and remembered Marc, and how he would never grow up. *If that mama cow is hurting any worse than I've hurt, I feel sorry for her.*

A tear slid down her cheek, despite her valiant effort to staunch the waterworks she knew were dammed up and threatening to overflow.

"I'm sorry," her visitor said. "Is something wrong?" He took off the cowboy hat to reveal a crowning mass of tangled, golden-red curls. "Where are my manners? I haven't even introduced myself. "I'm Ian Scarborough. We, that is my family, we own the farm down yonder." As he spoke, he pointed toward the southwest. "Been in the family since 1839."

Saralynn hesitated, almost afraid to speak for fear the tears would betray her again. But finally, she said, "Wow… 1839. That's a long time." *That makes my grandparents seem like the new kids on the block.*

"Eight generations," he said proudly. "We're one of the few farms in the county still owned by the family that homesteaded it. And I take it you'd be Miss Sallie's granddaughter?"

"Now I'm the one whose manners are lacking. Yes, I'm Saralynn Reilly." She put out her right hand. *My, but he's got a strong handshake.*

"Sorry to intrude on you, but when I heard mama making a racket this morning, I figured this calf had gotten out. Speaking of which, I'd best be gettin' her back home, only as soon as she gets her tummy full, I'm afraid she'll be out and gone again."

The visitor placed the suede hat back on his head, adjusted the angle, and said, "Come over and see us sometime. Some of us are always there." He walked slowly, holding the bucket at an angle that would allow the animal to smell the contents. "Come here. Got some a yer mama's milk for you."

Saralynn watched in awe as the man moved confidently toward the little animal whose eyes showed that it was torn between the prospect of getting something to eat and wanting to escape while it had the chance. In the end, the urge to eat won out, and in a matter of seconds, the farmer had the rope halter slipped over the little white head. Only then did he allow the calf's pink-tipped muzzle to drop into the bucket, where Saralynn heard the animal slurping the milk.

"She's sure not going to let that milk get away."

"It'll usually work, especially when they're this young. It won't be long before she gets wise to me."

When the calf had drained the bucket, the farmer tugged on the rope. "Come along, little gal. Let's get you back to your mama before she goes all to pieces." He led the animal past where Saralynn had seated herself on the back steps. "Cows are funny. They have a calf every year, but they can't seem to remember how it was."

"Obviously you've never been a mother."

"No… can't say that I have." His laugh was infectious, but the suffocating ache in Saralynn's chest wouldn't let her respond. *He just doesn't have a clue how badly a mother's heart can hurt, or how hard it can shatter.*

"Sorry to have bothered you, Saralynn. Don't forget to drop by to see us.

The man and his animal moved across the yard with a comfortable, easy gait that Saralynn found interesting. She watched until the corner of the house hid them from view.

Now what?

It was the earliest she'd been up since arriving in the south, and she found the morning mists to be almost intoxicating. *I don't even want to go back inside. It's like I could stay out here always.*

Yielding to the temptation that dogged her, she resisted the sensible urge to return indoors. The day could wait. Even the prospect of breakfast didn't entice her.

I'm hungry, but it isn't for food. Not right now.

Throwing caution to the wind, she cinched the belt to her robe more securely and set out through the yard.

The fierce morning sun shining through the rapidly evaporating mists created mini-prisms that caught her eyes as she moved through the orchard north of the house. *I can't believe I've been in Miss Sallie's house all this time and haven't already been out here. It's so beautiful.*

Beams of sunlight filtering through the trees caused patterns of light and dark to dance beneath her feet as she moved through the orchard she suspected had been producing fruit long before her grandparents bought the land. *Ian Scarborough said his family first settled here in 1839. Could these trees have been here even then?*

What struck her as she strolled through the lanes, now tangled with weeds and brambles, were the many variations and the intricacy of the sunlight patterns that spread themselves before her. They were magic to her soul at that moment, feeding a need she hadn't even known existed. Many of the designs reminded her of the beautiful stained glass windows she and Peter had seen in Europe.

I really miss painting. Just for the satisfaction of seeing the image emerge on canvas. I'm not certain Mama was totally right.

Those words out of her mouth were such a shock she had to seek support from a nearby pecan tree whose sturdy trunk provided a badly needed sense of stability.

It's been a long time since I've thought about using my talent as anything more than a tool for doing my job and making a living. But should I feel guilty for second-guessing Mama? She felt no shame and even that made her uneasy.

Vindicated, at least in her own mind, Saralynn felt safe to release her hold on the rough bark that had grounded her. She continued her stroll through the archway of trees, stopping often to survey the scenery from her artist's eye. More than once, she visualized what lay before her painted on canvas and hanging in a prominent place in a beautiful home. Once her soul was sufficiently fed, she realized that her physical body was calling out for satisfaction as well.

Mama always said that painting solely for pleasure was a waste of time. But how could anything that makes you feel so complete be wrong? That's part of Mama's problem now.

The gravity of her judgment call shocked Saralynn and she rooted in the small refrigerator for the yellow jug of milk, and then found a bowl and the box of cereal. Filled bowl in hand, she decided to eat on the front porch in the swing where she could continue to soak in the morning beauty.

Saralynn was midway to her mouth with a spoonful of cereal when the vibrating ring of her cell phone, momentarily forgotten in the pocket of her robe, caused her to spill the milky mixture into her lap. She juggled the bowl to her other hand and set it down on the swing seat beside her, as she rummaged in her pocket.

I should have remembered it was time for Mama to call. But the number showing on the tiny screen wasn't a Boston exchange.

"Hello."

"I'm glad to hear you sounding better this morning. Can we hope you've passed that bug?"

Bess Martin?

For a minute Saralynn struggled to understand what her caller meant. She then remembered, with a pang of guilt, the bogus virus from the previous evening.

"I'm much improved," she said finally, hoping that her caller wouldn't inquire as to the specifics of her brief illness. *I don't want to have to lie again.*

"That's great. Doug and I were worried about you. I told him before he left this morning that I'd be taking you in to the clinic if you weren't better. There's nothing worse than getting sick away from home and your doctor."

"I really appreciate your concern." Saralynn caught sight across the road of a deer standing with its nose high in the air. The animal's tense body intrigued her and she could feel her imaginary artist's brush painting in the muscles that lay beneath the butternut hide. Then with a twitch of its tail and a flash of the white underside, the creature disappeared into the woods at the same moment that Bess Martin said, "… so we'll see you at church."

Why do I do this? It's not just rude, it's going to get me in real trouble some day.

To her own surprise, Saralynn heard herself say, "I'm sorry, Bess. Run that by me again. I got distracted by one of the prettiest deer I've ever seen standing right across the road."

"They are beautiful animals, aren't they? Doug hunts, and so do most of the guys we know. But it's like I tell Doug, I promised to love, honor and cherish him. Shooting Bambi doesn't fall under any of those headings."

"You mean women deer hunt?"

"Sure. We know several couples that hunt together. It's just not for me."

"Gosh, I learn something new every day I'm here. But back to the other. What were you saying when I zoned out on you?"

Bess giggled, but it was, Saralynn thought, a delightful laugh that said its owner was so at peace in her world. "I said, don't forget we're all looking forward to you being with us tomorrow, starting with Sunday School."

Oops. I had forgotten.

"That's why I was going to haul you to the doctor if you weren't better. We don't want you sick. I don't think you have a clue how popular you are."

Me?

"But I hardly know any of you. How can I be popular?"

"Because you're genuine. Yankees usually aren't as friendly as you are."

Yankee. Is that how they see me?

"Saralynn? I didn't offend you, did I? I'm sorry. Often I

just don't stop to think before I open my mouth."

"No… no. You just took me by surprise. I don't guess I've ever thought of myself as a Yankee. In fact, I don't guess I've even heard the term that much." *Now I'm going to hurt her feelings.* "I take it Yankee isn't a very complimentary word down here?"

Bess laughed again, although not quite as confidently, Saralynn thought.

"Usually, no. Remember, we've got folks down here still fighting the war, and if you have to ask what war, you really are an outsider."

Saralynn snickered. "Well, I may be a Yankee, but I do know about 'the war.'"

"Anyway, don't worry," her friend advised, "you don't act like a Yankee, and something tells me even if you did, we'd still like you."

No one is Boston has ever told me they liked me. I've just always assumed that my friends were my friends.

Her phone emitted a squeaky beep, signaling an incoming call. "Hang on, Bess. Got another call."

"Answer it. We'll see you tomorrow. Bye, now."

Saralynn punched the transfer key. "Hello?"

"Are you safe this morning?"

"Yes, Mama." She pulled her robe closer around her. *If only I had a robe to protect me from Mama's obsessiveness.*

"Are you up?"

"I've been up for a couple of hours. In fact, I've been out for a walk in the orchard. One of our neighbors came over to get a baby cow that had gotten out, and I was talking to Bess Martin when you called. So, yes, I'm fine. In fact, I'm great."

"How you can be so cheerful when you're stuck down

there is more than I can understand."

She just won't get off it. But from this time on, I'm not going to bite. It takes two to argue.

"So how are things there?"

"Dreadful. Workmen can be so provoking. They aren't here today, just because it's Saturday."

"Mama! Merle's guys only work a five-day week. They earn their weekends off."

"I need this job finished and it won't happen if they take off every time you turn around. Haven't they ever heard about a work ethic?"

"I promise you, those guys have more work ethic than most. You just need to lighten up."

All I need is for Mama to damage my working relationship with Merle, especially after he's put her ahead of his other jobs as a favor to me.

"It's not your money and your time."

"That's right. It's not. But your expectations are unrealistic at any price. Please don't make those guys angry."

"I don't need my daughter lecturing me."

"I'm not lecturing, Mama. But I am advising you to cool it or you may be looking for another crew."

"Hhumph!"

One of us is changing, Mama, and I've got a sneaking suspicion it's me. I don't ever remember you being so obstinate.

"Do you know the Scarborough's who live on the next farm?"

"Are you changing the subject?"

"No, Mama. I'm asking a question before I forget it."

"Yes. I remember the Scarborough's. What about them?"

"According to Ian Scarborough, his family has lived here for the better part of two centuries."

"How did you meet him?"

"It was his little cow that turned up in the back yard this morning. He came over looking for it."

"Honey, that little cow is called a calf. I hope you didn't tell Ian who you are."

"Well, yes. I did. Why? Is there some reason I shouldn't have?

"Calf," huh? I'll bet he was laughing at me.

"The Scarborough's have always wanted Sallie's place. Seems like it was once part of their homestead, but one of them sold it off about a hundred years ago. They've always been so arrogant."

"Ian seemed real nice."

"Just promise me you won't get chummy with them. When we list Sallie's place for sale as subdivision property, they'll pay and pay well to keep it from going that way. After all, money's no object with them."

Do I detect an undercurrent of bitterness and gouging? Saralynn had a mental image of her mother as Mr. Potter in the movie "It's a Wonderful Life," and didn't like what she saw. *It's like Mama's sitting there now counting a stack of bills. I never realized how much she craves money.*

"I'll be careful, Mama." *I don't imagine I'll run in to him again, anyway. If his little cow… if the calf hadn't gotten out, I wouldn't even have known about him or his family.*

"I'll be back as soon as I can, but right now I don't know when that will be."

"Don't worry about me. I'm fine."

"Stay close to the house this weekend. You don't need to be wandering in places you don't know and don't understand."

"I'll take care, Mama. It's time I got my bath and got dressed for the day. Those boxes aren't going to pack themselves."

Chapter 9

The packing boxes were calling. But Miss Sallie's journals' screamed louder. *I told Mama I was going to pack, but there's plenty of time before she gets back.*

She made quick work of washing her cereal bowl and spoon and stowed the last of the milk in the refrigerator, before getting her bath. Then, dressed in jeans and a Boston Celtics sweatshirt that had been Peter's, she grabbed the entire suitcase and headed back to the front porch swing.

Miss Sallie's last entry was written just before Thanksgiving. I wonder if she was well enough to enjoy her meal.

Saralynn knew from other entries she'd read that the Sanatorium went to great lengths to make the holidays as special as possible for their patients. But if you couldn't even sit up, it must have been difficult to celebrate. Suddenly she had to know how her grandmother had fared so far away from home and family and

Broken Spirit

she began to search for that's day's posting.

I wonder if she was able to write anything. That would tell me a lot.

When she found an entry labeled Thanksgiving Day, it was like getting a precious gift. *She was able to write a few words.*

✏️

I didn't believe it would happen, but when Nurse Myra came by this morning, she exchanged the red card on my door with a yellow card. This means I can get up to go to the bathroom whenever I need to go. No more just getting up once a day. It is so hard to lay here in this bed day after day.

When Nurse Myra swapped my card, she congratulated me on my progress. I'll still have to spend Thanksgiving in my room, eating by myself, but at least I'll be able to sit up and eat.

✏️

Miss Sallie's earlier memoirs had indicated that patients were color-coded according to the severity of their disease. Over the course of the year's entries she'd read, her grandmother's condition cards had gone from white at the time she was admitted, meaning that she was critically ill, to orange, the best available. As her condition deteriorated in mid-year, she had gone back to white.

Getting back to yellow had to be a major encouragement for her. And coming on Thanksgiving meant she had something to celebrate. But how could one good thing make up for so many other negatives?

She flipped to the next page in the old Blue Horseâ tablet. *Miss Sallie evidently wrote in whatever book was available at the time.*

191

Only a few of them, especially in the early years, are identical. Somehow or another it makes them all more precious… more valuable.

There was no entry for the Friday following Thanksgiving. Saralynn feared her grandmother had over-exerted herself and was paying the price. Miss Sallie's next recorded thoughts were dated on Saturday.

⬤▭

I slept the best last night I have in weeks. Thank you, God, for Miss Dora. I don't know what I would have done without her. I don't guess I'll ever be able to pass a holiday without wishing I were home. But Miss Dora makes it almost possible to forget that things aren't normal.

I was so tired Thanksgiving night but I remember what a great day it was. Yesterday I had to have tests, and they wouldn't let me sit up. But Nurse Myra told me this morning that I can sit up in my chair by the window.

I saw that man, Ralph, working on the grounds. He must have been looking for me, because once he waved and I waved back. I hope he saw me.

After I'd had my afternoon nap on Thursday, one of the other nurses came to get me in a wheel chair and took me down the hall to the telephone. Mama and Papa were calling from Fishtrap Hollow. It sure was good to hear their voices, but I could tell by the way Papa talked that he still feels guilty because I got the TB. They have to go into Iuka to the telephone office to make the call, so I don't get to talk to them that much.

Dr. McCallum has told him that it's not his fault, but I don't think he believes it.

I am getting better, and now I believe that I will get well. It

may take a while, but I believe I will go home in a car. I'll ride in a car through the pass-way in the depot to a new life outside. I won't go home in a box!

When I first came here, I'd hear the train whistle as the engine pulled away from the little depot. Back home, I used to like to hear the trains as they passed through Iuka, but here, the sound is so cold and lonesome. It frightens me. Every time I hear that whistle, I wonder how many patients are going home in boxes on that train. And I wonder when one of them will be me.

⬤▷

Saralynn remembered her mother's story of the depot, now missing, that had been the entrance onto the grounds. Those fortunate enough to get well drove out. Those who didn't often went home in a casket on the train. She flipped back to see what else Miss Sallie had written.

⬤▷

When I first came here, I thought everything was hopeless. I wondered how long it would take to die. I just wished I could get it over with. But now that I've come so close, I realize I don't want to die. I want to get well and get out of here. Get married and have a family. And I believe that it will happen. Miss Dora…

⬤▷

The entry stopped there, without warning or explanation. *Why did she stop in mid-sentence? Was something wrong? What could have happened to give her such a change in attitude?*

Sunday's entry gave no clue as to what had happened the day before. She provided no explanation for the abrupt halt in her recorded memories. Instead, the few sentences scribbled under the date November 29, 1946, were upbeat and almost humorous, but there was no mention of Miss Dora.

I want to know more about that woman. She must have been an angel. Shocked at her own admission, Saralynn had to question if she even believed in angels.

Stopping only once to fix a quick sandwich, which she ate with one hand while turning ancient, yellowed pages with the other, Saralynn joined the close-knit community of tuberculosis patients more than sixty years before.

The sun was setting in the west and creating shadows on the front porch of the old house when she reluctantly closed the hospital door and realized how far her day's journey had taken her.

How can it be that the more I learn about my grandmother, and the more answers I find, that I also find I'm that much farther away from really knowing her?

There were three entries penned in the now familiar loopy scrawl she had come to love that she knew would stay with her always.

The first had been written in the spring of 1946, after the trees had come back into green, obscuring her view of the grounds beneath her second floor window. Miss Sallie had confided in her journal…

Today is my birthday and I'm eighteen. There was a letter

from Mama, wishing me a good day, but I could feel her pain so strong. It's hard to believe that Papa is gone. Been almost three months now since the sawmill accident. I just wish I could have gone home for his funeral. But Dr. McCallum said I wasn't well enough to travel. Miss Dora stayed with me for a long time. She said I could grieve right here, just like I could at the funeral, because God is everywhere that people are hurting.

I asked the doctor this morning when he came by how much longer I'd be here. I feel like I'm getting old in this place. He knew it was my birthday, and he said if I kept making progress, he thought I'd probably turn nineteen somewhere besides in this room.

That will feel so funny. It's hard to remember what it was like to live anywhere but inside these four walls. Miss Dora would say not to worry, that God will provide the time and the way, and the strength to cope. I hope I can get to know her God better.

⊷

Saralynn had been moved to tears when she read her grandmother's admonition that grieving could happen anywhere because God was everywhere. *That seems to say I could be here, getting on with my life, and still honor Peter's memory. Marc's, too.*

It was an entry near the end of October that same year that brought a huge smile to her face, at the same time that a lump formed in her throat and her heart felt like it would split anew.

⊷

I think I'm in love but I don't know for certain. I don't have any idea how it feels to be in love, so that makes it harder. It's Ralph, the grounds man. Even though I've got privileges and can leave my room, patients aren't allowed to socialize with the staff. Every morning, about nine-thirty, I see the top of a curly, red head coming into view outside my window. Ralph balances on one of the big branches and waves at me. Once I wave back, he gives me a big grin and starts to climb back down.

A couple of times Dr. McCallum has been here when Ralph showed up, and I think he knows what's happening. He told me the last time if Ralph wasn't careful, he was going to get so dizzy with love that he was liable to fall out of the tree and break his neck.

I'm trying to get up the courage to talk to Miss Dora about it, but every time I think I can, I get scared and chicken out. I don't want to get Ralph in trouble.

I can understand just how she felt. I still remember the first time I saw Peter. Even though he had been on the other side of the huge symphony hall, Saralynn remembered thinking that if his personality was half as attractive as he was physically, he was one fun guy.

Who would have ever thought that in less than two weeks, we'd find ourselves introduced when one of my clients threw an open house to show off her new living room and Peter was one of the guests?

From that first encounter, she had known she was smitten with the tall, lanky college professor. The only thing more beautiful than his handsome face was the mesmerizing brogue that proclaimed his Irish roots. *I was in love.*

Fortunately, Peter had been as smitten as she, and in a matter of weeks they had been on the slopes of the Swiss Alps, fulfilling every honeymoon fantasy. *I never had any clue it would end like it did. I guess I thought we'd always be together.*

For the first time since the most recent nightmare, Saralynn was powerless to stop the tears that consumed her. *Something's different. For the first time since Peter and Marc died, I don't feel so lost and helpless. I still love them... and I truly miss them. But I don't feel like my life is over. Could Miss Sallie's memories have been that thera-peutic?*

There had to be something more. *But what?*

If there was any clue she'd found so far in what she'd read, it had to have been the final entry of the afternoon's reading. It had gone in a direction that Saralynn wasn't expecting, but it did give her reason to question many of her philosophies.

October 10, 1948

I know that my life has undergone a tremendous change, but I'm at a loss to describe it. I just know that what I have now, I never want to lose.

In the months prior to October, Saralynn had read of her grandmother's discharge from the hospital and her employment by the Sanatorium as one of its switchboard operators. She boarded with a staff family that had a spare room, and outside of one brief trip to north Mississippi to see her mother, had made herself quite at home on the hospital campus.

Her entries began to mention Ralph more frequently and now that she was no longer a patient, the two had been free to date.

It's easy to see how very much in love she was with him. How did she find the strength to go on after he died? If I could answer that question, maybe I could get on with my life.

The October 10 passage continued…

⬤▭

Ralph just left me at the door. This has been such a wonderful night. We went to church at Rials Creek Methodist, and when they opened the altar at the end of the service, I knew I wanted some of the same faith Miss Dora talks about. I'm already a Christian, but I don't think I've always known the same God that Miss Dora knows.

Being sick can actually be a blessing, but it sure didn't look like it the day the doctor brought me to the Sanatorium. Scared as I was, I still wondered if there really was a God and if there was, what I had done wrong to make me so sick.

I see now that it wasn't God who made me sick. Instead, it was God who made me well. Dr. McCallum never doubted that God could take over from him, and Miss Dora kept saying if I had faith, if I truly trusted God to know what was best, that I'd either be cured on this earth, or by being taken to heaven to live with Him.

That's what the preacher talked about tonight, and that's when I knew that I wanted God close enough to walk with me and hold on to me whenever times get hard. If He can bring me through tuberculosis, He can bring me through anything.

Then, on the way home from church, Ralph stopped the car and asked me to marry him. He said he'd had it planned all week and couldn't hardly keep it to himself. I always thought whoever I married would have to ask Papa for permission. And if not Papa, then Mama for sure. It's hard to believe that they're both gone, less than six months apart. Uncle Art said Mama just grieved herself to death after Papa died. I'm all alone in the world, so when Ralph asked, I said yes. He said we'd talk tomorrow about when we can have the wedding.

I've sure got a lot to think about. But I know for certain that Ralph was sent to me because God knew that I needed someone. Oh, I love him alright. But I know that God sent him to me. He already had it planned when Ralph climbed up in that tree to rescue the cat. I'll bet Ralph didn't know it, though.

Saralynn re-read the last entry several times, only she found that the more she read, the more concerned she became. While she didn't doubt that her grandparents truly loved each other, it surprised her that there was an absence of emotion. Not even a hint of any passion. *Miss Sallie refers to her engagement almost like it was a business deal. Were times really that different then? I'd love to ask Mama, but I don't dare.*

After stowing the journals safely in the old valise, she made herself a light supper and then locked the house and took refuge in her bedroom. After all, she was obligated to attend church the next morning, and she needed time to ready her clothes. *What I really need is time to ready my mind. I'm not even sure I'll know how to act. Hope I don't embarrass these nice people. Evidently Miss Sallie didn't have this worry the first time she went to Rials Creek.*

Saralynn knew she would be attending a Methodist Church, but she wasn't sure what Methodists did. Or what she was expected to do.

As for this walking with God that Miss Sallie talked about

in her journals, that concept was totally foreign. *I'm not even sure I would know how to walk with someone I couldn't feel or touch. Or even see. How do you know what you're doing?*

When Alicia called just before bedtime, Saralynn found the courage to tell her mother that she was supposed to attend church with friends the next morning. "I'm nervous, Mama. I'm not sure how to act at a Methodist church."

"You should have said 'No'. I was so glad to get away from all those southerners that think they have a right to inflict their religion on anyone who will listen."

"These people aren't like that." She felt honor-bound to protest. "They haven't pushed. They've simply tried to include me in their activities and I don't want to make a fool of myself or embarrass them."

"You'll mainly just sit in the congregation. Sing when they sing, sit and stand when they do, and bow your head when they pray. Otherwise keep your mouth shut. In about an hour it'll be over and you can come home."

I'm not going to tell Mama they've asked me to spend the whole day with them.

"Thanks for the advice, Mama. I guess I'll do OK."

"So go, get your obligation out of the way, and then don't go back. Churches are no different than cults. They'll take every last dime you've got and enslave your time. It's not like you owe those people anything. So what do you care if you offend them?"

Saralynn didn't answer and her mother evidently didn't notice.

"Church is for losers and that's what my parents were. Look at what little they have to show for a lifetime of work and sweat and hardship and being there every time the doors opened."

"Good-night, Mama. I think I'm going to turn in now."

"I hope you didn't work too hard today. That's too big a job for one person."

"You don't have to worry, the work wasn't too much for me." *I didn't do any packing, but that would take more explanation than I'm prepared to give tonight.*

"Talk to you tomorrow, Mama."

After she ended the call, Saralynn lay on the bed looking at the ceiling. *You know, my knowledge of God, if there is one, doesn't go any farther than this ceiling. But there must be a God. These people down here live like He's one of their closest friends.*

Chapter 10

Saralynn borrowed her mother's travel clock for fear that for the first time she would actually oversleep and the entire day would get off on the wrong foot. *I wish I didn't have to go to this church, but I am kind of looking forward to spending the day with Donna and Dave and their friends. We had lots of fun at the Kennedy's.*

When morning dawned, however, she found herself hitting the off button before the tinny-sounding alarm even had a chance to ring. Her body might be up and at it, but her emotions were on a roller coaster she wished would quit.

Part of me wants to go and the other part doesn't. I've never been this way about anything else. She hoped it wasn't an omen of how the day would go. *Maybe I should just bow out. After all, like Mama says, when I go back to Boston, I'll never see these people again. What do I care if their feelings are hurt?*

Deep inside, however, she realized that while she couldn't

justify it, unless it was just a case of basic good manners, she didn't want to disappoint or offend her new friends. *I've had more enjoyment in the short time I've been here than I have in several years in Boston, if you don't count all the things I did with my two guys.*

She was still thinking about those two guys, as she climbed into the back of a red mini-van. There she found two other little guys that reminded her so much of Marc, her heart gave a lurch. *I forgot they had children.*

"Don't you look pretty," Donna crooned while Saralynn was fastening her seatbelt. "I told you there wasn't any need to dress up. We're pretty informal."

"I don't call this dressy." *Certainly nothing like what I could have worn.* But she noticed that Dave was sporting a shirt with an open collar and a pair of khaki pants. *She really wasn't kidding.* Donna, on the other hand, was wearing something comparable to the outfit Saralynn had on, and just for the moment, she felt comfortable with the situation.

Conversation in the van was spirited between the Hasty parents and their children and Saralynn found herself enjoying the sound of multiple human voices. *Maybe I* have *been out of circulation too long.*

Then before she realized it, the modest red brick church with white columns and soaring spire came into view. From where she sat, she could just make out her grandparents' headstones on the far side of the cemetery.

"Have you ever been here?" The question was posed by Dave, who'd been the quietest member of the party. "The original church was established in 1860.

"Just once. Mama brought me here before she went back to Boston. I wanted to know where my grandmother was buried."

"She was such a sweet woman," Donna volunteered. "This church has sure missed her."

I don't know if I want to do this or not. Everyone will compare me with Miss Sallie. How can I compete with someone I never really knew?

The impulse to run and hide was strong, but before she could act on her panic, Donna was pulling her toward a group of ladies who stood talking near the church steps. "Hold up," she called out. "Before we go in, I've got someone I want you to meet."

Saralynn and her hostess reached the group where Donna put her arm around Saralynn's shoulders. "This is Saralynn Reilly. She's Miss Sallie's granddaughter." Donna pointed to the nearest of the five strangers. "This is Cathy... don't worry about last names right now. Margaret..." she pointed to the next woman. "Louise... Amanda... and Patricia. You'll get to know them better as time goes by."

But I'm just visiting. I'm not here to stay.

"Your grandmother was the sweetest person I ever knew," one of the ladies offered.

Is she Margaret... or Louise? "Thank you," Saralynn replied. *I don't have a clue what else to say.*

Chimes began to sound and, as if on cue, everyone in the parking lot began to move toward the double front doors of the small rural church.

Saralynn was painfully conscious that she was on unfamiliar turf. *I used to wonder when I'd see churches from the outside, what they were like inside. But I was interested from a design standpoint. This little church is so pretty. Besides that, though, it feels so comfortable, so welcoming.*

"Our Sunday School class meets through there," Donna

explained and indicated a door to the left of the altar area. Others she'd seen in the parking lot were already ahead of them.

Sunday School? What does one do in Sunday School? There sure is a lot more to this church business than I ever realized.

Saralynn found herself directed into a small room with metal folding chairs lining the walls. Many of them were filled with men and women who were visiting and exchanging news. A small table at one end of the room was obviously where the leader... *What do they call that person?*... conducted the class.

"There's two chairs together right there. Let's grab them."

"What about Dave? Where's he going to sit?"

"He teaches a class of teenage boys, so it's just the two of us."

Don't you have to be a minister or priest or something to teach?

Soon after they were seated, a man, his arms loaded with several books, entered the room and positioned himself behind the table. Immediately the numerous conversations that had been underway concluded and the group turned its attention to the front.

"Good to see a full room again this Sunday. If we keep on racking up these numbers, we're going to have to ask for a larger space."

The various class members responded to his greeting in a very informal manner, Saralynn thought. *But definitely comfortable.*

"I see we have a visitor. I'm Donald Holcombe," he said by way of introduction. "We're real glad to have you with us."

Before Saralynn could even decide how to respond, Donna jumped in. "This is Saralynn Reilly, Don. Miss Sallie Watson was her grandmother."

"Well, if you're Miss Sallie's kin, you're certainly welcome here. Your grandmother was one of the pillars of this church."

"She sure was," another class member offered. "I used to wish she was my grandmother."

This is exactly what I was afraid of.

Saralynn took a deep breath. "Thank you for your kind words. I'm afraid that all of you knew her better than I did."

"Your mama hurt her bad, alright," another said. "But Miss Sallie wasn't one to hold grudges."

I wish I could get up and walk out of here. Mama, just what did happen between you and Miss Sallie? Everyone seems to know but me.

Once the introductions were past, the roll taken, and the lesson underway, Saralynn relaxed a little. The only other awkward moment came when the secretary asked if Saralynn wanted to join what she now knew was called "The Old Enough to Know Better" class.

"She says she's just visiting," Donna answered before Saralynn could find her voice. "But we're all going to try and get her to stay here and be one of us."

"You're all very kind," Saralynn answered. "But I am only visiting." She hesitated, not wanting to appear rude. "I'm very glad to be here, though, even for a short time." *I hope that sounded sincere, because I meant it that way.*

The lesson, which the guest discovered was taken from a small, bound paperback magazine that every member had in hand, was about someone called the prodigal son. Saralynn had never owned a Bible and suddenly felt very uncomfortable without one. *Not that I would know how to read it.*

"The scripture for today's lesson comes from Luke, chapter 15, beginning with verse 10." The teacher was writing the information on a small dry-erase board mounted on the wall.

Saralynn found her first Sunday School lesson interesting,

although she left the class forty-five minutes later pondering the reality of a parent who could forgive even the most despicable actions of an errant child. *He's right. There's nothing Marc could have done that I wouldn't have forgiven and still loved him. So why didn't Miss Sallie and Mama patch things up?*

Getting out of the classroom had been difficult because everyone, both the men and the women, wanted to speak to her, to shake her hand or hug her neck. "We'd sure like to have you stay with us," she heard more than once.

Finally, Donna touched her arm. "Look everybody, Saralynn's going to be at our house tonight for chili. We can all visit then."

With farewells that promised to pick up where they had left off, the class members dispersed.

"Now we go into the worship service."

People were filing in through several doors and finding seats throughout what Donna referred to as the sanctuary. *That's a good name. It feels like a sanctuary.*

"I usually sit here," Donna said indicating a blue-cushioned pew about one-third of the way from the front. "But we can sit anywhere you'd like. Some people like the very front and some prefer the back."

"This is fine," Saralynn said. "Where's Dave?"

"I'm a 'choir widow.'"

"I beg your pardon?"

Donna giggled. "Dave sings in the choir so that makes me a choir widow."

"Your husband has many talents evidently. He teaches a class and sings in the choir."

"He's also president of the United Methodist Men this

year, but that's how it is in small churches. Lots of people wear several hats because there aren't enough warm bodies to go around."

"I guess I never thought about people doing things in church. I thought churches had a staff and they did all the work. But then I haven't been to church that much."

"Really? You're serious?" Donna's shock showed. "Why?" She clamped her hand over her mouth. "Oops, sorry, there I go again. That's really none of my business."

"But you do find it odd, don't you?"

Donna hesitated, obviously struggling for an appropriate response. "I do, but I guess that's because I don't remember when I didn't go to church. It was always just as much a part of life at our house when I was a child, as it was to go to school Monday through Friday."

Now it was Saralynn's turn to feel uncomfortable. "Mama never had any use for religion, so I was grown before I truly realized that church wasn't a part of our lives. Besides, things are different in the north. You don't find people as connected as they are here."

"Guess I'm glad I don't live in the north, because I don't know how I'd make it without my church. I find God here and try to walk with Him until we come back the next time."

There's that walking with God expression again.

Saralynn jumped as the first peals of the organ near the front of the church signaled the beginning of the worship service. The congregation immediately ceased its chatter and visiting, and the visitor from the north could feel a change in attitude come over the entire room.

I don't have a clue how I'm supposed to worship, but Mama

said to just watch what everyone else did.

The choir, both men and women, filed into an area behind the altar, where they presented a short vocal selection that was a "call to worship" according to the printed agenda a man had given her. Donna said the program was called a bulletin.

Again, this worship word. I'm a college graduate, but I have never felt so ignorant.

After a welcome from one of the men in the church, where Saralynn was again introduced by Donna as Miss Sallie's granddaughter, there were announcements about the many activities for the coming week.

This is what Mama meant. These people go to church all the time. It's as much a part of their lives as their jobs. But they don't seem miserable or put-upon. It's like they want to be here.

Saralynn found the congregational singing of a song – the bulletin showed it was "Hymn 364" – very enjoyable, although the lyrics for *Because He Lives* reminded her once again that her husband and son no longer lived. *I'd love to have these words to read again when I'm back home. For some reason I find them strangely reassuring, almost warming.*

The remainder of the service passed without incident, except that she wasn't prepared with money for the offering plate, and the man had to wait while she dug in her purse.

I'm really out of my element. Was $5.00 enough?

The words to the opening hymn kept wafting through her mind as the service continued. She sought to understand a deeper meaning, wondering what they had to do with "Because He Lives!" *How can someone I can't even see help me survive what I've been through? Help me through tomorrow? Make my fear be gone?*

When the minister, Donna called him Brother Tommy,

got up to deliver the sermon, Saralynn braced herself. She had, a few times when she was channel surfing on TV, run across stations where people were preaching. She'd found their shouting and biting criticism most distasteful, and assumed that all church services were like that.

This is going to be the hardest part. I wonder how long it lasts?
But it wasn't hard at all.

"We're so glad to have you with us today," the young, bearded, sandy-haired minister assured Saralynn when the service was over and the congregation was filing through the doors. "Miss Sallie died before I was assigned to this church, but I've heard enough about her to make me wish I'd known her."

Is there anyone else who didn't know or admire my grandmother?

"Thank you for saying that," she said, as she shook the minister's hand. "Your sermon has really given me reason for thought." Only this time, she wasn't just being polite.

I don't understand everything I heard this morning, but there was something the minister said that connected with me. Donna, or probably even Dave, could explain it, I'm sure, but I'm not comfortable in admitting my ignorance.

The part of the sermon that spoke to her had come from a scripture in the Book of Proverbs. *I don't have a Bible, but Miss Sallie did. I can look it up in her Bible tonight.* She made sure to tuck the bulletin into her purse, for fear she'd forget where to find the verse. Still, as insurance she made a mental note: a book called Proverbs, Chapter 17, Verse 22.

It sounded so beautiful when the minister read the words. "A merry heart doeth good like a medicine; but a broken spirit drieth the bones." *That's what I have… a broken spirit… but I never realized it until he talked about how we can't get through difficult days without help. How did he know about me?*

The remainder of the afternoon was a blur of activity. Once she had finished speaking to what seemed like half the county, standing in the parking lot outside the church, the mini-van pulled away, headed for lunch.

If ever there was a couple with merry hearts, it was the Hasty's. Even though she told herself she shouldn't, Saralynn soon found that she was actually enjoying the company and the light-hearted manner with which they tackled life. Lunch at the "all-you-can-eat buffet" was as delightful as her hosts had promised. *Am I ever stuffed. And there's still chili and fixings to go. Can there ever be too much good living?*

At one point, late in the afternoon, she found the courage to question, "Is there ever a time when you two aren't upbeat and positive? Don't you have any problems?"

"Do we have problems!" the two hooted in unison. "Which list do you want first?" Donna asked. "His, mine or ours?"

"I'm sorry, that comes under the heading of none of my business. Please forgive me. I didn't mean to pry."

"No sweat," Dave answered. "Do you think that just because we laugh and carry on that our life is perfect?"

"Well... well, yes. I mean... how... how could you be so upbeat if you have worries or problems?"

The couple in the front seat exchanged glances. "Shall we tell her?"

Donna pulled her seatbelt to its maximum length so she could turn in her seat to face their guest. "Here's how it is. This van should have been traded a year ago, but because the kids had high medical bills, we had to do some repair work and drive it a while longer. Dave's employer is talking about closing some of the smaller offices in the region. We don't know how this might affect Dave and we're holding our breath on that. I'd love to take a real family vacation next summer, but I doubt that will happen. And yesterday my dishwasher went out. So, yes, we have worries and problems. Just like everyone does."

"They sure don't seem to faze you."

"You can worry about things you can't control until you find yourself paralyzed, literally frozen in place."

"So how do you deal with it?" *I guess I don't know how fortunate I've been. We always had enough money for anything we needed... or wanted.*

"We depend on God to provide what we really need. And He has never let us down," Donna added.

If I didn't know these people to be as genuine as they are, I would think they were over the edge. "You're serious, aren't you? Surely you don't mean God hands you money?"

Dave laughed and then quickly suppressed it. "I'm sorry, I'm not making fun of you. It's just the mental picture of cash materializing in front of me caught me off guard. Not that I'd object."

"Honey, it isn't that God gives us the money directly. Instead, he gives us the chance to get what we need through our circumstances and other people," Donna explained.

"I'm afraid I don't understand."

"Like yesterday when the dishwasher gave up the ghost, I was in the depths of despair. Not only did we not have a new appliance in this month's budget, but I'll have a mountain of chili bowls to wash tonight."

"We can help you wash..."

"Not necessary," Donna interrupted. "There's a brand new

dishwasher in my kitchen even as we speak. It's just waiting for those dirty bowls."

But she said they didn't have the money.

"God gave you a dishwasher?" *That sounds more ridiculous than giving them money.*

"Indirectly He did. What he did give us was a really good hay season and Dave has more hay in the barn than our cattle will need. About an hour after we declared the dishwasher DOA, a man with a long, lowboy truck pulled into the drive. His barn burned and he was trying to buy hay to get his animals through the winter. Dave sold him enough to buy a new dishwasher."

"So you believe God sent that man to buy your hay?"

"We sure do," Dave answered. "More than once in our marriage we've seen His providing hand in our lives.

This is almost like the cedar tree and the bedroom suite Miss Sallie had built.

"You have to experience it to truly understand how God puts people and events in our paths to answer our prayers," Donna added.

I don't know how people who don't know God personally get through some of the crises that come into every life." Dave piloted the van through a busy intersection and checked to be certain there was nothing coming, before pulling across the highway to head back to church.

"It can be difficult enough even when your faith is strong because God deals with things on His timetable."

"Is that why you go to church so often?"

"It isn't something we have to do," Donna explained. "There are times when we do miss, like if we're on vacation or if family comes in from out of town and will only be here for a short time. Then we may pass on church."

"You know what?" Dave asked. "Every time something like that happens, regardless of how good our reasons were, we all agree afterward that we missed it."

"I guess that does sound unusual to someone like yourself," Donna admitted. "Not that I'm criticizing, Saralynn. Really, I'm not." She hesitated. "In fact, I guess a lot of what you've heard today has been strange to you."

Saralynn was quiet, trying to form her words, because she realized she'd come to truly care for this family who had adopted her. "Strange? I wouldn't call it that, but definitely it's different from anything I've ever known. You see I was grown before I ever attended my first church service."

"That's so hard to believe. Not that I doubt you," Donna assured her. "So what did you think of us at Rials Creek? You can be honest."

To her surprise, Saralynn discovered that it wasn't difficult to answer her host's question. And she was honest. "Is everyone in the south so friendly? People acted like they had always known me. But the service was nothing like I expected."

"Why, what did you expect?"

"I'm not sure. For one thing, there wasn't nearly as much formality as I thought there would be. It was like everyone there was family, and everyone was on the same level. It was… it was… genuine. That's it! Genuine."

"Well, we do all feel like a family." Donna laughed. "Part of that could be because over half of the members are related on one side of their family tree or the other, either by blood or by marriage."

"I hadn't thought about that, but I guess that would make

a difference."

"Say...?" the woman in the front seat hit her forehead with the palm of her right hand. "How did that slip by me?"

She turned to her guest. "Miss Sallie's last name was Watson. Your grandfather was Ralph?"

"That's right."

"Then you've got cousins at the Rials Creek. And you're going to meet them tonight."

"Cousins? More than one? Are you sure?" *Mama never said anything about other family living here. I never thought about it either.*

"Yep, on the Watson side, but you're definitely related."

"Here we are," Dave announced as he swung the van back into the parking lot they'd left nearly six hours earlier.

"Let's go, Saralynn. Let's see if we can find your kinfolks."

Chapter 11

I'm not sure I want to meet family that I don't know. How will I act? What should I say?

The din of conversation that greeted the latest arrivals inside the small country church was one of warmth and welcome. There was no stiltedness, no standing upon ceremony. If anything, Saralynn realized, her earlier description of "genuine" still held true.

She felt her hand being grabbed and by the time she turned in the direction of the jerk, she was being led toward a group standing beside the piano. Dave was at the head of the line.

"Hey, folks," her host said, breaking into the conversation ongoing within the little covey of friends. "Did all of you meet Saralynn Reilly this morning?"

A couple in the group admitted they hadn't, while the rest greeted her as if she were a regular.

"Did you have a good time this afternoon with the Hasty Tour Service?" The question came from a man she hadn't met.

"Did I ever," she responded, surprised at the genuine enthusiasm she heard in her own voice. *There's that feeling again.* "They know every back road and every place that's any place."

"Dave has a pretty good tracking nose," one of the others quipped. "That, and he was born here," another offered. "He's older than some of those roads," a third joked.

Saralynn was trying to pay attention to the good-natured jabs that members of the group were tossing Dave's way, while at the same time, she was trying to understand why one of the faces across from her looked so familiar. *Could I have seen him at Boswell? He wasn't at the Kennedy's the other night, but I never forget a face.*

"I'm Bruce Harvey," a man standing next to the familiar face said. "I tried to get to you this morning to speak, but old speedy here whisked you away before I could get there." He extended his right hand, and Saralynn grasped it. "You didn't get to meet this fellow here, either," the man continued, pointing over his shoulder with his left hand and thumb.

"Ian Scarborough, meet Saralynn Reilly. She's Sallie and Ralph Watson's..."

"I know who she is," the mysterious gentleman replied, "she cornered one of my lost calves a few days ago."

Of course. No wonder his face was familiar. He surely looks different out of his farm clothes.

"It's good to see you again," her neighbor said. "Must I unfix that fence so my calf will wander over your way again, or are you going to take me up on that invitation?"

"I'm... I'm... sorry," she stammered. "Time has gotten away from me." *And if that's so, why can't I even remember what I've been doing?*

"Ian, where's your dad?" Dave punched Ian's shoulder. "Saralynn wants to meet all her kinfolks. If she's kin to you, she's kin to Hammish, too."

Saralynn couldn't hide her surprise. "We... I mean, you and I... we're kin?"

Ian's face erupted in a grin. "'Fraid so," he admitted. "Your granddaddy and my granddaddy were first cousins."

Saralynn was dumbstruck. "But your last name is..."

"Scarborough," he finished for her. "Mr. Ralph's mama, Catherine, and my great-granddaddy, Angus, were brother and sister. Mr. Ralph's mama's maiden name was Scarborough."

"So what does that make us?" *I'm in shock.*

"Close enough to be kin if we want, but far enough off that we don't have to claim it."

"Well, I never..." Saralynn said, finally, after she'd found her voice and retrieved her lower jaw from the floor. "Mama never told me we had any family here."

"She wouldn't have," one of the older women blurted.

"Why?"

"Phyllis, you ought not said anything," one of the men said hastily, dropping his eyes. "That's old water long gone over the dam."

"What water is he talking about?" Saralynn asked. *This is all so confusing.* Before she could further voice that confusion, a bell sounded and the group immediately began to disperse with calls of promise to see each other later. She felt Donna take hold of her arm.

"We'll go back through here to Disciple class," her friend explained. "It's a special Bible study that's been very popular here in this church." She nudged Saralynn and pointed her toward the rear of the church.

"But I wanted to ask Ian some questions," she confessed. "What was that woman talking about when she said that Mama wouldn't have told me anything about the Scarborough's being our relatives?

"I really don't know, honey. Dave probably does. Anyway, most of those in that group will be at our house after church for the chili social. You can ask your questions then."

The next hour was similar to the Sunday School hour. Conversation was spirited, and Saralynn was amazed to find that these people actually debated the interpretation of scriptures. *I always thought the Bible wasn't open to discussion. Why doesn't the pastor tell them what they have to believe?* She vowed to ask Donna. Later. *She's going to get so tired of me asking so many questions.*

The worship service that followed was even more informal than the morning's service. The choir didn't sit behind the pulpit and even the pastor was casually dressed. She sat with her hosts in the now familiar pew that felt almost like home. *I don't feel nearly as nervous.*

Saralynn found herself mesmerized as a vocal group composed of church members sang a medley of songs. While none of the titles were familiar to her, she sensed an aura of peace overcoming her as the group moved from one number to another.

One of hymns she found particularly touching was called "Amazing Grace." She wasn't sure she understood all the words or what they meant, but with each song, a calmness that she couldn't identify seemed to cradle her and protect her. *I'm a stranger here, totally out of the know with this religion business and with what they do. So why am I so comfortable?*

She was almost disappointed when their last number, *How Great Thou Art*, was finished. It was a title she'd heard somewhere before, but the words were totally foreign. One portion of the lyrics really touched her as she thought of Sallie's journal and how her soul had sung through them. *She surely understood how great God is.*

That's exactly how I feel right now…like my soul is singing. I wish I didn't ever have to leave this place.

Following a short sermon, where the minister talked about walking in the will of God, the service concluded with a closing chorus, *Take My Life, Lead Me, Lord*. Saralynn once again found herself surrounded by people wanting to visit.

Donna quickly took charge of the situation.

"Give the girl a break," she laughed. "Everyone will have a chance to talk with Saralynn back at our house." She pulled her guest toward the back of the church. "We've got plenty of chili. Last one there has to wash the pot!"

Chapter 12

*E*ven though she'd given Alicia her solemn promise that she would call when she got home, her cell phone began to vibrate in her pocket during church. Saralynn ignored the summons and finally lost count of how many times it interrupted. Once again Mama had paid no attention. *I'm not a child. But you surely have treated me like one.*

Seven calls, all from Alicia's cell, were registered in the missed call log. Knowing if she didn't call her mother, it was only a matter of time before call number eight. She did what she had to do. There was an interrogation coming.

Funny, I don't remember feeling smothered before, but I sure do now.

"I'm too tired to talk tonight," she informed her mother as soon as she could get a word in edgewise... No, Mama... I'm perfectly fine. It's been a full and exciting day and I'm just worn out. Even having fun can be tiring."

"We'll talk tomorrow, Mama. I've had a full day and I'm really tired," she said again.

"I can tell by your voice something's wrong. What has happened?"

Everything's wrong, Mama. But I don't have enough of a handle on it to be able to talk now. I'm sure I'd say something that I'd regret tomorrow.

As she readied for bed, Saralynn questioned why she even wasted time changing into her pajamas. *There's no way I'm going to sleep tonight. I might as well stay dressed. I don't know when I have ever felt so overwhelmed and confused. Peter and Marc's deaths were traumatic enough, but I feel like I'm caught up in a web of lies and cover-ups that are so much more confusing than death could ever be.*

At that moment, she craved the comfort of someone she could trust. As a reflex, she reached for the scarred brown case that held her grandmother's journals. Memories of a woman she never knew were, at that moment, preferable to any solace that a living, breathing human might offer.

She gathered the ancient notebooks into her arms and settled in the middle of the bed with the journals spread around her. *There is a lifetime of private thoughts and yearnings in these books, and it would take me another lifetime to read them all. At best, if I'm going to confront Mama, I only have until morning.*

The chili earlier had been delicious and filling. Obviously her hosts knew how to entertain, although the casualness of their home and their hospitality were a far cry from what Saralynn would have expected in Boston.

But I'm not in Boston.

No, she was in Simpson County, Mississippi, learning more

about her mother's family than she had ever imagined. Certainly if actions were any yardstick, it was more than Alicia had ever intended for her to discover. Saralynn wasn't sure how she was supposed to react.

I'm numb more than anything, and I'm not sure that I want feeling to return.

The story had come out in ragged segments as first one and then another added their contributions to the story behind Alicia and why she so disliked her home and everything connected with it.

The contents of the chili bowls had been enjoyed and emptied, more than once, before the close-knit group settled around the hearth where a blazing fire created a cozy setting. Shadows and highlights created by the flames cast fleeting but interesting expressions on the faces of those who called themselves her friends.

For some unexplained reason, Saralynn felt at home as well, but she realized that if she pushed too hard for the answers she sought, she risked destroying the comfort level she found so precious.

It was Ian's father, Hammish, who answered Saralynn's first question, although she had posed her query to the son.

"I'll tell you," the older Scarborough answered when his son hesitated. He glanced at the younger version of himself. "After all, it was me that started it all."

Those words brought Saralynn up short, for her thought process hadn't reached the point that she'd made a direct connection between the Scarborough's and her mother's actions. But as she looked more closely at the older man, she realized that Ian's father and Alicia would be about the same age. Apparently his outdoor vocation made him appear older.

"You started it all?"

"That I did."

"But how?"

"By proposing marriage, that's how?"

"You and my mother?"

"Don't look so shocked, missy. We weren't always old, you know."

"But I thought you were kin."

"We were. Still are. Only Alicia doesn't want to remember any of that.

"I'm… I'm sorry," Saralynn stuttered. "I'm getting more confused by the minute. Are you saying… are you my father?"

"I'd be proud if I were, but no, I'm afraid I can't claim that honor," the older man answered. He stretched his hands out before him and turned them over, although Saralynn wasn't sure what he expected to find.

"Perhaps I can help." The speaker was Walter Kennedy. "You're still too close to it, Hammish. Even after all these years." He moved over to where Saralynn sat and placed his hand on her shoulder. "Let me explain."

When no forthcoming objection was heard from the other man, Walter began to tell the story that Saralynn had longed to hear.

I'm not sure if I really wanted to know or not. But now that I do, what is my next move? Oh, Miss Sallie… no wonder your heart broke. How could you live with all that and still claim Mama as your daughter? She spoke aloud to the empty room. The young woman clutched the old notebook she still held to her chest. *Am I trying to console Miss Sallie or myself?*

Walter's words, while they were delivered with love and

concern, were nonetheless painful for Saralynn to hear. But through the pain, the young woman was finally able to understand many of the mysteries she'd only recently discovered.

"It might help me," Mr. Walter said, "if you tell me what you know about your mother's past."

"That's just it. I know basically nothing except that Mama had issues with her mother." She searched for words while the crackle of the fire made the only sound in the room. "It was like she found everything connected with Mississippi distasteful."

Oh, what have I said to these nice people? "Not that I feel that way," she assured her audience. "You've all been wonderful. Just wonderful."

"It's not hard to do," Mr. Walter assured her. "We were there for Alicia, too, only she didn't want us."

"But why? And how does Ian's father figure into all of this?"

"Okay, here goes."

It had been painful. But just as he promised, Mr. Walter told the story as it was, without embellishment.

Even after she heard it, Saralynn still had problems believing it. Yet she trusted Mr. Walter, so she had to accept the story he'd offered.

Mama jilted Hammish after their wedding date was set to elope with a wealthy patient just released from the Sanatorium. But his family objected to their new daughter-in-law, especially after they discovered she'd gotten pregnant on the honeymoon. Mama accepted a very generous cash settlement to seek a divorce and never make any other claims on her husband's family.

"Your granddaddy was already dead at the time," another older member of the group had volunteered. "Miss Sallie, she swallowed her heartache and welcomed your mama... she was pregnant with you... back with open arms."

"But Alicia wouldn't have nothing to do with it." The speaker was Hammish Scarborough himself. "I told her I still loved her and would be glad to marry her and make a home for her, and for you. And I would have, too. But she accused me of just wanting to get my property back without ever havin' to pay for it. Our family used to own Miss Sallie's farm, you know."

I simply cannot believe what I'm hearing.

"But you were cousins. Weren't you?"

"Distant cousins, we were. Still are, for that matter." Hammish grinned at her.

He must have been really handsome when he was younger. Was Mama crazy?

"But it was far enough off that it would have been legal. It didn't bother me, and I didn't think it bothered Alicia, either. I know Miss Sallie was all for it."

"She was so ugly to her mama, too," a woman from the group offered. "Told her she didn't want anything but to get out of here and never come back. Said she'd always hated this place. Even called us backward."

"Miss Sallie never gave up on Alicia, but that little lady had a mind of her own, even if she didn't have a heart when it came to Miss Sallie."

"Mama never told me any of this, I promise," Saralynn assured the group. "This is all news for me."

"And disturbing news, I'm sure," Mr. Walter consoled her. "Maybe we shouldn't have...."

"No... No... NO. I asked. I wanted to know. It's just that I never imagined anything like this."

"Alicia never came back here again," a solemn Hammish volunteered. "Except when Tony died and for that one time when Miss Sallie had surgery, about twenty-five years ago, and then when she came home for the funeral."

Uncle Tony's funeral... that would have been the first time I came. Funny, I don't remember anything about that trip. "She wouldn't let me come to Miss Sallie's funeral."

"She wasn't hardly here herself," a silver-haired woman in a blue checked pantsuit spoke up. "She came in here about lunch one day, made the funeral arrangements, and the next day, before Miss Sallie's body was even in the ground good, she was gone. Back to the airport. We never saw her again until the two of you showed up."

"She wouldn't even let us fix food or anything," Virginia Kennedy explained. "Said she didn't want any of our southern hospitality. And she didn't come to the funeral home viewing of the body, either."

Saralynn's head was whirling. *What do I say? How do I apologize for Mama?* Then the enormity of it all overcame her, and she was powerless to stop the tears that sprang from her eyes.

"I'm so sorry," she sobbed. "Please forgive me."

"You don't owe us any apologies," Bess Martin countered. She had made her way to Saralynn's side, as the story grew more critical. She put her arms around the shocked young woman's shoulders and hugged her close. "We probably shouldn't have told you."

Walter Kennedy knelt in front of her. "Just remember, honey, none of this makes any difference in how we feel about you. You're very special to all of us."

"And we don't hold it against Alicia, either." It was Hammish who had taken the floor again. "We don't agree with what she did, but that's between her and her God."

"If her mama could forgive her and still love her, how could we do any less?" The question came from the woman in the blue checks.

Saralynn raised her head and surveyed the somber group before her. It was hard to see through the tears, but there was no doubt in her mind that they spoke the truth.

"If Alicia came back today and wanted to be a part of us, we'd welcome her just like we did you."

"But how? She snubbed you and called you backward?"

"It's like this," Bess said. "We believe that if God can forgive us for all the wrongs we do… and He has promised us that He will… then we have to forgive Alicia."

"Besides," Walter Kennedy added, "hate only hurts the heart that holds it. So it gains us nothing."

Ian, who had been silent throughout the conversation, said, "We'd rather love you than hate your mother."

"That's for sure," Bess agreed. "Besides, my Bible says we'll be a lot happier with a merry heart. I don't know how a heart with hate in it could ever be merry."

"The other side of that verse that the pastor used today says that a broken spirit dries the bones," another member of the group agreed. "That's what Miss Sallie would always say every time she talked about Alicia and how she'd treated all of us."

"It broke her heart, you can be sure of that. But she wouldn't let it break her spirit."

I can't begin to imagine how much all of this must have hurt Miss Sallie. Her only daughter acting that way. How could Mama have been so cruel?

"Looking back," Mr. Walter said, "Alicia never was happy

here when she was growing up. I guess she figured if she married Hammish she'd be stuck. When she met Marshall Bankston, he fell head over heels in love with her and she saw her ticket out."

"She was so pretty," Hammish agreed. "I always thought I was the luckiest fellow to have snagged her, but she didn't see things the same way I did."

Marshall Bankston! That's the first time I've ever known my father's name. I never even thought to ask.

Now that she was back in her bedroom, the enormity of the evening's revelations overwhelmed her and she collapsed on the bed, crying so hard she feared she was totally going over the edge. At the same time, she didn't want to stop. *Because when I stop crying, I've got to decide what I'm going to do next.*

Despite her earlier belief that she wouldn't sleep that night, the emotional toll of the revelations she'd heard earlier in the evening, combined with the physical price of being on the go, non-stop all day, had drained her.

I've really gotten out of shape without Marc and Peter. I can remember when I would have gone twice as hard running my business, looking after the house and keeping up with a toddler. I've gone to wrack and ruin.

Still not believing that sleep was in the cards for her that night, Saralynn replaced the journals in the old case, brushed her teeth, and crawled beneath the covers.

The nights are starting to get cool. That fire tonight felt good. I may have to find another blanket before morning.

A few minutes later, after extinguishing the lamp, Saralynn was lost in a maze of dreams that blurred the borders between reality and imagination. Some she would remember at dawn's first light. Much of it would be lost to her forever.

I'll never be the same after tonight. Now that I know most of the answers, the next question is: What should I do?

Sleep prevented her from answering.

Chapter 13

*T*he trumpet tones of her cell phone lured Saralynn from her comfortable cocoon of slumber. *Mama... please. Won't you give me any peace?* Saralynn wondered for the first time if her mother's smothering concern for her daughter's safety was actually fear that Saralynn might learn the real story of all that happened so long ago.

But the caller wasn't Alicia.

"Have you forgotten that we exist over here?" The voice was familiar and friendly, but it took a moment for Saralynn to identify her caller.

"Katie! How could I forget you?"

"From the way you hesitated there, I figured you had."

"I'm just waking up," she confessed. "I'm afraid you'll have to forgive me."

"You are a lay-about this morning, aren't you? Or are the

rumors about northern women snoozing 'til noon when the maid brings a brunch tray really true?"

Saralynn laughed. "Believe me, I've never been able to get away with sleeping in." *Not even before Marc was born.* "Why? What time is it, anyway?" She pulled the phone away from her ear to look at the time display, but her eyes were still too glazed with sleep to focus on the tiny numbers.

"If you're just now waking up... you have really been a lady of leisure. It's nine- forty. Make that nine-forty-one now."

"Oh, my gosh. How did I ever manage to sleep so late?" *Mama must really be angry with me. She hasn't called this morning. Mama!* The revelations of the previous evening came flooding over her and Saralynn found herself in an emotional tug of war.

"...you think you'll be awake enough this afternoon to come for cake and ice cream?"

"I'm sorry, Katie, I missed the first part of your question. You'll have to forgive me, I've got something on my mind."

"It's Paul's birthday today, and I'm having a few people in to sing to him and share his birthday cake and ice cream. I'd love it if you could come." The caller briefly hesitated... "Are there problems? Is there something I can do?"

Can I handle seeing this little boy celebrate his birthday when Marc will never have another one? But she didn't say that to her friend. "Something's come up that I've got to deal with, but I appreciate the invitation."

"Then please say you'll come."

"What time?"

"He usually wakes up from his nap around three-thirty, so he should be in a real good mood by four."

"Tell you what. I've got several things I have to deal with

today, but I'll do my best to make it. Just promise you won't be hurt if I don't."

"I won't be hurt, but I will be disappointed."

"I just can't promise, because I don't know how my day's going to play."

"Even if you're running late, come on," her friend urged. "We'll probably hang out for an hour or so and I'll have plenty of refreshments."

"I'll try."

"Then I'll just adopt the attitude that you'll be successful and plan to see you this afternoon."

Saralynn was about to say good-bye when she remembered that this was a birthday celebration. "So what does Paul need? What can I get him?"

"He doesn't need anything. In fact, if he gets much more stuff we're going to have to find a larger house just to hold all his toys."

"I know how that is." *All of Marc's toys are still right where he left them. I couldn't bear even to touch them, let alone dispose of anything."*

"We never dreamed when we took this house and remodeled it that Paul would come into our lives. But sometimes you do what you have to; I couldn't let him go to strangers. Not under the circumstances." Her voice caught. "He's so precious and I don't begrudge him the space. But it does get a little tight at times."

Did she just choke back a sob? And what does she mean, "under the circumstances"?

"If I come, I'm bringing a gift... the biggest I can find, so you'd better clean out a room or else start adding one."

"If you'll come, we'll make it fit. Just please, don't go

overboard… on the price or the size."

"I'll see you by four."

After she punched the off button, Saralynn pulled her knees up in front of her and hugged them with both arms. She looked across the room, into the wavy old mirror on the oak dresser. Granted, her natural reddish-blonde curls always suffered from a severe case of bed-head. And without make-up, she had to acknowledge that time was showing its handiwork.

I definitely look better with make-up. She made a silent vow never to appear in public again without her face in place. *Yeah, like I wonder how long that resolution will last? But even without my beauty treatment, I'm not bad looking. So, if I've truly lost my mind and am about to do what I think I am, why don't I look like some kind of deranged old woman who needs to be locked up for her own protection?*

At the thought of following through on the impulse that had been a part of her for more than a week, Saralynn was suddenly too nervous to sit still. She unfolded her arms, threw back the handmade quilt she was certain had been crafted by a grandmother's hands, and headed to the bath.

"I'm gonna wash that idea out of my hair," she sang, as she worked shampoo into a generous lather. *"I'm gonna wash that idea out of my hair…"* She bent her head into the stream of water to rinse. *"And send it on its way."*

As she toweled off a few minutes later, Saralynn realized that the brainstorm, that had invaded her middle-of-the-night dreams once again, was starting to appeal to her.

"I've never actually stepped this far out before." *Mama wouldn't let me. Even after Peter and I married, she was still telling me what I should do.*

She had just criticized her mother, something she would

never have done only a few weeks before. *But then I didn't know everything that I do now.* Saralynn couldn't decide if what she felt was resentment, or justified displeasure. *One thing's for sure, my eyes have been opened. Things are not at all like I've been told.*

But now was not the time to confront Mama. Not until Saralynn knew how she was going to make everything work.

Might as well start with Mama, though. I can tell by her silence that she's angry.

The young woman dressed quickly in jeans and a sweatshirt and plucked the phone from it's resting place on the three-legged oak table beside the bed. She punched in Alicia's cell number and was finally rewarded by an aloof greeting.

"I wondered when you'd call. Are you rested enough to talk now?"

"I'm rested, but I'm not quite ready to talk. I've got some errands to deal with this morning. Just wanted to let you know that I'm just fine down here in the wilds of Mississippi."

"Are you angry with me about something?"

"Why do you ask?"

"Just the tone in your voice. You're not the same loving daughter you were before this trip."

You mean, I'm not totally under your influence? Immediately she regretted her harsh judgment. *After all, there are two sides to every story. Unfortunately, I heard several of those two sides last night.*

"Coming here has been the best thing I could have done. It's given me a totally new perspective on a lot of things."

"There's something you're not telling me."

"There are several things we need to talk about, Mama, but not now. I'll call you later. Maybe tonight. Or it may even be tomorrow."

"What things? What could we possibly have to talk about?"

There was a note of desperation in her mother's voice. It was a hardness Saralynn had observed before, whenever Alicia found herself backed into a corner.

"It's nothing to worry about. So how's your condo project coming?"

"How you deal with all these details day after day, on job after job, is more than I can figure out. I'd be half crazy. And you're not helping my sanity when you keep secrets from me."

"Sounds to me like everything's normal... as normal as it ever gets in the decorating game. There were many days when I felt like I was losing it."

"To have to deal with demolition and reconstruction, too. It's a nightmare. Won't you please tell me what's wrong?"

"Later, Mama. I promise. In the meantime, let Merle deal with all the construction details. That's what he's there for. You can depend on him."

"What choice do I have?"

"None, really. Now if you'll excuse me, I've got to go. I overslept and I've got to go buy a birthday present for a precious little boy and get to his party this afternoon."

"What little boy? Who all are you making friends with down there? Please be careful, Saralynn. There are some people down there you don't need to associate with. Take my word for it."

Why? Because I might discover things you don't want me to know?

Again, she was ashamed for her attitude, yet she believed she was on target with her feelings.

"Don't worry about me, Mama, I keep telling you. The

boy is Paul... his mother's Katie Brooks that we talked to on the grounds at the Sanator... I mean, Boswell, that day."

Alicia had more questions to ask, but her daughter quickly cut her short, with the promise to call again no later than the next morning.

She then placed her second call. "Mr. Walter? This is Saralynn Reilly. Do you have a minute?"

"For you, two minutes, three if we need them. I'm glad you called. I've been worried."

"Worried? Why?"

"I'm afraid we may have overloaded you last night."

I should have known he'd be worried. That's just how he is.

"I'm going to be fine, I promise. I will admit that in my wildest imagination when I used to wonder why my mother was so down on Mississippi, I could never have dreamed what really happened."

"We're not ones to carry tales," he assured her. "Unfortunately, most of us your mother's age and older were here then. We saw what happened. And we also saw how devastated your grandmother was when Alicia left before you were even born."

I didn't realize that my grandmother never got to see me until I was half grown. And the last time I was here, after Miss Sallie had surgery, Mama wouldn't let me bother her. So we barely got to see each other then.

"She worried about you, Miss Sallie did. Alicia kept in touch with her mama just enough to keep her concerned. You were about six months old before your mother ever told her that you had been born and that you were a girl. She wouldn't even tell Miss Sallie what your birth date was."

Oh, Mama. How could you have been so cruel?

"I never dreamed the situation was such."

"Your mama and daddy were only married about six or seven weeks before his family bought Alicia off, so Miss Sallie had a pretty good idea of when you should have been born. Every year, around that date, she'd put a bouquet of roses from her own yard in the church in honor of your birthday."

So that's why the cards never arrived right on my birthday.

Saralynn felt her knees buckle and she had no choice but to drop onto the still unmade bed. "You're kidding?" *She didn't even know me. How could she love me enough to do that?*

"You can't help what your mama did, but you deserve to know how much Miss Sallie loved you. She prayed for you every day, too. By name. Just like she prayed for your mama. She never give up 'til the Lord took her home. Of that I am certain."

"If only I could have known her. I wanted to. I wondered about her often."

"Several of us see a lot of her in you, and we're going to miss you when you go back north. Just promise you won't forget us. I'd like to think Miss Sallie's up there right now, smiling down on the both of us."

"Believe me, forgetting any of you is something I could never do. But that's why I called. Would you have time to talk to me this afternoon?" She thought about the birthday party. "Early enough that I could still make a late afternoon birthday party?"

"Why don't we have lunch? My treat. I'll pick you up."

"Lunch is fine, but remember, it's my turn."

"So you pay the next time. Big deal. Can you be ready by noon?"

Saralynn consulted the clock in the kitchen. Eleven-thirteen. "Yes sir, I'll be ready."

During the forty-five minutes remaining, she changed into nicer clothes and sat down to commit to paper some information she needed to share with her luncheon host. As she wrote, her hands shook. Her resolve was strong; evidently her hands weren't as convinced.

I can't believe what I'm about to do.

Saralynn and the older gentleman were soon seated at a table next to the huge picture window at The Covington House Restaurant in the nearby town of Collins. It had been Mr. Walter's suggestion, to give them some privacy.

How did he know we might want privacy?

"You're going to think I've lost my mind, Mr. Walter."

"I assume this isn't a purely social lunch." It was spoken more as a statement than a question.

How does he know?

The two had served their plates from the ample buffet that was the eatery's trademark, and were well into their meal when he asked, "So what is it you need to talk to me about? Not your mother, I hope. I've really begun to feel disloyal to her and yet, I really don't know why. Everything we told you was the truth."

"I know it was. And, no, this isn't about Mama. At least, not directly."

When she finished laying out her plan, Saralynn couldn't decide whether she was more surprised that he had anticipated her, or that he didn't think she was acting in haste or with poor judgment.

"Virginia and I have felt from that very first night when you came to our house for supper that you belong here."

"That absolutely astounds me. I don't think I even knew that this crazy idea was really worth pursuing until last night."

Mr. Walter chuckled. "Maybe we're just selfish people, but we wanted you to want to settle here." He reached across the table to take Saralynn's smooth hands in his own work-worn hands that were, she thought, the size of small shovels. "May I?" he asked, just before he touched her. When she nodded her consent, he continued, "You may not have ever known Miss Sallie, but it's obvious to those of us who knew her that you are her kin."

"I don't understand."

"Your spirit, for one thing." He hesitated. "You have a gentleness about you that reminds all of us so much of her." He grinned. "But it's more than that. You may not realize that you're very much like her physically as well. I would imagine that photos of the two of you at about the same age would bear a striking resemblance."

"I knew I didn't look like Mama, so I had always assumed I looked like my father. But since I've been here I've seen several pictures of Miss Sallie when she was younger, and we do look amazingly alike."

"You're a carbon copy of Sallie Watson and you even have some of her mannerisms."

"You're kidding?"

He grinned again, except larger this time. "Nope! Like when you encounter something that surprises you. You put your thumb between the first two fingers and then make a fist."

Unable to stop herself, Saralynn glanced down at her left hand, only to find it exactly the way she had known it would be. "I've done that all my life. I don't even think about it now."

"Your grandmother had exactly the same habit." Sensing her embarrassment, he added, "We both know you didn't copy her, so what other explanation is there?"

"So you don't think I'm crazy for wanting the house… for wanting to stay here instead of going back to Boston?"

"If you're crazy, then we all are. But are you sure? Don't let us color your decision."

"You aren't… but, yet… you are, too. I mean," she struggled for the words. "It's the welcome you've given me. I'm not sure what it is, but something's missing in my life. Something I didn't even know I wanted until I came here."

"We'd be glad to have you. As for what we've got that you don't have, it's just a sense of community and compassion. You know, concern for others. You've got that."

"No, there's something more," Saralynn asserted. "It's what you say, but there's still something else."

"It's called faith. Faith that no matter what happens, we can deal with it because we worship a God who has said He'll always be there for us."

"Mr. Walter? Can you explain that to me? Just what is this faith and how can you get it?"

"Surely an educated woman like yourself understands the concept of faith."

"But I don't. And if this faith is what makes the difference in how all of you act toward each other, then I want that, too." She hung her head, almost ashamed that she had revealed so much of herself.

"You've been in church, you should know as much about faith as the rest of us."

"But that's just it," she blurted. "I wasn't raised in church and I've only been to one a few times in my life." She caught the look of surprise in his eyes, causing her a moment's hesitation before admitting, "When I saw how all of you are like a family, I realized that church is really the people, not the building."

"Your mama didn't take you to church? She sure wasn't raised that way."

"I'd never even been in a church until after I started dating Peter. But those churches were just buildings and we mostly just went on holidays. I never felt like I did at Rials Creek on Sunday."

"How could Alicia stray that far from her raising?"

I didn't mean to get him off on Mama, although I know he means well.

"Then you have to stay here with us!" He pounded his fist once on the table, but once was enough to startle Saralynn and bring her back to the matter at hand."

"Then you'll help me... to stay here, I mean."

"And what would that involve? It should be a simple enough matter to draw up the deeds. You'll write Alicia a check and she'll sign the place over to you. You say you won't be going after a mortgage, at least not right away, so it can all be handled in the attorney's office, with a minimum of work and expense."

"But that's just it. Don't you see? Mama is going to hit the roof. That's why I've got to buy Miss Sallie's house through a third party. You know, a dummy buyer. I'll be glad to pay them something... you know, for their trouble."

A troubled look crossed his face. "You need to think about this, Saralynn. For starters, you're a grown woman. You don't have to hide from your mother. If you want the place, and can afford it, then buy it. It's as simple as that."

"But you don't understand. Mama doesn't let anybody dictate to her. The entire time she's been back in Boston, she's been a basket case because I'm down here alone in this 'foreign land' as she calls it. She'll never agree."

"Look, what you're proposing isn't illegal, but then it isn't totally ethical either. I can't be a party to anything like this." Seeing the stricken look on Saralynn's face, he went on, "Even if you buy it through a third party, Alicia is going to find out sooner or later. If she's that difficult to deal with, do you really think she's going to be happy when she finds out that her own daughter went behind her back?"

"It's just that I know my mama. I might as well pack my suitcase and go on back to Boston. She'll never sell me Miss Sallie's house."

The two had left the restaurant and were in the parking lot when Mr. Walter said, "Tell you what. Let me think about this overnight and let's talk first thing in the morning."

"Then you *will* help me!"

"I'll help you, but only if everything is out in the open and above-board. You don't want to settle here with deception on your conscience. Many a real estate deal goes down exactly as you propose, but it's not right for you."

"Oh, Mr. Walter, how can I ever thank you?"

"By doing this the honorable way so both you and I can sleep with a clear conscience."

On the way back to Magee, Saralynn shared with him her ideas for the house. "Down the road, of course. I'm going to have to take it slow and easy, especially if I pay cash for the property."

The two agreed that Saralynn would call him first thing the next morning so they could decide how best to approach Alicia. "That's a great idea because I told Mama this morning I had something to discuss with her. I promised we'd talk no later than tomorrow morning."

"Then we need to have our game plan mapped out by

then. How about if I work on several ideas and call you tonight? How late do you go to bed?"

"I'm usually up until about ten-thirty. My body is still on Eastern Standard Time, so by then I'm getting weary."

"I'll plan to call you around nine. That work for you?"

"I've got to go to Katie Brooks' house at four, so I should be home well before nine. It's Paul's birthday and she's invited me for cake and ice cream. I just hope it doesn't hurt too much to see such a happy little boy. I don't want to spoil it for them because I get emotional over Marc and Peter."

The autumn landscape was flashing by outside the Explorer's windows, and the blur that greeted Saralynn's eyes was on par with the fuzzy spirit she felt within herself. *I sure hope he knows what he's talking about, that he's got some idea that will help Mama to accept this. It is what I want.*

Saralynn was thinking about the birthday gift she needed to buy when her driver said, "A penny for your thoughts. You were miles away."

"I'm sorry. It's Paul. I was trying to decide what to get him for his birthday. He's almost a year younger than my Marc would be, and I'm wishing I could remember what his favorite toys were at that age."

"I'm sure he'll love whatever you get him. Kids that age are very accepting." He laughed. "It's when they get older their tastes become more... more discerning, shall we say?"

"Even so, I'd like to get him something that he won't out-grow in the next six months. Something he could enjoy playing with for a year or so."

"You don't know about Paul, do you?"

"What do you mean?" Saralynn was stricken by a cold,

nagging sense of foreboding. "Katie said something this morning, like things weren't quite right, but I figured I was over-reacting. Especially since I don't really know them."

"Here we are, back at your house," he announced as he swung the black SUV into the drive. "One day soon, it will be your house. We'll all come over and celebrate."

Is he trying to change the subject? That's what Mama would do.

"I hope you're right. I really hope you know what you're talking about."

"Just have faith."

There's that word again.

"Mr. Walter, what did you mean about Paul Brooks? There is evidently something I don't know, but I think I should."

Her new friend unbuckled his seat belt and turned in the driver's seat to face her. She had never seen such a study of pain as was mirrored on his kindly face. *This must really be bad.* Again, the chilly tingle of tragedy dogged her.

"Paul is dying," he said finally. Saralynn noticed a tear in the corner of his eye. *This is hurting him. People here really are like family.* And she said as much.

"We are family," he confessed. "Paul is our grandson. His name is really Paul Kennedy."

I guess I just assumed since Katie's last name was Brooks that Paul's was, too.

"Grandson. But how? Katie's not your daughter." *Have I missed something here?*

She wracked her brain to find the connection she was sure must be obvious.

"Paul's father was our son. He and Paul's mother... she was Katie's sister... were killed in a head-on crash about a year ago."

"Oh, Mr. Walter. You and Miss Virginia must have been devastated." *I know I would have been. What am I talking about? I was devastated! But for a minute there, I totally forgot about myself.*

"We felt like our world had ended. I don't think I've ever hurt so bad."

"I'd like to listen, if you'd like to talk."

"It's no deep, dark secret. In fact, Virginia and I talk about both Alex and Kathleen almost every day. It makes us feel better, like we still have them with us, if we don't bury the memories."

"That's what Katie told me to do with Peter and Marc, but I thought at the time she was either sadistic or insane."

"Actually, she was being wise far beyond her years, but it is something that every grieving person has to realize for himself or herself."

"I think I'm beginning to make that discovery."

As her friend began to talk about the recent tragedy in his family, Saralynn found herself mesmerized by a story that so closely echoed her own. At the same time, out of the corner of her eye, a glimpse of Ian Scarborough's calf with the wanderlusts caught her attention. *It's come visiting again. I'll have to call Ian as soon as I get back in the house. I don't want to interrupt Mr. Walter.*

"...we loved Kathleen like she was another daughter. She and Katie Brooks are twins, you know?

No, I didn't know.

We didn't think of her as an in-law, and she and Alex were so happy together. Then when Paul came along, it was sheer perfection. We all used to wonder if things could get any better."

Saralynn was bubbling over with questions she wanted to ask, but felt it would be impolite. She tried to squash her curiosity.

Instead, she said, "I know that feeling. That's how it was after Marc was born. Mama was somehow more mellow after that."

"Grandchildren. They're the magic solution to many an in-law conflict. Only in our case, Kathleen's parents doted on our son, and we felt like she had always been a part of our family. So when Paul was born, the already good only got better."

"I almost envy Alex and Kathleen and I didn't even know them."

The older man drew his hand across his brow and in doing so disturbed a lock of his snowy-white hair. "Then the good turned bad. Paul got sick and the doctors couldn't find the problem. For months we carried him from one doctor to another, until finally, a specialist in New Orleans at the children's hospital there diagnosed him with a rare form of leukemia. It's almost always fatal."

"Oh." Somehow her response seemed woefully inadequate, but she didn't trust her emotions to commiserate further.

"We were all shaken right to the core of our being. And we were angry, too. But in order to provide the best for that little boy, we were soon forced to put our anger away. We used all of our energies to deal with his needs instead."

"That must have been terribly difficult."

"It was. Still is. But we keep on keeping on."

"So what happened to Paul's parents?"

"Those two kids were devastated, as you might imagine. The families put their heads together and decided that Alex and Kathleen needed some time just for themselves, to give them a chance to come to grips with what they were facing. We sent them off to the Bahamas for a week, and Katie took Paul while they were gone."

"I thought she was his mother. She acts like a mother."

"Katie never was able to have children, but that doesn't mean she wouldn't have made a good mother. Besides, she loved Paul. We all did, but Virginia and I are too old to take on a toddler, as are his other grandparents."

"They're a handful alright." She laughed. *I never knew how demanding motherhood was until Marc came along and turned our entire house upside down.*

"Kathleen called us the same day they were killed, and Virginia said afterward that she heard some of Kathleen's characteristic optimism in her voice. She was even talking about new inspiration she'd found on the island for her fabric arts studio."

"Her fabric arts studio?"

"You've been in Katie's home, right? There's no way you could have missed Kathleen's art."

That's why she answered me the way she did when I tried to hire the artist for commissions.

"Her work is beautiful. I have clients who would pay dearly for some of those pieces. She was obviously very talented."

"Yes, she was. In many ways. And Alex was her equal. He was a certified community planner and was so good at what he did."

"Did they die on the trip?"

"Within an hour after Kathleen called home that morning. She and Alex were driving around the island when another tourist got confused and plowed right into them."

"Oh, how horrible." *I really do know how you feel.*

"Killed instantly, the authorities said. The man who hit them walked away and we've heard from him several times. He hasn't accepted it nearly as well as we have, even though we've assured him of our forgiveness."

"You forgave him?"

"Of course. In the first place, it was an unfortunate acci-dent. And even if it weren't, anger never hurts anyone but the person who harbors it. We had to get on with life, because we had a sick little boy who demanded our attention."

Am I supposed to forgive the truck driver that killed my Peter and Marc? I don't know where he is or if he even feels any guilt.

"That must have been hard."

"It was, in one way. But it was the right thing to do."

"I haven't been able to be that generous toward the man who hit my fellows."

"You might want to think about it. Hatred festers and poi-sons the soul when we're least aware of it."

I'm not even sure I want to know that man any better.

She changed the subject. "So what's Paul's prognosis?"

"Right now he's holding his own. Still, the doctors tell us it's only a matter of time."

"How do you deal with it?"

"When your child hurts, that takes precedence over your own feelings. That probably works to our advantage right now."

"You mean it takes your minds off of the bottom line?"

"Something like that. Not that it's ever far away from our thoughts. But he's such a delightful little boy until we've all pledged to make whatever amount of time he has left the best for him that it can be."

"He certainly is a live wire. I would never have guessed he was sick. Not terminally ill."

"We say our prayers daily, asking God to send us a miracle."

"Will He? I've never prayed that much?"

"God will answer our prayers. The only question is how."

"I don't understand."

"The miracle we're asking is for Paul to be healed. We want him left here on earth with us for many years to come. But that miracle could also come if God takes Paul to Heaven with Him instead. Either way, healing will happen."

"How will you accept it if he dies?"

Mr. Walter paused and Saralynn could see the battle that raged within him, the fight between his emotions and his sense of reality.

"We'll take it one day at a time, and trust that God knows what's best. The one thing that Virginia and I do know is that if we lose Paul on this earth, we'll see him again one day."

"You really believe there's another life?"

"Not just another life, but eternal life. God has promised it to those who trust Him in faith. And we know that if we're called on to shoulder that load of grief, God will be there for us."

"You say that like it's a guarantee."

"It is. I can show you in my Bible where God has made that promise to me, and Virginia. He made it to you, too."

"By 'be there,' do you mean like by public miracles or bolts of lightning or something?"

"There's always the possibility of such a grand display of God's power, but I think you'll find that most times, when God answers our prayers, He does it through the people He places in our lives."

Why do I suddenly feel so strange? Tingly, almost.

"I'm so glad you shared with me about Paul. I won't say anything to Katie about it."

"Not to worry. It's a common topic of conversation in all of our houses. Katie would have told you herself, eventually."

Yeah, like when I stopped feeling sorry for myself and crying on her shoulder.

"So, are you and Miss Virginia coming to the party this afternoon?"

"Wouldn't miss it," the grandfatherly man assured her. "We make Paul and his needs a priority in our schedule."

"Then I'd best let you get on your way. I didn't mean to keep you so long today."

"It was my pleasure," he replied. "And we will find some way to convince your mother to sell this place to you if that's what you want."

"That's exactly what I want. Now, more than ever."

"Why more than ever?"

"I'll explain it later. I need to think some more about it myself. Let's just say I'm inspired."

She opened the door and jumped down from the SUV's front passenger seat. "See you at the party."

"We'll be there."

As she navigated the stones that led toward the back door, Saralynn caught sight of the little red and white calf that was still making itself at home in the side yard. She stopped, created a viewfinder with the thumbs and forefingers of both hands, and framed a vignette of the little animal and the pin oak tree behind him.

There's one possibility right there. I need to think about this. It could work.

On her way to the house she scrolled the directory in her cell phone until she found the Scarborough's number, which she had recently added, and hit the "call" button. *I can just hear Mama now if she knew I had them on speed dial.*

"Ian… this is Saralynn Reilly. Your little red calf? She's come visiting again…"

Chapter 14

"You'd never know he was dying," Saralynn said to Virginia Kennedy later that afternoon. "The child's so healthy looking, so active."

The two were sitting in folding chairs placed to the side of the small living room, out of the flow of traffic, but still close enough to enjoy the antics of the blond-headed toddler who sat surrounded by oceans of torn wrapping paper.

"It breaks my heart all over again every time I think that we'll probably never get to see him grow up." The grandmother looked closely at Saralynn. "But I don't have to tell you about that pain, do I?"

"There's nothing that hurts any worse." *It is so liberating to be able to be honest about all that has happened.*

When the two ladies had hugged earlier, Virginia Kennedy shared, "I know Walter told you all about Paul... and Alex and

Kathleen. I just hope this won't be too painful for you."

Saralynn felt herself grow cold. "You know… you know about Peter and Marc?"

The older woman patted her shoulder and pointed toward the two chairs nearby. "Let's sit over there. Shall we?" She led the way and when they both were seated, she continued, "Walter told me. He said he didn't think you'd mind." She squeezed Saralynn's hand. "He also gave me the good news that you're going to buy Miss Sallie's house and put down roots here. I think that's the best thing I've heard lately."

"I want to, but it's a long way from a done deal. Mama's not going to be happy about this."

"I'm sorry Alicia feels so bitter about this place… and probably all of us here."

"You know, it's really been an eye-opener for me. Nothing here has been the way Mama described it."

"Don't be too hard on Alicia. Give yourself a break, too. Alicia has been unhappy for as long as I can remember. Don't forget, we went to school together."

"Do you mean that? Mama never was happy growing up?"

"She didn't really have any close friends. Never. She was pretty much of a loner. Some folks said Alicia thought she was better than the rest of us." She waved at the squealing little boy nearby. "Hey, Paul. Nana loves you." While still gazing with un-disguised affection for her grandson, Virginia Kennedy said, "We will get through this with Paul, because God is good and He will be there. He's been so gracious to surround us with people who love us, who rejoice with us and grieve with us. We are truly blessed."

Her children are dead and it's only a matter of time before this precious little boy joins them. How can she say, "God is good"?

The grandmother was rewarded with a toothy grin from the youngster who was clearly overwhelmed by the birthday bounty spread around him.

"He's such a love. Now, where was I? Oh, yes, Alicia… She didn't think she was better than we were. It took me a long time to realize Alicia didn't believe she was nearly good enough. Psychologists today would probably say she was insecure. I just know that whenever she had a problem, she could build a wall that no one could get around."

Insecure. Mama? "It's something to consider." *But she's right about that wall. It was really the third member of our family when I was growing up.*

"Think about it. I always said…"

The grandmother was interrupted when the birthday boy flung himself into her lap. "Wan' cake?" he gurgled.

"Do I want a piece of your birthday cake? Why, I most certainly do. Shall we go find your mommy and see how the refreshments are coming?" She rose, lifting Paul at the same time.

"'freshments," the child repeated in a sing-song voice. "'freshments… 'freshments." He turned to Saralynn. "Wan' 'freshments?"

"You bet I do." She instinctively reached for him and was surprised that he willingly left his grandmother's arms for hers. *Oh, Lord, it feels so good to hold a little one again. If only the ache weren't so bittersweet.* Then she realized what she had done. *I've called God's name before, but it was usually in anger or disgust… Even desperation.* She immediately felt guilty.

The next hour was a whirlwind of activity while Paul blew out his birthday candles and managed to smear cake icing over every surface within arm's reach. Only the quick efforts of both his grandmothers, armed with damp rags, salvaged the afternoon. No one, it seemed, had the heart to rein in the child's energetic antics.

After she had kissed Paul and wished him a final happy birthday, Saralynn hugged Katie's neck. "We need to talk. I'll call you."

Walter Kennedy, who had been standing nearby, called to her. "Saralynn. Wait up. Have you got a minute?"

"For you? Always."

"You're on your way out?"

"Yep, I never did like to bail on a good party, but I've got a bunch of things staring me in the face before tomorrow. I need to get home."

"I'll walk out with you. I've had an idea I want you to think about overnight."

"Oh?"

As they threaded their way through the jumble of parked cars that surrounded the small, brick cottage, her friend explained. "I've been studying how best to approach Alicia with this, and I'd like to be there in the morning when you call her. If you don't mind?"

"Mind? I'd feel like you saved my life. I wasn't looking forward to dealing with her alone."

"We won't hide anything, but if we approach her together, I think we can persuade her to see things our way… I mean, your way."

"Be at the house by nine. If I don't call her then, she'll call me. Remember, I'm 'all alone in a foreign land'…"

"I'll be there in time."

Saralynn turned the van toward home. *I realize now that Boston is just where I live. This is where I really feel at home. I can tell the difference.*

She had told Mr. Walter that she had a lot of work to do. In truth, she had been fighting the urge all day to delve back into her grandmother's diaries. *There are some stories there that I need to understand before I talk to Mama.*

Her original intent had been to read Miss Sallie's memoirs in something close to chronological order. Earlier in the day, however, she'd decided if she wanted to understand the split between her mother and grandmother, she had to fast forward to those months leading up to Alicia's ill-fated marriage.

Thanks to a second helping of the delicious birthday cake Katie had served and an ample bowl of Neapolitan ice cream, Saralynn knew she wouldn't want more than a sandwich before bed. *Besides, the sooner I get home, the faster I can get down to business.*

She wasted no time in beginning her search. *I know when I was born, so I need to go back about eighteen months and start from there. If Miss Sallie has held true to form, she'll have recorded all of her heartbreaks and thoughts in these notebooks.*

It took only a few minutes to find the journal that she hoped would finally share the story of what really happened. *If I'm so anxious to uncover the truth, why am I so hesitant to open this book?*

A knock from the back of the house rescued her from indecision and she hurried to the kitchen, almost appreciative for the interruption. Ian Scarborough stood on the back porch.

"Hi. It's your friendly, neighborhood run-away calf catcher. Where is the little booger?"

"Oh, Ian... I don't know." She knew the calf had been

there when she left for Paul's party. It was nowhere to be seen now, and she recalled with a shameful sense of guilt that she hadn't thought once about the little animal after she returned. *All I could think about was those notebooks.*

"Let's go see if we can find him. It is a him, isn't it?"

Ian laughed. "Actually," he grinned, "he's a she, a little heifer."

"Heifer. What's that? A breed of cattle?"

"Not quite," her neighbor answered kindly. "A heifer is a female calf. Once they have a calf of their own, they become cows. This one's a little heifer."

"What's its name?"

"Sorry, we don't give 'em names. Since they're a cash crop instead of members of the family, we don't get too familiar. Or too attached. Makes it too hard to enjoy those char-grilled burgers on a summer's evening."

"You eat them?"

"Where do you think we get steaks and roasts and hamburgers? They don't grow in the garden, you know."

"Yeah, but... I never had a steak where I knew it... you know... before."

Ian tried to hide the snicker that escaped his clinched lips, but Saralynn heard him anyway.

She colored red all the way to the scalp and even her coppery hair felt hot from embarrassment. "Don't laugh at me. I didn't know."

"I'm sorry," came the apology. "I didn't mean to make fun... or to hurt your feelings. I really do understand."

"Yeah, right. How could you possibly know how I feel?"

"Please... let me explain."

"There's nothing to explain. I'm a city girl, and from the north at that. Therefore I'm ignorant to how things are done here."

"Those are your words, not mine. None of us have thought that about you."

"But everyone will after you tell them how naive I am."

"In the first place, I don't have any need to repeat this conversation. And I don't think you're ignorant." He stopped for breath and, Saralynn thought, to temper his emotions before he said, "You should have seen me in high school."

"What's that have to do with anything?"

"It was like this..." he laughed. "It was my sophomore year in high school and I was in vocational agriculture. That spring, I was appointed to the livestock judging team."

"A livestock judging team? What's that?"

"The best cuts of that meat you used to eat in Boston have just the right ratio of fat to lean that makes them tasty and tender. Our team learned how to look at an animal and judge how close it came to being ideal."

"So?"

"Students in our class each raised a calf using a feed formula specifically designed for our individual animal. Then our entire herd was sold to a local supermarket and were taken to a nearby slaughter house for processing."

Ugh! Saralynn shuddered at the visual image that came to mind.

"Would you like me to change the subject?"

I would, but this little ol' city girl isn't about to let him know how close I am to throwing up. "No, please... go ahead."

"Anyway," he went on, "our teacher carried us to the processing plant so we could see how the special diets we'd fed our calves had translated on the carcass. Only thing, mine hadn't been slaughtered. About that time, they brought my steer into the kill area and did the deed right in front of me… I'll spare you the details."

"Thank you."

"I passed out cold," Ian laughed. "My legs buckled and that's the last I remember."

"How awful. Were you hurt?"

"Just my feelings. Can you imagine how cruel a bunch of high school boys could be in a situation like that?"

"They couldn't be any more vicious than a group of girls that age."

"I survived," he confessed. "At least until I got home. My mama had homemade hamburgers and I had to pass on supper and explain why?"

Saralynn was helpless to keep from laughing. "I can just imagine how uncomfortable that must have been."

"That was almost twenty years ago and my friends still rag me about it today."

He looked around the yard. "This place has always been here, longer than I've been alive. Do you know what's going to be done with it?"

"Mama says she's going to sell it." *I feel guilty about evading his question, but I'm not comfortable talking about my plans. There's too much that can go wrong. Like Mama's famous stubbornness.*

"Daddy said he was sure she'd sell. He'd buy it in a heartbeat, but he figures she would refuse any offer we might make."

And she'll probably refuse my offer, too. I just hope Mr. Walter can make her listen to reason.

"I'm sorry," Ian apologized, "it's getting late and I need to find that calf and get it home. I'm sure I'm keeping you from your supper. Where was she when you saw her last?"

Saralynn pointed toward the far side yard and watched as his long, confident strides in that direction quickly put distance between them. In just a couple of minutes, she heard a shout of success. In another minute, man and calf appeared. The little animal wasn't much taller than a large dog.

Saralynn ran toward them. "May I pet it? I've never seen a cow... I mean, a heifer, up close. We don't have too many in downtown Boston," she quipped.

Ian held up his hand traffic cop style. "Don't run, you'll spook her. Just walk toward us. Slowly..."

She complied and soon found herself on her knees, running her hands over the small, white head and down the animal's back. "She feels so soft and silky. So... so precious, almost."

"When they're little like this, they are just like babies. Unfortunately, they grow up and their demeanor changes when they've got several hundred pounds on you."

"What'll happen to her?" Saralynn asked. *Do I really want to know?* "She won't be eaten, will she?"

"Not to worry." Ian flashed his infectious grin. "This little lady will grow old with us and, hopefully, give us a number of calves as pretty as she is."

"I'm glad. But I still think she should have a name."

"Then you decide what it should be and we'll hang it on her before you leave. And now," he said as he gave a gentle tug on the rope he held in her hand, "name or not, little girl, we need to get you back to your mama before it gets too dark to see."

A man and calf, being slowly swallowed up by the late October evening shadows, was the image etched on her mind when she turned, finally, and made her way back to the house. It was an image she planned to remember. It could be her ticket to stay.

Chapter 15

*T*rue to his word, Walter Kennedy knocked at her door shortly before nine the next morning. "Good grief, Saralynn, are you ill? You're still wearing yesterday's clothes."

"Not to worry. Aside from a night of no sleep, everything's great. Sorry about my appearance, but I've been busy. And I have answers to some of the questions I've had my entire life."

"You've lost me."

"After we talk to Mama, I'll show you what I've found. I think you'll be as amazed as I was."

"I can't wait. Are you ready to make that call?"

"The sooner the better."

"Good. But before we do, there are two matters we need to deal with."

"We do?"

"Let's be sure that we are both on the same page with

everything. Price. Terms and conditions. Justification for selling to you. Just a few minor details." He grinned. "I've made a check list, so let's take a quick look."

He pulled from his pocket a single, folded sheet of white paper, opened it, and the two bent over it.

"Everything's just like we discussed," Saralynn assured him. "Now what's the other matter?" *What else is there?*

"We need to have a talk with God, a minute of prayer, before we launch this campaign."

"You want to pray about it?"

"Do you mind? I never begin any major undertaking without talking with Him."

"No… No, I don't have a problem. I've just never known anyone who prays like this, unless it's to ask the blessing before eating."

"Virginia and I believe that God is the third partner in our marriage, and we include Him in every aspect of our daily lives."

I am discovering so much I never knew. "If you feel that it's important, then by all means, let's pray."

Her mentor took her hands in his and bowed his head. *Gracious and loving Lord. We thank You for Saralynn and for bringing her into our midst. All of us here have come to love and appreciate her in this short time. Now she believes she wants to remain here to create a new life for herself. We would ask your blessings on that journey. Dear Lord, she's been through some of the darkest times anyone can experience on this earth. In so many ways, she's so much like her beloved grandmother who we know and rejoice is safe with You. Saralynn wants to buy this house and make it her home. We both know that her mother, who ultimately has the power to deny her this property, will not be a willing participant. Lord, we ask that Your hand will hold and guide us as we negotiate this deal. We have Your assurance that all we have to do is ask in Your son's holy name, and that You will hear us. Please guide our mouths, our heads, our actions and most importantly, our hearts, as we deal with Alicia. In the blessed name of Jesus, we pray. Amen.*

Saralynn was unable to speak, the lump in her throat threatening to implode and dissolve her into a sea of emotions that she wasn't ready to confront. But Mr. Walter seemed not to notice.

"I think you should call her, since you two normally talk each morning. Find out how she is, reassure her that you're fine. Tell her early on in the conversation that I'm here, and that I need to talk to her before you finish the call. Then, tell her that you've decided that you want to buy the property, at her price, and that you can close as soon as the deed is ready."

"She's going to explode."

"Probably. That's when you hand me the phone. I'm here to do damage control and bat clean-up, if you will."

"Then you've got a big job ahead of you."

"There's no job too big for me when I'm walking with God. Remember, He promised He would hear our prayer. If this is meant to be, it will happen."

There's that walking with God phrase again. "Let's call." Without waiting for a response, she punched in the number and was rewarded with the sound of Alicia's voice after only two rings."

"I was wondering if you were going to call this morning."

I'm going to ignore her barbed greeting. She's trying to drag me into an argument and get me on the defensive. "How is everything, Mama?"

"As well as can be expected when I've got a home that looks more like a bad replica of a war zone and all my treasures are packed away in some storage unit where who knows what may be happening to them."

"In other words, there are no major problems? Merle's guys are working out for you?"

"Everything is just a big headache."

"Construction projects always are. You're just spoiled, Mama. You've never been so close to basics before."

"Never, ever again, either. I've promised myself. If I'd had any idea how bad it could get, I'd have just sold this place as it was. I could have taken my insurance money and bought a new condo ready to occupy."

"Listen, Mama. Mr. Walter Kennedy is here with me. He needs to talk to you after we finish. But before I hand him the phone, I need to tell you about a decision I've made."

"What have you done now? You're still grieving, you don't need to be making any decisions without me there to help you."

"Mama, listen." *Don't plead, Saralynn. You're an adult.* "I want to buy this house and make my home here." *There. I did it.*

At first, there was no response whatsoever. *Have I lost the signal?* Then, when she wondered if her mother would ever speak again, Alicia's voice crossed the miles with a venom that even distance couldn't dilute.

"Never, as long as I have breath in my body! Those trashy people down there have brainwashed you. I warned you about associating with them. But would you listen? No! I'll be there by dark."

"Mama. Please calm down."

Mr. Walter tapped her on the shoulder and extended his hand for the phone. Saralynn indicated she wasn't quite ready to surrender the conversation. Not yet.

"Just because you don't like it here is no reason to deny

me the chance to live where I've found true happiness for the first time in my life. Surely you won't stand in my way."

"Oh, won't I? You seem to forget that I own that property, and if I choose to put a bulldozer to the whole place and then set fire to it, that's my call." Saralynn could hear her choking in rage on the other end. "And if I were there right now, that's exactly what I'd do."

Oh, Mama...

"I'll call you back as soon as I get my plane schedule. Meet me at the airport tonight. We'll leave tomorrow coming back. The sooner I get you out of there, the better it'll be for everyone. Most especially for you and me."

"Sure, I'll meet your plane. But you're not going to change my mind."

"And I'm not signing a deed for you, either. Now let me talk to Walter Kennedy. I'm about to give him his marching orders as well as a piece of my mind. I will not have those people interfering in your life. Or mine."

Saralynn made a gesture of cutting her throat and handed the small phone with the hot lady on the other end to her mentor. *Oh, Mama, if only you could see what you're doing and how it makes you look.*

"Good morning, Alicia. It's good to talk with you."

Saralynn could hear her mother's raised voice, but couldn't make out her words. *But I've lived with Mama long enough to imagine what she's saying.*

"Certainly, Alicia. I'll be more than happy to bow out and get out of your life. That's your call. But as for Saralynn, she's an adult, and she can decide for herself who she wants to associate with."

There was more squawking, louder this time. But still, Saralynn couldn't understand what was being said. Mr. Walter, meantime, still hadn't lost the smile that illuminated his craggy face.

"Of course, Alicia. In fact, Saralynn and I will both meet your plane… Oh, it's no trouble. Believe me, I insist."

Mama isn't accustomed to having her edicts challenged.

"Yes. I understand your position clearly. And so that we're both on the same page, let me give you something to think about on the plane. You can keep Saralynn from buying this house. But this isn't the only place for sale in Simpson County. There are even places to rent. And if this young lady says she wants to stay here, there are plenty of us who are prepared to help her. Just like we were here to help you, but you chose to do otherwise."

This time her mother's response could clearly be heard. "You go straight to h…"

"Alicia." For the first time he lost the affable smile that had been a fixture during the entire conversation, although his tone of voice never varied. "You will not speak to me in that manner. Now or ever. Do we understand each other?"

I've never heard anyone lay down the law in such a calm and unruffled voice. No one has ever talked to Mama like this. She's got to be in orbit.

"Call Saralynn as soon as you have your flight booked and we'll meet your plane."

Her mother evidently responded in some fashion, but Saralynn couldn't make out anything she was saying.

"It's been good to talk to you, Alicia. I look forward to seeing you again this evening. Maybe we can go somewhere for a bite to eat before we come home…. Safe flight. We'll see you tonight."

I'm in a state of shock. I'm surprised that Mama is even still breathing.

She looked at the kindly friend and announced, with obvious sadness, "Well, I guess God didn't answer our prayer."

"How do you mean?"

"She reacted just like I knew she would. I might as well spend the day getting my stuff together, because I'll be on my way back to Boston tomorrow."

"Come with me." He headed toward the kitchen door and Saralynn followed. Once outside, he pointed to the top step on the back porch. "Let's sit here and talk. It's not my intent to come between you and Alicia. That's your business. But you asked me for help and you're welcome to tell me to butt out whenever you think I've gone too far."

Go on."

"You'll always be your mother's child. Even though Alicia had nothing to do with her own mother, Miss Sallie, until the day she died, still loved your mama. Knowing her as I did, I can guarantee that at least one prayer for the two of you went up from this house every day your grandmother lived here."

"What does that have to do with anything?"

"Let me finish. Okay?" He looked out over the pastures that were grown waist high in weeds and a little grass. "You are an adult, regardless of whether Alicia treats you like one. And if you're both happy with that arrangement, then all of us would be wrong to interfere. But if you aren't happy, then you have the right to change things."

"Mama wouldn't let me."

"Saralynn, Alicia can refuse to change her own position

but she cannot stop you from asserting yourself. She probably won't approve. She might even disown you. But whether she likes it or not, you are an adult. It's up to you if you want to act like one."

He doesn't pull any punches, but I'm not offended. I wonder why? "But if Mama won't sign the deeds, I can't stay here, so what choice do I have?"

"Many choices, actually. Like I told Alicia, this isn't the only place around here for sale. And if you don't want to buy, we can find you something to rent." He gazed across the pastures and Saralynn sensed that his eyes were seeing what had been instead of the waste and destruction that now reigned supreme on the once proud little farm.

"Who is we?"

"All of your friends here. We have inroads into most of the county and we're all ready to help. Sure," he continued, "it would be sad if you had to buy something besides this house, but it's not the end of the world."

"I thought since you prayed it meant that Mama would cooperate. I sure didn't get the impression that she's anywhere close to seeing things our way."

The appraiser turned on the step to face the uncomfortable young woman. "God doesn't promise that life will be perfect when we believe in Him and ask Him to be a part of our lives. And He doesn't promise to do things by our timetable. It may be His will that you get this house later. And he may not intend for you to have it at all. Either way, He has told us He'll be with us, to give us the strength to deal with whatever confronts us."

"Is that how you got through Alex and Kathleen's deaths? And how you're dealing with Paul's illness?"

"Exactly. You know first-hand how bad that hurt is. And honestly, I don't know how people who don't have God in their lives deal with situations like that, because there were days in the beginning that we questioned if we could make it."

I almost didn't deal with it. I wanted to kill myself. It's only been since I've been here that I've been able to accept everything that has happened. Only thing is, I don't really understand why.

"So how did you make it? Did God send some kind of miracle?"

"He sure did, but not in the way that you mean it." He grinned at her discomfort. "Loving, compassionate, Godly friends helped to pull us through."

"How?"

"Just by being themselves and doing what they normally do. Some people stayed with us for several days. Others brought food. Still others prayed and sent cards or called. You should have seen the procession of cars from this community that met the plane bringing those two precious bodies back to Jackson. We didn't have to face any of that alone."

"And you think they were God being there for you?"

"There's a verse of scripture… I can't remember exactly where… that says something like 'when you do it unto one of the least of God's children, it's the same as doing it for God.' So you see, God uses ordinary people to answer prayers. And He's ready to use these same people to help you. If you want us."

Boy, he sure has given me a lot to think about. I guess in my mind I thought if I couldn't get this house, I couldn't stay here. But these really are two different issues.

"After what I read last night, I guess I better understand why Mama is the way she is. I do wish things were different, that she weren't so hard to reason with. But she's been that way as long for as I can remember."

"What you read last night?"

"I'll show you when we go back into the house. Miss Sallie kept diaries for most of her life. I found them and you're one of the very few I've told. Mama doesn't even know. She'd probably throw another fit."

"I'd love to see what our old friend had to say." He rose from the step and moved down into the yard. "Walk over here with me, there's something I want you to see."

Together, they walked toward an old tree at the edge of the orchard.

There's nothing out here that I haven't seen before.

"Look high up into the branches of this tree."

She did as he directed.

"Can you see that section right over there?" He pointed over their heads to the left. "See, those branches that are missing their leaves? Yet all around them the other branches look healthy and green."

Saralynn could. "Those limbs are dead, but the tree is still alive. However I'd guess that dead area is going to get larger as more of the tree dies?"

"Exactly. And it's the same way with people. When we shut others out of our lives, we deprive ourselves of the nourishment we need to survive and even thrive. And we die a little in the process."

"And you think that's what happened with Mama?"

"I do. Say, I want to see those diaries before it gets much later. I've got a lot of ground to cover before we meet Alicia's plane tonight."

"Then you're really going with me?"

"I am. Virginia's going, too. We both figured Alicia would hurt herself getting back down here."

"You don't know how relieved I am."

"Just consider us God's answer to prayer."

"You are. Yes, you certainly are."

As they mounted the steps to the back door, Saralynn said, "You know, your analogy about the dead part of that tree makes a lot of sense. It explains a lot to me. Both about Mama and about all the wonderful people I've met here. As for me, I feel like I've found a part of myself that was dead. Just like that tree."

"You know, there's another scripture that talks about that, and this time I know where it's found." He flashed his trademark grin that was fast becoming precious to the young woman from Boston. "It's found in Proverbs, Chapter seventeen. I think it's Verse twenty-one, but I do need to confirm that."

"I'll get Miss Sallie's Bible." The two had seated themselves at the kitchen table, and Saralynn dashed into her bedroom to retrieve the book that had obviously been an important part of her grandmother's life.

She placed it on the table in front of her friend. "I've been meaning to look through it, but I simply haven't gotten the chance."

Walter Kennedy opened the book slightly past the center. "Here's Proverbs."

This man knows how to find things without looking in any index?

He thumbed the tissue-thin pages. "Found it. Chapter 17, but it's Verse 22. Listen to this. 'A merry heart doeth good like a medicine; but a broken spirit drieth the bones.'"

There's that verse again. Then Mama's got dried bones. "I see what you're saying."

"And here's something else you need to see."

Saralynn walked around to look over his shoulder.

"See here." He pointed to a section of one page that was underlined with blue ink. "Miss Sallie has this verse marked. It meant something to her, although we'll never know what incident prompted her to underline the passage, or why it spoke to her."

"She apparently underlined a lot of things in that Bible. It looks like that would be desecration."

"Depends on why you're doing it. When God is at the center of your life, this book that He provides for us is where we can find many of the answers to the questions and crises that confront us. So marking specific passages is actually an indication of how much space God occupies in our lives."

"There sure is a lot to learn about this religion business."

Walter rose and put his arm around the young woman's shoulders. "Not really. All you need is faith, and the rest of it just falls into place."

"But I don't understand the faith part and that bothers me. I'm a college graduate."

"That's why God looks for faith like that of a young child. Education or IQ has absolutely nothing to do with it. In fact," he grinned again, "sometimes being too intelligent can actually get in the way."

"We need to talk some more about this."

"And we shall. I promise. In the meantime, let me explain it like this. Remember Paul at his party yesterday? He was a happy, unconcerned little fellow."

"He certainly was. That little guy didn't have a worry in the world."

"He knows when he's hungry. Or hurt. He also believes unconditionally that those responsible for his care will be there to answer whatever his needs are. So he's able to play and enjoy himself because he knows that his needs will be met. Paul has faith... he just doesn't know to call it that."

"You're right. That's exactly what he does. Marc was the same way."

"That's how God asks us to be. He doesn't promise that we won't be hungry or that we won't have pain and discomfort. But He does promise that He will meet those needs with us. All we have to do is to believe that He will keep his promise. And..."

"And He uses common, ordinary people to keep His promise," Saralynn finished for him.

Walter hugged her close. "He sure does. Just like He's used you to help some of us."

"Me? I thought He was using you to help me."

"He has. But you've done something for us as well. I'll explain it to you later, if you don't figure it out on your own."

She brushed her friend's cheek lightly with a kiss. "Thank you. Now. Do you still want to see those journals?"

"Lead the way. I'm very interested to learn what Miss Sallie had to say."

Chapter 16

*J*uly 11, 1970

Alicia is married. I didn't know anything about it until it was too late. And I doubt that it will last. She doesn't love him. You can't love anybody unless you love yourself first. Alicia never has. Now she's jumped out of the frying pan into the fire. She knows it, but she's so stubborn, so bitter, she won't let anybody help her. She's turned her back on all of us. First Ralph. Then Tony. And now Alicia. Lord, you've given this old woman a lot to shoulder. I'm just glad You're going to be here to help me tote it.

It hadn't taken Saralynn long the night before to find the diary entries she needed to fill in the blanks. Once she began reading... both the said and the unsaid... the entire story of what had happened between her mother and her grandmother more than thirty-five years before began to emerge with painful clarity.

"Poor Miss Sallie," she uttered more than once, as she read through one heartbreaking entry after another.

Walter Kennedy stayed almost another hour while she showed him the highpoints of her grandmother's memories. "It still doesn't justify Alicia's treatment of her mother, but it's easier to understand why she is so bitter today. Miss Sallie kept most of this to herself. Even Hammish doesn't know everything that's here." He shook his head, almost sadly, Saralynn noticed, and said he had to go.

Alicia had called while they were immersed in the Miss Sallie's writings. If Saralynn had doubted the depth of her mother's anger, the abrupt announcement, "My plane lands at five-fifty," followed by the beep of a disconnected call, removed all traces.

"Virginia and I will pick you up about four-thirty," Mr. Walter reminded on his way to the door.

After he left, Saralynn quickly moved into action. Her first stop was in the bath for a long overdue clean-up, followed by a change of clothes. *I've got about five hours before we need to leave for the airport. That's enough time to make a materials run.*

She turned the van into the Wal-Mart parking lot and headed directly for the crafts department, where she spent the next twenty minutes selecting fabrics. With each piece she chose, she envisioned how it would play into the design now engraved on her imagination.

She also purchased a number of other supplies. *On some of this I'm going to have to substitute, but at least I can create a prototype piece to see how well I do.*

Buying for her project made her remember Katie Brooks,

so on her way home, after she'd made a run-through for a Big Mac and fries, Saralynn dialed her new friend.

"Hello, Saralynn, I was hoping you'd call. Don't you just love Caller ID?"

Saralynn laughed self-consciously. "Guess I won't be making any more of those 'Is your refrigerator running?' calls to your house, will I?"

"So what can I do for you?"

"I just wanted to say how much I enjoyed Paul's party yesterday. He's such a precious little fellow."

"You weren't too uncomfortable, I hope?"

"At first, I was afraid it might hurt, but I was surprised. Paul made me remember Marc, more than I have in weeks, but it was a good kind of hurt."

"I'm relieved to hear you say that. I know that Mr. Walter told you about Paul. I'm glad, you know, because I'm going to need you before this is all over."

"I'll be here for you." *Gosh, that came out so easy, almost automatically.* She found she liked the feeling of contentment that enveloped her. *This means I have to stay here. I've made a promise.*

"I never doubted that you would."

"Listen, Katie, I need to talk. Tomorrow, if possible."

"Is something wrong? We can meet later today if it's that important."

"No can do. Mama's flying back in late this afternoon, and I've got a big project that has to be finished before I leave for the airport."

"Tell you what, why don't you call me when you can get free tomorrow and we'll get together. But you're sure nothing's wrong?"

"Not to worry. I just have an idea I want to bounce off of you. Thanks, Katie."

Saralynn brought the van into the drive at home and killed the engine. Then she unloaded her purchases and swallowed the now cold burger and fries, then cleaned off the kitchen table. She began to cut the fabric pieces into shapes that only her mind's-eye could see. *If I do this for real, I'll have to get a little more precise on my design, but this will do for now.*

Just before it was time to bathe and dress to go to the airport, Saralynn stiffened the last piece of cloth, shaped it, and applied another layer of starch. Then she stepped back to survey her work. *Looks good to me, but then I know what it's supposed to be. Wonder if Ian could recognize himself?*

She stored the project away in the parson's room in the front of the house, where she knew it would be safe and cleaned up her mess and stored away the leftover supplies. Following a quick dash through the tub again and a change of clothes, she actually had five minutes to kill before the Kennedy's red Lincoln Town Car pulled into the drive.

At least Mama will get to ride from the airport in a car luxurious enough to meet her criteria... That was cruel. Despite her guilt, Saralynn knew only too well how important a quality automobile was to Alicia.

"Hello, again," greeted both Walter and Virginia Kennedy in chorus when she opened the back door. "Your airport limo awaits."

"I really appreciate you doing this for me."

"We're glad to do it," Virginia responded. "Besides, I haven't seen Alicia. Remember? If what Walter tells me comes to pass, this may be the last chance I ever get to hug her neck and tell her that regardless of what she thinks, I do love her."

As Walter drove, keeping his eyes on the road, he said to his wife, "Give Saralynn that folder of information I brought with us."

I didn't ask him for anything.

The attractive woman in the front passenger seat extended a file folder back to Saralynn's waiting hand.

"If you're still determined to stay here, and your mother refuses to sell Miss Sallie's place to you, you're going to have to have a place to live. I took the liberty of checking the real estate on-line listings for houses in the same price range as you'd pay Alicia. Just in case you have to go that route. There's also a list of rental places, if you prefer."

"Thank you, but I'm hoping we can change Mama's mind. It's really Miss Sallie's house that I want."

"Would you change your mind about staying here if you can't make Alicia see things your way?" Virginia Kennedy's face showed her concern at the same time that she posed the question.

Saralynn didn't hesitate. "I've committed to myself… and others… to stay here. That's what I want. I just hope we can make Mama see reason."

"That's good to hear," Virginia said, the relief obvious in her voice. "We don't want to lose you." She reached over the seat to pat Saralynn's hand. "You've become very special to all of us, you know."

"I appreciate your nice comments, but I'm at a loss to understand it. All I've done is be me."

"And that's the explanation," Mr. Walter offered. "Whenever someone is genuine, it usually shines through. It's hard not to love someone when they're natural and don't put on airs or hide behind a façade."

Like Mama does?

The conversation in the Lincoln en route to the airport centered around renovations that Saralynn would like to make to the old house as funds permitted. "I'll be hard-pressed not to use your house for a model in some cases since you've done such a marvelous job of making a livable home out of an old barn of a house."

"Copy away," Virginia Kennedy offered. "Imitation is the sincerest form of flattery. Seriously, though, with these old houses, sometimes there's only one economical way to make these modernizations happen. Don't let that worry you."

Alicia's plane was right on schedule and as she came up the concourse pulling her wheeled-case behind her, Saralynn could read her mother's body language. *She is furious.*

"Here we are, Mama." The daughter waved to get her mother's attention.

Alicia saw them, the black expression already on her face becoming more stormy with each step.

Saralynn put out her arms to hug her mother, but the older woman ignored the gesture.

"It was a rough and exhausting flight. I hope the car is close."

"Mama, you remember Mr. Walter. But you hadn't had a chance to see his wife, Virginia, before you left."

The Kennedys both stepped forward but it was Virginia who spoke first. "Alicia. It's good to see you again. Welcome home. It's been…"

"Don't say it's been too long, Virginia. For me it hasn't been nearly long enough," Alicia snapped. "Let me make one thing clear right now. If you think you're going to brainwash my child and trap her in this god-forsaken place like everyone wanted to trap me, I will use every breath in my body to keep that from happening."

"Mama!" *She is so rude.*

"It won't matter… if you bring all of Rials Creek up here… to meet me. Saralynn's place is in Boston… I intend… intend to make certain… she goes back there… Tomorrow. Tonight if I could manage it." Alicia's rage was choking her speech.

She's going to have a stroke.

"Mama, please calm down. Nothing is worth getting this upset." She put her hand on Alicia's arm, only to have her mother jerk away.

"You and I will settle this privately, back in Magee. While we're packing."

"Let's all go and find something to eat," Mr. Walter suggested. "The car is this way." He reached out, "Let me take your case, Alicia."

"I don't need your help. Or your interference, Walter." Alicia stepped in front of the man and looked him directly in the face. "I consulted you professionally, and I'm not sure that what you've done doesn't constitute unethical conduct. We'll let the state licensing board decide."

I'm not going to take any more of this.

"Stop it, Mama. Stop it right now. You will not abuse these people who are guilty of nothing more than befriending me."

"Do you know who you're speaking to? You don't talk that way to me. I'm your mother and you'll do well to remember that."

"And I'm your daughter… make that your *adult* daughter.

Something you've never been able to remember."

Alicia's only response was to grab the handle of her wheeled luggage and stalk toward the nearest exit.

Saralynn felt her face redden with shame. "Miss Virginia… Mr. Walter, I'm… I'm so sorry. You don't deserve that." She felt her apology was both inadequate and long overdue.

"Honey," Virginia said quickly, and she hugged Saralynn as she spoke, "don't you worry about it. Alicia has never been cordial to any of us, although I will say that her behavior just now is the worst I've ever seen."

"That's right," Mr. Walter added, "we didn't expect her to greet us with open arms, but nothing she's done can change how we feel about you."

"But she was so rude," Saralynn observed. "There's never any justification for that type behavior. I'm just so embarrassed."

Mr. Walter put his arm across her shoulder. "Let's get out of here and see if we can find her. Just remember," he counseled the troubled young woman, "don't lower yourself to her level."

When they reached the sidewalk outside the airport, Alicia could be seen haggling with a cabbie nearby. "Why won't you take me to Magee? Money's not an object." They couldn't make out the driver's response, but it obviously wasn't what Alicia wanted to hear. She pulled away from the window of the yellow taxi and grabbed her luggage. Then she saw them.

"Everyone here is so ignorant," she screamed. "Stupid driver wouldn't take me to Magee. I informed him money was no object."

I don't have a clue what to do.

Evidently Walter Kennedy did. He stepped up to Alicia and grasped the pull handle on her case. "Alicia, we've tolerated your behavior so far, but that's about to come to halt. We've come to get you, as you asked, and despite your abusive behavior toward the three of us, we're still prepared to go somewhere for a nice meal, and then we'll take you and Saralynn home."

Alicia puffed up, her rage renewed.

Uh, oh... here it comes again.

"Alicia! That is enough." Walter Kennedy spoke in a tone of voice Saralynn had never heard him use before. "You have two choices. Lose the anger and come with us, or find your own way back to Magee. We're leaving. Now."

"Where's your Christian charity, Walter?"

Mama!

"You've been looking at it ever since you walked off the plane. And you're still looking at it if you choose to take advantage. My Christianity doesn't demand that I allow you to abuse me, or those around me."

Mama has never been talked to like this.

"So what'll it be?"

With poor grace, Alicia grabbed the handle of her case away and demanded, "Where's the car? I'm exhausted."

In short order the four exited the airport parking lot. Saralynn and her mother were together in the back seat. *There's that famous glass wall in place. She might as well be riding in another vehicle. What should I do?*

In the front seat, Walter and Virginia Kennedy acted as if nothing was amiss. "I thought we'd go to Capitol City Diner. As a decorator and an artist, we think you'll find it intriguing."

Throughout the meal it was a three-way conversation that broke the awkwardness surrounding the table. Alicia ate in stony silence and spoke only when she informed the server that her meal would be on a separate check.

She's not even offering to pay for my meal. My own mother.

Saralynn would have protested, but a look from Walter Kennedy silenced her and soothed her anguished emotions.

When Mama holds a grudge, she doesn't back down. I just wish she could understand how much damage she does when she gets like this.

Another awkward moment came when the food was served and Walter Kennedy asked the group to join hands for the blessing. Alicia refused to join them, and again the threesome said grace before they attacked some of the best food Saralynn had ever eaten.

"This place is great, Mr. Walter. I don't know which is better, the food or the décor."

"It is rather interesting, isn't it?"

"The decorator in me sees all sorts of very innovative and creative touches. Whoever did this knew what they were doing. In fact, they're much better than I am." Beside her, she could sense her mother's objection to that comment. *I'm a decorator because that's what Mama said I should be. I wanted to be an artist, but that wasn't exclusive enough for her. Oh, Mama… don't you see, you have to love what you're doing to be truly happy… that's when you're really successful.*

The ride back to Simpson County was dominated by Alicia's hostility radiating from the back seat of the Kennedy automobile. As he pulled into the drive, Walter announced, "Here we are, ladies."

"Thank you, Mr. Walter, for the company and for an excellent meal." Saralynn felt like she had to offer some comment and it was obvious that Alicia didn't intend to perform any of the requisite courtesies.

"We enjoyed it," Virginia answered. "Alicia, it was good to have a chance to be with you." The only response she got was Alicia's back heading for the kitchen steps. "Don't worry, Saralynn. We understand."

"I want to have a word with your mother, and I want you to hear what I have to say." Saralynn followed Walter Kennedy through the back door.

Alicia was standing in the middle of the kitchen. When they entered, she turned her back on them, pulled open the refrigerator door and busied herself inside.

"You don't have to look at me, Alicia, but you are going to listen to what I have to say." Walter Kennedy was showing a side of himself that Saralynn hadn't seen before.

Alicia didn't acknowledge his presence.

"If you want to report me to the state, that's your business. If you want to give this property to someone else to sell, that's also your business. But you will not browbeat your daughter because she's exercised her adult prerogative to determine where she wants to live."

Alicia still gave no indication that she heard.

Walter embraced Saralynn as he said, "If you need me during the night, you call me. You don't have to stay here and be subjected to her abusive actions."

When he had gone, Alicia finally withdrew from the refrigerator. "I thought he would never leave. They've always made me tired."

What do I say to her?

"I'm going to bed, Mama. We'll talk in the morning."

"We'll be packing in the morning. I want to be on the road by noon."

"You may be packing, Mama. But I'm staying here. At least for a few more days. Then I'll be back in Boston to get ready to move."

"How can you be so blind… so stupid? I gave you the best of everything and this is how you repay me." She turned away and began to fidget with items on the kitchen counter.

"We're two different people, Mama. You gave me what was best for you. I'm discovering that I'm a person who wants something different in life, and I'm going after it. Right here."

"Fine! So stay. Become one of them. But you won't be doing it in this house." When she turned to face her daughter again, Saralynn realized she'd never before seen the vicious expression that dominated her mother's normally attractive face. "No one makes me do anything I don't want to do. And there are no circumstances that can ever make me deed this house over to you."

"Then I'll get something else. But I'm staying in Magee. May I stay here tonight, or would you prefer that I vacated right now?"

The only answer was the slamming sound of her mother's bedroom door. She went to her own room as well and got ready for bed. *It's too early, but what else is there to do?*

For the first time since she'd arrived at Miss Sallie's house, Saralynn wished she were elsewhere. Anywhere, but under the same roof with her mother. *How could I have been so blind to what she's really like?*

Out of habit, she raised the lid on the small suitcase and removed several of the notebooks on top of the stack, the ones she'd read in the night before. *I should be falling over from exhaustion since I was awake all last night, but I'm not.*

There was one section in the journals that had particularly bothered her the night before, and she flipped pages until she came upon the passage where her grandmother had confided her most painful memories.

⌦

The lawyer the Bankston's sent down here from Jackson was back today with the papers for Alicia to sign. She ain't married no more, but she is one wealthy woman, which is what I think she wanted all along.

I knew we were headed for no good. Known it for months, but Alicia is out of control. She don't pay no attention to what I say, don't want to know what I think. Course she never would listen to me. Always did have a mind of her own. Told her it was gonna get her in trouble some day and now it's happened. Only I can't believe what she's done.

Her and Hammish Scarborough was engaged. He's a young man, a couple of years older than Alicia. Lives on the next farm. I was so happy when they decided to get married. I thought now, maybe, she would be happy. He would have made her a good husband. Except now she's been so ugly to him and everbody around Rials Creek is talking about it.

I should have never let her take that job at the Sanatorium, like I could have stopped her. I've begged the Lord many a night while I lay in my bed long after she should have been home to stop her before she come to no good.

Marshall is a nice enough man, but Alicia just used him. He comes from money and if there's one thing she's never been able to abide, it's being poor. Used to nag me day and night about wanting better than I could provide. Nothing I ever did was good enough.

Then she met Marshall and says she fell in love. But I'm pretty sure it was with his family's money more than it was him. Alicia is my child and I'll always love her, but she's selfish. She used to hit poor Tony, and him younger than her, to make him give her whatever she wanted. I never could punish her enough to make a difference, though Lord knows I tried.

The first thing I knew, she come in and announced that she was married. I never even got a chance to meet him first and I think he was kind of embarrassed to come in here to be introduced as her husband. I remember how it was when I first got out of the Sanatorium. You've been in there so long, wondering if you're gonna come out alive, that when it happens, it takes a few weeks to get situated again. That poor man hadn't been out but one day when Alicia and him run off up to Jackson and stood up before a justice of the peace. Didn't even have a preacher.

She looked all smug when she come in here to tell me, and then they went off on their wedding trip and ended up back to see his family in the Delta. The Bankston's are big farmers up there and his daddy is in the legislature. Only when they come home, I knew something was bad wrong. I let them move in here because neither one of them had any money to rent a place. That's when I knew there was going to be problems.

About three weeks later, he left and went back to his family, and the next week, the lawyer showed up. That's when I found out that my daughter was gonna have a baby and that his family didn't want nothing to do with Alicia or her baby. The lawyer wanted to know how much it would cost Mr. Bankston to buy Marshall's freedom back and never have to hear from Alicia again.

I ain't never been so ashamed of my child. You would have thought she was selling a cow or a piece of land. Not a husband and a baby. She told that lawyer, cause I heard her, that if the high and mighty Mr. Bankston wanted to buy her out of her marriage, he had better get out the big checkbook, cause it was gonna cost him plenty.

Before it was all over with, the Bankston's paid for the divorce and gave her fifty thousand dollars cash and a brand new car. And she made 'em set up some kind of account, she called it a trust fund, that would pay her something ever month for the rest of her life. I never will forget what she said to me after the lawyer left that day. She was dancing around the room waving the bank check in her hand. She looked at me, and she crowed, "I'm rich; I'm rich. I won't ever have to be looked down on again, and I can get out of here for good. Once and for all."

I'm so ashamed of her. But there ain't nothing I can do. Nothing but pray, and I've been doing that. It's out of my hands. Whatever happens, God's gonna have to put His hand on the situation. I've done all I can do.

Saralynn closed the journal. *Believe me, Miss Sallie, I understand how you felt.* She got up and changed into pajamas, brushed her teeth, and piled up in the bed again. The notebook was still where she had dropped it, and when she was comfortable, her grandmother's memoirs lured her back to an equally unsettling time.

The next few days' entries were rather brief. *Evidently she must have been so distraught she really poured out her heart that day. Even in those darkest moments, when she was a patient at the Sanatorium, she didn't write this much.*

But about a week later, the extent of Miss Sallie's grief was again measured in the amount of detail she recorded in her diary.

She's leaving. Alicia is leaving Magee. I told her when she got the divorce and the money that she and the baby were welcome here. I've lost my husband and my son. I didn't want to lose her and a grandchild I don't even know yet. I thought she had decided to do what I wanted.

Today she come in and announced that she's moving to Boston, Massachusetts. It's way up north, I'm not sure exactly where. When I asked her why, she said because she hates everything here and that she didn't intend for her baby to have to live like she had. She don't even have a job or anything. And she don't know nobody in Boston. Said she'd been to the library reading about towns all over the country and she likes the sound of Boston.

I begged her to change her mind. I even offered to give her this place if she'd stay, but she wouldn't have none of it. But to top it all off, Hammish Scarborough come over here and told her he still wanted to marry her, and that he'd be happy to make a home for her and the baby. He would have, too. She talked so ugly to him, I couldn't believe my own child could be so cruel.

She's loading that new car she got and says she's leaving tomorrow morning. Says she wants the Mississippi state line behind her before the sun goes down.

I asked her why she wouldn't marry Hammish and she said he didn't want her, he just wanted her money and this land. That wasn't so, but she was a fine one to criticize after she sold herself and her baby out of a marriage. She said if she married Hammish she'd always be a prisoner down here with people she hated. I asked her if she hated me too, and that's what really hurt. She said when I insist on living like the rest of the people here, she hates me for being like them. Said I could do so much better and that she don't want to end up some day like me.

Can you imagine any daughter saying that to her mama? It near about broke my heart. If I didn't have my God to lean on, I couldn't bear it. It hurts bad enough as it is.

✏️

If I didn't trust Miss Sallie, I'd think she was over-reacting, or that she was smothering. But between what my friends told me the other night, and the way Mama has been acting lately, I have no problem believing what I'm reading.

She closed the book and laid it aside. The small room, with its simple country furnishings illuminated in the light of the bedside lamp, had taken on a safe, comfortable, welcoming appearance. *I'm going to miss this room, because it appears that I will be moving out of this house. Probably tomorrow. But I'm at peace, if that's what has to happen.*

As she studied the architectural details of the corner bedroom, Saralynn remembered another portion of her grandmother's memories that had been particularly painful. *If I remember right, it was in the next notebook.* She quickly located the page.

✏️

My grandchild is here. A little girl named Saralynn Alicia. I don't have a clue where Alicia got the first name. There's nothing like it in any of our family. It's been months since I've heard from my daughter. I knew about when she got in the family way, and if I'm right, the baby is about six months old. She couldn't let me know when it happened, I guess. But at least she's safe and I know that I have a granddaughter. I'd love to see and hold the precious little thing. But that won't happen.

Alicia made it very plain in her letter that I will never know my grandchild as long as I live here. Said if I wanted to sell out here and move to Boston with her, we might could be family again. But she said until I decided to do that, that she didn't want to hear from me unless I was ready to do what she wanted.

She don't understand what it would take for me to pull up here and go up north with her. I still don't know for sure exactly where Boston is, but from what I've heard about folks up north, I wouldn't be happy there. I can only hope that Alicia's happy. Nobody deserves to go through life as unhappy as she was growing up.

So I'll stay right here. At least I can pray for my two little girls ever night. My God lives right here with me, and I lean on Him so hard some times.

Sleep was finally starting to claim Saralynn, and she put aside the journal before turning out the lamp. Even though there was conflict as close as the next room, she was at peace with her plan. In the darkness, just before she surrendered to the fatigue, she surprised even herself. *Dear Lord, I feel really awkward, because I don't really know how to pray and I'm not sure if I'm even doing it right. But Miss Sallie believed in You then, and all my friends here still believe in You today. And I want what they have. Please be with me tomorrow when I have to deal with Mama and make arrangements for a place to live and find a way to earn a living. Thank you for loving me. Amen.*

Then she slept.

Chapter 17

The sunrise through the eastern windows in the little bedroom was a morning event Saralynn had come to treasure. When the first rays awakened her, she lay there, basking in the warmth and welcome and taking her time before joining the rest of the world.

What was that?

The sound of a door closing elsewhere in the house startled her and brought fear and a lump to her throat. Then she remembered... *I'm not alone. Mama's here. In her house.*

Breakfast was a mostly silent ordeal. When Saralynn entered the kitchen, her mother was at the stove and the fragrance of fresh-brewed coffee wafted about, assailing, enticing the young woman to come in. *It's sad the real welcome isn't as wonderful as the smells in this room suggest.*

Without saying a word, Alicia pulled a cup from the dish cabinet near the sink, poured coffee into it and set it on the table in front of her daughter. "You know where the cream and sugar are."

"Thanks." Saralynn doctored her coffee and fixed herself a bowl of cereal before she sat down. Alicia took the chair opposite her. Each woman concentrated on her breakfast. Finally, unable to stand it any longer, Saralynn offered, "It's nice to have you back, Mama."

"Is it?"

"Well of course it is. You're my mother and I love you."

"Do you?"

"Mama, can't we put an end to this insanity?"

"The only insanity going on around here is your insistence that you're going to give up everything you've worked so hard for in Boston and exchange it for a backwoods life in this God-forsaken state." Her voice broke with a sob. "Don't you understand, Mississippi will always be twenty years behind the rest of the country?"

"Aren't you being a little hard?"

"Look, it's time you faced facts. This state is a loser. Always has been and always will be. And that goes for everybody in it. Why do you think I got out?"

Why did you, Mama? I think Virginia Kennedy was right. It's not the state you're ashamed of, you're ashamed of yourself.

"I haven't found it that way, Mama. There are some warm and wonderful people here who have made me feel like family. I've been able to come to grips with the loss of Peter and Marc." At the look of horror on her mother's face, she was quick to add, "I didn't say I'd forgotten them, because there's never a day I don't think about them, or look for Peter to share something with him. But I'm not paralyzed any more, like I was in Boston."

"Which means you can go back with me and pick up your career... your very successful career, I might add."

"Successful how, Mama?"

"Financially, of course. You can't even count all the satisfied clients you've worked with, or the beautiful homes you've given them. Face it, you're one of the most sought-after decorators in the city. There's no way you can afford to jeopardize that."

"But what if I'm not happy? Not fulfilled?"

Alicia banged her coffee mug on the laminate-topped table. "Happy! What do you mean you're not fulfilled? Of course you are."

It's a good thing that cup was heavy pottery. We'd be cleaning up a mess. "No, Mama, I'm not happy. You are."

"I wish I knew where you got this craziness. Certainly I'm happy that you've done so well. That's what mothers do. They find... fulfillment, as you put it... through the accomplishments of their children."

Saralynn picked up her dishes and walked to the sink, where she carefully disposed of her cereal bowl and cup, before she turned and faced the woman she knew would soon reject her. She weighed what she was about to say. She still felt the peace that had been her constant companion since she made the initial decision.

"Mama, I love you and I had hoped we could find middle ground on this. Obviously that isn't going to happen. So let me be very clear with you about how I feel and how I plan to proceed."

As she spoke, she leaned against the copper-colored metal sink unit and found strength in its sturdiness against her back. "I am not happy in Boston and haven't been for a long time." She held up her hand when she saw Alicia's mouth open. "Please let me speak and then you can have your say."

"But you're…"

"I really want you to understand how I feel, but if you won't let me explain, then I'll just proceed with my plans and you can get on with yours."

"Fine. Have it your way," Alicia snapped. "You're going to anyway."

This is one of the few times I've ever known Mama to give in.

"Thank you. And I promise, you'll get your chance to speak." She took a deep breath before she continued. "I was very happy married to Peter, and when Marc came along, I didn't think I could ever be happier." Try as she might, tears sprang to her eyes as she said this, and the lump in her throat prevented her from talking. She gripped the edge of the sink for support.

"When I lost them, I thought my world had ended. Even my work didn't interest me. I didn't care if I ever picked out another fabric swatch or matched a paint color. You didn't know this, but I wanted to join my two guys. I couldn't even manage to take my own life."

Alicia gasped and her hand went to her mouth. Saralynn could sense her mother's impatience. She hurried on before her captive audience could seize the floor. "After I got here, away from everything familiar, I discovered things about myself that have amazed me. I don't like Boston. I feel at home here in a way that I've never known there. My successful decorating business may have made money, but it didn't do anything for me internally. I know now that I'm a decorator because that's what you told me to do. I don't want to do that any more."

Alicia half rose from her chair.

"Not yet, Mama. I'm not quite through. If you don't like Mississippi, that's fine. That's your choice. But I do. I like the state and I like the people. I don't see it as backward. It's developing, which is exactly what I'm doing. Now, here's how it all shakes out. I'm going to stay here. I'm going to sell my business and lease out my house for the time being, and I'm going to relocate here, where I have friends… real friends. Where I feel at home."

"I will not allow…" Alicia sputtered and rose from her chair. Purple rage consumed her face.

"It's not your decision to make, Mama. It's mine." Saralynn said this firmly, but not unkindly. "You can block me from buying this house, but this is the only property in Simpson County that you control."

"Just go back to Boston with me, and I'll give you the money from this house."

Where have I heard this deal before? It's come full circle.

"Sorry, Mama. Boston just isn't in the picture for me. Not any more. If I can't have this house, I'll find another one. But I'm staying here and I hope you can be happy for me."

"People here are backward. They don't use decorators. They buy accessories at home decorating parties. You'll starve."

"Doesn't matter. I'm not going back into decorating."

"What'll you do?"

"Follow my first love. I'm going after the art career that I've always wanted."

"You're crazy!"

"That's your opinion, and you're welcome to it. But my mind is made up and as far as I'm concerned, the subject is closed. Now about this house… will you sell it to me?"

"I can be just as stubborn as you. You will never own this house. Mark my words on that."

Saralynn had moved away from the sink and was standing

in the kitchen doorway when Alicia delivered her verdict. "Fine, Mama. Do what you will. I'll be out by lunch." She turned and headed for her bedroom, then stopped to face her mother again. She reached into her robe pocket and fingered the keys to the van she'd placed there for just such an eventuality. "Here. These belong to you, too. You'll need them to get the van back to Boston." She tossed them to Alicia and heard as they hit the worn linoleum floor.

After she shut the bedroom door and turned the old skeleton key in the lock for the first time since she'd been there, she grabbed her cell phone and punched in the Kennedy's number.

"Good morning, Saralynn."

Caller I.D. again.

"I'm glad you called. Virginia and I have been concerned. We trust that things are better this morning."

"Mama and I have come to an understanding, which is why I'm calling. Could you drive me somewhere that I can rent a car? We've agreed to disagree and I'm vacating."

"Of course I'll come. When?"

"Give me… let's see, it's almost nine-thirty now. Let's say ten-thirty. I'll be ready and waiting."

"Ten-thirty it is. I'm sorry, Saralynn. We thought surely Alicia would bluster a while and finally see reason. Obviously the years haven't mellowed her."

"Thanks, Mr. Walter. I'll see you shortly."

Her next call was to Katie Brooks.

"I was wondering when you'd call. You've got my curiosity aroused, you know."

"Hope you won't be disappointed when reality doesn't match your anticipation."

"So when are you coming over? Please don't keep me in suspense."

As she talked with her friend, Saralynn moved around the small room collecting her belongings and laying out what she would wear that day." *Sure puts a different emphasis on the phrase "going away outfit."*

"Will you be available this afternoon? Say around two… maybe as late as three?"

"We'll be here all day. Charlie said he could watch Paul, so we've got as much time as you need. You call it."

"Let's say two, then. I've got some business I need to deal with first. That should give me enough time."

"See you at two then."

Saralynn disconnected the call and finished packing, being sure to tuck Miss Sallie's bulging Bible and the old family photos she'd discovered into her travel bag. She made certain to latch the overnight case that held her grandmother's journals. *Don't want to forget this.* Then she unlocked the door and listened. There was not a sound anywhere in the house and the door to Alicia's room was shut.

Don't want to forget my handiwork. She pulled her door closed and went quickly to the front of the house, where she retrieved the fabric art she'd fashioned. *Good! It's still holding together. Wish I had a box for it, but I'll just have to be especially careful."*

Back in her room, she took one last look around and headed for the tub. By ten-twenty she was dressed and had all of her belongings on the back porch, just minutes before Walter Kennedy's SUV entered the drive. He got out and came to where she stood. Without saying a word, he put a supportive arm around her shoulders and pulled her close.

Oh, thank you, Mr. Walter, thank you. This almost hurts worse than losing Peter and Marc.

"Is this everything?" He bent to pick up the luggage. "Surely there's more in the house."

"Nope. These are all my worldly possessions. At least it's all I have here."

"Then you're ready to go? Where's Alicia?"

"I haven't seen her since breakfast. The van's still here, so I guess she's locked in her room."

"You need to tell her goodbye."

"But it's so hard."

"Most things worthwhile in life are, one way or another. You go in there and tell her you're going and I'll get everything loaded." He grabbed two cases and headed for the car.

Saralynn went back into the house to her mother's still-closed bedroom door. She knocked and waited, but there was no response. When she tried the knob, it was locked. "Mama. I'm leaving now. Please call me before you head back to Boston so I can know you're on the road. It's a long trip for you to make by yourself."

There was still no response from the other side.

"Bye, Mama. I love you." Her eyes filled with tears when she realized that she and her mother might never speak again. *But I'm doing what's right. There's no question about it.*

Once in Mr. Walter's SUV, Saralynn brought him up to date. "I'm afraid I've cost you Mama's business."

"I'm not worried. At least not for myself. Don't give it a second thought."

"Still, I hate that it's turned out like it has. So where is the nearest place I can rent a car?"

"At the airport in Jackson. That's where we're headed now. But where will you go? You're going to need a place to stay."

"As soon as I get wheels under me, I'll come back and get a motel room. It'll only be for a few days. I've got to go back to Boston to deal with matters there so that I can come back to stay."

"I don't mind taking you to rent a car, but you're not going to any motel. Not as long as Virginia and I have three spare bedrooms at our house."

"Oh, I couldn't."

"And why not? Give me one good reason."

"I'd be imposing."

"I said a good reason. So that's settled. You'll come back to our house."

The two rode in comfortable silence for a short while until her driver asked, "Have you given up on buying Miss Sallie's house?"

"I know Mama." If I push her far enough into a corner, she'll come out fighting. I think the best thing to do is back off. Right now, she'd give the house away before she would see me have it. I don't want to push her that far."

"So you're not giving up?"

"Not just yet. But I do have to have a place to live."

"You haven't asked my advice, but I'm glad you're not giving up on Miss Sallie's house."

"Maybe if Mama can see that I'm happy, and it hasn't already sold, I can make her see reason. I can't abandon my goal just yet."

"I have a lot of respect for you. You know what you want and you go after it."

"Before you shower me with accolades, you need to know that this is probably the first time in my life that I've ever taken a stand. I realize now that everything I've done has been because Mama said I should... or shouldn't. How could I have been so blind?"

"It wasn't hard. Alicia loves you. There's no doubt about it. But she carries a lot of baggage with her, and directing your life gave her a reason for living. Because you didn't know any differently, you went along with it. Now that you've defied her, she's probably feeling at loose ends."

"I hadn't thought about it like that. You don't suppose Mama's any danger... to herself, I mean?"

"The way she feels right now is exactly how Miss Sallie was when Alicia drove off to Boston. Only your grandmother had her friends and her church... she had her God to help her through it. Alicia doesn't have any of that.

"She doesn't, does she?"

The SUV was approaching the round-about at the entrance to Thompson International Airport and the driver ceased talking while he negotiated the tricky turns into short-term parking.

"We'll have to go inside, next to baggage claim. This is pretty close." He eased the Explorer into a space and the pair headed for the airport's lower pavilion. "You need to reach out to Alicia on a regular basis, whether she responds or not. When you left this morning, her whole world caved in."

"I will, Mr. Walter. It'll be hard, but I'll do it. You haven't steered me wrong yet."

"It's the right thing to do."

Renting the car was a speedy, fairly painless ordeal. The agency had a week-long special – pay for five days and get seven.

Saralynn calculated that it would take her a week to get all the arrangements made for her return to Boston. "I'll be driving my own car back."

"See you back at our house?"

"I've got one quick stop I need to make and then I'll be right on."

"Want me to take your luggage with me?"

"Sure. I won't be far behind."

"You remember how to get there?"

She laughed. "You can't lose me now, Mr. Walter. I'm home."

At the roundabout, Mr. Walter went straight, while Saralynn hung a right and began to consult directions she'd jotted down earlier that morning. Within just a few minutes she was pulling into a parking space at the renovated fire station that housed the Jackson Chamber of Commerce. A smiling young black woman piled her arms full of information about the area's interior designers, architectural firms and more.

"I won't lack for reading material," she assured the clerk. "Thank you."

"Call us if you need anything else. That's what we're here for."

Saralynn negotiated her way out of the city. *Man, this place is a breeze compared to getting around in Boston. I'm going to enjoy coming here.*

Try as she might, thoughts of Alicia and her actions kept intruding on Saralynn's concentration as she drove south on Highway 49. "When you left this morning, her whole world caved in." Mr. Walter's admonition echoed in her head. *I still love Mama, and I wish I could feel guilty, but I don't. I am an adult, and I'm entitled to live my life in a way that gives me peace. Why do you have to try to live your life through me, Mama?*

As she approached Mendenhall, she found the exit and made her way through downtown, headed toward the Kennedy's spacious country home located between the county's two largest towns.

When she saw the Mendenhall Grocery & Grain sign, she remembered her vow to come back and spend some time there. *That place is bound to be worth half a day's time.*

Her hosts had been watching for her. Virginia Kennedy, followed closely by Walter, headed toward her car, her arms outstretched in welcome.

"You come right on in this house." Virginia gushed as she hugged her guest. "By the time you get unpacked, I'll have lunch on the table. Just don't expect too much, we usually eat light in the middle of the day."

"Now you aren't to go to any extra trouble. Promise me, please?"

"We normally eat about this time everyday," Walter Kennedy assured her. "I put your things in your room. Come and I'll show you where you're bunking while Virginia dishes up the food."

Saralynn followed him into the older portion of the house, to the largest of the bedrooms that had a private bath attached. The walls were butter yellow with cream trim. Traditional country tab curtains with hand-stenciled hems showcased the two towering windows and the ancient glass panes that let in the mid-day light.

"We thought you'd like this room. It's yours for as long as you need it. So unpack and make yourself at home."

"I already feel at home. In every sense of the word." *It will be hard to tear myself away from this room. It could be a page in a decorator's portfolio.* Instead, she said, "I hope I won't need it very long. I'm anxious to get settled in my own space." *Wherever that is.* She began to unpack the suitcase that already lay on the burled walnut bed as she talked. "I want to find a place to rent before I go back to Boston to close out things there."

"We can talk about that while we eat. I've got some ideas."

"I can never thank you enough for all you've done."

"We're not doing anything we don't want to do, so don't get to strung out on appreciation. You'd do the same for us."

And I would. That's what's so funny. Before I came here, I wasn't even conscious of anyone else's needs. It would never have occurred to me to offer to help.

"Say, I'm hungry. Virginia's had time to get things on the table. All your stuff will still be here after we eat."

The three were soon seated around the antique oak table Virginia explained had been in her family for several generations. "We've enjoyed many a meal around this old table. And today's lunch will be yet another one."

"You've done too much," Saralynn said as she surveyed the dishes her hostess brought to the table. "Beef roast, baked potatoes, green beans, garden salad and homemade rolls. Some snack."

"Well," Virginia admitted sheepishly, "we didn't know if you got any breakfast this morning and I decided you might be hungry."

"I did have a bowl of cereal, but you know what, I am hungry." After Mr. Walter had returned grace, she ladled generous helpings onto her plate and began to eat. "This is soooo good."

Everyone ate in silence until Walter asked, "So you want to rent rather than buy?"

Saralynn speared another bite of lettuce and swirled it in a small pool of dressing that had collected in the bottom of the bowl. "If there's any chance that I can get Miss Sallie's house, that's what I want. I can always buy something else later, if things don't work the way I hope they will."

"Then I won't even show you anything for sale. Instead, we'll look at rental, and I've got a place that Virginia and I think would be perfect, but we're going to need to move fast."

"Why?"

"Because, my dear, rental property is in short supply here. Anything available always goes quickly," Virginia explained.

"Are you available to look at this place the minute we finish eating?"

"You do mean to move fast, don't you? Only I can't go until after Katie Brooks and I get together. I'm supposed to call her at two o'clock." She took one last bite of baked potato, which she'd dressed liberally with real butter and sour cream. "This potato was so good. In fact, everything was. But I can go as soon as Katie and I finish."

"We're not trying to pry, dear, but is your business with her something you could do here?" Virginia, already clearing the table, posed the question. "If so, you're more than welcome to invite her over."

"That is an idea. Let me give her a quick call." Saralynn returned to her room and dug the small silver phone out of her purse. *Well, Mama hasn't tried to call. I guess I didn't want to admit to myself that I hoped she would.*

Her friend answered on the second ring and quickly agreed

to come to the Kennedy's. "But why are you there?"

"I'll explain everything when you get here?"

Saralynn finished unpacking and picked up the brightly colored piece of fabric art that she hoped would be her ticket to a new direction for her professional life and headed back to the great room at the other end of the house. Through the French doors that opened onto the screened porch, she could see Mr. Walter talking on the cordless phone. *He looks so sad.*

In a matter of minutes, Katie's car entered the drive and Saralynn dashed out to meet her friend. "Thanks for coming. I've got so much I need to talk to you about."

"You said nothing's wrong, but that's not what your eyes say. From the way you hugged me just now, you're hurting. What's the matter? Does it have something to do with Peter? Or Marc?"

"Come in the house and I'll explain." The two walked arm and arm across the neatly manicured yard and up the rear steps. "Let's just say that things aren't as good as they could be."

Once inside, both Walter and Virginia greeted Saralynn's visitor warmly and suggested that they would be outside in the yard for a few minutes.

"That's not necessary," Saralynn assured them. "I have no secrets from any of you, so please stay if you were leaving to give us privacy."

"If you're sure?" Virginia questioned.

"Then please sit, while I bring Katie up to speed on what's happened so far."

As concisely as she could, Saralynn recounted for her friend the decision to stay in Mississippi and about her mother's refusal to support her wishes. "In short, she won't sell me Miss Sallie's house, so I moved out. I'm staying here with Mr. Walter and Miss

Virginia until I can make other arrangements."

"I'm so sorry, Saralynn. You didn't need all this additional grief."

"But I will make it."

"Of course she will," Miss Virginia volunteered. "Because we're all going to help her."

"So where will you live?"

"Later this afternoon we're going to look at a piece of rental property that Mr. Walter knows about. I don't want to buy just yet. Maybe..." Saralynn paused. "Maybe over time Mama can be made to listen to reason."

"Well, if you're needing a place to rent, has Mr. Walter..."

"I've got the perfect place for her," the gentleman in question interrupted. "In fact, if you have time, you might want to go and look at it with us."

"Could you?" Saralynn quizzed her friend. "I'd love to get your reaction."

"Sure. I've got all afternoon. Paul will go down for his nap shortly, so I can be pretty flexible for the next couple of hours."

"Great. We'll all get to go."

"But there was something else you wanted to talk about, because you called me yesterday. That was even before your mother landed last night."

Saralynn rose from the comfortable over-stuffed loveseat and disappeared around the corner, to re-emerge with her fabric art."

The collective gasp from her audience of three was sufficient proof that her creation had the impact she'd hoped it would.

"It... it looks like a man leading an animal on a rope or a leash," Miss Virginia offered. "But whatever it's supposed to be, it's absolutely breathtaking."

"It is exquisite. Did you do this?" Katie inquired, her voice dropped almost in reverence. "And when?"

"This old man doesn't dispute that it's beautiful, but just what is it?"

"Oh, Walter. Honestly," his wife chided him. "It's a three-dimensional fabric tapestry, like Kathleen made. And an excellent one it is." She reached out and brushed the piece with the tips of her fingers. "Why didn't we know that you could do such as this? You've been keeping secrets."

They really like it. Maybe this idea isn't half-baked.

"In truth, you three are the first ones to see this. I only did it yesterday, before we went to the airport to get Mama. I can see several rough edges on it, plus I took several production short-cuts on this one because I lacked some of the materials I needed. Not to mention I was up against time."

"I assume you make these and sell them there in Boston?" Mr. Walter was fingering the artwork, running his fingers over the puffed-out areas of cloth that created the raised design.

"In truth, I've never made one until I decided to tackle this one yesterday."

"Saralynn," Virginia charged, "you need to tell us something we can believe."

"You can believe this, because it's the truth."

"Then where did you get your inspiration? I can't imagine that you see many guys leading calves around in Boston," Katie challenged.

"Then you do see a man leading a small calf? That makes me feel better. I was afraid I might be the only one who could understand what it is."

"We all see it," Virginia said. "Now tell us about it. You've got my curiosity aroused."

"Well, first of all, I guess it's fitting that I'm showing this to the three of you at the same time. You see, I have all of you to thank for the idea."

"We remind you of a man leading a calf?" Mr. Walter asked, confusion evident in his voice. "I don't understand."

"No... no," Saralynn laughed. "I got the idea after seeing Kathleen's exquisite work at Katie's house, and hearing the two of you talk about her art and how creative she was."

"So who's the guy with the calf?" This time it was Katie who posed the question. "Come on, inquiring minds want to know."

"That's Ian Scarborough and... and his run-away calf. He told me to pick out a name...it's a little girl... he called it a heifer. But I haven't had time. But that's not what's important."

"So what is important?" the audience of three chorused.

"Ian came the other day to get this calf that had run away. As he left, I thought it made an especially poignant picture, and I was trying to think of some non-traditional medium that I could use to capture and preserve it."

"I would never have thought about doing it this way, but it's very effective." Virginia traced her index finger around the various pieces of cloth that made up the composition. "It's almost like a patchwork quilt, only it has a... a multi-dimensional quality about it that brings it to life."

"It's breathtaking, Saralynn." Katie continued, "I didn't get the first smidge of artistic talent... Kathleen got it all, as you saw. But I know what looks good and I know what I like. This I like very much."

"So why did you want to talk to us?" Mr. Walter asked.

"Kathleen was my inspiration. When I saw what she had done with a needle and fabric, it was like a part of me I had never known suddenly opened up. I always wanted to pursue an art career, but Mama wouldn't hear of it. That's how I ended up in interior design."

"That's a real compliment. We were so proud of Kathleen," stated Virginia. "It's gratifying to know that she can still influence people."

"Yes, and that's why I want your blessing for what I'm considering."

"Why would you need our blessing?" Katie asked.

"I don't want to feel like I'm copying your sister. Or that I'm using her as a springboard. But when I saw her creations at your house, I knew I had clients back in Boston who would pay big money for some of her pieces. I think I can create a market for custom tapestries through designers and architects. This type art would work in commercial buildings as well as in private homes."

"But my sister isn't here any longer. She didn't have any legal claim on the talent she had, tremendous though it was." Katie was now on the floor examining Saralynn's creation in closer detail. "If she could know you as we have come to know you, she'd be the first to encourage you to follow your heart and to make the most of your talent." She looked to Virginia and Walter for affirmation. "Don't you both agree?"

"Remember, Saralynn...remember that God often answers our prayers through the people we encounter and the situations in which we find ourselves." Walter had risen from his chair as he spoke, and made his way across the room, where he selected a framed photo from among many displayed on the bookshelves that flanked the fireplace.

"Here, look at this picture. It's the family portrait they had made just days before Paul got sick. Meet Alex and Kathleen Kennedy. Paul you know."

"They were a beautiful family. I don't know how you all were able to go on in the face of such tragedy."

"It's because of people... people just like you," Virginia explained. "They are what made the difference because they were put here by God to minister to us in their own way, with their own human limitations. Any time a human gives his all in God's name, the results are so much more powerful than any mere mortal could achieve alone."

"You mean you think I was put here by God to help you? Until I came here, God was something mysterious, almost a supernatural being that lived way up on a remote summit that you used if you needed Him and then put Him away. You act more like He lives with you."

"He does," Mr. Walter affirmed. "In all of our homes, it's easy to include Him as one of the family, because He lives first in our hearts."

"So you're saying that even though I didn't know who God was, He still used me to help you?"

"May I share the conversation we had just a few days before I first met Saralynn?" Katie looked to the couple across from her for permission, and Saralynn saw them smile.

Katie continued. "Less than a week before I ran into you and your mother on the grounds at Boswell, Virginia and Walter had come to the house to get Paul. We were looking at several of Kathleen's later pieces and lamenting that none of us had the talent to pick up where she left off. Now you're here."

I never dreamed that I might be fitting into a bigger picture. I thought that what I was doing would enable me to stay here and earn a living.

Virginia scooted over to Saralynn and hugged her. "So you take it and run with it. You have our blessings and if Kathleen could speak, you'd have her support as well. It's just so gratifying to know that even in death, she's still touching others with her God-given talent."

"I'm overwhelmed," Saralynn admitted. "I never dreamed our conversation would take the course it has. But I am grateful to you for your love and support."

"If I dig back far enough," Katie said, her face twisted in deep thought, I'll bet I can find some of her client files, because she had already begun marketing herself."

"You would share those with me?"

"Of course. You're one of us now."

"Your work is beautiful, Saralynn. You have a priceless, God-given talent and you should use it. But right now, we need to go look about a place for you to live," Mr. Walter said. "Don't want this to get snatched away from us do we, Katie?"

They have an understanding among themselves about whatever this is. If I didn't know them as well as I do, I'd think I was being set up for a practical joke.

"We can go in our car," Walter volunteered.

"What is this we're going to see?" Saralynn asked. "I've got a two-story home in Boston. Anything I can't use is going to have to be stored."

"I figured as much. If you like this place, it should work well for you."

They rode for about five minutes from the Kennedy's, back toward the Rials Creek Church. Walter turned into a paved drive that wound through a dense stand of tall pine trees. Saralynn couldn't help herself when she first caught a glimpse of the house.

"Ohhhhh. You must be kidding. This place isn't for rent." She surveyed the New Orleans style façade of stucco and wrought iron and stone and took in the double galleries across the front. "For sale, definitely, but never for rent."

The car had stopped in the circular drive, in line with the double carved wooden front doors, each one with leaded glass insets. Both Walter and Virginia turned in their seats to face Saralynn, and Walter began to explain. "This was Alex and Kathleen's house. None of us can bear to sell it, and because of insurance, the mortgage was paid off when they were killed. It has set here all this time, while we've tried to decide what should be done with it."

Virginia broke in. "Ordinarily, we'd protect it for Paul, but since nothing short of a miracle will see him live to be old enough to need it, we had made up our minds to lease it."

"The ad is already at the printers for the real estate book and if we're going to pull it, it has to be done before five o'clock today. That's why we were insistent that you see it this afternoon."

"I'm totally in shock. I don't even know what to say."

"Say you'd like to see the inside," Katie hastily advised. "It's almost three o'clock now."

"That does sound like a winning idea," Walter agreed. He opened his door and got out with the others following suit.

As she stood in the elegant, towering two-story foyer, Saralynn immediately felt at home.

"We've already removed all of their possessions. And it's been cleaned. All you'd have to do is transfer the utilities and move in," Virginia commented.

"Before we start through the house," suggested Walter, "let me give you a run-down on what's here. You've got a formal living and separate dining room... breakfast room/kitchen combination... a family room. Upstairs there are four bedrooms and three baths. There's another full bath down here, along with a laundry room and Alex's home office. Out back is a screened porch, an attached two-car garage and the studio."

"Kathleen's studio?"

"Would you like to see it first?" Katie offered. "The rest of this stuff is pretty standard."

The four trooped across the huge garage toward a room on the other side. "I don't know how many cars you have, but this is an oversize garage. Anything you couldn't accommodate in the house could be packed in here and save you having to rent a storage unit," Mr. Walter proposed.

As Saralynn said later, it wouldn't have mattered what the rest of the house was like. When she saw the studio space, with it's bank of eastern windows and skylights and the large work tables where the late Kathleen Kennedy has crafted her art, she was hooked.

"I'll take it," she bubbled with excitement. "It's perfect." *But is the price perfect? This place would bring a premium price as rental property to some executive.*

"Don't you even want to see the rest of the house?" asked Virginia.

"Oh... sure. Of course. Only I still want to rent it. That is, if I can afford it."

"It's affordable," was Mr. Walter's only reply.

"No, let's talk serious business here. This isn't some little apartment that would go for a few hundred dollars a month. I'm afraid to even guess what the fair market rental value would be, for I know it's not cheap."

"Would you pay eight hundred a month?"

"I'd be a fool not to. Double that still wouldn't be full value."

"And you'd be right. But in this case we're asking eight hundred. Do you want it at that price?"

"Certainly. Yes. Of course I do."

"Good. Then we have a deal. Your rent will start the day you move in."

They made quick work of closing up the house and resetting the security system. On the way back, Walter said, "I'll give you a key and the security code when we get home. That way if you need to go in for anything before you head back to Boston, just go. There's no need to ask permission."

"Don't' get me wrong, because I'm very grateful, but why are you doing this for me? You could come out so much better to rent it for what it's really worth."

"If money were the only consideration, you're right. But to get that big money, we'd have to rent it to a stranger. You're like family, and money isn't the first priority. Paul's expenses are assured; we don't need the income as much as we need someone in the house we know will treat it like their own. And, we need for you to stay here among us because we believe that God sent you our way."

"I'm still in a daze," Saralynn confessed. "But of course, you know, if Mama should come around to my way of thinking, I still want to buy Miss Sallie's house."

"That's a given," he assured her. "But I have to tell you that I took a call earlier that has a bearing on that matter. It was from an attorney in Jackson. Evidently Alicia didn't let any grass grow under her feet after you left this morning."

"What do you mean?"

"Mr. Johnson's call was to inform me that I have been removed and that if I am caught setting foot on the property, I'll be arrested for trespassing. He also said that Alicia was at that very moment listing the property with a Jackson realtor and that for sale signs will go up on the place today."

"Mama never has given up without a fight. It didn't matter what it was. I'm just sorry she's come down on you like she has. She blames you for my insanity, as she calls it."

"I'm not worried," he said. "But I wouldn't get my hopes up, because there are a lot of city folks, with deep pockets and an unrealistic concept of country life, who would pay more than the place is worth. A status thing, you know."

"Yes, I had plenty of clients like that back in Boston. Were they ever a pill to work with."

Katie, who had been quiet throughout the conversation, finally spoke. "But if God means for you to have that house, it'll be there for you at some point, some way you can't even imagine right now. The question is, can you entrust it to His keeping, and be content to say, 'Thy will be done…' while getting on with building your new life here?"

"That's a toughie. How do I do it?"

"It's called 'faith'. That's all that it takes."

Everything seems to revolve around faith. I just wish I knew how to do it.

"You make it sound so simple."

Katie laughed, "It is simple. It's our complex human mind that overrides our heart. We decide if something is too simple, there must be something wrong. I'm going to tell you something, Saralynn. You already have faith. We've seen it. You're the only one who hasn't."

"I want it. I really do."

"And you'll find that you have it within yourself. Just like you'll find the patience to wait to see if you're meant to have Miss Sallie's house. In the meantime, you're set on this end. All you've got to do is deal with matters in Boston. In your heart, you're already at home here... all you lack is getting mail."

She's right. Everything has fallen into place. I'm embarrassed by the way Mama has acted, but it's obvious that my friends here aren't holding me accountable for her vindictive actions.

Before the car came to a stop in the Kennedy drive, Saralynn extended the invitation. "Here's how it is," she said, "we need to celebrate and we're long overdue for me to treat. So dinner tonight is on me. Katie, you and Charlie and Paul, and you two, Mr. Walter and Miss Virginia, you're my guests for tonight."

"We can go," the Kennedy's chimed together.

"We can, too, but I think I'd better get Aunt Toots to keep Paul. He doesn't do restaurants yet. But we'd love to go."

Once inside, Saralynn excused herself and went to her room.

"You've had an exhausting day," Virginia agreed. "Perhaps you'd like to nap for an hour or so? I'll be glad to wake you."

"A nap sounds great. Yes, if you would, please check on me about five-thirty."

The bed looked extremely inviting as she lay across it, knowing she wouldn't stay awake for long. *But before I doze, I have to say thank you, God. I'm still not sure I know how to pray, but I'm anxious to learn.*

Chapter 18

*D*inner that evening was characterized with high spirits and much overeating. The five adults traveled to Jackson in the Kennedy Lincoln, to Dennery's, one of the capital city's signature eateries.

"If I gain ten pounds off this meal, which I probably will," Katie Brooks charged, "I hope you can live with your conscience," she told Saralynn. "There was enough shrimp on my plate to stock a small ocean."

"It was delicious," Virginia added, "but that's why Dennery's has lasted all these years. They have excellent word-of-mouth advertising."

Over their more than ample servings of shrimp and prime rib and salads, the five-some discussed Saralynn's upcoming move and the merits of one transfer company over another.

"One of the chain do-it-yourself movers used to have a

slogan on their vehicles that said 'Adventure in Moving'. I always thought that was such a drastic understatement," Walter Kennedy observed. "Moving is just plain hard work, even when you have movers."

"I hate to confess," Saralynn told her dinner companions, "but I don't have the first clue of how to begin. Most of what I have was brought into the house in Boston one piece at a time. Peter and I came out of an apartment into that house. Then, when Marc came along, that changed the dynamics of everything. I'll just have to let the movers handle it all."

"Say," Katie asked, "we've all heard you talk about Peter and your little Marc, but we don't really know them. You wouldn't happen to have pictures in your purse, would you?"

I do, but it's been a long time since I've had the courage to look at them. But they showed me the photo of Alex and Kathleen....

"Sure, I've got pictures. I just haven't had the...."

"If it's too painful, don't," Katie hastened to say. "We understand. I probably shouldn't have asked."

"Nonsense. You're the very people who've shown me that it's possible to go on. I'd love for you to see my boys." She dug a black and gold-trimmed wallet-size photo album from her purse and opened it to a picture Peter had made just a few weeks before he died.

"Oooh... good looking. Where'd you find him?" Katie was flipping on through the pictures. "This is Marc, right?" She pointed to a small, blonde-headed boy with Peter's chiseled features and a broad grin."

"That's my Marc. He was just about the same age Paul is right now when that was made." She laughed, easily, she realized. "Marc was a photo ham. He always wanted his picture made and would beg anyone he saw that had a camera to aim it his way."

Everyone at the table joined in the laughter. "They are so precious when they're little and innocent," Virginia Kennedy said. "I remember when our daughter, Emily, was about Paul's age, we bought her a pair of red, frilly, ruffled panties. When we came out of church one morning, our guest minister who was none other than the Bishop, complimented Emily on her pretty dress. Before we could stop her, she offered to show him her new red panties, too, and she turned her bottom up and flipped her skirt to give him a good look."

"Mama and I were mortified," Walter chimed in. "Everyone else thought it was a hoot."

"It has gotten funnier with the passing of time. I wouldn't take anything for that memory now," Virginia affirmed.

Conversation turned to Saralynn's planned business. "You'll need to define what you're doing, you know," Katie explained. "I think Kathleen would have gotten more commissions than she did, but her hobby had suddenly evolved into a business, and she wasn't sure what she wanted to happen. So she didn't push it."

"I won't have any choice, I'll have to push mine. I'm giving up a lucrative design practice to go in a different direction. But I know how to speak the language, so I think that will give me an in, if I can just get a few commissions to help me establish a portfolio."

"You've got a lot facing you," Virginia agreed. "But if you need us, for anything, we're here for you."

"I know that. I wish you were in Boston to help deal with all those loose ends. I've got to sell my practice, find a tenant for the house, sell Peter's car, give up my studio and arrange for transporting all my worldly goods. I hope I can accomplish everything within two weeks."

Despite her reservations about sleeping in a different bed, Saralynn slept soundly that night. She awoke the next morning ready to get on with the business at hand. The Kennedys had encouraged her to leave local details alone until she got back from Boston and was ready to settle in.

After one of Virginia's country breakfasts, which was considerably more than the bowl of cereal that had been her daily fare for so long, Saralynn got to work. Her first call was to one of the other designers in Boston, a larger firm that had approached her on more than one occasion about joining forces.

"Saralynn… it's soooo good to heah your voice," the other woman gushed when Saralynn reached her at home. "We were simply devastated to leahn about Peter and Marc's unfortunate deaths. How ah you holding up, my deah?"

As she listened to the older woman who was quintessentially old Boston, she sensed unspoken triumph in her competitor's voice. LaRay… "just LaRay, dahling…," would be gowned in one of the many flowing, multi-colored caftans that were her trademark. *I can see her now.* Underestimating someone who looked so unconventional, almost like an over-the-hill hippie, had been the undoing of many a novice designer new to the Massachusetts decorating scene.

LaRay chews up the competition before they even know what got them, spits them out, and moves on to the next one. Fortunately, I never let her appearance put me off my guard. But I know of several accounts she's taken from me.

"Thanks, LaRay, I'm doing well, which is one reason I'm calling."

"You've finally decided to join me. You won't regret it.

We'll make an unbeatable team and this town will sit up and take notice. I'll have the papers drawn up this week."

She hasn't changed a bit. That's how she gets half her commissions, by steamrolling over her clients and when they come to, they've signed on the dotted line. I've got to walk this tightrope carefully.

"LaRay... LaRay!" She had to break into the older woman's monologue. "I'm not interested in joining forces. I've decided to relocate out of state. Do you want SAB Interiors, or do I offer it to Harvey Hanson?"

"You wouldn't sell to that cretin!"

It's amazing how hard and common her voice can get whenever things don't go her way.

"I've worked too hard to see my business just disappear from the landscape. You need my clients, but Harvey will be glad to get them."

"Have you talked to him yet?"

"No, but he's next on my list. My goal for today is to find a buyer. Are you interested?"

LaRay's voice had lost all of its charm. "How much? I don't intend to be held up."

"And I won't sell out for less than my business is worth. I'll take one hundred seventy-five thousand today."

"Surely... you... ahen't... serious." The curt words were bitten off and spit out.

"Why wouldn't I be? SAB is worth every dime you'd pay." *I've never wheeled and dealt like this before, but I'm actually enjoying it. Thank you, Mr. Walter, for the coaching.* "Tomorrow it'll be one hundred eighty thousand. Remember, you're getting all my files, customers and equipment."

"I wouldn't give over one hundred thousand on the best

day of the week."

"Let me call Harry and if he isn't interested, I'll get back to you."

"You drive a hard bahgain. Don't call Harry."

"Like I said, my goal is to sell this business today."

"I'll give you one hundred thirty thousand, and that's my final offer."

"I'll bet I can get one-fifty from Harry."

"Would you take one-fifty and forget Harry?"

"Provided you sign a sales contract today, and put down ten percent, with the balance due in ten days, I'll let it go for one hundred fifty thousand."

"You drive a cut-throat deal. You know that, don't you?"

"I prefer to think of it as an honest deal. At any rate, my attorney will have a contract to you before the day is out. Have your check ready."

I did it. I did it!

Empowered by her success, she put in a quick call to the home of her attorney, Lawrence McCollough, where she dictated terms of the sale and instructed the lawyer to get LaRay's signature and earnest money before the temperamental designer had time to change her mind. "I'll get back to you Monday with all the details."

After all the business I've given him, he can do a little work on Saturday just this once.

Her next call was to the landlord of the building where her studio was located. Because she'd been a tenant for many years, the man grudgingly agreed to cancel the lease if she paid two months' additional rent as damages and forfeited her deposit. "I'll send you a check as soon as I'm back in Boston next week."

Peter's friend, Ashley, had always admired the classic Volvo that had been Peter's pride and joy. He rarely drove it, preferring instead to pamper that car in favor of a later model BMW. *That's the car they were killed in.* She called him next.

"Saralynn! Where have you been? We've been calling for days and you ahen't returning messages."

"I'm sorry, Ashley. I've been out of state for a few weeks, trying to get a handle on things. And that's why I'm calling. I want to sell Peter's Volvo. Would you be interested?"

"Of course I'm interested. May I ask, ah you having financial difficulty? We heahd you'd been left comfortably."

From anyone else, I'd take offense, but Ashley and Peter were as close as brothers. He's asking out of concern.

"No, no… it's nothing like that. I'm going to relocate to another state, and I don't need two cars. I thought of you for the Volvo. I think Peter would want you to have it. But don't feel obligated."

"Of course I'll buy it. Just name your price."

Saralynn did, and when he accepted without debate, she promised to call as soon as she got back to Boston to finalize the deal.

Her next call was to a real estate agency where one of her former clients worked. "Linda, this is Saralynn Reilly."

"It's so good to hear from you. How are you faring these days? I was just sick when I heard what happened."

"Thankfully, I'm doing better each day. It was pretty rough those first few weeks. And there's not a day goes by that I don't think about them. But I'm trying to get on with my life."

"So what can I help you with? You ready to sell that gorgeous house? I can find you something where you can start over with new memories."

"I'm quite content to keep the memories I have. They're precious to me. But I am going to relocate. What I'm calling…"

"I'm way ahead of you and I'm already on the computer looking to see what's out there. I'll call you back."

"No… wait. I've found exactly what I want, and it's not in Boston."

"Not in Boston? Saralynn, what have you done?"

"I'm moving to Mississippi and I need to lease my house. I'm not quite ready to let go of it completely, but I am willing to give someone a lease with a purchase option."

"Mississippi?"

"Hey, if you haven't been to Mississippi, don't prejudge it. There are some wonderful people, which is just one of the reasons I'm going to settle here."

"I'm sorry." There was uneasiness in her voice. "When will it be available?"

"It'll take me about two weeks to get everything out. How much rent can I get?

"You taking all the furniture?"

"Everything except the kitchen appliances. I'll even leave the refrigerator since I'll have one in the house I'm renting. Everything else goes with me."

"Hmmm… I think we could easily get thirty-five hundred."

"Then go for it. Put out the word that it's available. I'll call my carpenter who has a key and ask him to drop it by to you. I'll stop in to sign the papers when I get back in town next week."

"I'll have everything waiting when you arrive. Meantime, I'll starting marketing it today."

"Thanks, Linda. I knew I could depend on you. And Linda,

you ought to take a few days vacation and come see me after I get settled. I'm serious. I'd love to show you my wonderful new state."

It had taken the entire morning to make those contacts, but it was, in Saralynn's opinion, a very productive day. When she shared her accomplishments with her hosts over lunch, both Walter and Virginia were astounded. "When you set your mind to something, woe be unto any grass that tries to take root under your feet," Walter observed dryly. "I've got a list of tasks I've been working on for two weeks. You want to help tackle those this afternoon?"

Saralynn knew he was teasing her so she replied with a totally straight face, "Oh, no, I only work miracles before lunch. Tomorrow, perhaps?"

"So what are your plans for the afternoon," Virginia asked.

"I thought I'd go down to the house and go through it again. I need to look carefully at where I'll place furniture."

"You've got the keys and the utilities are on, so go make yourself at home. Stay as long as you like," Walter said. "Just don't forget to enter the security code within a minute after you open the door."

When Saralynn set out on foot a little later, Walter, who was in the garage, called out, "Aren't you taking your car? Do you need me to drive you?"

"Not to worry, Mr. Walter. I want to walk. I'm in no hurry and I want to stroll along and take in my new neighborhood."

"Have fun, then. And if you decide it's too far to walk back, call me and I'll come get you."

"Thanks, but I'll be fine."

And she was extremely fine for the entire afternoon as she wandered from room to room, visualizing all her furniture and accessories in various configurations. Just as the sun was starting to fall lower in the sky, just in time to make it back before dark caught her, she set out on foot again, this time with a fair idea of where big, burly men would set every piece of her furniture on that glorious moving day to come.

Then I can really be at home.

Chapter 19

While her day had been both full and extremely satisfying, Saralynn found that night was her enemy again, as she grieved over the broken relationship with her mother. *It's like another death.*

At church the next morning, when she had a chance to pull Donna Hasty aside, she confided to her the events of the past few days and her heartbreak over the way she and Alicia had parted company.

"You're exactly correct to look at is as a death, because that's what it is… the relationship you two once enjoyed, however flawed or off-balance it might have been, is dead."

"I hadn't thought about it like that."

"There's no use grieving over what has happened, because it can never be re-created again. Both of you are different people now."

"I just can't believe Mama and I will never be close again."

"And you shouldn't believe that. It would be the greatest mistake you could ever make." She led Saralynn away from the crowd, out a side door and into the churchyard next to the cemetery. "I want to show you something that I think might help."

"Whatever it is, share it with me, because I'm hurting. I've never been without my mother."

Donna hugged her close and pointed to the far side of the cemetery. "See those trees over there, the ones that are losing their leaves?"

I'm not sure where she's going with this, but I'll stay along for the ride. Does everybody around here use trees to make their point? "What about them?"

"Every fall, those trees lose their leaves. They stand bare and exposed for the entire winter. And in the spring, tiny green buds appear and soon those trees are in full greenery again. Not the same leaves they had before, but new leaves."

"I think I see where you're going with this. Are you saying that my relationship with Mama is like the trees? What we had is falling away but in time it will come back?"

"That's part of it. But there's an even bigger part that you need to own, before you can find the peace to build that new relationship."

"Now you've lost me."

"You've mentioned to several of us that you want to fully understand the faith that we have."

"That's true. All of you have something that I want but I don't know how to get it." Saralynn clutched her friend's arm, as if to emphasize her confusion.

"Let me ask you a very simple question. Do you doubt for one minute that come next spring, those trees will burst forth with new, green leaves?"

"You forget, Donna," Saralynn laughed, "I come from New England where I've watched four different seasons change for as long as I can remember. I would never think to question it."

"Then you've already shown faith, whether you knew what you were doing or not."

"Surely it can't be as simple as that."

"Sometimes we get too smart for God. All faith is, when you boil it down to its most basic, is the belief that God will do what He says."

"But there's a lot of difference in leaves and lives."

"Not in God's eyes. So you see…" she took Saralynn's hands in hers and looked directly into her face, "just like you trust God to bring new leaves to those trees next spring, you've got to trust Him to restore your relationship with your mother. In His own way and in His own good time. And in whatever form He designs."

Oh, Donna, how did I ever get so fortunate to find you for a friend? But then she knew. *Thank you, God… for Donna… and for dying tree leaves.*

The two hugged again. "We'd better be getting back. It's almost time for Sunday School."

"Thank you. That seems so inadequate for such a huge lesson."

"Hey," her friend said as she tucked her arm through the crook in Saralynn's elbow, "that's what we're here for. God put all of us here for a purpose."

"I wonder what He's going to use me for?"

"He has, already. In time you'll see that."

The music that morning was glorious and it joined the

song in Saralynn's heart as she thought again about faith and about the leaves she would be at Rials Creek to see next spring.

Virginia Kennedy had refused Saralynn's insistence that they eat out as her treat. "I've already got our meal in the stove and it will be ready shortly after we get back from church."

As promised, the casserole was cooked to perfection and lived up to every expectation Saralynn had regarding Virginia Kennedy's culinary skills. "This is soooo good," she exclaimed when, at last, she lay down her fork and crumpled her napkin on the table beside her plate. You are spoiling me."

"The pleasure is all mine," Virginia chuckled. "It's been nice having someone else to cook for. I really miss those days when the children were home and we had three full meals together everyday."

"Gosh, as much as I loved Marc, there were times I consoled myself with the thought that I wouldn't be cooking forever." *That hurt, but not so much since I feel free to talk about those two guys because they're still a part of me.*

"There's not a mother out there who hasn't said the same thing. It's natural when you're overwhelmed to look for the light at the end of the tunnel. But once they're out and gone, you miss that responsibility. It anchored me."

"You know, I just realized... I haven't cooked one single meal since the dinner I was working on the afternoon Marc and Peter were killed. And I have a professional kitchen in Boston."

"You'll find yourself back in the groove once you get here and get settled. I'll bet you're a great cook."

"I thought I was, but after sampling your food on several different occasions, I'm beginning to wonder if I don't need to take lessons."

Walter, who had adjourned to his recliner nearby, offered, "When we got married, Virginia couldn't cook."

"Now I don't believe that. This woman is a wonderful cook."

"Now I am, and I don't mind saying so. But in the beginning, Walter's right. What I did to food was a sin. Thank goodness his mother took pity on me and helped me learn the basics. Now I really enjoy it. And the larger the crowd, the better time I have preparing it."

That's what I can do. "What are your plans for tomorrow evening? For eating?"

"To eat," Mr. Walter answered promptly. "I try to do it three times a day, whether I need to or not."

"From the looks of your waistbands lately, I'd say you don't need to eat that often," his wife interjected. "But Saralynn was asking a serious question. We've nothing planned. Was there something special you wanted to do?"

Miss Virginia is very protective of her kitchen. Dare I ask? "I'd like to prepare tomorrow night's meal, and invite Dave and Donna Hasty and Katie and Charlie to join us. If that's not asking too much?"

"You're welcome to ask anyone you'd like. But you don't owe us a meal."

"Well, whether I owe it or not, I'd still like to give you a night out of the kitchen and find out if I can still cook."

"Let her do it, Virginia. Saralynn needs to feel like she's one of us, and I think she's found that we do a lot of bonding around the table." Walter got up from the tan, suede recliner Saralynn had identified early on as his special chair. He came and put his arms around her shoulders. "Our kitchen is your kitchen."

"But I know how it will be to cook in a strange kitchen," Virginia chimed in. "You don't have your own containers and layout, so if you can't find something, just ask. Otherwise I promise to leave you to it. And I know we're going to really enjoy the meal. Any idea what you'll serve? My taste buds want time to anticipate."

What will I serve? All my recipes are back in Boston and I don't trust my memory for much more than cereal and toast.

"That's a secret," she said. *Right now I don't even know.*

Saralynn spent the afternoon making out her menu and finding recipes on the Internet. By the time they left for church, she was comfortable with what she would cook and even had her grocery list made.

She was able, later that same day, to find Donna soon after arriving at the little red and white brick church, and was pleased when her invitation was immediately accepted. "See you at seven o'clock then," she called as the two went their separate ways.

The service was again a joy for her to behold, and after she got home, just before bed, she placed a call to Katie Brooks. "I hope I waited long enough for you to get Paul down for the night. Many of my decorating clients knew I had a small child, and still they would call just as I was trying to get him to sleep. Usually it was for something that could easily have waited until the next morning."

"He's just dropped off. What can I do for you?"

Saralynn related her plans for the following evening, and received an immediate acceptance. *This is working out even better than I had hoped.*

Before they hung up, Saralynn broached a subject she'd wondered about more than once since she and Katie first met.

"Do you mind if I ask you something?"

"Sure… what is it?"

"You don't go to Rials Creek Church like the Kennedy's, do you?"

"I used to… when I was growing up. But when Charlie and I married, he was the music director at another church here in the county, so we go there. You'll have to visit us sometime."

"That would be great," *Only I don't think I'll ever find another church that gives me what I get at Rials Creek.*

Monday dawned bright, but with a definite nip in the air.

"Cold weather comes later to Mississippi, but it does get here eventually," Mr. Walter said at breakfast. "I'd say it has staked out its territory."

Saralynn, who hadn't packed any cold weather clothing, had to scramble to find something to wear. Finally garbed in her own clothes and a couple of donations from Virginia, she was off to the grocery store and to run a few other errands. Then it was back to the country and an afternoon of cooking. *I don't know which feels stranger, being back in the kitchen, or being in a kitchen that belongs to someone else.*

The meal, consisting of marinated beef tenderloin, potato casserole, fresh, steamed broccoli, glazed baby carrots and homemade rolls, was a big hit.

"You've just made a big mistake," Donna informed Saralynn after the seven people gathered around the table had eaten their fill, including a dessert of homemade key lime icebox pie. "Now that we know you can cook, everyone at church will be waiting to see what you bring to church suppers."

Mama said Miss Sallie always took half the kitchen to church every time there was covered-dish meal. Guess I'll follow in her footsteps.

The thought of Alicia made her sad, but only for a moment. Mr. Walter had learned earlier in the day that her mother left Mississippi the same afternoon she listed the property with the new agent. *I guess she wanted the state line behind her before it got dark.*

"Cooking's not her only talent, as we've all seen," Katie announced. "Charlie has a big surprise for Saralynn. It's one I think will make her very happy." She grinned a conspiratorial smirk.

Her husband, whom Saralynn had already guessed wasn't quite as outgoing as Katie, colored slightly before he began. "You all know how persuasive Katie can be. Not that she nags," he added quickly. Ignoring his wife's provoked expression, he continued, "I've arranged for Saralynn to volunteer in the arts and crafts program at Boswell. We think that she can make a real difference in the lives of those people she'll be helping."

"But how?... When?" Saralynn sputtered.

"Don't worry about the details now," Katie reassured her. "We'll work all that out as soon as you're back here and settled. Just go to Boston knowing that you're both wanted and needed here."

"On that cue, I guess this is as good a time as any to tell all of you that I'm headed back tomorrow morning to begin closing that chapter of my life. I hope to be back within a week... ten days at the most."

"You can do it that fast?" The question was Mr. Walter's.

"All the detail work is done. I've even talked with the movers and have an appointment with their estimator for the day after tomorrow. All that's left is to tie up the loose ends. Just pray that the couple interested in leasing my house follows through."

"You can depend on us to be praying," Donna promised. "We already have been, you know."

"Oh, I know it all right. There's no way the pieces could have fallen together so perfectly otherwise."

"Then we'll be counting down the days 'til you're back," Virginia assured her. "You really have become one of us."

"That's because you reached out to me."

"But you reached back," Dave Hasty reminded her. "It takes two."

Sleep that night didn't come easily either. *This night feels like Christmas Eve when I was a child, waiting for morning to see what Santa brought me.*

Morning did come, and after another one of Virginia's bountiful breakfasts, the Mississippi transplant found herself on the way to the airport. As the plane streaked skyward after lift-off from Jackson, Saralynn leaned back in her seat and relaxed.

The assent had been smooth and if the blue skies outside the plane's window were any indication, the flight would be equally comfortable. Even turbulence couldn't disrupt her good feelings, because she had both peace and purpose. No doubt she would encounter her mother once they were both back in Boston. She was prepared for that, as well.

She had reached out to Alicia that morning by dialing her cell phone, since she didn't know her exact whereabouts. Alicia had answered, but instead of a stilted conversation, which was usually the case when Mama was getting over being angry, Saralynn got a venom-laced barrage that denied her any chance to speak.

"You are no longer my daughter!" were Alicia's final words and then the phone went dead.

Well...

Her hand strayed into her purse, to a folded piece of paper she had placed there earlier. She retrieved it and opened it to the words she had typed only a few hours before.

While she had spent many hours reading her grandmother's memoirs, she knew that many more days of study would be required if she was to cover half a century of journal entries. Just that morning, even, when she snatched a few minutes to further explore Miss Sallie's past, she chanced upon a few lines she had overlooked earlier.

While it was dated September 3, 1968, it turned out to actually be her grandmother's recollection of the day she was released from active patient status at the Sanatorium. After she read Miss Sallie's words, Saralynn knew she needed to keep those thoughts close to her for strength and inspiration in the days ahead, as she wrapped up thirty-five years of life in Boston.

Unwilling to risk losing the precious journal by taking it with her, she borrowed her hosts' computer and quickly transcribed her grandmother's words.

She was particularly taken by the opening sentence…

⬤▷

I felt like a bird set free from the nest.

I was released from the Sanatorium 21 years ago today, so this is my anniversary. Dr. McCallum came to my room the day before with the news I had often wondered if I would ever hear. I was cured, and I could leave the hospital and go home. He offered to call Mama in Fishtrap Hollow to tell her the good news, and to make arrangements to get me home. Only I wasn't going back to north Mississippi. Not to live, anyway.

He didn't act surprised when I told him. Instead, he asked if Ralph Watson had anything to do with my decision. I know I blushed,

because I was already in love with Ralph, only we hadn't been able to date because I was still a patient.

I don't think Mama understood completely when I called her. She seemed happy that I was well, but I couldn't make her understand that what I had gone through had changed me. I promised to come for a visit, but I tried to explain that my family and my home was here in Simpson County now. When you walk as close to death as I did, and see as many people taken all around you, like I did, it makes a difference. Miss Dora said it could change you for better or for worse. Some people left cured, but forever bitter. Others left knowing that God had spared them for specific purposes. I like to think that God had something else for me to do.

After you've been bedridden and confined for months, living under rules you didn't make and don't understand, like I was, when you walk out the door of the hospital building for the first time, knowing that you're free to do whatever you want, it's an almost scary feeling. You're on your own and there's no one to tell you what to do. I'm thankful that Miss Dora had already offered me a room for as long as I needed, because I sure didn't have any money. I didn't even have a job.

As I walked across the campus, headed to the grounds building to tell Ralph I was released, I kept expecting someone in white to grab me and put me back in bed. It took a while to adjust to normal life again. But I found Ralph and he was as happy as I was. He asked me for a date that night, and I agreed. When you've almost died, you don't want to waste any time.

While I was waiting for Miss Dora to come pick me up, there was a copy of the Clarion-Ledger newspaper on a table in the lobby where I was sitting. I picked it up to pass the time, and found a poem written by a young pilot during the early days of the War. It described his feelings as he flew high above the earth, like a bird. That's when I realized that's how I felt, like a bird set free. For sure, his last words describe my feelings too, when he said he reached out his hand and touched the face of God.

Saralynn didn't doubt for one minute that Miss Sallie was honest when she compared her experience to touching the face of God. She had that close a relationship with Him, because she knew that medicine alone had been insufficient to cure her.

As the jet carried her closer to Boston, and closer to Alicia, whom she knew had left several days earlier, Saralynn stared intently out the plane window. Try though she might, she couldn't see the face of God. But for the first time, she could say without hesitation that she believed He was there.

It's called faith. Katie was right. I did have it. Only I didn't know it. It took an entire community of God's people to show me how to find it.

"How are you going to handle things with Alicia?" Walter Kennedy had asked as she was leaving for the airport. "You're going to be on her turf, you know."

"I've prayed about it, and I'm at peace. I'll call her when I get there and let her know I'm in town. And I'll call her just before I leave. In between, the ball's in her court. I'll be glad to see her, but I won't allow her to abuse me."

"I'd say you've grown a lot in a short time. You didn't even know how to pray when you got here. It sounds like music to my ears to know that you've learned to trust God to do what He promised to do, to help you through these hard times."

"What can I say? I had some excellent teachers. But I still

need to learn how to let Him walk with me on a daily basis. I'm not sure how I make Him a part of my home."

"When you get back, we'll talk about that." He hugged her. "We'll all be praying on this end as well. There are a lot of folks at Rials Creek who are looking forward to you becoming a permanent part of our family."

"That goes double for me. And I'm also excited about the volunteer work I'll be doing at Boswell. I hope I can make a real contribution."

"I know you can. Safe travels, Saralynn. Call us if you need us. In the meantime, we'll be waiting."

Emotionally, Saralynn had already closed the door on Boston. *I just have to make it official. Then I'm coming back to Mississippi, where my heart is happiest.*

As she scanned the clouds and marveled at the reflection of the bright sun once again, Saralynn understood how her grandmother had felt. *I'm like a little bird, free and soaring above all the confusion below.*

The plane soon began its descent into Boston. *At any other time, the sight of my hometown from overhead would have thrilled me beyond words.* Only she'd found a new hometown, and she was painfully aware that in the city below, lived a woman who was miserably unhappy.

Mama's problems aren't mine, but that doesn't mean I'm going to give up on her. I'd be fooling myself if I thought she and I could pick up where we were. I don't think I'd want to. But I've got to find a way to reach her broken spirit if we're ever to have any kind of a relationship again.

The pilot announced their approach into Boston, and Saralynn began to prepare for the landing. While her hands were occupied with securing the tray table and restoring the position of her seatback, her mind, and her heart, were miles removed.

Somehow I've got to find the faith to believe that we can be mother and daughter again. "So Lord, You're going to have to show me the way."

About the Author

John Shivers began his writing career at age 14, stringing for his home-town newspaper. During those same formative teen years, he wrestled with a call to ministry, finally choosing to pursue a writing career instead. A freelance writer, editor and storyteller, John's byline has appeared in over 40 Christian and secular publications, winning him sixteen professional awards.

Hear My Cry, his first book, was published in 2005, and paths converged; his goal of becoming a published novelist was realized and with it, came the realization that writing could be a ministry. John explains that once his definition of ministry would have been defined and confined by structural and denominational walls. His writing allows him to minister to readers of all faiths and stations.

Broken Spirit is the first volume in the Renew A Right Spirit trilogy and he is at work on the second volume entitled *Merry Heart*. Coming next in 2007 is *Paths of Judgment*, the second volume of the Create My Soul Anew trilogy, the continuation of the story begun in *Hear My Cry*.

John, his wife, Elizabeth, and their Cocker Spaniel, "Miss Maddie," live on the family farm in Calhoun, Georgia where the wooded hills supply him with nourishment for his soul and his creativity.

www.johnshivers.com